Nora Roberts published her first novel using the pseudonym J.D. Robb in 1995, introducing to readers the tough as nails but emotionally damaged homicide cop Eve Dallas and billionaire Irish rogue Roarke.

With the In Death series, Robb has become one of the biggest thriller writers on earth, with each new novel reaching number one on bestseller charts the world over.

For more information, become a fan on Facebook at
/norarobertsjdrobb

Titles by J. D. Robb

J. D. ROBB

RANDOM
IN DEATH

PIATKUS

PIATKUS

First published in the United States in 2024 by St Martin's Press,
an imprint of St Martin's Publishing Group
First published in Great Britain in 2024 by Piatkus

1 3 5 7 9 10 8 6 4 2

Copyright © 2024 by Nora Roberts

A CIP catalogue record for this book
is available from the British Library.

Hardback ISBN 978-0-34943-739-2
Trade Paperback ISBN 978-0-34943-740-8

Printed and bound in Great Britain by Clays Ltd, Elcograf S.p.A.

Papers used by Piatkus are from well-managed forests
and other responsible sources.

Piatkus
An imprint of
Little, Brown Book Group
Carmelite House
50 Victoria Embankment
London EC4Y 0DZ

An Hachette UK Company
www.hachette.co.uk

www.littlebrown.co.uk

Bloody, bawdy villain!

Remorseless, treacherous, lecherous, kindless villain!

—William Shakespeare

To be choked with hate

May well be of all evil chances chief.

—William Butler Yeats

RANDOM
IN DEATH

Prologue

Gimme Avenue A 'cause they slay.

Pleased with the rhythm in her head, Jenna Harbough rocked her hips to the beat.

They may be old, but they rock and they roll.

Probably they wouldn't like the "old" bit, but from her sixteen-year-old perspective, anyone heading toward, like, forty or whatever hit *old*.

I mean, jeez, even her parents liked their music. Which was why they'd agreed to let Jenna come, with her two besties, to the club to hear them live and in freaking person.

Avenue A played twice a year at Club Rock It, and for one night in the summer Rock It locked up the alcohol and opened the club to the under-twenty-one crowd.

Anyone who knew their music history was up on how back in the long-gone day, like in the 2040s (talk about old!), Avenue A had their first real gig at Club Rock It. So they paid that back twice a year, even though they were totally rock gods *EXTREME* who played for sold-out crowds in stadiums and huge concert halls.

Though she'd campaigned to go on this once-a-year night for three years, she'd gotten the absolute, no-way no. Until this time!

Now she danced with Leelee and Chelsea while Avenue A *slayed* with "Baby, Do Me Right."

And she danced close enough to the stage that she could see the sweat on Jake Kincade's face. For an old guy, he was still looking frosty extreme. Maybe because he was really tall. She liked the way the lights hit the blue streaks in his black hair—and how they sort of matched his eyes.

Dr-ream-y!

But more, she loved how his fingers just freaking flew over the guitar strings.

One day hers would do that. She knew she'd improved. She practiced every day, and knew, just *knew*, one day she'd stand onstage and slay the crowd with her music.

She had a demo disc in her purse. Her biggest dream of the night involved finding a way to get it into Jake Kincade's hands. She'd only put one song on it, the best she'd written, and she'd worked really hard on the demo.

Maybe it wasn't all studio slick and professional, but you had to start somewhere. And the guys of Avenue A had been about her age when they really got going, so, maybe.

They segued into "It's Always Now," a classic crowd-pleaser, and more people swarmed the dance floor.

Jenna didn't mind—the more the better. And she was so caught up in the music.

Then, just for a second, for one tiny second, Jake's eyes met hers. He smiled; she died.

On a squeal, she grabbed Leelee's hand.

"He looked at me!"

"What?"

Then she grabbed Chelsea's hand as Jenna's face flushed so deep she felt the heat in her toes. "Jake Kincade looked right at me. He smiled at me!"

"On the real?" Chelsea demanded.

"So on it! Holy shitfire!"

She bounced and bopped with her friends to the last song of the set.

"Me and a rock god locked eyes. We had a moment."

"You've gotta find a way to get him your demo, Jenna. You totally smashed it," Leelee assured her.

"Maybe I could— Ow!" When something stung her arm, she closed a hand over it. Some guy shot her a hard grin and the middle finger before he melted into the crowd.

"Asshole jabbed me!" Then forgot him and just danced.

"I've got to sit a minute," she said when the song ended. "Make a plan, and— Whoa, I'm sort of floaty. That look!"

"I'm dying." Chelsea put a hand on her throat, stuck out her tongue. "Need sweet, fizzy hydration."

"Go, grab our seats, Jenna, and we'll get drinks. We'll help with the plan."

"Solid."

She felt a little woozy as she tried to get through to their tiny table. Floaty, she thought.

Then the heat came back, but like a million degrees. As she tried to breathe it away, she rubbed at her arm where it felt like a big, pissed-off hornet had taken a bite.

Need that sweet, fizzy hydration, she thought. But then her stomach cramped, and terrified she'd puke and humiliate herself, she tried to bolt to the bathroom.

Jake swiped at sweat as the band's drummer, Mac, grinned at him. "We still got it, boss."

"Ain't never gonna lose it. I'm going out to catch some air. Jesus, you'd think Harve and Glo could get a decent temp control in here."

"And lose this ambiance?" Renn, keyboard, tossed Jake a tube of water.

"Thanks. Back in five."

He glanced out at the crowd as he had during the last song in the set, but still didn't see Nadine. Probably headed for the john—and good luck with that, he thought.

She earned big points for coming with him tonight. Rock It wasn't a dive or a dump, but as clubs went, it clung to its Alphabet City roots.

Never going to be fancy, never going upscale. And proud of it.

But his ace reporter, bestselling writer, fucking Oscar-winning lady had come on a night that remained important to him and his friends, his bandmates.

It reminded them of their roots, their beginnings. And just how far they'd come.

He made his way through the back of the house—such as it was—and slipped out the alley door.

And breathed.

Even in the sweltering summer of 2061, the air outside blew cooler than in.

He cracked the tube, drank deep.

He smelled the overstuffed recycler, but that didn't bother him. It, too, reminded him of his roots, the skinny, gangly kid from Avenue A who'd worked after school and weekends to save enough for his first guitar.

He'd written music when he should've been studying because the music had been first and last for him. Always.

He remembered busking in subway tunnels with Leon, then Leon and Renn, before they'd hit fifteen. And watching Mac play the drums at their high school's band concert. Then Art slid right in, and they became Avenue A.

Practicing in the storage room of the apartment building, then in Mac's uncle's garage.

Then fast-talking Harve into letting them play, just one gig, before they were old enough to buy a beer.

That one gig turned into two weeks that summer, and ended with a recording contract.

So yeah, an important night to him. Avenue A had a lot of beginnings—that first guitar, Mac's uncle letting his nephew bang away on an old drum set. His mom telling him to grab a dream and ride it.

A lot of beginnings, and Club Rock It ranked high.

He started to turn to the door, but it flew open. A girl stumbled out.

The kid had a mass of pink-tipped brown hair and wore a tiny black skirt with a midriff-baring red top. Her face was white as chalk, her big brown eyes glassy.

She said, "I got sick."

"That's okay, honey. It happens."

Glo might have been vigilant about keeping the club alcohol and drug free on the underage nights, but kids found a way.

He sure as hell had.

"Let's get you back inside. There's a place you can sit down in the quiet, have some Sober-Up."

"Not drunk. Can't breathe right. He jabbed me! He jabbed me!"

Jake reached for her arm. Then her eyes rolled up white.

He caught her before she hit the pavement.

"Who jabbed you?" As he spoke, he noted her face wasn't white but slightly blue. She shook with cold.

A needle mark, red and raw, stood out on her left biceps.

"Goddamn it. Jesus." He yanked out his 'link as he lowered to the ground with her. Hit emergency. "I need an ambulance." He rattled off the address while he checked the girl's pulse.

Weak, he thought as he struggled not to panic. And getting weaker.

"You stay with me now. Look at me, okay? Look at me."

For a moment her eyes fixed on him. But blindly.

"Come on now, hold on. Help's coming. What's your name, baby? Tell me your name."

But he felt her go as he sat on the alley floor and cradled her in his arms.

Laying her down, he started CPR.

The alley door opened again. "Hey, Guitar Hero, Mac said— Oh my God, what happened?"

Nadine dropped down beside him.

"She's not breathing. I can't get her back. Her arm, look at her arm. She said someone jabbed her."

"I'll get an ambulance."

"On the way. Her arm. Needle mark. Only junkies who can't score a pressure syringe use needles. She's not a junkie. Come on, kid, come back. Fucking come back."

Beside him, Nadine looked at the needle mark, looked at the staring brown eyes of the girl on the ground.

She didn't tell him to stop the CPR, but laid one hand on his back as she took out her 'link.

"Jake, I'm tagging Dallas."

When he looked at Nadine, the despair simply covered him. "She's just a kid."

One, Nadine thought, who wouldn't get any older.

Chapter One

When Lieutenant Eve Dallas wasn't working a case, Saturday evenings often meant a vid, popcorn, and sex. With a Summerset-free house, as Roarke's major domo and the hitch in her stride had the night out with friends—whoever *they* were—the sex portion of the evening arrived early in the game room.

She'd bet Roarke she could beat him two out of three in pinball. She lost.

Or did she?

In any case, after dinner on the patio, a walk through the gardens, sex in the game room, they settled down on the sofa, with the cat curled at their feet.

She had Roarke, popcorn, wine, and an action vid with plenty of bangs and booms to cap off a Saturday at home.

Knowing Roarke, she expected a second round of sex as an encore.

And that suited her just fine.

He talked now and then of adding a media room to the castle he'd built in the heart of New York City. But she liked this routine, stretched out or curled up together on the sofa in their bedroom sitting area with the cat purring in his sleep and her husband's excellent body warm against hers.

Her life had taken a radical turn when he'd walked into it, she thought. She'd never get all the way used to it. Before Roarke, her life had been the job, and the job had been her life.

Now she had two things she'd never expected, never looked for.

Love and a home.

And those two things, she'd come to realize, made her better at the job, better at running her division, better at standing for the dead.

At a pause in the action, he reached over for the bottle, topped off both their glasses.

"We're going through a lot of wine, pal."

"Safe and snug at home." The mists of Ireland wove through his voice. "Something I intend to take advantage of in a bit of time."

"Is that so? Freeze screen," she ordered, and rolled on top of him.

So ridiculously gorgeous, she thought, with the carved-by-benevolent-gods face, the sculpted mouth, the wildly blue eyes. "No time like the right now."

She took that sculpted mouth, slid her free hand into the mane of black that framed his face.

Roarke set his glass beside the bottle, then nipped hers out of her hand to do the same.

She laughed as he flipped her over, and with a grumble, Galahad slid off the couch.

Then his hands were on her, slipping under her baggy Saturday-at-home T-shirt. And as the kiss turned greedy, she felt her need, the wine, the moment tie together in a single perfect thrill.

Nipping at his jaw, she worked her hands between them to flip open the button of his jeans.

Her 'link signaled.

"Oh, come on!"

Roarke angled his head to read the display on her 'link. "It's Nadine."

"Fine. I'll get back to her. Eventually."

But when she started to pull him down again, he shook his head.

"Eve, how often does Nadine tag you on a Saturday night near to eleven?"

"Never. Shit. Damn it."

When he eased away, she sat up, grabbed the 'link.

"Unless somebody's dead, I—"

"She is. I'm sorry, Dallas, we need you. We're at Club Rock It, the alley behind the club. Ah, it's on Avenue A, but I don't know the address."

"Who is she?"

"I don't know. A girl, teenage girl. Jake—they're playing a special under-twenty-one thing. I came out—alley at the back—and he was doing CPR. He'd called an ambulance. The MTs just got here. He said she said someone jabbed her."

Eve's brown eyes went from mildly annoyed to cop flat. "She's stabbed?"

"No, no, a needle mark, on her arm. Or maybe a really thin blade. It wasn't really bleeding, but it looked raw."

"Tell the MTs not to move the body. I'm calling it in, and uniforms will respond, secure the scene. I'm on my way."

"Thanks," Nadine began, but Eve cut her off.

She noted Roarke had brought out brown khakis and a jacket, a navy tank, boots, belt.

She didn't complain about him picking out her clothes as she grabbed her communicator and called it in.

"You didn't tell them to notify Peabody."

Eve tugged the baggy summer Saturday shorts off long legs, pulled on the khakis. "No point screwing up her night until I know what it is." She dragged on the tank, then shoved at her choppy brown hair. "Sorry it screwed up ours."

"Lieutenant, it's what we do. She sounded frazzled," he added as he changed his shirt. "She rarely does."

"Yeah, I caught that."

She moved quickly, efficiently, a long, lean woman with an angular face, a shallow dent in the chin, and her mind on murder.

She pocketed her badge, then hooked on her weapon harness. "I'm not drunk, but—"

"A lot of wine, so Sober-Up all around." He detoured into the bathroom, came out with a pill for each. "I'll drive. I know the club."

She sent him a look as she shrugged on her jacket. "Is it yours?"

"It's not, no. But the building is. Ready?"

"Yeah."

They went downstairs and out to the car he'd already remoted. Her DLE, she thought, in case she had to stay on the job.

In the passenger seat, she put the window down. The fresh air, especially at the speed he'd drive, would give the Sober-Up a solid kick start.

"It's a club for teenagers?"

Roarke streaked down the driveway, through the gates.

"No. But every year, in the summer, Avenue A plays there one night for the teenage crowd. He told me about it just the other day. He gave a workshop at the school. Apparently, they had their first paying gig there when they were still of that age.

"They lock up all the alcohol," he added before she could comment.

"Maybe. Who runs the club? I want to run them."

"I don't have those names in my head at the moment."

"I'll find them."

Taking out her PPC, she got to work.

"Harvard Greenbaum and Glo Reiser. Harvard's not a name, it's a school. And what kind of name is Glo? Not seeing any criminal on Greenbaum, age sixty-three, New York native, married to Reiser for about twenty years, no offspring. She's got a fifteen-year-old assault ding, charges dropped. Age sixty-one, also a native New Yorker.

"The club's got a scatter of health department violations over the twenty-odd years they've had it. All addressed. No citations for serving the underage. Not one."

"Jake said they're fierce about that issue."

Maybe, she thought again.

The Sober-Up and the air whipping through the open windows cleared her head and gave her a nagging yen for coffee. She used the in-dash AutoChef to program some for both of them.

"You wouldn't know the max capacity for this club, would you?"

"I wouldn't, but recalling the size of it, I wouldn't say over two hundred."

"Two hundred teenage suspects, great."

"Some of those would be staff, maybe some parents."

"We're going to need Child Services," she said, and pulled out her 'link. "Even if it looks like an accidental OD, we'll need someone. Two's better."

"Someone else is about to have their Saturday night screwed."

She spotted the cruiser and the ambulance in front of the club. Easy to recognize the club, she thought, as it had a rainbow sign lit up with the name, and music notes jumping around it.

"Just double it beside the cruiser."

"Loading zone just there," he said, and pulled into it. "I'll get your field kit."

She flipped on the On Duty light, got out to take a look at the club.

The graffiti on the old brick seemed purposeful. Guitars, drums, a bunch of figures crowded together. Dancing, she decided, and walked to the uniform stationed at the front door.

"Lieutenant," she said.

"Officer."

"No one's attempted to go in or come out since we arrived. The owner, apprised of the situation, is keeping things calm inside by having patrons join the band onstage, like an open mic. Mr. Kincade and Ms. Furst are still in the alley with the victim and the medicals. My partner is there."

"That works. I've notified Child Services to assist with any interviews involving minors. You can direct them to the alley."

"Yes, sir."

"Stand by, Officer."

Taking the field kit from Roarke, Eve walked around the building to the alley.

Halfway down, the medicals stood with the uniform. Nadine stood with Jake, hands linked, a few feet away.

When Nadine spotted her, Eve held up a hand to keep her back.

"Stand by, Officer. What do we have?" Eve asked the MTs.

"Victim's fifteen to seventeen years old. We didn't go into her purse for her ID, Lieutenant, to keep the scene as clean as possible."

"Appreciated."

"Can't give you a definite COD, but it looks like an OD. Got a blue tinge to her skin, and the needle mark's fresh. But I suspect a used needle due to the redness around it. She doesn't have any other visible marks. Looks to be a healthy weight, decent muscle tone. The ME'll be able to give you a better picture.

"We responded at twenty-three-oh-four, and she was already gone. Jake, ah, Mr. Kincade was attempting CPR when we arrived. But she was gone."

"All right. Again, I appreciate you preserving the scene as much as possible. I'll take it from here."

The second MT looked over at Jake. "You did everything you could."

Eve looked down at the body. Five-three maybe, weighing a buck and some small change. Dressed for fun with a tiny, shiny bag worn cross-body.

Eve opened her kit to seal up. "Roarke, why don't you take a walk with Jake and Nadine? Get them some coffee." She looked at Jake—pale, his eyes full of grief and a hint of shock. "I'll need to talk to you, both of you, but right now, I need to take care of her."

"She just . . . she just stumbled out the door, and—"

"I'm sorry this happened, Jake, but you need to leave her with me now."

"Come on, Jake." Nadine slid an arm around his waist. "We have to let Dallas do what she needs to do."

When Roarke led them away, she crouched and carefully opened the little bag.

A mini 'link, lip stuff, her ID, a key card, a little cash, and a disc marked DEMO FOR JAKE KINCADE.

She thought: Well, shit.

"ID in the purse on the victim is for Jenna Harbough, age sixteen, mixed race. Brown and brown, five feet, three inches, a hundred and six pounds. Photo matches."

Minus the pink tips in the brown hair, and the life in the big brown eyes.

After bagging the contents of the purse for Evidence, she took out her Identi-pad to make it official.

"Prints match." She read the address into the record, and realized it had to be next door to their friends Charles and Louise. "Parents, Shane and Julia Harbough, younger sibling, male, Reed, age twelve."

She took out her gauges. "Time of death, twenty-two-fifty-eight."

After putting on microgoggles, she leaned down to get a good look at the wound on the arm.

"Somebody jabbed me, she said, and yeah, that sounds accurate. The wound on the arm's fresh. It's also puffy, inflamed. Potentially, she could have self-inflicted, but there are no works on her person and no signs of illegals abuse. ME to confirm."

A boyfriend or girlfriend, maybe, who pressured her into trying something new? A rebellious, youthful impulse that went terribly wrong?

He jabbed me.

Or something else.

Gently, she turned the body, found no visible wounds.

Sitting back on her heels, she took out her 'link, tagged Peabody. Then straightening up, contacted the morgue, the sweepers.

"Have you been inside, Officer?"

"Yes, Lieutenant, briefly."

"An estimate of how many are in there?"

"Well, sir, it's packed. Gotta be a couple hundred."

"Okay. I need you to stand by here until the dead wagon comes to transport the victim. And the sweepers arrive to process this scene. After that, I'm likely to need you and your partner inside to help with crowd control."

"Yes, sir. It's a damn shame, Lieutenant. I've got a grandkid about her age. You hate to see a kid. I'll look out for her until they come to take her."

Since she wanted to interview Jake next, Eve walked back down the alley. She saw him with Nadine and Roarke standing by her vehicle. She stopped to give the second uniform instructions, then walked down.

"Nadine, how about you walk around the block with Roarke?"

"I don't want to—"

"I need to talk to Jake. Just Jake. Then I need to talk to you. Just you."

Nadine opened her mouth, then on a nod closed it again. She turned to Jake, lifted onto her toes, and kissed him.

As Roarke led Nadine away, Jake turned to Eve. "She thinks I'm going to fall apart, and she's not far wrong. I couldn't get her back, the girl."

"Did you know her?"

"No. I saw her. I realized I'd seen her out on the floor, dancing. Right before the end of the set. She looked so happy."

"You'd never seen her before tonight?"

"No."

"Her name's Jenna Harbough. Is that familiar?"

"No. Jenna." He repeated it, softly, then pressed his fingers to his eyes.

If you took away the misery, he looked like the rock star he was. Faded jeans and black high-tops, black tee that showed off a damn good build, the careless mop of dark, blue-tipped hair.

But his misery hung in the air around him like a haze.

"I went out for some air. It's frigging hot in the club. We were taking a fifteen-minute break between sets, so I went out, chugged down some water, got some air. And she stumbled out the alley door."

"Stumbled?"

"Yeah."

Eve heard him breathe in—the sound of a man steadying himself.

"She just sort of tripped out, you know? She said she'd been sick, and I figured she'd found a way to get some booze in. Glo's got a hawk eye there, but you have to figure some will find a way if they want to bad enough. I guess she looked a little drunk because I figured she was. I was going to take her back inside, into the office, get Harve or Glo. They'd be pissed at her, but they'd take care of her, call her parents, whatever."

He closed his eyes, and Eve let him have the silence. He was telling her what she needed to know without her asking.

"I didn't notice the needle mark right away, I guess because I was looking at her face. She was so pale—but then she said, 'He jabbed me. He jabbed me.' Twice, like that. And I saw the mark, I saw she wasn't white so much as that faint blue?"

"Yeah."

"Yeah." Now he passed a hand over his face. "I'd seen that before. On tour, one of the roadies. They brought him back, they got him in time and brought him back. But she just started to go down. I caught her before she hit. Her pulse was barely there, and she just . . . I called for an ambulance, but . . .

"I've never seen anyone die before, just . . . leave. I was holding her, talking to her, trying to get her to talk to me, tell me her name. Anything to keep her here. And she died. I could see it, but I thought, CPR. She's young, she'll come back, and the MTs are coming. Nadine came out looking for me, and when she said we needed Dallas, I knew the girl—Jenna—wasn't going to come back. Maybe if I'd—"

"Jake, what you just ran through for me couldn't have taken more than two or three minutes."

"Yeah, it was only a couple minutes. Felt longer," he murmured. "But yeah, it was so damn fast."

"I'm going to repeat what the MT told you, and you should listen because we deal with this every day. You did all you could do."

His eyes met hers. Not the wild blue of Roarke's, but a deeper blue now drenched in sorrow. "It doesn't feel like it."

"Do people—fans, groupies, like that—ever send or give you demo discs?"

He smiled at little. "Oh yeah. Why?"

"Something I need to look into. Can you tell me when you went outside, about what time?"

"I can tell you because I checked to make sure I got back before the fifteen was up. It was ten-fifty-five. We had one more short set before we closed out at midnight. We could go over a little, but when we're doing these, we try to hit last number at midnight. Kids have curfews."

"Right." She saw Roarke and Nadine coming around the corner. "I need you to come into Central tomorrow, to follow up. Let's make it ten."

"Okay, sure. Listen, does she have family? I know you can't tell me specifics, but—"

"Yes. I'll notify them tonight."

He closed his eyes again. "If they want to talk to me—I was with her when . . ."

"I'll let them know. It's your turn to take that walk."

"All right. Dallas, what she said? If somebody did this to her—"

"It's my job to find out. One more time around," she said to Roarke, then turned to Nadine.

"I've never seen him like this. He's always in control. I need to get him away from here, Dallas."

"Then let's make this quick. What time did the band break?"

"Oh, I don't know, just before eleven, I think. I knew the break was coming, so I made a dash to the ladies' before a hundred teenage girls had the same idea. When I came out, I looked for Jake, and Renn said he'd gone out to the alley. So I went out. I saw Jake doing CPR on the girl. I was going to call for the MTs, but he said he had. And, Dallas, I could see it was too late. He was trying so hard to save her, but she was gone. And I said I was going to tag you.

"And he looked at me when I did." Taking a breath, Nadine dashed a tear away. "And he looked at me as if I'd broken his heart.

"You can't suspect him of doing something to that girl. You know—"

"I don't, but at the same time, there's a procedure that has to be followed to clear him of any suspicion. You know that."

Nadine swiped at another tear, this time impatiently. "It's different when it's your person. You know that. And I know you," she added. "So I know you'll find out who did this to that poor girl."

"At this time, I can't conclusively say anyone did it to her."

Nadine pushed a hand at her streaky blond hair, gave Eve one long look with those shrewd green eyes. "You can't say it, but you know it."

"And you know the fact that Jake Kincade and Nadine Furst were in an alley with a dead minor female is going to explode all over the media."

Nadine set a hand on the hip of a pair of tight black jeans. "I'm a freaking reporter on the crime beat, so I know that very well. Only another reason I want to get him the hell away from here. We'll handle it."

"No interviews unless I clear it."

It took only that for Nadine to look and sound more like herself. "You have heard of a little constitutional amendment we call the first?"

"If someone did this to her, wouldn't it just bring on a happy dance if they found their ugly little deed all over the celebrity gossip channels? Her name was Jenna. Let's keep her and your person away from that until we can't."

"You're right, and I wasn't going to do interviews. I just don't like being told I can't. Here they come. Roarke's a goddamn rock, Dallas."

"I know that, too. Take Jake home. He's coming in tomorrow morning for a follow-up. With some luck and Morris, I'll have a COD by then."

She glanced back at the club. "And with a shitload of luck, maybe a suspect tonight."

"What about the rest of the band? He'll want to know. They're family."

"I need to talk to them, then they can go. It's a process, Nadine. And there's Peabody with McNab. Take Jake home," she repeated, and headed in the opposite direction to meet her partner and her partner's person.

In his striped baggies and neon-pink tee, Detective McNab, one of the Electronic Detectives Division's stars, looked like he should be riding a unicycle and juggling.

His earlobe glittered with studs and tiny hoops; the tail of his long blond hair swung as he pranced her way.

Peabody clumped in her pink boots. She may have worn more sedate black trousers and quietly pink shirt, but she still sported those red streaks through her dark, and currently all flippy, hair.

"We've got a dead teenage girl in the alley waiting for the dead wagon. Inside," Eve continued, "we've probably got a hundred or more teenagers currently being stalled by the rest of Avenue A. There may be closer to two hundred with staff, any parents or guardians."

"How's Jake?" Peabody asked.

"He's holding up. We've got to start carving through the people inside, releasing them—and Child Services hasn't shown up yet. The victim's parents need to be notified. I have to take that now. Peabody, tag CS again, and tell them to get somebody's ass over here or I will fry any number of asses. Until that ass or asses are here to represent the rights of the minors, stick with adults, or with minors in the company of a parent or guardian.

"McNab, talk to the band, get times, locations. They took a break about twenty-two-fifty-five. Get the security feeds, front and back."

She described the victim and what she wore. "See if anyone saw her, saw anything. I'll be back as soon as I can."

She walked back to Roarke. "Appreciate you circling the block like that."

"It's a lovely night for a walk, if an ugly reason to need one."

"It's going to be a really ugly night for the victim's parents. I'm going to go do the notification."

"Without Peabody?"

"I can't spare her for this when we have all those potential wits and suspects in that club. Look, I don't know how long we'll be at this so—"

"You're about to go tell a mother and father their child's dead." He took her field kit to put it in the trunk. "I'm with you, Lieutenant."

He closed the trunk. "Have you run them?"

"Not yet."

"Why don't I drive while you do that?"

She paused to breathe, to let the night air blow away some hard.

"That works. They live next door to Charles and Louise."

"Do they now?" he murmured. "Whenever you marvel how big the world is, it reminds you how small it can be. Odds are they know each other."

"Yeah." She slid in the car. "Odds are. The victim had a disc in her purse. It was labeled. Demo disc for Jake Kincade."

"Ah well. Did you tell him?"

"No, it's need to know right now until I check it. I ran him through did you know her, have contact, recognize her name. All no. He said he saw her on the floor during the last song before they broke, dancing. I believed him. I'd have believed him even if I didn't know him. Plus, the timing's going to check out, which means he couldn't have stuck a needle in her arm, if he'd somehow hidden the fact from someone like Nadine, from me, from you that he's a vicious teenage girl killer."

"But it concerns you."

"It's a complication, a possible connection between Jake and the victim. His story rings true, and again it would even if I didn't know him. Add the timing. But it's a complication."

One she needed to unravel.

But first she had to forever change the world and the lives of three people.

They drove into the quiet Lower West Side neighborhood with its dignified brownstones and summer-green trees. She noted a couple of lights on in the house Charles and Louise shared. At least twice as many glowed in the Harbough residence.

Waiting up for their daughter, she thought. Probably checking the time, anticipating. She knew parents worried—she'd met enough of them—and some imagined the worst.

But none believed the worst until it came knocking on their door.

"She's a doctor," Eve told Roarke, "so that ups the odds she knows Louise. He's an exec at a Wall Street firm, heads his own division. They're twenty years into the marriage. She has an assault charge—she'd have been about her daughter's age. Unsealed at her request."

As she spoke, Eve got out of the car to stand on the sidewalk and study the house.

"She punched a guy picketing a woman's health clinic when he tried to bar her and her mother from going in."

They walked to the door flanked by carriage lights that gleamed.

Solid security, Eve noted as a matter of habit, and thought of the key card she'd bagged that Jenna Harbough would never use again.

She rang the bell, and felt Roarke's hand press briefly against her back in support.

The man who answered had a thatch of brown hair threaded with gray. Over his thin build, he wore gray sweat shorts and a T-shirt that read:

BECAUSE

His narrow face had what Eve took to be a weekend stubble. Though he offered a pleasant smile, curiosity filled his hazel eyes.

"Can I help you?"

"Mr. Harbough, I'm Lieutenant Dallas with the NYPSD." She held up her badge.

Before she could say more, he winced. "Oh Jesus, is she in trouble? Teenagers at a rock club, what could go wrong? Jule! Looks like we've got to post bail. Sorry, come in. She's missed curfew," he went on, "so the hammer's going to come down there."

"Mr. Harbough," Eve began again as they entered a foyer with a living area through a wide case opening on the right, a smaller den on the left with a set of stairs leading up.

"She's not answering her 'link." A woman walked down the hall, frowning at her own 'link. Mixed race, a lot of wavy brown hair with shimmering highlights, and the big brown eyes she'd passed to her daughter.

"That girl is—"

She broke off as she looked up, saw Eve and Roarke.

Her eyes went blank, and her face took on a shade of gray.

"I know who you are. What happened to Jenna? Where's Jenna?"

"Dr. Harbough—"

"Say it." Julia reached out to grip her husband's arm.

"I regret to inform you your daughter is dead."

"What?" Shane's voice punched out, breathless and angry. "That's ridiculous. You need to leave, right now."

"Shane." Julia turned, wrapped around him. "Our baby. Our baby."

"It's not true. Stop this. Jenna's fine. She'll be home any minute. I'm going to go get her. I'm going to go get her right now."

"Shane." With tears streaming down her cheeks, Julia pulled back enough to look at his face.

And what he saw in hers had the anger in his draining into shock, denial, and terrible grief.

"No," he said. "No, no, no."

As he slid to the floor, Julia went with him, stayed wrapped around him.

"It's a mistake." Shaking, he sobbed it out. "It's a horrible mistake. She'll be home any minute."

"Shane. Shane, you have to help me. You have to hang on and help me. We have to know what happened."

"I don't believe it. I won't believe it. Julia, it's Jenna."

"I know. I know." Framing his face now, she kissed his cheeks. "Come on now. Stand up. We have to know. It's Jenna. We have to know."

She helped her husband to his feet, then faced Eve. "We have to know what happened."

"If we could sit down, I'll tell you everything I can."

Chapter Two

The living area held style with a few antiques, moody paintings, a fireplace framed in blue-veined white marble.

The Harboughs sat together on a couch that picked up that blue veining. Eve took the wingback white chair that faced them.

"Are you sure it's her? I know the answer," Julia said, "but I—"

"Yes. I'm very sorry for your loss."

Eve often wondered if those words sounded as empty to loved ones as they did to her.

"At approximately eleven this evening, Jenna walked out the alley door of Club Rock It. According to the witness, she was in severe physical distress and collapsed. The witness contacted nine-one-one for medicals and attempted CPR."

"But—but— She's healthy. She's only sixteen," Shane objected. "Julia, you just gave her a full physical a couple weeks ago."

"The medicals responded within five minutes, but Jenna was already deceased. She had a fresh needle mark in her left arm."

"What!" Shane lunged to his feet. "You're going to sit there and try to claim our little girl used illegals? That she's a junkie?"

"Shane, stop. Stop now."

"This is bullshit, Julia. It's cruel."

"Mr. Harbough, from my on-scene exam, I saw no signs to indicate your daughter was a habitual user of illegals. I believe the medical examiner will confirm that, but I have to ask if you know or suspect she experimented."

"I know without question she didn't. I'm a doctor, and I gave both our children a complete physical less than three weeks ago. As a doctor, I'd know. As her mother, I'd know. And you said needle. She's phobic about needles. She even has issues with a pressure syringe, but she'd never willingly use a needle syringe. She'd never inject herself."

"Sit down, Shane. This is Lieutenant Dallas. She's a friend of Charles and Louise. And she's with Homicide."

"Homicide." He sat slowly as his face lost all color. "Somebody killed our baby? How the hell could that happen? It's a decent club. Julia and I have been there, and we made sure to go there only last week, to be sure because we were letting Jenna go."

"I haven't determined homicide. We are investigating. I have detectives interviewing everyone who was in the club. I interviewed the witnesses. I can't give you solid information as yet. I felt it was important to notify you as quickly as possible."

"Is she still there?" Julia linked hands with Shane, gripped tight. "We need to see her."

"No. I've asked the chief medical examiner to take care of her, and I can assure you, no one will look after her with more compassion. I know it's difficult, but it would be best if you wait until tomorrow, until he contacts you."

"You know it's difficult? Have you ever had some stranger come to your door and tell you your daughter's dead in an alley?"

"Shane." Julia looked over as she heard feet on the stairs. "It's Reed. Stop him, Shane. Take him back up. Don't tell him. Please, we'll tell him in the morning. Together."

After he hurried out, Julia turned back to Eve.

"I'm sorry."

"Don't be. Dr. Harbough, it would be helpful for me to see Jenna's room, to have your permission to look through it."

More distress showed as Julia gripped her hands together. "Her room's just across from Reed's."

"Tomorrow's fine."

"They fought, as siblings do, but he looked up to Jenna. They fought and squabbled, but they had such a bond. I don't know how we'll tell him. Or her grandparents, or . . . God, she went with Chelsea and Leelee. Her friends. Are they all right?"

"As far as I know, and there was police response quickly. I'll check on them when I get back."

"You said there was a witness." Julia used both hands to swipe away tears. "Could they have done this?"

"I don't believe so. The timing doesn't point to that, and his statement, and that of a second witness, check out. Dr. Harbough, we're in the very earliest stages of our investigation, so I have more questions than answers. You said Jenna went to the club with friends."

"Yes, and I can vouch for them. I know them, I know their families."

"Was she dating anyone?"

"Not really. She's gone out now and then, to the vids, that sort of thing. For the most part in groups. She's interested in boys. She's sixteen. But Jenna's all about music. She wants to be a songwriter, a performer. It's one of the reasons we let her go tonight. She worships Avenue A. They're doing what she dreams of, and they started when they were her age. They're role models. Especially Jake Kincade."

She smiled a little. "What teenage boy can compete with a rock star?"

"Has she ever met him?"

"Another dream, though I think she might pass out cold if she ever did. She actually made a demo—and it's good. I say that as her mom, but she's got talent. She imagined herself finding a way to give it to him tonight. Then, of course, he'd listen to it, and help make her a star. I couldn't discourage her. Dreams matter."

She pressed her hand to her lips, rocked herself.

"Dr. Harbough." Roarke spoke gently. "Can I get you something? Some water? Is there anyone I can contact for you?"

"No, no, thank you." She took a breath. "Thank you. I know how strange this sounds, but I almost feel I know you. Charles and Louise—you must know they live next door—they speak so highly of both of you. And then the vid—the *Icove* vid. We watched it, the whole family. Will you really work that diligently to find out what happened to my little girl?"

"I'll answer that." Roarke laid a hand over Eve's. "She will. She won't stop until she finds the answer."

"We need to know," Julia said again. "But even when you give us those answers, you can't bring Jenna back."

"No, I can't bring her back. But I can bring her justice."

When they left, Roarke waited until they'd reached the car. Then he turned, wrapped his arms around Eve.

"Give me a minute." He lowered his forehead to hers. "I need it. Of all you do, of all I've seen or been part of, this duty, this horrendous weight, is the one I don't know how you carry."

"You just have to keep lifting it up. But I swear to Christ, Roarke, every time you do, it's just a little heavier.

"The lights are still on next door. I'd like to do a quick run-by with Charles and Louise on Jenna Harbough, get their take on her."

"All right. I'd have to say the parents' rang true. To my ear as an expert consultant, civilian."

"Yeah, but they're still her parents. I'd like to see if Charles and Louise agree. Then I can more or less shut off the self-inflicted angle."

He took her hand, started to walk with her down the sidewalk. "Which you don't believe."

"Belief isn't fact. This won't be, either, but it'll add to it. And give me an impression of the Harboughs from opinions I respect."

They went through the gate, down the walkway in the tiny courtyard where she'd once seen Dr. Louise Dimatto planting flowers in the spring.

They sure as hell bloomed now.

When they rang the bell, Charles, former licensed companion, now sex therapist, answered.

"Well, look at this. Good to see you, Roarke. Lieutenant Sugar. Come on in. Louise just went to open another bottle of wine."

He stepped back, tall, slickly handsome in silky black lounge pants and a loose shirt the color of blueberries.

"Have to rain check the wine," Eve told him. "On duty."

"Oh. This isn't an impulsive drop-by."

"No, sorry."

"I went for the sauvignon blanc, and if we take this upstairs, I'll . . ."

Louise, elegantly sexy in white silk pants and skinny-strapped white top, stopped, a bottle in one hand.

"Oh. Oh," she repeated, and sighed. "Who's dead?"

"Jenna Harbough."

"Jesus, no." Charles dragged a hand through his hair. "Goddamn it, she's just a kid. And it can't be an accident if you're here."

"Should I go over to Julia?" Louise set the wine down before she walked forward.

"Maybe check tomorrow. Can we sit a minute?"

"Of course. Did something happen at the club?" Louise asked as they went into the living area. "I know Jenna was going to Club Rock It with a couple of her friends tonight. Avenue A does an under-twenty-one night there in the summer."

Wineglasses stood on the coffee table, along with the remains of a cheese board. The pillows on the sofa showed signs of weight.

An experienced investigator, Eve deduced there'd been recent sexual activity.

Louise fluffed at the pillows before they sat.

"God, this is horrible. Jenna was all in on tonight. She ran over to have me approve her outfit." Squeezing her eyes shut, Louise reached for Charles's hand. "Apparently, she considered me a better fashion consultant than her mother."

"You're friendly with the family?"

"Almost from the minute Charles bought the house."

"And Louise talked Julia into volunteering at the clinic twice a month," Charles added. "What happened to Jenna?"

"OD."

"That can't be." Gray eyes clear and direct, Louise shook her head. "She didn't use."

"You're sure of that?"

"Absolutely." Louise looked at Charles, who nodded. "There's no way that girl used illegals. First, Julia's a damn good doctor and would've seen the signs. She's also a good, involved mother. They're a tight family. Very solid. And I'd have seen the signs, Charles would have."

"It only takes once," Eve pointed out.

"Not Jenna," Charles insisted. "Especially tonight, when she's been angling to go to this thing for months. And she's basically a rule follower. The last thing she'd do is try illegals on a night she's been looking forward to the way she was tonight."

"I take it Morris hasn't done the autopsy yet. It won't be an OD."

"It will," Eve corrected. "But it's looking as though it wasn't self-induced."

"Someone drugged her?"

"Injection, needle syringe."

"She'd never have used a needle. And yes, I'm sure about that, too," Louise said. "Jenna was scared of needles. Someone did this to her, Dallas. Someone did this to that sweet, young girl."

"Do you know if she had any trouble with anyone?"

"No, I don't." As she thought it through, Louise pressed her fingers to her temple. "She dated some, but casually. Her big love? Music. When I told her we'd actually met Avenue A, and that Jake was involved with a friend of ours, she practically fell at my feet. Then there's the Mavis connection. She literally lost the power of speech."

"I know she made a demo and hoped to get it to Jake tonight," Charles put in. "Just like I know if she didn't manage it, she planned to talk us into giving it to him."

"Yeah," Louise agreed. "I knew that was coming. Dallas, she was a really sweet, interesting kid. She had a truly lovely voice, and though I'm no expert, a talent for songwriting. She had a good, stable home life, good friends, did well in school. I don't know why anyone would hurt her."

"Okay, that helps. I have to get back to it."

"Can you keep us informed?" Louise asked as they rose. "I know there are limits, but whatever you can share? And if there's anything we can do."

"They're going to need someone to lean on," Roarke said.

"We'll be there for them," Charles assured him.

"That's enough for me," Eve said as they walked back to the car. "It's not fact, but it solidifies everything else."

"You didn't tell them about Jake."

"I didn't need to, not to get what they gave me. They'll find out soon enough. You should go home. I'm going to be at this for a while."

"I saw her, too. A young girl dead in an alley." He got in the car. "I'll stick."

Accepting that, accepting him, she leaned her head back, closed her eyes.

"They'd had sex on the couch."

"Well now, we were about to do the same."

It made her smile. "Good thing we got an earlier start in the game room when I let you beat me at pinball."

"You'd like to believe that. I tanked the first game to give you a chance."

"I call bollocks to that, and demand a rematch."

"You'll have it."

When they pulled up to the club, she saw Peabody had ordered up barricades and more uniforms. A number of people stood behind those barricades.

"Kids texted their parents," Roarke surmised. "Now parents are flooding down to get their kids."

"I should've thought of that."

"You were thinking of one kid."

"They'll have interviewed and released some of them by now. Let's see what we've got."

Eve approached the door just as two teens—one of each variety—burst out.

From behind the barricades came the shouts.

"Darlie! Tanner!"

The kids rolled their eyes at each other, but sprinted toward the shouts.

And those kids, she thought, unlike the one, would sleep in their own beds tonight.

She went inside.

The lights, turned up full, showed some dinge. Worn tables, a scarred dance floor, a bar with empty back shelves where the alcohol normally stood.

The place smelled like candy and sweat.

No surprise on the sweat, she supposed, as the temp control must've read close to eighty.

She found some relief seeing she didn't have to deal with a couple hundred. Easily down to about fifty, she estimated. At least in the main club.

She saw McNab talking to a couple of kids at a table while others sat in chairs. They buzzed with conversation and nerves. Some tried to look bored or rebellious, but didn't quite make it.

A man who looked like an accounting nerd with his baggy jeans, floppy sand-colored hair, and belly paunch, hurried to them.

"You're Lieutenant Dallas. And Roarke." He took Roarke's hand, pumped it, then did the same to Eve's. "I'm Harve Greenbaum. This is my place. I'm sick, just sick about what happened here. We never had anything like this happen, all these years. We've had to bounce out a few, sure, but nothing like this. And on the kid night, too. That poor kid."

"Mr. Greenbaum."

"Harve, just Harve. Mr. Greenbaum's my old man."

"Harve. Has anyone taken your statement?"

"Yeah, yeah. Blondie over there." He pointed at McNab. "Sure don't look like a cop, but he's got that going when he gets going. He talked to me and Glo. My partner, in life and business."

"Did he tell you you're free to go?"

"We're not leaving until the last kid gets out, and please God, gets home safe. It's our place where this happened. Glo says I should shut up about that, and we're going to get our asses sued. But Jesus on an airboard Christ, it's our place."

"Understood. Can you tell me where to find Detective Peabody?"

"Yeah, Pretty in Pink. She's back of the house talking to more kids. Staff's done, and the band. Holy God, poor Jake. Jake and the boys, they don't forget their roots."

"Can you take me back to Detective Peabody?"

"You bet. Oh, hey, you own the building, right?"

"That's right," Roarke confirmed.

"Well, I hate to mention it at such a time, but just today something went wonky with the temperature control. We didn't have a chance to report it, but—"

"I'll take care of it."

"I appreciate that. Anytime something goes wonky, your people are right on it."

"Maybe you can see if McNab's had a chance to check the security cam on the doors," Eve said to Roarke.

"Gave him a copy of the feed," Harve said.

"Take a look at it, will you?" And leaving him to it, Eve went with Harve.

"It ain't much back here. It's not like we run to dressing rooms and all that."

"This is fine."

They walked past the restrooms, down a short corridor, past the alley door, where she caught a whiff of vomit under fresh cleaning fluid. And to what he called the back of the house.

About eight kids sat in chairs lined up against a wall. She saw another door with a STAFF ONLY sign, another space with some rolling clothes racks, then a door that read OFFICE.

"She's taking them in there. How about I get you something cold to drink? It's a little hot in here. I don't mind it myself, but it's pretty hot."

"I could use a Pepsi."

"You got it." He knocked on the door, then stuck his head in. "Boss Cop's here."

She stepped into an office smaller than her bedroom closet. Though windowless, it was overly bright to her eye, and fiercely organized. Peabody sat at the desk facing the door. Two kids, one with hair as brightly pink as Peabody's boots, another with hers sharply divided into purple on one side, that same pink on the other, sat in chairs.

Eve figured the makeup each had piled on had to weigh ten pounds.

"Okay, Gabby, okay, Apple, that's all I need, thanks. Your mom's waiting outside, Gabby. And your mom cleared it, Apple, for you to stay the night at Gabby's as planned."

"Now we probably won't get to go clubbing again until we're twenty. This totally gales it," Gabby added before she and Apple walked out.

"Gales it?"

"Blows hard."

"Maybe they should consider it gales it for the dead girl. Status?"

"We hit some luck actually. I talked to the two girls who came with the vic."

"Chelsea and Leelee."

"Yeah, those. Believe me, they more than consider Jenna's death gales it. After I brought them down from hysterical, I got some timing and steps."

Peabody leaned back, shoved her hands up her face, back into her hair. "Sorry, it's been a mess. Bitchy, scared, sulky, snarly, weepy. I've hit every one of those and more."

The knock sounded before Harve stepped in. "Brought you another fizzy, PIP."

"Harve, you're a prince."

"Got your Pepsi, Boss Cop."

"Thanks."

"You want I should send in another kid?"

"Give us a minute," Eve told him.

"You got it. Just give a shout if you need anything."

"PIP," Eve said when he went out. "Pretty in Pink."

"Hey, you got it!"

"He already called you that. Where's our luck?"

"Both girls had the same story. They were dancing, turned out to be the last song before the break. Jenna got the squeals because she told them Jake looked right at her and smiled. He's her god-hero, according to Leelee. And they both said she had a demo disc in her purse and was going to find a way to get it to him. She's—"

"Into music, songwriting. I got all that."

"Anyway, they said she totally whooshed—their term—meaning she got all flushed and giddy. She was going back to their table to recover, and they were going to the bar to get drinks.

"Alcohol's locked up tight, Dallas. No problem there. Chelsea stated that between what they call The Smile from Jake and the end of the song, the talk about getting drinks, Jenna grabbed her arm. She said somebody or something jabbed her."

"While they were on the dance floor?"

"That's right. And Leelee stated Jenna looked around, maybe saw somebody. That's a maybe because neither girl really noticed. But Jenna said, 'Asshole.' Then they danced the rest of the song, talked a minute, split up."

Pausing, Peabody took a long drink of her fizzy.

"They don't know how much time it took for them to get the drinks. But a while. When they did get to the table, they thought Jenna had gone to the ladies' or—they got whooshed thinking maybe she'd gotten to Jake. Then they went to the ladies', and that took a while. By the time they got back to the table, Avenue A, minus Jake, was doing the open mic thing.

"They looked around for Jenna, figuring she'd go up, wow the crowd.

They both texted her, Leelee made another trip to the ladies' to look for her. And about that time, McNab and I came in."

"Did they see anyone else they knew?"

"Yes. A few from their school, a few from their neighborhoods. This is a big deal for their age group downtown."

"Did Jenna have a boyfriend, a girlfriend?"

"No one special."

"Did she blow off anybody recently?"

"They said no. But she only danced a couple of times with boys who asked. She just wasn't interested in hooking it tonight, so they mostly danced as a group, and Jenna said 'no, thanks' a lot."

"If someone stuck a needle in her tonight, they had the syringe and what was in it. It doesn't feel like you'd carry that around, then decide: 'Won't dance with me, bitch? I'll kill you.'"

"No, it doesn't. Nobody's come through here carrying works. Everyone we've interviewed agreed to empty the contents of pockets or purse—and McNab reports the same. The sweepers haven't found anything yet. Oh, shit—I did. Fresh puke out there, near the alley door."

"Yeah, I caught the smell."

"I marked it, and the sweepers took a sample. It might be hers. Probably hers."

"All right. Take a break. I'll talk to the rest you've got waiting. We need to get them home."

"I could use a break. I'll grab a couple minutes, then split the rest with McNab. Some of them want to come in pairs. Most of them didn't come solo tonight, so they're in pairs and groups."

She rose. "We started with the youngest, like twelve to fifteen. We're on sixteen and up now. Only a handful, compared, over that. McNab got a copy of the security, but we wanted to get the interviews first, so he just glanced."

"Roarke's going over it."

At the next knock, Eve turned, opened the door to one of the sweepers.

"LT, we may have something in the boys' john."

"I'll take my break later," Peabody said. "I've got the next here."

Eve followed the sweeper out, then into the boys' john. One that smelled like stale piss and staler farts.

"See the scuff marks under the window there?"

"Yeah, I do." She crossed over for a closer look. "Fresh marks. Somebody boosted up, climbed out this window."

"Caught their shirt or pants." The sweeper held up a small vial. "Left a few threads behind. Window that size? Have to be small or agile enough to get up and out."

"It would come up close to the mouth of the alley. Away from the door cams." She studied the scuff marks. "Any way to get a partial on the shoe?"

"We'll give it a shot. No prints on the wall or window."

"Smart enough to seal his hands. Didn't think of the feet. Make sure Harvo gets those threads."

"Nobody but the Queen of Hair and Fiber on it. Vic was just sixteen, right?"

"Yeah."

"I hate that shit. We'll work on the scuffs."

Eve stepped back.

Jabbed her on the dance floor, then walked away. Headed into the boys' john, so that meant a male—unless.

She went out, walked to the ladies'. Same setup—though it smelled like cheap perfume and face gunk. Had the window, but . . .

Maybe someone was in the room, in a stall, by the mirrors. Girls spent more time in johns.

Still, she thought the odds were male. A male who brought the weapon with him and had an escape plan in place.

Jab, walk away, go into the john, climb out the window.

You didn't need to see her die, Eve thought.

Killing her was enough.

Chapter Three

She went out to hunt down Roarke.

And found him sitting behind the bar, a glass of sparkling water at his elbow, working on his PPC.

"No one left by the front or back doors during the time period," he began. "Factoring fifteen minutes before Jake went out the back, and the uniforms arrived."

"Forget that. He went out the window in the men's john. We'll run it back to when the bar opened, then try to find someone who didn't leave by either door. I'll pass it to EDD to try face recognition."

"As I'm here, I'll get a start on that. You're sure about the window?"

"He left scuff marks on the wall, fibers caught in the window frame. He's going to have a slight build. Height won't matter, but he's not a big guy. Couldn't be to fit through that window."

"Could be female."

"I can't discount that. I need to talk to McNab."

She crossed the room, tapped his shoulder, then held up a finger to the teenage boy he was interviewing. "Hold a minute."

"Man, I gotta get home."

"Yeah, me, too." She drew McNab a few steps away. "Have you let the interviewees use the johns?"

"Yeah, otherwise we'd have a hell of a mess in here."

"Alone?"

"No way. We're sending the girls in threes—three stalls—and the guys in fours—two urinals, two stalls. Each group goes with a uniform. Peabody's group has a shot, then mine, then hers. Like that."

"The uniform goes inside with them?"

"Yeah, sure." When he turned his head, his forest of ear hoops glittered like stars. "Don't want any shenanigans, right?"

"Exactly right. The suspect left by the window in the men's john."

"Well, shit! You can check with the uniforms, Dallas. Officer Grady for the guys, and Officer Loren for the girls. They're instructed to go inside. They're not rooks."

"I'll check, but the suspect left before we got here."

"Well, shit twice."

"Finish the interviews. Somebody might have seen something. He'd have slipped out during the last song before the break."

"Got it."

She checked with the two uniforms, and both stated they, as ordered, escorted each group to the assigned restroom, accompanied them inside, then escorted the group back to their interview waiting area.

Then she started a hunt for Harve.

She found him and a woman built like an Amazon in the bar kitchen. The woman, with a soiled apron over a spangly, skintight dress, scrubbed viciously at a prep counter.

The room smelled of grease, onions, and chemical lemons.

Harve stopped his studious mopping of the floor, leaned on the handle. "Get you something, Boss Cop?"

"I'd like you to switch the lights in the bar to whatever you had going during that last song before the band took their break."

"Sure, sure, I can do that. Glo, this is Boss Cop Dallas."

"I figured." When she straightened, Eve judged her at a solid six feet—add another three with the sparkly heels she wore. She had skin like polished oak, eyes like green lasers, and what looked like a mile of corkscrew curls tied up on the top of her head.

"The other cops said the kitchen staff couldn't clean in here till they processed. Whatever the hell that is that leaves an even bigger mess."

"Did they finish? Clear you to clean?"

"We're cleaning, aren't we? You gonna arrest us for cleaning so the frigging health department can cite us for not?"

"No, ma'am, I—"

"Don't you 'ma'am' me!" She stabbed a green-tipped finger at Eve. "I'm not your ma'am."

"Now, Glo." Leaning his mop on the counter, Harve came around it to pat her. "Everybody's just doing their job."

"I'm doing mine right here, and don't need some fancy badge coming in telling me how to do it. We've run this place for more than twenty years. You know how many times we had to have the cops in? I'll tell you," she snapped before Eve could respond. "Three."

She jerked up three fingers in case Eve needed to count.

"Three times in more than twenty years. We run a decent club, and don't put up with any bullshit. Somebody crosses a line, out they go. Nobody—"

She broke off, covered her face with her hands.

Given the length of her lashes, it surprised Eve they didn't spider their way through her fingers.

"Oh Jesus, Harve. A kid died here. A kid."

"I know, babe." He put his arms around her, and though his head barely reached her shoulder, seemed to provide the rock for her to lean on.

"Just kids," she said. "Just kids. We've been doing these kid nights for years. A kid tries to sneak in some booze, we take it, dump it. They get one warning. Screw up again, and out. Try to sneak in illegals, same deal. If it's hard stuff? No warning, banned and that's that.

"Now a girl's dead, in our place, and you cops are saying it's an overdose, and maybe even somebody did it to her. How the hell did that happen?"

"It's my job to find out," Eve told her. "Ms. Reiser."

"Ah, fuck it. I'm Glo, and I'm going to half—only half—apologize."

"I'll half accept," Eve countered, and got the faintest smile. "Glo, I've corroborated that your alcohol is and was securely stored away during this event. Your beer taps locked and secured. I have no reason at this time to conclude that either you or your partner are responsible for the circumstances that resulted in Jenna Harbough's death."

"She died here."

Because she understood, Eve nodded at the simple statement. "Let's find out how and why. My detectives are nearly through the interview process, and the last should be released momentarily. I'd like to see how the club area looked during that final song."

"I'll get the lights for you. We'll get through this, Glo."

"Yeah, we will. Sure we will. You want the music, too? We've got the boys on the house loop. I can cue up the song. It's not tonight's live version, but it'll be close."

"That would be helpful. Before we do that, let me check, see that the interviews are complete."

When she went out, McNab had only a handful left.

"Peabody took another six or so a few minutes ago," Roarke told her.

"Any luck with that?"

"Not so far, and it's going to be problematic."

At his gesture, she walked over, looked at the screen.

"A lot of groups, and a lot—primarily boys—with their heads down, hair flopping over, hands in pockets."

"Trying to look frosty. Bet you did that back when."

He smiled. "If your head's down, you might miss a pocket ripe for the picking. In the game, it's more important to look invisible, or at least innocent, rather than frosty."

"Right." He'd have looked frosty anyway, she decided. "I'm going to check with the sweepers—they should be about done. When the last kid's out, I need to do a run-through."

As the sweepers packed up, she got a report.

No sign of the syringe inside the club, in the recycler, in the alley. They'd analyze the puke and work on the scuff mark. The Queen of Hair and Fiber would take the bits of fabric retrieved from the window frame.

No other evidence collected.

When she came back, McNab and Peabody sat at a table drinking fizzies. Roarke, with his sparkling water, joined them.

She walked back to the kitchen.

"I could use those lights, the music, too."

She went out to the table.

"They're going to cue up a recording of the song they were playing when Jenna said she got jabbed. And set up the lights, so I can see how it looked. You can both write your reports in the morning. Peabody, yours after we talk to Morris. Morgue, eight sharp."

"Nothing like starting the day at the morgue."

"How it goes," McNab said. "When somebody kills you to death, a murder cop gets no rest."

"Ha," Eve said, and walked out on the dance floor.

Lightning white-and-blue streams crisscrossed the stage. In the club, the lights dimmed to blue as the music blasted out with a manic guitar riff.

She'd seen Avenue A play, so envisioned the setup. Drums back some and centered, the three guitars in front. One left, one right, another center.

Keyboard thing a bit to the side, and the one playing that switched off now and then, grabbed some other instrument.

All but the drummer moved around the stage a lot, she recalled, switching places, dancing around, playing to each other, playing to the crowd.

On the dance floor, under those blue lights, movement. Feet, hips, arms. Bodies brushing, bumping.

That smell of candy and sweat and teenage lust notes.

He's watching her while she dances with her friends, surrounded by other bodies in motion.

Did he know her? Maybe, maybe not.

A pretty girl in a tiny skirt, bare midriff, hair flying, eyes bright.

Why her when there were so many others?

He knew her, or . . . he had to pick one, and she drew the short straw.

The lights shift from blue to red.

Onstage, Jake looks out at the dancers. All those young faces, those young bodies, caught up in the music. She looks at him, and he smiles.

And oh, her heart jumps. Her skin goes electric.

She squeals out the thrill, babbles to her friends, can barely find her breath.

He saw her!

Then, a quick, sharp pain in her arm.

Seeing it, feeling it, Eve closed her hand over her own.

Somebody jabbed me.

And looks left.

He sees her. Is he pleased with her angry look? He's already slipped the syringe back in his pocket, but doesn't he take that one moment to look at her, maybe to meet her angry eyes before he melts away?

He doesn't run, running draws attention, but walks—as Eve does now—off the floor, brushing and bumping others as he does. It's crowded, it's loud, the lights are dim and red.

Skirt the tables, keep going.

Straight to the men's room. Already scoped it out, planned the way out to avoid the security cams. Cops would look hard at anyone leaving in this time frame.

Music pumps against the walls.

If somebody's there, use the urinal, use a stall, just wait. If not, move fast now.

She lifted her hands, boosted up. She didn't need to brace her foot on the wall, and had no trouble easing through the window to the alley.

She could still hear the music, dimmer now, but still playing as she looked down the alley.

She walked back and went inside just as the song ended.

"Want we should play it again?" Harve asked when she stepped back into the club area.

"No, that's fine. You can shut it down. We'll get out of your way. We appreciate your cooperation."

"We're going to stay closed tomorrow, out of respect. But Blondie has our contacts if there's anything we can do. And when you find out that how and why, we'd sure like to know."

"I'll be in touch."

She walked back to the table. "We're clear here. We'll give you a lift home. McNab, can you pick up the face rec from where Roarke left off?"

"I'll be on it."

Outside, she let the night air wash over her. "He had a plan. It would've taken him less than ninety seconds to get off the dance floor and into the men's room after he injected her. And it's timed," she continued as she got in the car. "Last song before the break. After the break, the bathrooms are going to be swamped, lines into the hall."

"And the song's a classic," McNab told her. "It's one of those that has people pouring out on the dance floor. Art said they generally play it before a break. Art's the married one. He was on the 'link with his wife during the break. They're expecting their second kid pretty soon. I verified that."

"Good. Okay, so the chances the john's clear go up. He timed it. He'll be a teenager or look like one. An adult would've stuck out, even a parent."

"Parents danced, too." Peabody stifled a yawn. "But from my interviews, they stuck to the fringes, gave the kids the floor."

Filing that away, Eve nodded. "Slight build, shorter than me, or sloppy core. He had to work to get out the window, use his feet to boost up. I didn't. But he knew the club well enough to know he had that route out. He knew the band well enough to know how to time the attack and the escape.

"We can't be sure yet if he knew the victim or just picked her out of the crowd."

"If he didn't know her, what's the motive?"

Eve gave Peabody a shrug. "To be determined. Morgue, eight hundred sharp," she added when Roarke pulled up at the apartment building. "Thanks for the assist, McNab."

"I go with She-Body."

He got out, then leaned in her window. "You know how Feeney feels about kid killers."

"I do."

"And how he feels about Avenue A."

"Yeah."

"He'll want a piece of this one."

"He'll get it. Go to bed."

As Roarke drove away, she leaned back.

"What do you think on motivation?" Roarke glanced at her. "You have a thought on it."

"She rebuffed him. If I'm wrong and it's a female, then it's some sort of crazed jealousy, or maybe, again, a brush-off. But I don't think she knew him, or her. Him, damn it. Either way, Jenna didn't know or feel anything toward this person."

"Why not?"

"She said, 'Asshole.' She didn't say, with her friends right there, 'that asshole Bob' or 'that bitch Jane.' She didn't say, 'That asshole Bob jabbed me.' And she said 'he' when she said it to Jake. 'He jabbed me.' I'm saying she saw the one who did, the one who did's a male, and she didn't know him. Doesn't mean he didn't know her.

"They could go to the same school," she continued, "but he's not in her circle, not on her social rung, so she doesn't see him or notice him. There's a pisser. Or he came ready to kill in that place, with that method, and had to pick somebody. Maybe Jenna was a type. Maybe he asked her to dance and she blew him off. And that's a pisser."

"You're a marvel."

"It's just logic."

"It is when you lay it all out that way, yes. So you likely have a teenage boy with a homicidal grudge against either Jenna or teenage girls. One who has a slight build and is somewhere under five-nine, who can access whatever substance he used to kill."

"And is smart enough, organized enough to have worked out a plan." With her eyes closed, she ran it through. "Smart enough, I think, not to have come into the club alone. He's thinking about the cameras, so he slides in with a group. Head down, face turned away. But he didn't come with a group so no one's going to notice when he's gone."

When she felt herself drifting off, she straightened up again. "We're not going to lock him in with the face rec—we won't see his face. But maybe the build and his clothes, the hair. Process of elimination. Who with that build, those clothes, that hair didn't walk out again?"

She huffed out a breath. "Is that going to be as complicated and time-consuming as I think?"

"Probably more so."

"Well, Feeney's going to want a piece. McNab's not wrong. He can sure as hell have that one."

"No one better for it." He glanced at her again.

Cop adrenaline fading, he noted. When fatigue hit her and hit hard, she went so pale. At times so pale he imagined he could pass his hand through her.

"You know it's near to three and tomorrow's Sunday."

"This is not news."

"You could start an hour or two later in the morning."

"When it's hot, you work it hot. Who caught the weekend?" Trying to pull it out of her head, she rubbed her eyes. "Who caught weekend duty? Carmichael and Santiago. Baxter and Trueheart on standby. I'll know more after I talk to Morris, and if they're not working one, I can pull them in if I need them."

When he drove through the gates, she let out a sigh. "So much for a lazy weekend at home."

"We had almost half of one."

"Next time we both have one free, let's make sure we get a whole one. We could go to the island."

When he parked, he leaned over, kissed her. "The very next."

"Deal. Just leave the car. I'll be back in it soon enough."

Inside, they walked up the stairs. "I should get up by six."

"Why, now? It won't take you two hours to get dressed and get downtown."

"I'm too wiped to write my report tonight. And I want to open the book, put up a board. It'll keep it clear in my head when I get to Morris."

"Six it is then."

"You don't have to get up at six. You have a free day."

"To paraphrase Ian, I go with the Boss Cop. No, not to the morgue." Since she was fading, he guided her to the bed, where the cat sprawled. "But I'll get you up, Lieutenant."

"'Kay."

She yanked off her boots, her clothes, and would've fallen facedown on the bed if he hadn't pulled the spread off first.

She was out before he slid in beside her.

The cat stirred enough to rearrange himself.

Roarke brushed his lips over her hair, closed his eyes. And dropped into sleep with her.

At six, he woke her with coffee, and even through the grogginess, she decided he was the most magnificent human in the history of humans.

Enough so she set the coffee aside, crooked her finger. "C'mere."

With her arms around his neck, she kissed him, long, slow, deep.

"That's exceedingly unfair when you're soft and sleepy and naked."

"I know." She dropped her heavy head on his shoulder. "For me, too, and you're not even naked."

Then she pushed him back, grabbed the coffee.

"Thanks for this. I'm going to blast myself awake in the shower. Five minutes. And for the second time in a row, I won't bitch if you pick out some clothes."

He knew her idea of blasting away meant calling for the shower temp to hit close to boiling. It nearly made him shudder as he strolled to her closet and considered.

Another hot one forecast, he thought, and opted for linen trousers in pale gray, a crisp white shirt with half sleeves, a dark gray vest, boots and belt to match, with a pale gray linen jacket if she did fieldwork and needed to cover her weapon.

Both the vest and jacket had the Thin Shield lining, so she'd be as safe as he could make her.

And look crisp and fresh while she went about it.

He laid out the clothes just as she opened the door, a bit flushed from the heat of the drying tube.

"Great, thanks. Need more." "More" meant coffee, and she hit up the bedroom AutoChef before she dressed.

"You'll eat something while you work."

"Yeah, sure."

He only lifted his eyebrows. He'd see she had a bacon and egg pocket, with a bit of spinach she'd hardly notice.

"What're you going to do while I'm at Central?"

"I imagine I'll find something to occupy myself."

As she hooked on her weapon harness, she lifted her eyebrows at him. "You're going to work, aren't you? Maybe buy a small country."

"Only a small one?"

"It's Sunday, so on the small side."

"Ah, I see. Actually, I may wander out and take a look at your new property. You'll need to think of a name for the club there. You won't want to call it Stoner's."

"That asshole. There you go. We'll call it Stoner's an Asshole."

"Truth doesn't always ring."

When she grabbed the jacket, he walked out with her.

"I don't know how to name things." Or actually own them, either. "You do. You name it."

"It's your place."

"You bought it."

"Ah well, we'll think of something. Why don't you print out what you want on your board? I'll set it up for you."

Grateful she didn't have to think about owning a building, she sat at her command center, opened operations.

She ordered the printouts, and while that worked, started her report.

He set a plate with an egg pocket beside her unit. "Fuel, Lieutenant."

"Yeah, okay."

It smelled good. She suspected spinach, but it smelled good.

She ate while she worked. Once she'd completed the report, she opened the murder book.

Between the coffee, the fuel (despite spinach), and the work, she felt fully awake.

She heard Roarke talking to the cat in the little kitchen. The cat, she thought, who'd been dead asleep when they'd left the bedroom.

Obviously, Galahad's superpowers included scenting food, especially bacon, regardless of the distance involved.

She rose, studied the board. Jenna's ID shot. Vibrant with youth and possibilities. And the crime scene stills with all that wiped away.

She'd added the two friends, the club owners, Jake and the other band members, Nadine, and all the bits of evidence.

The demo disc, the close-up of the needle mark, the vomit, the scuff marks, the open bathroom window.

Now she added the timeline she'd worked out.

Not much, not yet, but she'd get more.

She thought of a mother's face turning gray, of a father simply dissolving onto the floor.

She'd get more.

"You should add your description of him," Roarke said from behind her.

The cat, she thought, made more noise than the former cat burglar.

"Speculation. But . . . maybe. We'll see what we find today. I have the morgue, and I want to go through the victim's bedroom sometime today. I'll tag the lab to see if Harvo's on, but it's Sunday so not likely."

Sunday, she knew from experience, would be a pain in her ass on a hot day.

"I might want to talk to her two friends again, see if either of them noticed anyone at school, or wherever they hang out otherwise. Definitely need to talk to Feeney. And Jake's coming in this morning, which I'm betting means Nadine."

"She's in love with him. It shows."

"Yeah." She let out a breath. "Yeah, it shows, both ways. I just looked at the security feed, the alley door."

And watched a young girl die.

"His statement's accurate," Eve commented. "The time's as close as it gets. When he stepped out, when she came out. Stumbled out, just the way he said she did. He tried to help her. He did everything right. Everything he could to help her."

"I know. I watched it as well."

She turned now. "But there wasn't anything he could do, because she was dead when she fell out that door. It was already too late to save her."

"I thought the same."

Eve shook her head. "Not think, is. I know what death looks like, and it was all over her. She never had a chance. Not once whatever was in the needle went into her. She stayed on the floor and danced another couple minutes, but she was already dead."

She rubbed her hands over her face. "Okay. Okay. I've gotta go."

"Tag me, will you, when you're done for the day. Or before, if you can use me. If I'm wandering, I may wander by the Great House Project. I'll be downtown having a look at your property in any case."

"All right."

When he kissed her goodbye, she leaned into him.

"I probably won't put in a full day. It's harder to shake people loose on a Sunday."

"Either way, take care of my cop."

When she left, he turned to the cat. "What's your Sunday look like then?"

After a quick ribbon through Roarke's legs, Galahad jumped on the sleep chair, stretched out.

"Just as I expected."

Chapter Four

Because the day started mild but wouldn't stay that way, Eve kept her window open on the drive downtown. No matter what the hour, New York had its sights and sounds.

The quick yips of a trio of cat-sized dogs prancing ahead of their human walker, who bopped behind them, probably to the beat of whatever played in her earbuds.

The dogs had collars embedded with shiny things that shot back the sunlight like lasers. She assumed rhinestones, but hey, you never knew.

The laser beams made her wish for her badass sunshades. Considering, she checked her jacket pockets, and yeah, there they were. Points for Roarke, she thought, and slipped them on.

A maxibus blatted and wheezed as it pulled to a stop. Sleepy people filed off; sleepy people filed on.

She wondered, as she often did, why sleepy people didn't find a way to live closer to work.

Then again, here she was, living uptown, driving downtown to the job. Life would throw its curveballs.

She caught the scent of glide-cart coffee—reminiscent of burnt cardboard—ignored the sounds of horns as somebody didn't move fast enough when a light went green. And watched a bike messenger risk life and all four limbs as he wove through building traffic. He sped through a yellow as it turned red while the pedestrian he nearly splatted at the crossing shot him the finger.

Metal rattled as a shopkeeper lifted his metal security doors, and someone blasted thrash metal through their own open windows.

A sidewalk sleeper, license to beg displayed, set up against a building, tossed a few coins in his bucket to seed it, and began to play a harmonica.

One block down, a woman in a breezy summer dress and skyscraper heels strode out of the street doors of a silver tower. She slid fluidly into a sleek black limo while the doorman and the driver loaded her mountain of luggage.

In New York, the carelessly rich and the quietly desperate breathed the same air.

When Eve got to the morgue, she programmed a large go-cup of coffee. Carrying it with her, she entered the long white tunnel with its echoes, its scents of death and disinfectant.

She'd made good time on her commute, so she'd arrived a few minutes early. And knowing Peabody's aversion to watching Morris dig into the dead, she expected her partner might arrive a few minutes late.

When she pushed through the double doors, Morris stood over Jenna Harbough. Her body lay naked, split open by his precise Y-cut.

The music he played, for the dead as much as himself, Eve knew—Avenue A.

"I appreciate you coming in on a Sunday morning, and brought coffee."

"Endless gratitude," he said.

Since Jenna's blood coated his sealed hands, she set it on the counter by his sink.

Rather than his usual suit under the protective cape, he wore jeans—black—a T-shirt—white. He'd twisted his long black hair into a single braid.

Walking back, Eve flanked Jenna on the other side of the slab.

"Young, pretty, a bud that will never blossom." After removing the liver, Morris weighed it, scanned it. Behind their clear shield, his eyes held the compassion she'd assured the victim's parents he had.

Eve looked down at Jenna. "No external indications of illegals or alcohol abuse."

"And no internal indications that I've found. The lab will do a full tox, of course, but my preliminary conclusion is we have a healthy dead girl. Teeth, bones, skin, muscle, organs show good nutrition and exercise. Her hymen's intact, so any sexual activity didn't include penetration."

"Calluses on her fingertips. Guitar player?"

"I can't say, but music was her thing."

"You'll see a slight blister on the side of her left pinkie toe. My conclusion—new shoes. Otherwise, only the needle mark on her left biceps."

"She had two friends with her. Both of them state they were dancing together near the stage. The victim grabbed her arm, said somebody jabbed her."

"I'd take that as truth."

He walked back to the sink to rinse his hands, then picked up the coffee.

"Ah, is there a richer nectar of all the gods and goddesses?" He drank, then set the cup down again. "*Jabbed* is an accurate word. The needle went in hard—enough that the impact caused mild bruising before death. And, from your on-site, began infection in only minutes. Not just a needle, Dallas, a dirty one. A dull one."

Rather than microgoggles, he used the scanner, brought the wound on-screen, enlarged.

She studied the image. The site showed swelling, a raw red fan circling the puncture, and that mild bruising he'd spoken of.

"No matter how I play it, it couldn't have been ten minutes from the time the needle went in until she was dying in the alley. What does this that fucking fast?"

"We haven't found a syringe or needle yet, so I can't analyze them. But from the wound, the rapid spread of infection? I think not just a dirty needle, but one treated with a substance, a bacteria or virus."

Her eyes narrowed at the image on his screen. "Is that what killed her? Inside minutes?"

"No, simply caused her more pain and distress. We'll need that tox report, but again, my preliminary indicates a mix, a deadly one. From the blue tinge to her skin, nails, lips? Likely heroin, but—"

He broke off when Peabody came in.

"Good morning, Peabody."

She gave him a wan smile and studiously avoided looking at the body. "I chugged a double espresso, so it's almost good. It's only two minutes after eight," she said to Eve.

"I made good time. But?" she said to Morris.

"Given the rapidity of reaction, the narrow window between injection and death? I believe they'll find at least one other agent in the mix. What can you tell me about her actions, reactions, symptoms within that window?"

While Eve ran it through for him, Morris nodded, moved back to lay a hand on Jenna's forehead.

"If the timing's correct, and I trust it is, an injection of street Junk wouldn't have caused such rapid death. Not alone, particularly since she wasn't a user, was healthy. The MTs arrived quickly, and could have given her an opioid antagonist injection. Purer heroine, a massive dose? Still within that narrow window?"

He shook his head. "I think they'll find a cocktail, one that quickly began to shut down her organs, stopped a healthy heart from beating."

"Why not just shoot her up with poison?" Peabody wondered.

"Well, didn't he, essentially?"

"This is more . . . exotic," Eve speculated. "More special. Like a signature?" Eve looked back at Jenna. "She didn't know him, or at least didn't recognize him. I don't know if he came to kill her, specifically, or just whoever caught his eye.

"If it's a cocktail," Eve began, and she'd bet a year's pay on Morris's analysis, "he'd need access to illegals, controlled substances, the means, the way to create them."

"He would."

"Somewhere to start. Her family, they'll contact you this morning."

"I'll make sure she's ready for them."

"Thanks for coming in on Sunday."

"She's more than worth it," he said, "to all of us."

As they went out, Eve rolled it all around.

"Morris said he used a dirty needle, and one probably treated with a bacteria or virus to cause the rapid infection at the site."

"Jeez! I was going to say overkill much, but it's just snarly."

"Snarly?"

"Like mean and petty and piling on all together in one."

"It's all that. Thinking of, accessing, and knowing how to mix the substances, access to bacteria or viruses? We have to reconsider adult. The victim, the snarly, the venue? That all reads teenage boy. But . . ."

"Maybe an adult who can pass for a teenager."

Maybe, Eve thought as they got in the car. "Or maybe a kid who's around junkies, or around people who work with chemicals, controlled substances. Somebody who works in medical research, or is around those who do. Maybe an adult using the boy as the trigger."

"Somebody snarly."

"Somebody snarly," Eve agreed, and started the drive to Central.

"You want coffee? I want it, but I should lay off for right now due to double espresso."

"I want coffee."

Peabody programmed black coffee for Eve and stuck herself with water.

"When we get in, contact the Harboughs. Find out when it's most convenient for them to let us go through the victim's room. Jake's at ten, so block off an hour there. The Harboughs live next door to Charles and Louise."

"They do?"

"They know each other. They're friendly. The mother's a doctor and does some of Louise's free clinic time. They knew the victim."

"They'll be good people for the Harboughs to lean on."

"They still had some lights on, so we stopped in after we did the notification. I wanted another perspective on the family, the victim."

Pulling into Central's garage, Eve aimed for her slot.

"Solid, same as my impression. Close-knit, stable. Louise hit absolutely firm on Jenna not using. No teenage romances, nothing specific or serious. Music, songwriting. Both the parents and Louise and Charles said Jenna made that demo, hoping to get it to Jake last night. They all stated she'd never met Jake or any of the band before. If she had, she'd have told them and everyone else she could tell."

"I know we know Jake didn't do it, but that adds weight to what we know."

"So does the alley security cam. It went down exactly as he said."

And she'd seen everything he'd felt, from the initial amused concern to the alarm, the panic, the desperation, then the grief.

"We need to follow up. He saw her dancing. He remembers smiling at her. He may have seen something else that didn't get through the shock last night."

"Maybe one of the other band guys saw something. I know McNab interviewed them, but maybe, on a follow-up."

"Yeah, we'll cover that. I'm going to see if Feeney wants to take them."

Peabody grinned as they walked to the elevator. "You're a good pal."

"He's a good cop."

"Yeah, he is, and if any of them saw anything that relates, he'll know the buttons to push to jog memories. It'll also give him a mega lift."

"Good, he's going to need it to run the security tapes to try to find somebody who was there, then wasn't."

She considered the empty elevator a perk of working on a Sunday morning.

She walked in to find Santiago and Carmichael playing cards at Carmichael's desk. Eve looked at Santiago with pity.

"Is there a bet?"

"I'm winning."

Carmichael shook back her hair. "Not for long. Hey, LT, Peabody, didn't expect to see you bright and early on a Sunday morning."

"Obviously, or you'd be working instead of scamming your partner at cards."

"Not scamming." Carmichael swiped a finger over her heart. "I'm just better at them."

Santiago gave his partner the hard eye. "I'm winning."

"Uh-huh. We caught up on paperwork yesterday, caught two—one ruled accidental. Victim tripped into the street in front of a Rapid Cab. Great shoes." Carmichael spread her thumb and forefinger apart to show how high.

"See, those things are lethal."

"Well, she was pretty drunk, too, which didn't help her balance."

"The other was a domestic," Santiago added. "A pissing match over a possible dalliance with an ex-girlfriend escalated when the current girlfriend stabbed the boyfriend with a kitchen knife. A fillet knife. I'm dating a chef, and you pick up these things."

"Make sure you don't dally," Eve advised. "I don't want to have to break in another detective."

Carmichael snickered. "She tried to claim it was an accident, how she'd turned around to say something and he sort of ran into it. That might've been the case on the first hole she put in him."

"But since there were four others, we deduced deliberate. So both cases closed."

"Good. Then you've got time to do some runs. I'll send you a list."

"What did you catch?" Santiago wanted to know.

"Fill them in, Peabody."

She went into her office to set up her board and book. Then she dumped everyone who'd been interviewed the night before on her detectives.

She knew the killer hadn't been among them, but it needed doing.

Then, checking the time, she tagged Feeney.

"Yo," he said when his face came on-screen. Sunday or not, she noted he wore one of his shit-brown ties, a beige shirt, shit-brown jacket. His wiry silver-threaded ginger hair looked like he'd spent the night in a lightning storm.

But his hangdog eyes were fully alert.

"I'm on my way in. The boy tagged me, filled me in. How's Jake?"

"I'll find out in about an hour. I know the e-work's time-consuming, but if you can carve out a little more?"

"What else you got?"

"I want to hit it while memories are fresh. I've talked to Morris, and we've established somebody on the dance floor stuck the needle in the victim. An infected needle on top of whatever was in it."

"Fucker. Going after a little girl."

"Yeah, there's that. Jake saw her on the dance floor during that—what is it—set. Toward the end, close to, it appears, the time she was attacked. We need to reinterview the rest of Avenue A, in case they remember seeing someone or something that relates."

His already alert eyes went bright. "I'll take that for you, sure."

"I'd appreciate it. I need to go over Jake's statement, get into the victim's room, reinterview the two girls she was with last night."

"No problem, I've got it. I'll set up the search in the lab, get that going. I can contact Art, Renn, Leon, and Mac. If they can't come to me, McNab can keep on the search while I go to them."

"That works."

"Pulling into the garage now."

"I'll check back with you later today."

When she clicked off, she thought she'd cut back her workload, put the interviews in expert hands. And as a bonus made the EDD captain and her former partner's day.

Not bad.

Since she'd dumped the runs, passed on the interviews, she had time to contact the lab and try to nag her way to results.

It didn't get her much, and since Berenski, the chief lab tech, had the day off, she couldn't even try for a bribe.

Because Sunday.

Maybe, maybe, the Sunday crew would get to the tox screen before the end of the day. But everything else stayed on hold until Monday.

So she took five minutes, put her boots on the desk, and studied the board.

Nice girl, solid family, big night out with friends.

Did he expect her to be there?

No way to be sure, either way.

She goes for the music, some hero worship there, and a big dream. Dances a couple times with others, but primarily with her two girlfriends.

No boyfriend or romantic relationship with a girlfriend. Still a virgin. Not looking for sex, for hookups, casual or serious.

He comes prepared to kill. It took time, had to take trouble to create whatever he had in the syringe. Had to know how to handle viruses or bacteria, and have access.

That pointed to an adult, but screw that, she thought, it wasn't.

At least not emotionally, she considered. Or if it was an adult using a kid to kill.

A Mira question, which had to wait until the next day.

He knew how to get in, knew how to get out. Nothing impulsive there.

If they didn't know each other—and she couldn't yet nail that as firm— how did he pick her?

Her face, her body, the way she moved, her outfit? Because the kill hadn't been impulse, either. He'd waited, timed it, to near the end of the set.

He'd had a timetable, an agenda, and a target.

He'd had plenty of time during the event to pick his target—if he hadn't chosen Jenna previously. What made her the one?

She swung her boots down as Peabody's clomped toward her office.

"Jake and Nadine are here. I can throw myself on the sword and block Nadine."

"No need. She may have seen something she didn't think of last night."

"Good, because I hate throwing myself on the sword."

"Why would anybody do that?"

Peabody hiked her shoulders. "Death before dishonor?"

"Death ends you. You can come back from dishonor. Let's do this in the lounge."

When she went out, she saw Jake had washed the blue out of his hair. Shadows dogged his eyes, and he had the look of a man who'd had a very rough night.

She imagined he had.

Beside him, Nadine stood camera ready in a black suit. Though the makeup hid most of it, Eve saw shadows there, too.

"Working?" she said to Nadine.

"It leaked, which we had to expect. I went into the station, did a quick in-studio on it. It would help if we could do a one-on-one. It's not for the damn ratings, Dallas," she snapped at Eve's cool stare.

"Come on, Lois." Jake took Nadine's hand, leaned down to kiss the top of her head.

"I'm aware of that, Ms. Lane. Like you're aware there's not much I can say about an active investigation, especially at this stage. Add the fact we have a relationship, and I know Jake."

"Anything. Anything to take some of the pressure off. Hell, Dallas, the media's even got his mother's house staked out."

"It's okay." Jake gave the hand he held a squeeze. "She'll handle it. We'll handle it. Somebody else's mom lost her daughter. This is nothing."

Not comparable, Eve thought, but not nothing.

"Let's take this to the lounge. When we're done, you can have a brief— very brief—one-on-one with Peabody."

"Peabody and I have a relationship," Nadine countered. "Peabody knows Jake."

"But she's not the boss of this division or the primary in this investigation."

"Valid, and thank you."

"Let me say this," Eve continued as they walked. "Jake, you're not a suspect. You're a witness. Evidence clears you absolutely."

"I wasn't worried about that. Wasn't thinking about that."

"See, I have to, because Boss Cop, as Harve dubbed me. Shit, I forgot coffee."

"I'll spring for some." Jake turned to the Vending in the lounge.

"No, Jesus, don't drink that swill. Peabody, use my code—if you dare— get me a Pepsi. Don't go for the house coffee," she told Jake.

"Just water." He shoved both hands through his mop of hair. "Water's fine."

"I'll have what Dallas is having—the low-cal variety." Nadine sat, linked her hand with Jake's again. "I could use the boost. We didn't get a lot of sleep."

"You talked to her family. I'd really like to talk to her family, if they'd let me."

Eve nodded at Jake. "I'll test those waters. Is there anything you want to add or amend to the statement you gave me last night?"

"I can't think of anything. I've played it over and over in my head, from the time she came out the alley door until . . . until the MTs pronounced her."

"Let's go back from there. You saw her on the dance floor."

"Oh, yeah, right. Thanks," he said when Peabody gave him a tube of water. "She was close to the front of the dance floor. You try to make a connection to the audience when you can. She was cute, and she was dancing, but staring up at us, so I smiled at her."

"That was the last song in the set?"

"Yeah, pretty sure on that. When we broke, I sort of glanced back toward where Nadine was sitting. Figured she'd gone to the ladies', or the bar."

"How long from the time you looked at Jenna to the end of the set? Approximate."

"Ah . . ." He closed his eyes. "Let me think back. No, I've got it, because Mac was just starting the drum solo, and I moved stage right to open it up for him. That's when I looked out and saw her. So we'd have about two minutes left. Now and then Mac gets into it, goes over a little. But no more than two and a half minutes."

"Two to two and a half minutes. Not much less, not much more?"

"No, between that's close."

"She was dancing with two other girls. Did you see them? Did you see anyone move toward Jenna—a boy or man?"

"Dallas, they're packed together. Everybody's dancing with everybody unless they're on the edges or manage to clear a space. I looked at her because, well, she was right there, and she had heart eyes on me.

"Shit." He paused a beat. "It doesn't cost me to smile."

He paused again, drank some water.

"You just sort of pick someone out, make that contact, that connection, but you're focused on the work—the music, the moves."

He shifted, leaned in a little. "It doesn't matter how many times you've played that song, hit those notes. When Mac hits the last beat of the solo, I come on with a riff, right off that last beat. Then we hit the vocals, bang, four-part harmony."

He leaned back again. "You've got to focus on the work. I couldn't tell you anything specific about the other girls, or if somebody moved in on her, because I was totally focused. But it was just a couple minutes before we closed the set and I announced the break. Before I looked back for Nadine."

"Okay. Nadine, you went to the john."

"Right after they started the last song. I've seen how people crowd the floor for that one, so I grabbed my chance."

"How long were you in there?"

"First, it took me a while to get there. The place was packed, and I stopped for a few seconds to talk to Glo. She was helping serve, because packed. I know I could hear the music when I got there. Lots of yelling and applauding when I was still in there doing a quick makeup repair. I was just coming out when I heard Jake do the taking-a-break thing, and they'd started the house reel."

"Did you see anyone going into the men's room?"

"Not when I went in. When I came out, let's say I had good timing because there was a stampede of teens, both genders. I got through that, then went backstage to ask about Jake. Leon said he went out to the alley for some air. It was freaking hot in the club."

"When you were in the john, did you hear anybody in the men's?"

"With that music going? Not hardly." Then her eyes sharpened. "Why?"

Eve sat back. "Lois Lane can't use it."

"Off the record," Nadine said. "Anything you want off the record's off the record. It's not business, Dallas. It's personal."

"And the reason I'm going to tell you, both of you, is because it's personal. He went out the window in the men's john, and the timing tells me he went out while you were in the women's."

"I didn't see anyone in the alley," Jake began.

"Because he timed it. He injected her during that two, two and a half minutes, walked to the men's room, and went out the window before you ended the set and went outside."

And, Eve thought, was very likely on the street before you announced the break.

"Jake?"

He looked up, met Eve's eyes.

"Nothing you could've done, once he put that needle in her arm, would've have saved her. That doesn't just come from me, but from the chief medical examiner. But because of you, she didn't die alone."

Chapter Five

E ve took a moment to let him settle again.

"Because it's personal, and off the record, I think there's something else you should know. Jenna Harbough had aspirations toward songwriting and performing. She had a disc in her handbag, labeled demo disc, to give to you if she managed it."

Emotions ran over his face, surprise, sorrow, guilt. "Can I listen to it?"

"It's in Evidence. Once it's been processed, her personal items belong to her parents. Let me see what I can do."

"Will they talk to me? I don't know what I'd say, but I feel like I should say something."

"I'll see what I can do there, too. Meanwhile, Feeney's going to talk to the other members of Avenue A. Now that we've established a specific timeline, we know when and where she was injected, they may remember something. May have noticed something that didn't make an impact on them at the time."

"We went over it all last night, but maybe something'll click."

"Now I'm going to tell you something else, and you need to hear me."
She watched him brace.

"Okay."

"You made a difference. You don't feel that now, and maybe you never will. But I'm telling you as someone who deals with death every damn day. And Peabody, who does the same, will back me up."

"All the way on this. What you did mattered."

"She wasn't alone," Eve continued. "In those minutes when she was afraid and confused and hurting, someone was there with her. You were there with her. She heard your voice, she may not have understood the words, but she heard your voice. She saw your face, she felt your arms around her, and knew she wasn't alone.

"You need to understand and believe that. We're cops. We're murder cops, and personal dealings aside, we've got no reason to bullshit you on it."

"She's ours now," Peabody added. "In her last minutes, she was yours, and you did your best for her. Now we will."

"I want to say I don't think she recognized me. If that means anything. I mean anything helpful to you."

"With the drug in her system, the distress from it, that's not surprising. You've been around long enough to know the media's going to be all over this because they do recognize you. They already are, obviously. And as you said, I figure you and your group know how to handle that."

Face grim, he picked up his water again. "Yeah, we'll handle it."

"You need a statement."

"Pete—PR's working on one, but—"

"He's bucking PR," Nadine interrupted. "I'm working with them because Jake's idea of a statement was and is a mess."

"I don't want some hollow-ass, two-sentence nothing." He snapped it out. Eve figured this marked the first time she'd heard him snap out anything.

"And you can't feed the public an overemotional, guilt-ridden soliloquy," Nadine responded with absolute and utter calm.

Before Jake could snap again—because she could see it coming—Eve held up a hand. "I'm going to bet the answer's between those two. You do want to keep it brief," she added. "You don't want to say too much, for Jenna's sake, her family's, and for the investigation. And you don't want it to sound like someone else wrote it. I don't know your PR people, but I'm going to say it'd be smart to give Nadine the lead on this."

"I'm backing up the lieutenant on this one, too," Peabody commented. "Nadine knows how the media works, she knows how we work, and she knows you."

"I'd like to look it over before you release it," Eve said. "You don't have any obligation there, but—"

"I'd actually appreciate your take," Nadine told her. "I'll send you a copy of what we've drafted."

"I don't want it to sound cold." With a wince, Jake looked at Nadine. "Sorry, really sorry. I didn't mean you're cold, or sound like it. It's just— You need to cut me some slack."

"All you need. This time."

"I have to get back to it. Peabody, do the one-on-one, then you get back to it."

Jake rose as Eve did. "I know you're not big on . . . cut me some slack," he said, and hugged her. "Thanks."

"Okay. Keep it short," she told Nadine. "We've got work."

She headed back, then turned into the bullpen. Both her detectives sat at their own desks. "Status?"

"They're kids. Few dings." Santiago shrugged as he worked. "Shoplifting, underage drinking, truancy. Kid crap."

"I took the adults first." Carmichael mimicked her partner's shrug. "Few little dings. Nothing pops."

She imagined either of them finding something that broke the case hit the same odds as Santiago beating Carmichael at cards.

In her office, she contacted the parents of each of the victim's friends to arrange a follow-up interview. It didn't surprise her both agreed to come into Central.

A lot of people didn't like cops in the house. Bonus? It saved her time.

What did surprise her came in the form of a lab report in her incoming.

Somebody had spent Sunday morning analyzing vomit.

And had matched it to the victim's DNA.

The contents, other than cherry fizzy, soy fries, gummy candy, included a junkie's dream stash. The heroin both she and Morris had suspected, along with ketamine, a trace of potassium chloride—something she knew had once been used in lethal injections before the outlawing of capital punishment.

And the surprising addition of Rohypnol.

Why add in a date-rape drug when death was the goal?

The heroin, confirming Morris's take, wasn't Junk, not street-level, but high-octane, and not cut with any of the usual cheap agents.

Death was the goal.

But why the other drugs? Why the roofie? Why the dirty needle?

Playing? Experimenting?

She got up, programmed coffee, and drank it standing at her skinny window, looking out at her view of New York.

To add to the symptoms? The speed of reaching the goal? Pain, dizziness, confusion, possibly hallucinations, potentially a seizure. And death within minutes.

He'd wanted all of that.

She turned as she heard Peabody coming.

"She vomited up—DNA confirmed—a lethal mix of drugs, heavy on the heroin—not Junk, the pure stuff. He added ketamine—again, not street-level Kettle. Traces of potassium chloride—the last step in lethal injections back in the day. He added a roofie."

"A roofie?"

"There has to be a reason for it. He wasn't going to rape her—she'd be dead."

Peabody's face showed a mixture of distress and disgust. "Unless he . . . ick, after she died?"

"I don't see how. He'd already taken off, out the window. And he couldn't know she'd go outside, couldn't know where she'd die. But there's a reason for it.

"She wasn't sexually active, so maybe she blew him off there. Maybe she didn't see him." Eve closed her eyes, took herself back to the club. "Maybe the 'asshole' comment was just knee-jerk. But damn it, it's all fast. It seems like she'd have caught a glimpse."

"Maybe, with the lights, the crowd, she didn't catch a good one."

"Yeah. We'll set up in the lounge again. The vic's friends are coming, each with a parent, for a follow-up."

"The victim's mother's going to contact us when they're ready. They want us to go through her room when they're not there. So when Morris is ready for them to come in."

"That works. Go ahead and check with McNab, see if he's getting anywhere."

She sat again, added the notes from her follow-up with Jake to her book.

And studied the timing again.

Yes, crowded floor, dim, atmospheric lights. But he had to get right next to her to use the needle. The jab hurt, she turned toward the direction of the hurt.

How could she not have seen him?

She imagined herself the killer.

Move in, palm the syringe in your hand.

Am I excited, nervous, angry, detached?

Depends. If it's just an experiment, detached would work.

But if it's the finish line? Excited seemed more likely.

She's dancing, turned away, bouncing with her friends.

Shove the needle into her arm, hit the plunger, pull it out.

It takes a couple seconds when you're not worried about the niceties.

Sitting, she mimed the act.

Pressure syringe would've been faster. But the needle hurts more. That's a choice, that's intent.

Two seconds to inject? Three, maybe four before the syringe is back in your pocket.

How long did it take her to turn?

Ow. Jolt, pull back from your friends, slap a hand on the sting. Just seconds, a few seconds. Turn around.

Didn't he want to see her face? He wasn't going to watch her die, but to not even see her face?

Even if just an experiment, that had to be part of the data, didn't it? Action/reaction.

"She fucking saw him." Eve pushed up, paced. "Even if he was turning to get gone, she had to see him.

"Why am I stuck on that?" Annoyed with herself, she scrubbed her hands over her face.

Peabody came back. "McNab's on it, but nothing yet. Feeney's taking the rest of the band at their studio. They're not suspects, so he's taking them all at once, to see if one maybe sparks a memory with the others."

Exactly why she wanted to take both the friends together.

"And the victim's friends, their mothers, are on the way up."

"Have you ever given anybody a shot?"

"Jeez, no." Peabody shuddered at the thought. "Sometimes you have to give animals meds or whatever. I didn't like doing that, usually found a way to get out of it."

Free-Ager, Eve thought. Farm animals.

Close enough.

"You've got a syringe in your pocket, and I'm the target. You come up behind me, on the left while I'm all freaking giddy and distracted."

Eve turned away. "Jab me. With your finger."

"Okay, but since it's a needle, I have to take off the tip—you know, the little protective tip so I don't jab myself. Then tap it so there's no air bubbles, and—"

"He doesn't give a shit about air bubbles. Jab it, shove the plunger down—fast. Get it back in your pocket and get away."

Peabody obeyed.

"Ow." Eve jerked back, looked down at her arm, slapped a hand on it. "Somebody jabbed me." Turned.

Peabody just started to turn to move away.

"You're barely a foot away."

"Well, I was pretending I'm on a crowded dance floor."

"Exactly. She saw him. Even if just that glimpse. He's a planner, and you bet your ass he rehearsed this, in a variety of ways. He had to know she'd catch that glimpse."

"He had to know she'd be dead in minutes, so he didn't care."

"But she could've said, 'That butthead John Smith jabbed me.' She didn't just collapse and die right then and there. She's with two friends. 'Somebody jabbed me,' turn, see, and say, 'That asshole John Smith.' No way, at this point, to know if he knew her, but she caught that glimpse, at least a glimpse, and didn't know him."

"You're worried he didn't know her, either, because if he didn't, she was random."

"If she was random, if she was just a type, just a girl, and he reached the goal, he's going to want to reach it again. Let's go take the friends. Maybe we'll get lucky."

"Leelee's mom's Maddie Spencer. Chelsea's is Audrey Fine."

"Got it."

They walked into the bullpen just as the four entered.

"Ms. Spencer, Ms. Fine. Lieutenant Dallas, Detective Peabody." Eve extended a hand to both. "We appreciate you coming in so quickly."

"We want to do everything we can to help," Maddie said. "Jenna was like part of our families."

"We've all known each other since the girls were in middle school." Audrey kept her hand on Chelsea's shoulder.

"If you'd come with me."

"We have a lounge on this floor," Peabody told them, talking directly to the girls. "It'll be pretty quiet in there today. I know this is hard. You were both really helpful last night when we talked."

"We didn't know she was sick." Leelee's eyes flooded. "We just didn't know."

"You couldn't have. Let's take the big table there." Peabody had already pushed two together in anticipation. "Would you like something to drink? Vending has lemonade this time of year, but it sucks beyond." Peabody smiled at the mothers. "The coffee goes beyond the beyond."

"We could use a round of Cokes. Okay, Maddie? Nobody got much sleep last night." Audrey, a freckle-skinned redhead, took a seat, drew Chelsea with her swollen blue eyes and purple-streaked blond hair down beside her.

"We'll relax the rules." Maddie, a dark-skinned brunette, her brown eyes a near match with her daughter's, did the same while Peabody went to Vending.

"I know you talked with Detective Peabody last night, and as she's already said, you were very helpful. I'm sorry to ask you to go over it again, but sometimes people remember things, just some little detail, they didn't think of."

"Mom says it can help Jenna, but I don't see how anything helps." Now Chelsea's eyes filled. "We're never ever going to see her again."

"Someone hurt her," Eve began.

"It wasn't Jake Kincade!" It all but exploded out of Leelee. "We saw stuff on the Internet. Bogus extreme, and—"

"It wasn't Jake Kincade. He did everything he could to help her."

"You're not going to arrest him?" Chelsea watched Eve with shadowed and suspicious eyes. "Mom says cops can lie. She's a lawyer."

Since Eve had already run a background on the families, she was aware. "We've established conclusively, through solid evidence, Mr. Kincade was not, in any way, responsible for Jenna's death."

"Mom?"

"Lieutenant Dallas has no reason to lie about that, baby."

Leelee elbowed her friend. "Plus, we saw the clone vid and she was totally iced getting the bad guys. You were, too," she said when Peabody brought the drinks.

"Maybe." Chelsea swiped at tears. "But I *know* Jake and Leon and Mac and Art and Renn were all onstage when Jenna said somebody jabbed her, and they're saying illegals killed her, and some fuckwads—"

"Chels!"

"I don't care, Mom." The girl's voice rose in pitch and volume. "It's freaking me because they're fuckwads saying she OD'd, and she was a junkie."

"They're fuckwads," Eve agreed, ignoring the mother, giving the girl her attention. "And they're liars looking to stir up ugliness about someone who can't defend herself. We've also concluded, conclusively, through sold evidence, Jenna did not use illegals."

"As if," Leelee muttered. "Illegals are for losers and flakers. Jenna wasn't, ever."

"But someone did jab her, and she did overdose—through no fault of her own. I want you to think back to that last song before the break."

"We've thought and thought."

"And it's hard," Peabody put in, "hard to keep thinking. But that's when and where he hurt her."

"We were all there, all three of us. This close." Chelsea held her hands up, a foot apart. "And she was so mega juiced because Jake looked at her, right at her, and smiled. I mean that was the ult!"

"She wanted to meet him so bad," Leelee continued. "She knew he'd take the demo and listen to it if she could."

"And it was then, when she was happy, when she told you he smiled at her, just after that, when she said someone jabbed her? Is that how you remember it now?"

"We were all juiced because it's just the ult, and I looked at the stage. Maybe one of them would look at us again, you know? So I looked that way," Chelsea continued. "Then Jenna sort of yelled, half yelled, I guess. Like 'Ow!'"

"She did. I was mostly looking at her, and her eyes got really big, and she sort of jerked."

"You were looking at her, Leelee? Did you see anyone behind her?"

"All kinds of people. Everyone was dancing and shouting or singing or clapping, whatever. Avenue A slays that song, and we'd never heard it live, which is slay it max. I thought somebody like stepped on her foot or bumped her hard. That's what I thought."

When tears dripped again, her mother cracked the tube, urged it on her. "Drink a little, then take a breath."

"'Kay. I guess she looked mad. Mostly when you get bumped it just happens, but she looked mad, and she did that little jerk. That's when she said about getting jabbed. I still thought it was just like somebody caught her with an elbow or something."

"What did she do then?"

"Ah. I think I started to say chill, but she grabbed her arm. Like this." Leelee pressed a hand to her biceps. "So then I thought, I guess somebody's elbow really jabbed her, like ouch. Then she kind of turned around, and looked behind her. She said 'Asshole,' then she like brushed it off, and we kept dancing. So I still thought elbow jab. A hard one."

And maybe so had she, Eve realized.

"Before she brushed it off, and she turned around to look, what did you do?"

"I guess I was sort of dancing, and I looked at the stage because I wanted to watch."

"You didn't notice anyone leaving the dance floor, just about that time? Right after Jenna turned around to look."

"I really didn't. We were all still riding that smile and the music."

"I maybe did."

Eve shifted her focus to Chelsea. "You saw someone moving off the dance floor."

"Maybe."

"Stop and think," her mother told her. "Are you seeing someone because Lieutenant Dallas suggested it, or because you think you did?"

"I think I did. Like I wasn't really paying attention because we were totally wrapped. But he was sort of . . ." She rocked her shoulders side to side. "Like, ah, showing off, like guys walk when they think they frost it. But he wasn't dancing, he was walking away, and I thought: Dooser can't wait until the end of the song, which was ripping it, to take a piss. Sorry."

Audrey cast her eyes to the ceiling. "Rules relaxed."

"Can you describe him?"

She shrugged. "Dooser. I think black baggies and a black shirt, maybe. He had his hands in his pockets, like he was frosting it."

"Was he tall, short?"

"I dunno, maybe sort of short. I dunno."

"How about hair color, skin color?"

She shrugged. "The lights were all swirly and red. It was only a couple seconds. I just noticed he walked like a dooser. I didn't even think about it last night. I swear."

"We didn't know to ask you about it last night," Peabody said in her I-understand tone.

"We never thought anybody hurt Jenna. We were all feeling so mag, and Leelee and I said we'd get some cold drinks."

"Because Jenna wanted to go sit down, work it out how to meet Jake. She said she was all floaty, but we thought it was The Smile."

"I bet she did, too." Peabody reached out, gave Leelee's hand a squeeze.

"We never saw her again. When we finally got back to the table, we thought she'd gone looking for us, or gone to the bathroom. So we went to the bathroom, and the line took forever. If we'd looked for her sooner, or looked faster, maybe—"

"Chelsea." Eve cut her off. "It wouldn't have mattered. As much as you would've wanted to help her, you couldn't have. No one could."

"Are you sure? We would've called for help, an ambulance, the police."

"Jake did that. He did that only a handful of minutes after whoever hurt her walked away. The medicals arrived only a couple minutes after that, and they couldn't help her, either."

"Why did he do it? Why did he kill her? She never hurt anybody. We're only sixteen years old."

"We're going to do everything we can to find out why, to find out who, and to put him away where he can't hurt anyone else. Can you think back again, earlier? Did anyone try to pressure Jenna to dance?"

"We danced with some guys, some other girls a few times. Mostly everybody just bops, right?" Leelee's brow furrowed as she tried to think. "I guess we all said 'no, thanks' a couple times because we were doing something else? Like we wanted a drink or had to pee or whatever. Mostly we danced together."

"Did anybody get, ah, snarly?"

The girls looked at each other, both shook their heads.

"How about farther back, before last night. Anyone she dated who wanted more than she did?"

"She'd have told us that for sure, and she didn't. She didn't have the mood to date-date yet. She wanted to stay loose because she had plans. Songwriting, practicing, putting an act together. She figured to solo artist because she didn't know anybody who wanted what she wanted, or not enough."

"Someone who wanted to go out with her, and she said no?"

"I can't think of anybody." Chelsea looked at Leelee, got another head shake. "I mean if somebody asked, and she wasn't into something, she'd go out. We'd probably make it a group. Leelee's got a guy."

"We're not wrapped." Leelee spoke quickly, with one sidelong glance at her mother. "We mostly hang. But he's on vacation with his fam, so he couldn't go last night. Anyway, if you mean like back in school, she never had a solid, didn't want one. But she got along, you know? She wasn't a wheeze, or like the weebs some of the bruisers pick on, or the tots who flaunt it."

"Or a teaser or geek."

"Maybe sort of a music geek."

Chelsea managed a smile. "Yeah, maybe sort of."

"All right. If you think of anything—any little thing, any incident, anything—you can contact me or Detective Peabody."

"Lieutenant," Maddie began, "both girls would very much like to see Jenna's family. When it's appropriate."

"We'll see them later today. I'll let them know. I'm sure they'll contact you. Again, we appreciate you coming in, appreciate all your help. Do you need transportation?"

"No, we're fine." Audrey rose, offered her hand. "It's hard for us, and we appreciate your understanding. I know your reputations. I'm going to say please find him, Lieutenant, Detective. Please find him."

They walked the group as far as the bullpen, waited while they caught a glide down.

"What the hell is a dooser?" Eve demanded.

"Oh, a cross between a dick and a loser."

Eve considered. "That's a good one. Do I need to know weeb and tots? The rest was self-evident."

"No, but basically boring or awkward for weeb and tots are slutty types."

"All right then, we're looking for a dooser in, probably, black baggies, maybe shortish, no further description."

"It's more than we had."

"It is that. And she didn't react, not violently ill, at least for a couple minutes. Time for him to book it, for the song to end, for the three girls to separate. Jenna very likely thought the elbow jab initially. What kid's going to think that dooser stuck me with a needle full of heroin and whatever the fuck else he could think of?"

"And she was riding on The Smile. It plays out. She's excited, head-spinning giddy. It's hot, she's breathless. She's sixteen and going to live forever anyway."

"It probably didn't really kick in until she was headed back to the table. Felt floaty, okay, The Smile, the heat, the dancing. But now, feel sick, feel wrong—turn off for the ladies', but it's bad, and there's that line ahead of her."

"Try for the alley," Peabody continued. "Can't make it before her stomach heaves up."

"By then her arm's probably burning, and some part of her thinks about the jab. Sick, confused, hurting, she stumbled out into the alley.

"We've got the timing. We've got the drugs he put in her, and got a glimpse at a dooser in baggies."

"We've got that her two best friends can't come up with anybody who'd want to do this," Peabody added. "Nobody at the club that night, nobody before last night. I'm saying you're right. She didn't know him."

"We need to find out if he knew her. We can start with her school and her neighborhood. Contact the school, see if we can line up her teachers from last year. We can put uniforms out on the neighborhood after we check her room."

"I'll get on it."

"There's a reason for the roofie in the mix," Eve speculated. "Maybe he watched her, wanted her. She didn't blow him off so much as not see him. Too good for me, she thinks, doesn't even know my name. That builds up until he decides, she'll notice me now. She'll pay for ignoring me. And nobody will have her. Ever."

"Extreme."

"Yeah, shooting her up with a heroin cocktail's pretty damn extreme." She pulled out her signaling 'link. "Text. Julia Harbough. They're ready for us. We're in the field," she called out to Santiago and Carmichael, then headed for the elevator.

Chapter Six

On the way to the garage, she checked in with Feeney.

"No luck here," he told her. "I'm about to head in."

"Try asking if any of them noticed a shortish dooser type, black baggies, hands in pockets, kind of strutting off the dance floor toward the johns near the end of the set. Or anyone like that near the victim prior."

"I'll roll it out."

"We're on our way to check out the victim's bedroom. Carmichael and Santiago are doing runs on interviewees."

"If I hit with your dooser, you'll know. Otherwise, I'll work with McNab awhile."

"Keep an eye out for that description, such as it is, when you do. Thanks."

"Letting McNab know about the dooser," Peabody said, then slid her 'link back into her pocket. "I'm not going to speculate how many black baggies walked into that club last night."

"We take what we get as we get it."

They crossed the garage to the car.

"He has to have a source." Pulling out, Eve aimed for the exit. "Or the means, knowledge, and facilities to create that kind of cocktail. Her school first, going with the she-didn't-notice-him angle. But if he was trolling, looking for a target, maybe college. The eighteen-to-twenty type. Better equipment in colleges, more time to study, practice."

"So maybe a chem major, maybe a TA. Could even be younger and in college—one of the supersmarts."

"Anything from that to a kid living with a chemi-head, a dealer, a cook and learning the family business. We start with the most probable. He knew the target, or wanted to, used source and/or knowledge to create the murder weapon. We work from there, then spread it out."

It struck her that finding space to park barely three yards from the Harboughs' rated as another Sunday thing.

She'd take it.

"Getting steamy," Peabody commented. "But no bitching about it because I love summer. And love it more now that we've got an actual garden. Oh, and I love how Louise made a classy cottage garden out of the little front courtyard."

"Why are they courtyards? Do people judge them? Hold court in them? They call them dooryards in Ireland, and I don't get that, either, but at least there's a kind of yard outside the door."

She rang the bell.

Caught up, Peabody asked, "Why are they yards? It's not like everybody's is a multiple of three feet."

Eve poked her shoulder. "Right. Why are they yards?"

She filed it away for later contemplation when Julia opened the door.

She looked like a woman who hadn't slept in days. She'd pulled her hair back, leaving her face, its color dull, unframed. Shadows, like deep bruises, spread under her eyes reddened by weeping.

"Please come in."

"Dr. Harbough, my partner, Detective Peabody."

"I'm very sorry for your loss, Dr. Harbough."

"Thank you."

Like her color, the words were dull. "We're in here."

Shane sat with his son tucked under his arm. While Jenna had her father's coloring, it looked to Eve as if the DNA chefs had mixed up the parents' codes to make a near-perfect blend of both in one boy.

His mother's coloring, his father's eyes, his mother's mouth, his father's hair.

While his sister had been pretty, the boy was striking.

Charles and Louise sat nearby, and Charles stood as they entered.

"Louise . . . Louise is going with us," Julia began. "I asked Charles to stay while you . . . I'd like to have someone we know in the house while we're gone and you're here. I don't mean to imply—"

"It's no problem," Eve assured her.

"I'd like Reed to stay—"

"I'm going." Teary eyes diluted the impact of the mutinous tone.

"Dr. Morris said it's allowed, but . . ."

"You need to see her, to say goodbye." Peabody stepped toward him. "You know it'll be hard, but you have to see her, for yourself."

"She was supposed to come back. When she left, I said she looked okay, for a wheeze."

Though a tear slipped down Shane's cheek, Peabody focused on the boy. "Then you did your job. I've got brothers, and they always do their job."

"She laughed."

"You'll remember that. It's important to remember she laughed."

"When you catch who killed my sister, will you hurt him?" Reed shifted his gaze, intense now, to Eve. "Hurt him bad."

"It hurts bad to spend the rest of your life in prison."

"It's not enough."

"Come on now, Reed." Shane pressed a kiss to his hair. "We need to go now."

Reed stood. "I saw the vid about you," he said to Peabody. "So I know you're the nice one. You can be mean," he said to Eve. "You have to be mean to the bastard who killed my sister. Check it?"

"I've arrested a lot of people. None of them thought I was the nice one."

"Reed, you and Dad go on out. I just need another minute."

"You just want to talk about stuff you don't want me to hear, and I—"

"Please, Reed." Tears filled Julia's voice now. "Not today. Please."

The anger on his face dropped away. He just nodded and went with his father.

"It's so hard for him," she murmured. "They could bicker until I thought my head would explode, but they loved each other. I wish he'd stay here, but that's selfish. What you said, Detective, and what Louise already had, is right."

She took a deep breath. "I need to know if you've learned any more. I can filter that for Shane and Reed. And I can promise any information you give me won't leave this house."

"We know when and where your daughter was assaulted. We know she was injected with a lethal cocktail of drugs."

"What drugs?" At Eve's hesitation, Julia stood firm. "I'm a doctor. I'm her mother. I understand fully your need to keep information out of the media. Such as Jake Kincade's involvement, which you didn't tell us before."

"Let me start with this. Heroin, ketamine, potassium chloride, Rohypnol. The needle was, we believe deliberately, tainted."

"God." Julia shut her eyes tight. "My poor girl." She steadied. "You didn't say she was sexually assaulted."

"She wasn't. I can't tell you the purpose of the inclusion of Rohypnol, but Jenna wasn't raped. She died within minutes of the injection. Jake Kincade's involvement was limited to being in the alley when she came out, sick, confused, and as a medical, you'll understand already dying."

"But—"

"When she collapsed, he caught her. He tried to help her, called for an ambulance, attempted to revive her with CPR—as was witnessed by Nadine Furst, who came out shortly after, and the medicals when they arrived, again, shortly after."

"He really was with her? He stayed with her?"

"Yes. All of this is verified, conclusively, by the security feed from the door cam."

"I want to see that."

"No."

"I have a right to—"

"No, you don't. She wasn't alone in those last minutes, and that's what you need to know. I'm going to ask you again, was there anyone who bothered her, made her uncomfortable, that she dismissed? Or anyone you noticed paying too much attention to her? Most likely a male between fifteen and twenty."

"No. I swear I'd tell you. And I'm sure she'd have told me. But if not me, she'd have told Chelsea and Leelee. You could ask them."

"We have. They say no."

"Then it's no. Jenna wasn't a secret keeper. I'm not saying she told me everything. Girls that age don't share everything with Mom. But they do, girls like Jenna, with their best friends."

"Okay. Chelsea, Leelee, and their families would like to see you or speak with you, when you're ready."

"Yes. Tomorrow. Maybe tomorrow."

"Jenna made a demo she hoped to give to Jake Kincade. He's asked if he could hear it."

Tears flooded her eyes, spilled from them. "That was her dream."

Armed with tissues, Louise walked over, slid an arm around Julia's waist.

"You said he was a good man."

"Yes. He is," Louise assured her.

"He stayed with her. He stayed with Jenna?"

"Dr. Harbough, she died in his arms. He held her, he called for help, then he tried to revive her. He never left her."

"He held my little girl when I couldn't. He stayed with her. Yes, of course he can hear her demo. She made it for him, after all. I need to go. They've been waiting too long."

Eve waited until Louise led her out, then let her shoulders relax.

"Neither of you could've handled that any better than you did. I don't know how you do it," Charles added. "I won't get in your way, but if I can help, I'm here."

"First help? Where's her room?"

"Upstairs, to the right, second door on the left. I know my way around the kitchen well enough to get coffee if you want it."

"No, but thanks."

With Peabody, she went up. A glance up and down the wide hallway showed her every door closed.

It made her itchy. She understood the desire for privacy with cops in the house, but as a cop she'd have preferred a quick look behind those closed doors.

She opened the door on the left.

"Well, wow." Peabody's eyes popped. "It's like a music studio with a bed. And the wall color, that's an energy color."

Though posters—Avenue A, Mavis, and other music luminaries—covered most of it, what Eve could see looked like the color you might get from crushing ripe purple grapes.

The bed stood on one side, covered with a white duvet, mounds of pillows in various colors, and a couple of stuffed animals she figured made the teen cut from childhood.

As Peabody said, the rest of the room Jenna devoted to her dream.

The computer desk held two screens. A guitar stood on a stand, a keyboard on a smaller counter with headphones beside them. Yet another counter held more equipment, another set of headphones.

"This is prime stuff," Peabody told her. "It's smaller scale and lower end than what Mavis has in her studio at the house, but it's prime. This is serious stuff, and it says her parents supported her with this. A kid couldn't afford all this."

She walked over, tapped some control board.

"This one? She could mix various instruments, record her voice and overdub, and all that."

On that, Eve took Peabody's word. "It's organized, clean. Cooler in here than the rest of the house."

"For the equipment. It should stay cool, and you don't want dust and crumbs, liquids getting into it."

Eve opened a door. "Okay, closet. Not as clean and organized."

She opened another. "Small bathroom, clean, but with all this hair and face stuff all over the counter."

"Getting ready for the big night."

"Yeah. You know more about the equipment, so you start there. I'll take the closet and the bathroom."

Eve studied the closet. Like many females Eve knew, Jenna had a thing for shoes. Skids, kicks, booties, sandals, fancy shoes, clunky shoes. High-tops, low-tops, airboots.

She hadn't stinted on clothes, either. Mostly pants—baggies, jeans, crops. A handful of dresses, more skirts, some barely longer than a dinner napkin, others that would've hit her ankles.

Skinny tops, oversized tops, flowy, clingy—and everything in between.

She found nothing in pockets, nothing tucked secretly in the toes of footwear or in any of the half a dozen handbags—all small, all cross-body style.

As she worked, music filled the room behind her.

"I found some recordings," Peabody called out. "This is a mash-up with Avenue A's 'In the Dark' and one of hers she titled 'Going Down.' It's good, Dallas. It's really good. Listen to her. She overdubbed so she's singing harmony with herself. She had a serious range."

Eve heard the voices wind around each other, blend, a kind of defiant, edge of angry mix that suited the lyrics about booting someone out of her life.

Then Avenue A took over, crashing guitars, and yeah, defiant and angry male voices.

Same theme, she realized, different viewpoints.

"She's got mash-ups in this section." Peabody pointed toward the screen. "Another area for originals. Another where she's done covers. And one more for works in progress.

"She's got a laptop, put away. It looks like it's strictly for school-work. At least that's all I found on it with a quick scan. Nothing's passcoded."

"Closet's clear—no hidey-holes. She had some cash stuffed in one of her bags. Under a hundred. I didn't find any T-shirts, no underwear in the closet. There's no dresser."

"Drawers under the bed. I haven't looked there yet."

"I've got it."

She found tees, tanks, sweatshirts, shorts in one drawer, underwear—simple, pretty, but not overtly sexy—in another.

On the other side, there were notebooks.

For lyrics, for stray thoughts and ideas. Doodles, and the occasional sidebar.

Reed can be such a brat!

The 'rents are mega strict!! I'm FOURTEEN!!!! It's just one tat, ffs! But all I get is the big NO. Ugh!

She'd obviously gone back to revisit lyrics, thoughts, sidebars, as she'd added to them.

Sixteen today! And I still want that damn tat. Two more years!!

Eve settled down on the floor, flipping through the notebooks, hoping a clue jumped into her lap.

While she searched, Peabody switched the music.

A kind of ballad, solo, with the dead girl's voice as clear as bells, pure as angels.

Glancing over, she saw Peabody's eyes had gone shiny as she searched the desk. She could tell her to cut the music, Eve thought, but that voice, the heart in it helped her—helped them—see the girl they stood for.

She found other quick notes. Leelee got her hair cut. Chelsea got blue highlights. Everybody got mani-pedis.

She went out to the vids with someone named Jay.

I like when he kissed me good night. It felt all mmm in my stomach. Maybe we'll go out again sometime. But music's first!

Everything she read confirmed statements. No serious relationship, nobody who pushed or pressured, no one she blew off—that she wrote of or realized.

And in the final book, she found a final note.

*Tonight's the night!!!!! I can't believe it's finally here. I worked
my BUTT off on the demo for Jake and the guys. It's mag, I just
know it. I must find a way to get it to him. Oh, it's going to be the
abso-ult! Seeing Ave A in person!!!!! Woo! I love them so much!!
(esp Jake!) I helped L and C pick out their outfits, and they helped
me with mine. We are going to look so iced tonight!! I hope I don't
blubber and act like a wheeze when I meet Jake and give him the
demo. I want him to know I'm a serious musician and songwriter.
It's going to be the best night of my life!*

Eve put the book back, took the next drawer.

The junk drawer. Guitar picks, packs of guitar strings, bottles of half-
used nail polish, pencils, markers, empty notebooks, scissors, sunshades,
and other debris.

No secrets, no threatening messages.

She got up to take the bathroom.

"I'm not finding anything, Dallas. Her music's extensive and organized. She's got plenty of tunes from groups and artists she liked—a hell
of a collection, really—and some pretty technical review notes on some
of them. Some vids of her practicing, like performing in here. Trying
different styles, trying to work up like a signature, she called it."

"Copy some of those. I'll take a look later. Emails, vid calls through
the comp?"

"Nothing much, but her age group lives by the 'link. I'm nearly done
here."

"Just the bathroom."

As she went through it, Eve told Peabody about the notebooks, the
quick comments in it. And the last Jenna had written.

In the bathroom she found mascara in every shade imaginable and
beyond. Enough lip dye to turn an entire building any shade of pink. Eve

shadows, liners, something called highlighter, cheek color, and more. And the stuff used to set the stuff, the stuff used to take off the stuff. Stuff to put on after taking off the stuff.

Jesus, how much did a sixteen-year-old face require to looked iced?

As she finished up, Charles rapped knuckles on the bedroom doorframe.

"Sorry to interrupt. Louise texted that they're about to come home. I thought you'd want to know."

"Yeah. I'm done here. Peabody?"

"Same."

"Let's get out. They don't need us to be here when they get back. You could let them know, Charles, the room's cleared. That we appreciate them allowing us into Jenna's personal space."

"I will."

They started downstairs together.

"Can I give them a sense of what you found?"

"Take this, Peabody."

"You can tell them we found Jenna to be a lovely young woman with an extraordinary talent. We'll work very hard to find out who took her from them."

"That's perfect." Charles wrapped around her. "It's good to see you, Dee, even in these awful circumstances."

"Come by the house again when you and Louise can. More progress since you saw it last."

"We'll make a point of it."

"One last thing," Eve said as she and Peabody stepped outside. "They'll hold a memorial for her. We need to know when and where."

"You think whoever did this might show up?"

"They often do."

"I know they have family they asked to come in—not everyone lives in or around New York. They want to have the memorial date set. Louise and I are helping, so we can let you know when it is."

"All right. Later."

"I'm with Reed," Charles called out. "When you find the bastard, hurt him."

"After going through that room, it's hard not to feel the same."

"Not how it works," Eve reminded Peabody.

"I know, but it's hard not to hope maybe it'll be necessary, under the law."

In the car, Eve sat back a moment.

"I'm going to check in with EDD. Unless they hit something, there's nothing left on this today. We need to set up with her school, and we can check other chem labs—other schools, colleges.

"I need thinking time."

"My brain's out of thoughts. And my stomach's just as empty. Yours has to be, too."

She hadn't thought about food, but had to admit the fatigue had hit her brain.

"You contact EDD. Even if they hit, we can either work it from home, or we turn around and grab up whoever they found. I need to tag Roarke. He asked me to when we finished, and we're finished."

"We put in a good day, Dallas. We made progress."

They made their tags.

"Nothing yet. A maybe, but head down, no face. They're flagging black baggies, black shirt, but there are more than one. They're about to knock off, let it run on auto. Any hits, it'll signal their 'links."

"So far, the only mistakes he made were leaving those scuff marks and the fabric on the window. We follow up there tomorrow. Roarke's at the house—your house. I can take you there or to the apartment."

"There please! I can make something to eat. You've gotta eat. My craft room's painted—I went with the neutral so the yarns and fabrics give the pop. And the main bedroom and bath on Mavis's side is finished. So's Bella's room. Oh, it's going to be so sweet when it's furnished."

Since she couldn't think anyway, Eve let Peabody ramble as they drove.

The gates of the Great House Project opened when she pulled up to them.

The exterior looked as it had the last time. Finished, homey, happy. Flowers and trees, green grass, the wide porch, the tall windows.

As she parked, Roarke walked around from the back of the house. Odd, she thought; though it had been only hours since she'd left him, it felt like days.

Roarke took one look at her. "You're tired, Lieutenant. As are you, Peabody. We're on the back patio. Come sit awhile."

As they walked around the house, down a paved path that sort of meandered, Peabody talked about doing some shade plants, naturalizing with bulbs or something.

Eve wanted to lay her head on Roarke's shoulder and shut her eyes. For several hours.

Then Bella raced around the back corner and shot at Eve like a missile.

Oh God, she thought, but with little choice caught the girl in red shorts and a shirt with a unicorn jumping over a rainbow as she leaped.

"Das! Das! Das!"

Cupping Eve's face, she slobbered kisses on both her cheeks. Then leaned back. Her face, pretty as that rainbow, crumpled into sympathy. "Aw, Das seepy. Nap."

"If only."

Bella laid her head on Eve's shoulder, patted her arm and sang something sweet and incomprehensible.

"It's a lullaby," Peabody told her. "Mavis sings it to her at bedtime."

Eve gave up. Even for a kid-phobic cop, Bella hit irresistible.

Her mother sat at a patio table, one hand on the growing Number Two and the other holding a glass of what looked like lemonade with a sparkle.

Leonardo sat beside her in a flowing, sleeveless shirt over flowing cotton pants. He looked like a man absolutely content with his world.

Despite the baby bump, Mavis sprang up, gave a bounce on the purple sneaks that matched her current hair color.

"We were hoping!"

She didn't leap into Eve's arms, but threw her own around her. "You look washed, both of you. You're going to sit down, stretch out your legs, have some wine."

"I really should—"

"Have some wine before we put our spanking new grill to work making burgers—with cow meat provided by Roarke. We've got real potatoes, too. Not from the garden, yet, but real ones."

"Woo. I'll make fries. Fresh, hand cut."

"We've got some in the AutoChef. Peabody, you're washed and wasted."

"Just the idea of burgers and fries perks me right up. So does the chance to cook in my own gorgeous kitchen."

"Then I'll make a salad—and that is from our very own mag garden. But first, wine for everybody." Glowing with happy, Mavis patted her baby bump. "Except me, Number One, and Number Two."

"Bella Nummer One!"

"Come sit. We're going to have our very first dinner party. McNab?"

"He should be here before too long."

Leonardo rose, kissed Eve's cheek. "I'll get the wine."

She drank wine. And since Bella shouted, "Watch me!" she watched the kid go down the slide on her playset, listened to the waterfall in Peabody's seriously amazing water feature.

And because the happy and homey demanded it, put murder aside for a little while.

She knew nothing about gardens, but walked out with Mavis and watched the urbanite, the music sensation, the former street grifter, pluck tomatoes off the vine, pull carrots out of the ground, snip lettuce.

"I wanted a minute to ask how Jake's doing. It's so beyond awful."

"He's okay. He'll get better."

"And that poor kid won't."

"No."

"But she's got you and Peabody, and McNab and Feeney. Roarke, too." Mavis walked along, plucking, twisting, snipping stuff to go in her basket. "You'll find out who did this."

"That's the plan. Isn't that a lot?"

"Not once you put it all together. I make magalicious salads." Much like her daughter, Mavis threw back her head and laughed. "Who knew?"

"Not me."

"There's McNab. Look at Bella go. Nothing she likes better than having people all around. She'll be sixteen one day."

"Mavis."

"No, I'm not like, what is it, projecting. I just mean you have to start letting them go, bit by bit, so, so soon. You have to because that's part of it. It's bitching scary, Dallas, those bit by bits, but you gotta, and that's that. And the whacked of it? They're scary, but they make you stupid proud at the same time."

"You and Leonardo are great at this."

"We freaking are. And now we have all this to give Bella, and Number Two, and all the ones who come after."

"All? After?"

"Oh yeah, bet your ass. There'll be more. There goes Peabody, off to make fries from potatoes. Jesus, Dallas, she's teaching me so much."

Mavis beamed at Eve. "Want me to teach you how to make a magalicious salad?"

"I absolutely don't."

Instead, she had more wine, got a quick update from McNab, and put it all away again.

She ate a salad made by her oldest friend, burgers Leonardo cooked—

mostly—with Roarke showing him how it was done. And ridiculously excellent handmade fries fresh out of Peabody's kitchen.

She figured Leonardo had a right to feel perfectly content with his world. The music sensation, the designer, the cops, and the kid (and the one on the way) had created a damn good one.

Chapter Seven

More than happy to turn the wheel over to Roarke, Eve kicked back in her seat as they drove home.

He gave her leg an affectionate rub.

"It meant a lot to them, having you stay for wine and burgers."

"I figured we'd stay five minutes, and it ended up closer to three hours. But it meant a lot to me, too. It's the happiest damn unfinished house."

"Another six to eight weeks, it will be finished, and I expect happier yet."

"Mavis pulled carrots out of the ground. She knew they were carrots even though the carrot part's in the ground, and knew how to yank them out. Of the ground. Then what to do with them after that."

It both baffled and amazed.

"When I first met her, the closest she'd have come to a carrot would've been sliding by them in a market on her way to steal a candy bar."

Eve considered. "After she'd lifted somebody's wallet."

"It was a lovely salad."

"She put those flowers in it. The nasty ones."

"Nasturtiums."

"Right, those. It's weird eating flowers even though they're, well, tasty. And you're showing Leonardo how to cook burgers, Peabody's making fries from potatoes, McNab's dancing around with the kid on his shoulders.

"Where does she get that laugh?" Even now, Eve could hear it. "It's like somebody on happy juice in an asylum."

She started to close her eyes, then realized if she did, she'd be asleep before she opened them again.

"The victim's bedroom? Peabody called it a music studio with a bed, and that's accurate."

"She was serious about the music then?"

"Deeply. And, Jesus, Roarke, the kid had a voice. Peabody went through her equipment, her recordings. Jake wants to listen to the demo she made. The one she brought to the club, hoping to get it to him."

"Of course he does."

Of course for Jake, Eve agreed. But plenty of others would want just the opposite. Self-preservation.

"It'll cut at him. Listening to her today cut at me, and I know better. It'll cut sharp at him."

"Tell me about her. You know her now."

"Young for her age. Part of that's the parental shield, and part's her focus on music. At the same time a maturity. She had her goals lined up. She liked boys, but wasn't interested in hookups. Tight with her two friends and their families.

"She wanted a tat," Eve remembered. "Musical notes—she drew three of them in her notebook. On her wrist." Eve tapped the inside of her wrist. "Big no from the parental shield on that, which pissed her off. She wasn't a wheeze or a weeb or a tot or a flaker or a bruiser."

"What language are you speaking?" Roarke asked as he approached the gates.

"Teenage. She got decent grades, stayed out of trouble, liked cherry fizzies. She wished she had longer legs and bigger boobs. The usual complaints about the parents being too strict or the little brother bugging her, but it comes across she loved them.

"She had a serious talent and big dreams for building on it."

Because the towers and turrets of home had a big bed inside them, she let the fatigue wash over her again.

"I think, I really think, she'd have grabbed those dreams if some dooser hadn't killed her."

"Translate *dooser.*"

"Combo of *dick* and *loser.*"

"That's a good one."

"What I said."

"How do you know he was a dooser, specifically?"

"One of the friends caught a glimpse of a guy—black baggies, black tee—strutting off the dance floor in the direction of the johns right after Jenna got jabbed.

"Can't give it a hundred percent," she said as she pushed out of the car into air that felt as if it floated like a slow-moving river.

Or maybe she floated in it.

"I'm giving it a solid ninety. The timing just locks. It's still Sunday, right?"

"It is."

"Why is it Sundays when you just laze around don't last as long as Sundays when you don't?"

"Hardly fair, is it?"

"Bites."

He led his exhausted wife into the house where Summerset waited with the cat at his feet.

"I hope you enjoyed your time with friends after a difficult weekend."

"We did. It was just the thing to lift a hard load for a bit of time."

"I heard Jake's statement earlier. Brief and compassionate while keeping the focus on the child. I sensed your touch at least around the edges, Lieutenant."

"More Nadine's," she said, and kept going toward the stairs.

The bed was up there.

Then she thought: He'd lost a child. A daughter, brutalized and murdered.

And the cops did nothing. The cops did less than nothing.

She turned, met his eyes. "I'm going to get him. I'm going to put him away."

"I have no doubt of it."

As the cat raced up the steps ahead of them, Roarke scooped her up.

"I can walk. Jesus, I . . . Okay." And giving in, she dropped her head on his shoulder.

It felt too good, too damn good to finally let her brain go fuzzy and her body limp.

"What do you say to a nap?"

"Affirmative."

The cat had already claimed the bed when Roarke carried her in, set her on the side of it. He stopped her before she could just twist and flop over on her face.

"You won't need your weapon."

"You didn't get any more sleep than I did," she said as he unhooked her harness.

"So I'll have a bit of a nap with you. Let's have the boots."

"Is it really still Sunday?"

"It is, yes, and for several hours more."

"Good. That's good." As he set her weapon and boots aside, she rolled and flopped on her face. "Wake me when it's Monday."

After shedding his shoes, he stretched out beside her with Galahad guarding her other flank.

"No dreams, darling Eve," he murmured. "No dreams now. Just sleep."

She woke disoriented in dim, dying light. She heard Roarke's quiet murmur, and blinking, watched him give the cat a few of the treats Galahad craved like a junkie craved the funk.

After rolling over, she stared through the sky window over the bed, trying to gauge the time.

Gave up, sat up.

"Yes," Roarke said. "It's still Sunday."

"How long was I out?"

"Nearly as long as we were at Mavis's, and you look considerably better for it."

"Did you sleep?"

"I had a solid, recharging hour."

She swept her hands over her face and back over her hair. "I should have coffee, update the board."

"Tell me, will updating it now change anything for your investigation or your victim?"

"No."

"Then let's try this. Why don't we cap off that much-needed nap with a swim? After that, if you're still anxious about the updates, I'll give you a hand with them."

"That's a good deal." Maybe, marginally, even better than coffee. "I could use a swim."

"Grab something more comfortable than your work clothes to change into after."

"Is that like that old line?" She slid out of bed. "Putting on something more comfortable?"

He looked at his wife, her whiskey-colored eyes alert again, her body loose instead of limp.

"It could be, though that wasn't the original intent. I had in mind a T-shirt and lounging pants."

She pulled both out. "Like these?"

"There you are."

Taking her hand, he drew her to the elevator.

Inside, she leaned companionably against him. "Have you ever pulled carrots?"

"You're oddly stuck on that, aren't you?"

"Well, it was so weird. Have you?"

"I have not." He shot her a cautious look. "Are you telling me you'd like to plant carrots so you can harvest them? Or, as you said, yank them out of the ground?"

"Jesus God, no." The idea of it, and the accompanying image of the two of them doing just that, made her laugh. "We planted that tree by the pond, right? I think that covers us for the duration."

"I enjoyed planting that tree, but agree. It covered us."

They stepped into the tropical air of the pool house with its potted palms and brilliantly blossoming vines.

The water sparkled, a perfect blue.

"If I don't work in a swim every few days, I forget how good it feels in here." She shed her vest. "I figured on hitting the gym, then the dojo, then the pool today. But one out of three's not bad."

"Should I feel guilty I managed all three?"

She glanced back as they both undressed. "No. I'll catch up eventually. I bet you worked, too."

"A little here, a little there. The progress on shoring up the infrastructure of your building's coming along well."

On that, she rolled her eyes and dived into the water.

On her first lap, she heard him dive in. He swam beside her, an easy pace. While sleep had been a desperate need, the swim, the cool water around her, her muscles warming and stretching, relaxed her, body and mind.

After six laps, she surface dived and did the last two underwater.

Then, she came back up, sucking in air before rolling over to float.

"I could do a cop bar."

Rather than float, he lazily treaded water beside her. "You could, as it's yours, but it's more than a bar, isn't it? The space is a music venue, a club. I'll add you have the Blue Line only so many blocks away for brews and fake burgers and such."

"Yeah. Well, cops like music. And not just for cops."

"Which would limit your patronage."

"Clubs are noisy. You wouldn't go there—a cop wouldn't—to bounce around the sticky parts of a case like you do at a bar like the Blue Line. Same with civilians. They're not going to brainstorm a work problem, or talk shop, right? People go to a club to blow off steam or look for somebody who wants to get laid. So . . ."

She rolled again, treaded water with him. "Off Duty."

"Clever. I like it. Your waiter who's put in a long day serving others is off duty there as much as the cop who's spent the day on the job. Your admin, store clerk, and so on. They're all Off Duty."

"Great. Now I don't have to think about it anymore."

"I'll have some design options tweaked to suit for you to look over in a few days."

At that, she just sank beneath the surface.

On a laugh, he went under, grabbed her. And pulling her to him, met her mouth with his. Still locked together, they surfaced.

Legs lazily kicking in tandem with his, she studied him.

"You didn't want me in something more comfortable. You wanted me naked."

"I'd be mad not to."

"And your cap off to the nap included pool sex."

"Well now, naturally."

"Plus, it's still Sunday."

"With more than enough time for Sunday pool sex before it's Monday."

"How long can you hold your breath?" On the question, she fixed her mouth to his, and pulled him under.

Long enough, she thought, to pump heat into her blood. Long enough for him to take them both deep, into the water, into the kiss, then push off the bottom so, wrapped together still, they shot back up into the air.

"How long can you?" On another kiss, he took them both back under, where they rolled together, a playful dance, hands sliding and seeking. Sliding and seeking still as they kicked up together.

"We could time it." She fixed her teeth on the side of his throat. "See who has more lung power."

"Winner takes all?"

"Win or lose, we're taking all."

"In that case."

He pulled them under again, and slipping a hand between her legs, shot her to a fast, unexpected peak.

She surfaced, weak and gasping. "That's cheating."

"I heard no mention of rules."

Fair enough, she thought, and kept her eyes on his as she stroked her hand down all that wet, sleek black hair. "You'd break them anyway."

"To have you? I'd break every one of them."

But when he started to draw her close, she shot away, went deep, pulled out the speed, and aimed for the far end.

She swam like a fish, he thought, and gave chase as he knew she intended. No, a mermaid, he corrected, with all that grace and power in the water.

The chase stirred his blood as much as the feel of her skin under his hands, the taste of her on his tongue.

When he caught her—no simple feat—he heard her laugh bubble out. When they surfaced again, they were both breathless.

"I'd say we're even."

He felt her heart race against his. "I'll take a draw."

"Then you take me; I'll take you."

Now she wrapped her legs around him and stole the rest of his breath with her lips.

She bewitched him, delighted and enchanted him. And aroused him beyond all comprehension.

When he gripped the edge of the pool, he pressed her back to the wet wall. "Mine." He touched his finger to the little dent in her chin, then skimmed it down, and down. "You're all mine."

"Same goes. Now show me. Show me how much you want me."

He took her mouth first, let the hunger come, let it fill him to aching while she answered with equal fervor. And when her arms locked around his neck, she filled him.

He drove into her and watched the pleasure rush into her eyes, heard the echo of it in the catch and release of her breath.

"Show me," he said.

Wanting to, wanting him, she kept her arms locked tight. Her hips moved, meeting and matching his thrusts while the water sparkled around them.

His eyes, bluer, deeper than the water, held hers as everything in her opened for him, opened to him. It built and built, that glorious thrill, the dazzling and welcome heat rising, spreading until the long, slow climb took her to the peak.

Then spilled her over.

Still, she held him. She gave him more.

"I love you." On her words, the return of that love swirled into his eyes. When she tried it in Irish, his lips met hers with such tenderness her heart all but wept.

"*A ghrá.*"

He pressed his lips to her shoulder, to the side of her throat. And on love, took them both over.

Blissful, she clung to him. She could feel his heartbeat slow again, as hers did. Whatever she'd faced during the long day, whatever she'd face on the next, she had right now.

"That was a really good cap." Sighing, she stroked his hair. "And we've probably still got some Sunday left."

"We do."

He'd have given the rest of his to help her set up her board, to let her bounce theories, timelines, whatever she needed.

And for right now, knowing he would was enough.

"Why don't we get some popcorn, more wine, and finish that vid?"

He eased back, looked at her face. "That sounds perfect."

When they stretched out on the sofa, with popcorn, wine, and the cat, Eve thought: Everything else can wait until Monday.

The annual Battle of the Bands in Memorial Park drew a solid crowd. It lacked headliners, but the music was free, and it gave a chance for bands—usually garage or basement bands—to play to a real audience.

By the time they got to this summer night, most of the seriously crap ones had been weeded out, so the half dozen finalists could hold their own.

Most had some paying gigs in their pockets—school dances, backyard parties—that barely covered the subway fare and a fizzy.

But tonight, the big prize was ten thousand actual dollars, and more, a guest shot on *Here's Talent,* a professional production of a vid/disc, plus Internet exposure.

Each group performed three songs. An original, unless it blew, usually chalked up extra points from the panel of three judges.

You had your rockers, your poppers, your thrashers, and your hick stompers.

And every one who walked onto the stage knew the crowd's reactions played into the judges' scoring.

They played hard.

Arlie hooted and cheered along with the crowd. Some of the bands— three so far—were better than she expected. Better yet? Being here on a summer night with her boyfriend of four entire months.

His friend played bass guitar and did vocals in Arrow, the last band of the night. She and Moses, her friend Nikki, and Nikki's girlfriend, Dawn, were going to scream like crazy for Arrow.

As much as she loved the free music, the night out, she really enjoyed judging the costumes and outfits.

She'd just turned seventeen two weeks before. One more year of high school, and hey, *senior* year, and she'd head off to college to study design.

She had a small college fund, and had saved what she could working summers, a lot of weekends, and breaks at her mother's shop.

Since her mother was a tailor, and a damn good one, it was solid experience. But she didn't want to fix clothes. She wanted to design them.

She hoped for a scholarship, so she didn't have to work every damn break and every damn weekend in college. Unless she got a solid internship.

But all that was down the road, like her mother said. Right now, the music blasted, and like most of the others she was on her feet, dancing or clapping.

She'd heard Arrow, and they were pretty mag. But she worried they wouldn't beat the band onstage now. The all-girl band Sisters, who rocked it into fricking orbit.

She didn't want Moses—she was just wild for Moses—to be disappointed.

To prove it, she tempered her applause, and kissed Moses. Kissed him under the stars with the music blasting.

He so did it for her! And they'd done IT four times now.

Tonight, since his parents were out of town visiting friends, and her mom said she could spend the night with Nikki, would be the big fifth.

An all night long, since Nikki would cover for her and she'd spend the whole night with Moses.

They'd never actual slept-slept together before, or woken up together. The thought of it had Arlie's romantic heart soaring.

When Sisters rolled into their third song, Arlie lifted her arms high, waved them.

"They're good, Mose."

"Yeah, can't lie. But Arrow's going to bring it. And they're going to take it."

He turned to say something to Dawn, and Arlie gave her attention back to the band.

If she'd designed their outfits, she'd have put the lead vocalist in red leather skin pants. She had the body for it. She'd have paired that with—

Something stung her arm. Her first thought was wasp, and in reaction she squealed. But the sound didn't reach over the music and shouts.

She *hated* wasps, actively feared them. So she had to brace herself to look down, with her teeth gritted as she braced more to flick it away.

She only saw a red mark, which relieved her even as she thought: Bastard. Go sting somebody else.

As she rubbed at it, she saw some jerk grinning at her.

"You think it's funny?" As she shouted it, Moses turned back to her.

"What? What's funny?"

"Nothing. I got stung by a frigging wasp, I think, or a bee, I guess, and that guy—"

She broke off as, when she started to point him out, he wasn't there.

"Forget it. Doesn't matter. Just some jerk."

"You got stung? Let me see."

"It's no big." She didn't want to spoil things because she was a baby about stupid wasps. But she pressed her hand to the mark, tried to ease the nagging pain.

"Come on, let's have a look." Moses nudged her hand away, turned her arm. "Whoa, that was some wasp. I bet it really hurts."

"Yeah, feels hot, too."

"I'm going to go get you some ice for it."

"You're so sweet." It had her kissing him again. "Wait till the break between bands. It's just a sting."

But when the song ended to wild cheers, her legs didn't feel right.

She had to sit on the ground while Moses went to get the ice. Ice would help because she felt really hot.

"Let me see." Nikki, with her eye on medical school, took her arm. "Holy shit, Arlie, that looks infected. And it doesn't look like a wasp or bee sting."

Now her head didn't feel right. It felt like it could roll right off her shoulders. Her arm was on fire. She thought she saw flames coming right out of it.

"There's a rabbit over there. Where did a rabbit get those clothes?"

One look at her friend's eyes had Nikki's heart thumping.

"Dawn, call nine-one-one. Call an ambulance."

"Is she allergic to bees?"

"No, but I think it's a needle stick. Nine-one-one, Dawn. Fucking now. Here, Arlie, lie down."

"I don't feel right. I can't breathe right."

She gagged. Nothing much came out before she went all the way down. "I can't breathe. I can't breathe."

"Take it slow. Dawn, go up there, have them use the mic to see if there's a doctor."

Because her friend's lips were turning blue, and she began to seize.

"Hurry! Hurry!"

With thoughts of the media reports of the girl at Club Rock It, tears spilled as she started CPR.

"We need help." She shouted it as she continued compressions. "We need a doctor!"

One came even before the MTs arrived.

But it was too late.

Chapter Eight

On-screen, the main character, kick-ass woman, kicked ass as she battled both bad guys and the clock. The other main, nerdy guy, raced against that clock, leading hostages—including tiny, innocent children—out of the target building seconds before it exploded.

Though wounded by shrapnel, he proved his mettle, emerged from the clouds of smoke with a toddler in his arms.

Given the distance, Eve figured they'd all—including said toddler—have gone up in pink mist. But she put that aside as she enjoyed the visual.

Just as the music swelled, Eve's communicator signaled.

"God. Goddamn it."

Saying nothing, Roarke rose from the sofa to walk to her closet.

"Dallas."

Dispatch, Dallas, Lieutenant Eve. See the officers at
Memorial Park. Minor female, DOS, apparent OD.

"Do we have an ID on the victim?"

Nine-one-one caller ID'd victim as Arlie Dillon.
Dallas to confirm.

"Notify Peabody, Detective Delia. I'm on my way. Dallas out."

He'd taken out lightweight gray trousers and a sleeveless top, with a waist-length jacket the color of the smoke the nerdy guy emerged from.

He'd added the boots, the belt, and had already begun to change himself.

"It's going to be another late one," she began. "You don't have to—"

"I'll drive." He pulled on a fresh T-shirt. "You'll want to run the victim, hoping to find some connection to Jenna Harbough. Otherwise, it's random, isn't it?" His eyes met hers. "And that's worst case."

"Don't get bitchy when I say you think like a cop when you think like a cop."

After strapping on her weapon, she grabbed her badge, her 'link.

He heard her mutter another curse as she shoved things into her pockets.

"What is it?"

"Nothing. Let's move."

"A bit short, are you?"

As she walked out, she gave an irritable shrug. "I didn't expect to work Saturday night through Sunday. Through freaking Monday morning. I had other things on my mind besides pulling out more cash.

"I can tap Peabody until I hit a machine."

"Stop." As they went down the stairs, he took out a money clip, peeled off bills. When she didn't stop, he just stuffed them into her pocket.

"Don't get bitchy when you run out of the ready, and I haven't."

"As if you ever could."

She wanted to fight about it—again—but she couldn't spare the time or energy.

Instead, she got in the passenger seat of the waiting car, started her run.

"Need a connection," she muttered. "Same school, same neighborhood, same something."

"They may have frequented the same places. Clubs, arcades. Had a mutual interest."

"Unlikely on the places, as the first victim lived Lower West and this one's Upper East. Damn it. Maybe a connection through the parents, friends.

"Why was she in Memorial Park at, what, around eleven on a Sunday night?"

She did a search there for events.

"Battle of the Bands. Music. Maybe they knew each other through that mutual interest. Music. Arlie Dillon's next of kin, Tisha Dillon, mother. Single, never married, a tailor, her own business. No father on record, no other offspring. The Harboughs might use a tailor, though I can't see why they'd go that far for one, any more than I see the Dillons going downtown for a doctor. But maybe."

Since she had the drive time, she dug deeper.

"No bumps on the victim. Seventeen, just a couple weeks ago, so nearly a year older than Jenna. Medical . . . nothing major, but confirmation Julia Harbough isn't the family doctor. Works part-time at her mother's shop, impressive grades in school.

"Got some social media here."

After a scan, she shook her head. "Music's not her thing. It's fashion. Designing. Damn it. Got a boyfriend. She'd already posted pictures from this band thing. *Ready for the battle!* with her and a guy, tall, white, about the same age. And another group shot with two other minor females. A couple, from the body language. So a group of four."

She put her PPC away as they approached the park. "We'll hope one of them saw something."

What she saw when they walked toward the police barricade were Jamie Lingstrom and Quilla Magnum.

Jamie, college boy e-genius, stood with his hands in his pockets. He'd let his fair hair grow just long enough for a stub of a tail.

Quilla, Nadine's teen intern, reporter in training and student at Roarke's An Didean, stood beside him in hot red shorts, purple high-tops that matched the current color of her hair, and a T-shirt featuring a guy with hair down to his ass manhandling a guitar.

Eve badged her way through, said, "What's this?"

"We were here." Quilla burst out with it. "A bunch of us from the school. Crack and Ms. Pickering came. We're going to put a band together for next year, and we got to come if we wanted to see how it all works."

Eve shifted to Jamie. "Don't you go to Columbia, when you're not interning in EDD or for Roarke?"

"Well, yeah. I tagged along. We weren't near the incident, Lieutenant."

She gave him credit for using her rank, and the carefully modulated cop tone.

"While we didn't witness the assault, we were moving in that direction. Quilla and I were, as she took videos."

"So we could study them," Quilla added. "And so I could write a story about the event." She offered Eve a disc. "I made a copy for you. In case there's something, um, relevant."

"Okay." Eve took an evidence bag out of her pocket. "Where are your adults?"

"They took everybody back. I mean they were over there." Turning, Quilla pointed. "And it happened over there. Nobody could've seen anything. But Ms. Pickering said everyone would be available for interview."

"All right. Why are you still here?"

"I got permission, because Jamie's with me, and you were coming. And I tagged Nadine, and she said to document, and she's coming."

"Do you think it's connected to the murder at Club Rock It?"

Eve gave Jamie one long, flat look. "You're too smart to ask me that question at this time, in this place."

"Yes, sir."

"Stay here."

"Ah, sir, I could assist if—"

She cut Jamie off with that same look. "This is a minor female. She is in your charge."

"Bogus" was Quilla's opinion. And the opinion got her a swift elbow jab from Jamie. Which resulted in a massively exaggerated eye roll from Quilla.

Rather than dignify any of it, Eve walked away.

"They're dating, aren't they?" The idea made her twitchy. "How can they be dating?"

"Well now, that usually begins with mutual attraction, perhaps a mutual interest."

"Shut up."

She saw the body on the grass, gauged its proximity to the now-empty stage. Far enough back, she judged, there would have been people in front of them.

She stepped up to the two uniforms near the body.

"Let's hear it."

"Sir. The call came in at twenty-two-forty. The MTs, standing by for the event, responded within two minutes. A witness, Nikki Lieberman, was performing CPR on the victim, and a doctor, Dr. James Marcell, took over from her. The MTs attempted to resuscitate the victim, but weren't successful. Several uniforms assigned to the event, including myself and Officer Danby, also responded. Danby and I arrived just as the MTs took over. We secured the scene, while other officers moved the crowd clear."

"How much of a crowd?"

"Estimate about twenty-two hundred, Lieutenant," Danby told her, "not including the performers, judges, vid crew, concessions, souvie stalls.

"We have the three individuals who came with the victim, Lieutenant. We've also secured the performers and the vid crew, and others who worked the event. Most of the crowd disbursed. A lot of kids, Loo," he added. "And if they came with adults, the adults got them gone. We had some panic to deal with, but felt securing the scene had priority."

He'd have been long gone anyway, Eve thought.

"Where are the people she came with?"

"They've got a couple tents behind the stage. Their parents gave permission for the interviews. There's an officer with them in one of the tents. They're pretty shook."

"All right. Let's get some shields around the body. I don't want to see this dead girl on the morning media."

She looked to the skirted table—judges' table—and concluded from that vantage point they'd have seen nothing to help. "I want someone to interview the judges, get their contacts. Release them. Anyone who was back of the stage, in one of the tents, the same. Hold the video crew, and whoever was onstage. Either my partner or I will talk to the victim's friends as soon as possible."

With her field kit, she crouched by the body. A pretty girl, her hair in long braids with blue woven with the black. Blue, like the undertone in her skin, like her mouth.

Eve took out her Identi-pad.

"Victim's ID confirmed as Arlie Dillon, mixed-race female, age seventeen. Resides 1205 Third Avenue. Victim's skin, mouth have a blue cast. The only visible wound, an apparent needle mark, reddened and raw, left biceps. My on-scene concludes the same method, same drug cocktail, administered without her consent as Jenna Harbough."

She took out her gauges. "TOD, twenty-two-forty-two. Two minutes after the nine-one-one. How much longer from the injection? Not much. It won't be much."

Arlie also wore a cross-body bag, a larger one than Jenna's. Opening it, Eve read off the contents for the record.

"Purse contains victim's ID, twenty-six dollars in cash, a 'link, two key swipes, some makeup, a roll-on scent, a toothbrush, two condoms sealed in their packs, a change of underwear."

Roarke handed her an evidence bag.

"Weren't going home tonight, were you, Arlie?"

"Peabody and McNab are coming."

"About damn time."

She took out microgoggles to get a closer look at the injection site. Same damn thing.

"Dallas, sorry, sorry. I didn't put the comm by the bed like I always do. We were dead asleep. Neither of us heard the comm for I don't know how long."

In the big scheme, Eve thought, it didn't really matter.

Another teenage girl wouldn't go home again.

"Bring in the morgue, the sweepers. Got a little puke there, so mark it. Sweepers aren't likely to find much in this mess. Over two thousand people stomped around."

"Media's swarming," Peabody told her.

"Yeah, I bet they are."

"Nadine's out there with Quilla and Jamie. Jamie asked us to ask you if he could assist, since Nadine's here."

As she rose, Eve let out a sigh. "Go ahead and bring him in, McNab. He sticks with you. Take whatever group was onstage at the time of the attack. They're holding them behind the stage in tents. Tell him to keep his mouth shut, his ears and eyes open so he can learn something."

She stepped around the shield the uniforms had set up.

"Peabody, with me. She came with three people, and one of them was trying CPR. Are you sticking?" she asked Roarke.

"Can I be useful?"

"You could review whatever footage the vid crew has. They'd have panned over the crowd a few times. You see the angle here, and you know what we're looking for. That would be useful."

"All right then."

Peabody lengthened her strides to keep up with Eve's. "I'm really sorry for the delay. I should've been here before you. We hung around the house longer than we should have, then we just crashed."

"I'm not pissed. I was going to be, but we've been on with hardly a break for twenty-four. I ran the victim on the way here. No connection I can find to Jenna Harbough other than age. Even then, this vic's about a year older."

"He hit them both downtown. Not in the same sector, but that may say he lives or works downtown."

"It may. Hold on." She stopped at the stage, climbed the short steps to it. Then looked out.

"She wasn't as close as Jenna, but if you're standing up here, you could see her if you looked that way. You could see someone moving in on her, or dooser-walking away."

She jumped off. "We've got her boyfriend and two female friends. They're not suspects, so we'll take them together. One might jog something out of another's memory."

Well behind the stage she found three tents that had probably once been white. She stopped a uniform.

"Which one has the people who were with the victim?"

"That one there. Officer Casey's with them."

"Thanks."

She'd barely gone another three feet before she heard the weeping.

"Shit."

"I can take them, Dallas."

"No, no, just do what you do to try to settle it down."

She pushed aside the tent flap.

One boy, two girls sat close together on a ragged-looking sofa. A folding table on the side held mostly decimated platters of food—little sandwiches, fruit, cheese, some raw veg. Soft drinks and water poked out of ice melting in a tub.

A circulating fan did very little to dispel the heat.

Eve showed the uniform her badge. "We'll take this now, Officer."

"Yes, sir. Nikki?" The uniform put her hand on the weeping girl's shoulder. "You've got my card if you need to talk. That goes for you, too, Moses, and you, Dawn. Lieutenant, if I could have just one minute outside?"

Eve stepped out again.

"Sir, Nikki—Nikki Lieberman—has known the victim the longest, and she's the one who attempted CPR, told Dawn, her girlfriend, to call nine-one-one when she saw the wound. They're all very shaken, but it's hit her the hardest at this time. She's planning to go to medical school, or has planned, and now feels she's already failed. I thought it might help for you to know."

"What division are you in, Casey?"

"The one-five-three. Sir, if I overstepped—"

"You didn't. You stepped just right. Locate civilian consultant Roarke. You can assist him by doing preliminary interviews of the vid crew while he reviews their footage."

"Yes, sir. Right away."

Eve stepped back in where Peabody crouched in front of Nikki and held both her hands.

The boy had wept, too, Eve noted. A good-looking kid, Caucasian, his white-blond hair worn in a skullcap. While red rimmed his light blue eyes, they now looked shell-shocked more than tearful.

The girl on the other side of the weeper had a tear spilling out fresh, had her arm around Nikki. She had dark skin over sharp bones and her glossy black hair in long dreads.

Nikki's hair hit somewhere between maroon and Quilla's current purple, and she wore it nearly as short as the boy beside her.

Her eyes, miserably swollen, tipped up at the corners. Her face, blotchy from crying, made Eve think of Leonardo's burnished copper.

"I'm Lieutenant Dallas," she began, and Nikki pressed her face into the other girl's shoulder.

"Oh God, it's really happening."

"Nikki." Eve tried to get somewhere in the vicinity of Peabody's I-feel-for-you tone. "This is hard, I know. We're sorry for your loss, but we need your help."

"I *tried* to help her. I didn't."

"I'm going to tell you differently. You recognized she needed medical attention and directed Dawn to call for it. You attempted CPR."

"I must have done it wrong."

"You didn't, and a doctor wasn't able to revive her. The MTs weren't able. All of you did what you could. Someone injected her, and that injection was lethal and fast-acting. But you did all you could, and because of that we're here quickly."

"Why would somebody stick a needle in her?" Dawn demanded. "She didn't use. Maybe I've only really known her a couple months, but I know she didn't use. I know what it looks like. My uncle's been in rehab three times. I know what it looks like when somebody's using."

"Anything and everything you tell us will help us find out why, find out who."

"I wasn't even with her." Moses's lips trembled, and Nikki reached for his hand. "I wasn't even with her. I went to get ice. She said a wasp stung her, and when I looked, it was all red, so I went to get ice for it. And when I came back . . ."

"I'm sorry, I don't have your name."

"I'm Moses, Moses Rowe."

"Moses, it's hard, but can you tell me exactly what was happening when Arlie said a wasp stung her?"

"We were watching the band."

"Which band?"

"Sisters. Girl rock band."

"They were on their third song," Dawn added. "Every finalist gets three."

"And she said a wasp stung her?"

"She said . . ." Moses trailed off, then continued. "I remember it was really loud, everybody's into the music, and I heard her say something about being funny. No, she said, like, 'You think it's funny?' And I asked what was funny. She said about the wasp, and how some guy, and pointed. But said he wasn't there now."

"She's really scared of wasps," Nikki told her. "Regular bees wig her, but wasps? Freak time."

"It looked all red," Moses continued. "And like it really hurt. I said I'd get ice, but she said wait until they finished the last song. No big. She seemed okay, and I didn't go for the ice until the break between bands."

"You didn't see anyone near her?"

"It's crowded, sure. Lots of people. We're all watching the Sisters."

"All right. Nikki, Dawn, can you tell me what happened when Moses went for ice?"

"She said about the wasp, and I said let me see. It didn't look like a sting. I want to be a doctor. I volunteer at the hospitals where my dad works—he's a nurse. It was too big for a stinger, I thought. I thought it looked like a needle stick. I've watched vids where they use or used needles instead of the pressure syringe, and it looked like that. Only bad, infected."

"Arlie started to feel wrong," Dawn added. "And she said something about a rabbit wearing clothes, and sat on the ground. She puked a little.

I want to say I kind of froze, and it was Nikki who yelled for me to call for an ambulance. She had to tell me twice even, because I froze. And Arlie's eyes looked all glassy and then I could see all the whites, and she started shaking."

"Before, she said she couldn't breathe." Nikki took her own breath slowly. "And I tried to get her to look at me and breathe slow. But I heard about the girl at Club Rock It, and I was so scared."

"You were scared," Peabody put in, "but you did CPR. You were scared, but made sure Dawn called for help."

"She told me to run and find somebody, get them to go on with a mic and say we needed a doctor. But by the time I did . . ."

"The doctor came. The MTs came," Nikki murmured. "And the police, and nobody could help her."

"You're helping us now. The four of you came together tonight."

"Yeah. My friend plays in Arrow," Moses told her. "They're finalists, slated to go on last."

"What time did you get here?"

"Ah, we grabbed some pizza. We rode the subway downtown and grabbed some pizza. Then walked over. I guess, maybe like nine? Maybe a little before because we wanted a decent spot. It was already pretty jammed."

"They don't start until after the sun sets," Dawn explained. "Then the winning band from last year does a short set to get everybody going. We were here for that."

"Moses, how long have you and Arlie been dating?"

"Oh, um, like four months about."

"Was she seeing anyone before that?"

"Oh, well, um, we don't talk about exes much."

"Do you all go to the same school?"

"Yes." Steadier, Nikki gave Moses a modified eye roll. "Um, Dawn graduated, but we did. And yes. Before Moses, she and Wes Burke went around for a couple months, but they weren't totally locked, right? She decided if she was going to be with somebody, it should be a lock, so she told him to go on and keep seeing other girls, but none of them would be her."

"How did he take that?"

"He said, 'Fine, your choice.' He's a total cruiser, so it wasn't a bfd for him. Before that, she went out with Aaron Kowosky for about ten minutes. Then his dad got transferred to Atlanta or someplace, so move on. She dated some other guys, but none of them locked. Not like with Moses."

"Anyone you know who wanted to date her and she didn't?"

"There was Zeke, but that was back freshman year. He was a total wheeze back then. He completely pined for Arlie. Then he made the swim team, and whoa! If I went for guys, I'd go for Zeke. But he's abso-nutso for Sharleen. They've been locked for like a year."

Trying to finesse details, Eve took them through it again.

"Okay. Arlie didn't plan to go home tonight, did she?"

Moses blushed to the roots of his white-blond hair. "Ah, well. We were sort of planning go to my place. My parents are out of town till Tuesday."

"Her mother was aware?"

"No." Nikki spoke up. "I was covering for her. We said she'd spend the night with me. Do you have to tell her mom? I hate for her mom to know she lied to her."

"Not unless it proves relevant. Detective Peabody's going to arrange for all of you to be taken home. You've been very helpful."

"I didn't want to say before because it's, like, lame, but . . ." Dawn looked at the other two. "We saw the vid, didn't we?"

"I read the book, too," Moses said. "Both of them."

"Moses is a big reader." Nikki struggled to smile. "I guess we're hoping it wasn't all bullshit."

"The part about the detective and me, and everyone else involved in this investigation, doing everything we can to find who did this to Arlie and seeing they pay for it? That isn't bullshit.

"If any of you think of anything that might help, contact me or Detective Peabody."

"If you'll wait here a few more minutes," Peabody told them, "an officer will come and drive you home."

"Wasp," Eve said when they stepped out. "Arlie thought wasp, Jenna thought jab. And they both brushed it off so they could keep having fun. Why wouldn't they? And it wouldn't have mattered," Eve added. "I guess a couple more minutes of fun's better than more panic.

"I'm going to check with Roarke, see if there's anything we can use on that vid feed."

"I'll get that transpo."

"When they're on their way, come get me. We have to notify the next of kin."

Before she headed to another tent, she saw Roarke sitting on the edge of the stage, studying his PPC.

He glanced up. "Fresher out here. I have the original of the vid. This didn't please the operator."

"It's evidence. Anything on it?"

"It's a great deal of video. A pan at about the twenty-one hundred mark caught the victim."

He cued it up. "The closest one to her in this pan is a tall boy with short, nearly white hair."

"That's the boyfriend." She studied the screen, watched Arlie wave her arms in the air and laugh.

"He came up on the left side again."

"I've tried that angle. It's a very large, enthusiastic crowd, so difficult. And the timing? When or about she was injected, given the TOD, the operator focused on the stage. After the band finished, there's another long pan. You can see the one you've identified as the boyfriend—the hair's distinctive—trying to get through the crowd, moving toward the concessions."

"He went to get ice. She thought she'd been stung by a wasp."

"Ah. As consultant, I'd advise you to have EDD take this. They'd have the equipment to enlarge, pull in more than I can do on this portable."

"Yeah, I'll do that." Scanning the park, the stage, the screens set up for those who couldn't see the stage, she jammed her hands in her pockets.

"It's a crapshoot, but I'll do that. Or you could give the original to McNab before you leave."

"Am I leaving?"

"There's nothing you can do here now. Go get some sleep. Peabody and I have to do the notification. I'll be home after that."

"You said the mother lives uptown?"

"Right."

"Which means Peabody would have to go uptown, then down yet again."

"It's the job."

"In which I'm officially an expert consultant, civilian," he reminded her. "Let her stay with McNab, Eve. I'll do the notification with you, then we'll all go home and get some sleep."

She scrubbed at her face, shoved at her hair. "All right. All right, logistically it's better. She stays downtown, and she can drop into Central and write this up, then go home and get some sleep."

"You're very strict."

"That's why I'm LT. Peabody!" she called out, gestured. "Give her the original of the vid," she told Roarke. "Bag it, Peabody, give it to McNab. I need EDD all over it. Looking for the shortish dooser in the crowd shots. Tell him to find us a miracle. In the morning. Tonight, he can go with you into Central. Write this up. I'll copy my on-scene recording.

"Roarke and I will do the notification."

"Oh, sure. Are you sure?"

"You're down, we're up. Morgue, eight sharp."

"I won't be late."

"Don't be. I've got a picture of her from her friends," Eve said as she and Roarke walked away. "I don't see a junction with Jenna. Different types, different interests, different schools. Arlie definitely made time to date. Solid grades—they had that, I guess. But Arlie worked part-time, wanted to go into fashion design. Only child, just her and her mother, no father in the picture. Different looks, so it's not a type, not that way, he goes for."

She hissed out a breath as she saw Nadine doing a stand-up, with Quilla and Jake off to the side. Every other reporter doing stand-ups turned as Eve approached the barricade.

And every one of them shouted questions.

"There will be no comments at this time. Shout yourselves hoarse for all I care. The NYPSD has no comment on the investigation at this time. You"—she pointed at Nadine—"over there. You"—now at Quilla—"stay put."

As she stepped to the far side with Nadine skirting the barricade to join her, she called back to Quilla.

"I can feel your eyes rolling at me. And oh!" She glanced back, slapped a hand on her heart. "It burns."

She heard Quilla laugh, ignored it.

"First, you bring the rock star?"

"I might've been able to stop him if I'd had your stunner. Might, possibly."

"Second, you keep the kid here?"

"The kid," Nadine countered, a little pissy with it, "is my intern, and has permission from the school to stay until I see her safely back. Which is momentarily. What—"

"One question, just one at this time on this investigation, and I block you for a month. I'm fucking serious."

"I get that. I just want anything I can tell Jake. Off the record, whatever you need. Just anything I can tell him."

"There's nothing, Nadine." She held the look. "Nothing, and even the nothing's off the record, that ties the two victims together except method."

Nadine nodded. "Understood. Thank you. Should we wait for Jamie?"

"He's with McNab and Peabody. They've got him."

"We'll take Quilla back. If you need any research, need anything—it stays off the record."

"I'll let you know. Roarke? With me."

Ignoring cameras and questions aimed at her, Eve pushed her way through.

Roarke waited until they sat in the car. "You told her, without telling her, it's random."

"Ten minutes researching both victims, she'd know anyway. The difference is? She won't go on air with it, not until tomorrow. Not until after the notification.

"Let's go get this done."

Chapter Nine

"Tisha Dillon." Eve looked deeper into the victim's mother as Roarke drove uptown. "Age thirty-nine. Pretty young when her daughter was born. No marriages, no cohabs. Started as a seamstress in the Garment District, worked in alterations at a high-end boutique, then started her own business about fourteen years ago.

"Does okay," Eve noted. "Employs one part-time seamstress—and that's her mother."

She set the run aside.

"He chose two crowded events geared to a younger crowd. One indoors, one out. There's nothing, at this point, that connects the two victims, other than him. It's not impossible he knew both of them, but I don't have to do a probability to know it would hit low. Lower yet that they knew him."

She closed her eyes. "Okay, okay. Music event. Same age group. Both mixed-race females, but different builds, different coloring, different interests. One uptown, one down. And for a lot of people that's like living on different planets.

"First vic, private school, second, public school. And that's different planets. First vic, no serious romantic or sexual relationships. Second dated regularly and had a serious boyfriend of a few months. She was either sexually active or about to be."

"You're hoping for common ground."

"And not finding it, not beyond the surface. If it's not who they are, it's what. I can't find a what beyond their age group, gender, and being pretty."

As he hit a red light, he glanced over. "Maybe that's all he needs."

"And that makes it a nightmare. Because he plans, Roarke. He plans. The mix of drugs, the delivery system, selecting the kill spot, the timing. But his victims are chosen on the spot? No real stalking time, no particular research? He could've known both were attending an event—that's possible. Finding Jenna in the club, not hard. Just hang out awhile, wander awhile, hit the dance floor. But finding Arlie in a crowd of a couple thousand? I don't buy that one. Not her specifically, not beyond finding a pretty teenage girl."

"And that makes it a nightmare," Roarke repeated. "As what would be two successes in his mind means he's got no reason to stop, does he?"

"More. Two successes on consecutive nights. No cooling-off time, no downtime, no sitting around whacking off on it. Just back to it."

Roarke found street parking on Third, which made her wonder why he always seemed to have better luck there than she did.

It probably connected to the fact he was a gazillionaire, and she wasn't.

She got out, walked the half a block with him while she studied the building they approached.

Midsize, post-Urban, a mix of residential and commercial. Standard buzz-in security, which was, she thought, useless.

Rather than buzz in, she mastered into a small, more than reasonably clean lobby with a pair of elevators.

She gave them a dubious study.

"She's on four."

"You want the stairs," Roarke concluded.

She did, but . . .

"I'll risk the moving cage."

It smelled like Thai food—spicy Thai food. She concluded somebody had gotten a very recent delivery or brought home takeaway.

"You'll be Peabody, right? You know what I mean."

"I do, and I will."

He took her hand, squeezed it. She squeezed back.

"This is hard for you, too. And you've done back-to-backs."

She stepped out.

"Four-oh-four."

At the door, she pressed the buzzer.

After midnight, she thought. Probably sleeping.

She waited, considered buzzing again. Then saw the shadow move over the Judas hole in the door.

"Yes?"

"Ms. Dillon. Tisha Dillon?"

"Yes."

Eve held up her badge. "Lieutenant Dallas, with consultant. NYPSD."

Even as she finished identifying herself, she heard the rattle of the security chain, the thud of locks.

Tisha yanked open the door.

Her skin, a few shades darker than her daughter's, was beautifully clear and smooth. She'd passed on the bone structure, the shape of the eyes, the build.

Now those eyes held fear.

"Arlie."

"May we come in, Ms. Dillon?"

"It's Arlie. I had a pain in my heart, a terrible pain in my heart. I—I went to bed early, and this pain woke me."

She stepped back, not so much to let them in as to step away.

"Something happened to Arlie."

As Roarke closed the door quietly behind them, Eve looked into a mother's terrified eyes.

"Yes, ma'am. I regret to inform you your daughter's dead."

"No." Using both hands, she covered her mouth, just shook her head.

"You should sit down, Ms. Dillon." As gently as Peabody, Roarke took Tisha's arm, guided her to a chair in cheerfully striped blue and green. "Could I get you some water?"

She looked at him. The plea in her eyes, the one that said, so clearly, *Say it's not true*, died away.

"No. No, thank you. How can you be sure it's Arlie?"

"I identified her fingerprints. In addition, she had her ID in her bag." Eve sat across from her on the edge of a sofa with a green back and arms, and cushions that matched the chair. "She had three friends with her."

"Nikki, Moses, Dawn."

"Yes, ma'am."

"Was there an accident? At the contest, on the subway? Where is she? Where's Arlie? I need to go to her."

"Ms. Dillon, I know this is hard. Arlie was murdered."

"What?" Tisha gripped both arms of her chair. "How? Why? No, no, this is a mistake. She was with Moses. He's a good, responsible young man. And Nikki and Dawn."

"I'll explain as much as I can. Do you recognize the name Jenna Harbough?"

"No. Why?" Fire flashed over her face. "Did she kill my baby?"

"No, ma'am. Jenna was killed last night. There have been extensive reports in the media."

"I worked today. I had to work because a client . . . Doesn't matter. I had music on. What does it have to do with Arlie?"

"Though the investigation is ongoing, we believe they were both killed by the same method, and the same person."

"What method? Who?"

"I can't tell you who, and can only assure you that the NYPSD is working diligently to find this individual. Arlie was injected, without her knowledge or consent, with a lethal mixture of illegals."

"Illegals? Arlie never, *never* used illegals."

"Without her knowledge or consent, ma'am," Eve repeated.

"Why would anyone do that? I know there were police there, and medicals." When her lips trembled, Tisha pressed the back of her hand against them, steadied them. "Why didn't anybody help her?"

"Both medicals and police responded quickly once contacted. Moses, corroborated by Nikki and Dawn, stated Arlie thought, and said, she'd been stung by a wasp."

"A wasp." Now Tisha closed her eyes. "She's afraid of wasps. One got into her bed somehow. She was just a little thing, about six. It stung her four times. I ran in because she was screaming, grabbed her up, and it was still on her arm. I killed the hell out of it. She's been afraid of them since."

"Believing that, she more or less ignored it. When Moses looked at her arm, it was very red at the site. He went to get her ice."

"He's a sweet boy," Tisha murmured.

"It was a few minutes after the injection, and he was getting the ice, when the reaction set in. Nikki stated that was when she herself looked at the arm, and believed it was a needle stick."

"Nikki wants to be a doctor."

"Yes. She acted quickly, Ms. Dillon. I want to stress that. She directed Dawn to call for help, and tried to help Arlie, including administering CPR."

"They tried to help her."

"They did."

Her eyes filled as she nodded. Eve could all but see the force of will that held the tears back. "They tried to help her. It's good to know that."

"I understand how difficult this is, but I need to ask you some questions. And at some point, I'd like to go through Arlie's room."

"Why her room?"

"I may find something to help find who took her from you, Ms. Dillon."

"She doesn't know any killers. You can look all you want. Arlie's a miracle. My miracle. I don't mean she's perfect. I wouldn't want that for her. Just like I know she and Moses had sex. She's seventeen. I remember what it's like. I was twenty-two when I had her. The boy I thought I loved and loved me said we'd get married. I believed him, and we made plans for a wedding, for a baby.

"Then he left. Arlie's more careful and a lot smarter than I was. She has ambitions, good friends, she's working hard to try to get scholarships. She didn't know anyone who'd do such a horrible thing."

"Sometimes you don't realize you know something. Did she ever indicate someone pressured her?"

"Not Arlie. She'd have told me. Not because she told me everything, God knows, but because for Arlie, she said when, how much, yes, no. She makes her own choices and doesn't tolerate bullies."

She folded her hands in her lap. "I could use that water now, if you don't mind. Over in the kitchen there. I'm sorry. I should've offered you both something."

"We're fine," Eve assured her as Roarke rose to get the water.

"When did Arlie decide to go to the event tonight?"

"It's been a couple weeks, I think. Moses has a friend whose group made the finals. So once that happened, I think she wanted to go more for Moses than herself, really. Not that she didn't want to go. Thank you."

She looked up at Roarke as she took the water. "You look very familiar. Have I tailored for you?"

"You haven't, no. You taught Arlie your craft."

"Like my mama taught me. She had the touch, too, and the eye. More, she wanted to design clothes, go to school to learn more. She'd draw and draw her ideas. Sometimes she'd draw something for me or herself and we'd make it. A Dillon original."

"Ms. Dillon, is there someone I could contact for you? Your mother?" Roarke suggested.

"No, let her sleep. It'll be hard tomorrow. She dotes on Arlie so. I don't want anyone right now. I don't want to talk to anyone, not right now. I need to be alone with her because she's here and here." She pressed a hand to her heart, her head. "That's what I need."

"If I could give you my contact? You could let me know when it's best for us to go through her room."

"All right. But I need to see her. I know her spirit's flown. I think that's why my heart hurt. But I still need to see my daughter."

"I've requested that the chief medical examiner take care of her. He'll contact you tomorrow, so you can go see her."

"Chief? He's the best?"

"Yes. In every way." Eve dug out a card. "You can contact me anytime. If you have questions, if you think of anything, however insignificant it might seem."

Eve rose. "We're very sorry for your loss, Ms. Dillon."

"Yes. Thank you."

Halfway to the elevator, Eve heard the first keening wail.

Despite the hour, when they got home, she updated her board, her book.

"Lieutenant, you need sleep."

"I need sleep. I need thinking time and I can't think. I'm sending a request to Mira—she'll get it in the morning. I need a consult on this. I need a profile, and no one's better.

"I can't see him, and I need to. I don't mean how he looks, but—"

"I know what you mean."

She sent the request to arrive at eight, then shut down.

"At least it's not Sunday anymore." As she rose, she pushed at her hair. "So I can start badgering the lab, have this consult, start working on chem labs, chem students. He's going to at least look like a teenager or college kid," she added as Roarke steered her out of the office.

"He blends, so . . . I need to find out what other events like these two are coming up. Geared to that age group. Crowded events. Maybe I should pull in Detective Willowby. She can pass for that age group."

"You'll decide tomorrow."

"I'll decide tomorrow," she agreed, and began to undress. While she did, she planned out her agenda.

Then, as she had her command center, she did her best to shut down her brain as she got into bed.

"Make room, Tubbo," she told the cat, then sighed when Roarke wrapped an arm around her. "I can't see him."

"But you will."

"I will."

The dreams took their time weaving into sleep. They came with music, crashing guitars, pounding drums. With lights flashing.

The two dead girls danced with the crowd around them no more than a frantic blur of motion and energy.

"We're young!" Jenna said.

"And we'll never get old."

"I wanted to write songs that made everybody want to dance. I'd be a rock star."

"I'd design your costumes," Arlie told her. "You'd look so frigging mag in Dillon originals."

"We had another hundred years coming, right?"

"Damn right. We got screwed, totally."

"It hurt when he jabbed me." Jenna pointed at the needle in her arm.

"Tell me! It hurt when he stung me." A wasp the size of a golf ball sat on Arlie's arm.

"Asshole."

"Jerk."

"Dooser!" the girls said together, and laughed as they danced.

"You saw him. Give me something," Eve demanded. "I need to see him."

"Asshole. Jerk. Dooser," they said together.

"Why should we pay attention?" Jenna shrugged.

"He's not in our club."

"What club?" Too hot, Eve thought. Just too hot in here. Out here. Where was here?

"Like normal." Jenna bopped her shoulders, her hips.

"No wheezes, weebs, flakers allowed. Normal, living our life, so no you, either, Boss Cop."

"She's old," Jenna reminded Arlie. "We're not."

"Wasn't a normie when she wasn't old. I mean Jee-sus! Just skulking around when she was our age. No friends, no fam, no nothing. No normie."

"No normie," Jenna conceded.

"It's not about me," Eve began, and the music stopped; the light held bright.

Then she stood in that bright light in the buzzing hallway of her state school.

She could smell it: sweat, cheap cologne that couldn't cover the sweat, hints of—forbidden—gum and candy. Whiffs of the even-more-forbidden Zoner wafting from the bathrooms along with the faint aroma of piss.

Other kids brushed past her. Some sneered, some snickered, some ignored her as beneath notice.

She preferred being ignored.

She wore the ugly blue uniform—the pants too short because her legs kept growing, the top baggy because her frame stayed too thin.

She'd tried to cut her hair, and made a mess of it, so even pulled back it looked ragged and uneven.

She just wanted to get to class. Get through the next class, and the next. Get through the day, get through the night. And mark another off. One day closer to freedom.

Freedom came in twenty-two months, one week, and three days.

She'd take the money she'd saved from the stingy monthly stipend—the money most of the others blew on snacks or smuggled-in Zoner—and she'd go to New York. Into the Academy.

She'd be a cop, and when she was a cop, she'd be somebody.

She could get through twenty-two months, one week, and three days more, as long as at the end of it she climbed on a bus headed for New York.

Thinking of it, dreaming within the dream of it, she didn't pay attention. She knew better.

"Uh-oh," Jenna said, and snagged her attention.

"Here it comes." Arlie winced. "No bruisers allowed, either. But you'll live through it. We didn't."

She saw the bruiser, a girl who'd earn the title at five-ten and a solid one-sixty of muscle and mean.

"Shouldn'ta sassed me, bitch."

She didn't have time to block the punch before it landed and shot waves of pain from her jaw to her toes.

It shoved her out of sleep so that she reared up, a hand on the jaw she swore felt that fist.

"Lights on, ten percent. What the fuck time is it? Display."

The lights glowed low. On the display she saw five-twenty-two.

"Okay, fine." Galahad crawled into her lap, bumped his head on her arm. "It's fine, it's fine." She gave him long, slow strokes to comfort them both. "Should get up anyway."

Seconds later, wearing one of his king-of-the-world suits, Roarke rushed in.

"I'm okay, I'm okay. God, you didn't have to break off from buying Australia or whatever. I'm fine."

"I'd just broken off—though I still lack owning a continent."

"Only a matter of time."

"You . . . well now, you yelped." He sat beside her, stroked her hair as she had the cat. "Grabbed your face and shot up in bed like an arrow out of a bow. A dream, I take it."

"Yeah, ending with Big Bitch Brenda—she called herself that—sucker punching me in the face."

She wiggled her jaw. "I swear, I felt it."

Because he believed her—her dreams came so lucidly—he brushed a kiss over her jaw.

"And is this Big Bitch Brenda real, or just a dream person?"

"Oh, she was real. Back at school. She bloodied me a few times. Me and whoever else she decided needed bloodying. She had a low threshold there," Eve remembered. "So hardly a day went by without somebody getting bashed."

"Ah." Leaning in, he kissed her jaw again. "And what did you do about that?"

"Nothing for the better part of a year, hoping she'd get tired of it. She didn't. So I spent a few weeks studying boxing vids, practicing, trying some martial arts. The next time she went at me, I kicked her ass. Mostly, I think, because it threw her off I fought back. But she tried again later, and since I kept practicing, I kicked her ass again. She didn't have any form. Just force.

"After that? She left me alone."

"And where is Big Bitch Brenda now? You know."

"Doing fifteen—her second round inside. Felony assault. Anyway, since I'm awake, I should get moving."

"I'll get your coffee, as I want some myself."

"Hold mine till I shower."

He turned to stare at her. "Did you say hold the coffee? Did the dream punch from Big Bitch Brenda knock something loose?"

"The dream punch woke me up. Bang. So yeah, hold that."

She rolled out, jumped in the shower. Maybe she was running more on adrenaline than sleep, but she was running.

When she came out, he not only had coffee but breakfast under warming domes.

"You don't have another meeting?"

"I do, and it's breakfast with my wife. Pancakes, because whoever topples Big Bitch Brenda deserves them."

"I'm in." She plopped down beside him, and when he removed the warming domes, drowned her pancakes in butter and syrup.

"Is that all you dreamed?"

"No. The girls, both of them."

She ran it through for him while she ate, and since it was right there, hit the bacon.

And he kissed her cheek, so damn sweetly.

"Okay, yeah, it tossed me back. They had it right. I wasn't a normie. No club for me back then. He's not in one, either."

"Bullied, you think?"

"Maybe, and probably, but not by those two."

No, she thought, she'd have gotten the sense of that if they had been.

"They're not the type. Ignore, shrug off, not see, maybe snicker at. Yeah, that might play. But they weren't bullies. And they didn't know him. I'm coming down on the pretty damn sure he didn't know them."

"Back to the type then?"

"Possibly a popular, pretty girl bullied him, or ignored him, or broke what he thinks of as his heart. But he's wrong, he's wired wrong, Roarke. Not just that he kills, but how he does it."

"You're thinking again."

"Like I said, the punch woke me up. So here's to Big Bitch Brenda."

She lifted her coffee in toast. "He needs the venue—one that offers easy escape. He needs the crowd to blend into, and a selection of targets to choose from."

She polished off the pancakes. "At least that's my current morning thinking."

"You're starting to see him."

"Maybe. I'm not sure. I was bullied, Mavis was bullied. Neither of us would've been welcomed into Club Normal. It takes more to hunt and kill, to plan and follow through. The drugs, that plays in. Access or ability to create. He understands chemistry, even if it's just a dealer's understanding."

She rose, went into her closet, and considered the fact she had to put the work deal together herself.

"It's raining, and will be most of the day," Roarke told her.

"Great."

She grabbed black pants—because, damn it—and a simple black tee, also because. But to avoid The Look, pulled out a light blue jacket.

She dressed, avoiding The Look primarily, in her opinion, as Roarke was busy warning the cat not to try the feline combat crawl and pounce on the breakfast plates.

"I'm going to head out."

"I have another meeting shortly. Hold a minute."

He stacked both plates under one dome, then put them on top of a highboy.

"He can't jump that high."

And yet, halfway to the stairs they both heard the dome rattle to the floor.

"Bloody hell. He's relentless."

"He should get points for figuring out how to get up there."

"I'm leaving him to Summerset." He grabbed Eve's shoulders, pulled her into a kiss. "See you take care of my cop."

"I'm too old for him. Plus, I'm the one who took down Big Bitch Brenda."

"You are indeed. There's an umbrella in your car, not that you'll use it."

"Nice to know it's there." She paused, looked back. "If you walked by and saw a sidewalk sleeper with his ass parked against one of your buildings while he played the harmonica, what would you do?"

"I'd give him a bit of the ready for the song and his situation. Why?"

"No reason."

He would do exactly that, she thought. She'd seen him do exactly that. Because people weren't invisible to him.

Who were you invisible to, Dooser? Who pulled your trigger? Or, hell, were you just born to kill?

She walked out into the rain—a warm, soaking one that only added to the humidity. In the car, she drove downtown through miserable traffic loaded with people she decided would never, ever learn how to drive in the rain.

She took her thinking time, but even when she got to the morgue, she still didn't have a clear picture.

She sat a moment, listening to the rain.

She could see herself, as she had in the dream. Pants too short, frame too thin, hair all wrong. Trying to be invisible.

Don't notice me, don't talk to me, just let me get through this and get out.

"But that's not you, is it? No," she muttered. "No, that's not you. You want people to notice, to look at you. You want attention. You're craving it. And from girls—has to be from girls most especially."

Sex, she thought. Sure, especially if he hit in that same age range. But attention, admiration, too. But you're blocked from the club you want into so bad.

Attention, she thought again.

"Well, hell, you're getting plenty of it now. The venues? Maybe not just for convenience. For the attention."

Nodding to herself, she got out of the car. Not a clear picture, not yet. But it was coming.

Chapter Ten

S he'd grabbed Morris coffee from the in-dash AutoChef before
she headed down the tunnel.

Another day, she thought, another teenage girl on a slab.

The ME wore a suit under his protective cape, one in pale, pale blue
with a white shirt that had that same tender blue in needle-thin stripes.
His tie, a bolder blue, coordinated with the cord he'd woven through the
braid he'd rolled into a loop at the back of his neck.

She wondered if he dressed with such stylish formality for himself, for
his position, or out of respect for the dead.

And decided all three.

He played rock again, but lowered the volume when Eve came in.

"Two in two days." Eve gestured with the coffee before walking back
to set it beside his sink.

"Another bud who will never bloom." His eyes, enlarged behind the
microgoggles, met Eve's. "There's a saying about youth being wasted on

the young. I don't agree, and hope she made good use of that youth while she had it."

Eve thought of Big Bitch Brenda. "I like my youth just where it is. Behind me."

"No stray thoughts of recapturing it?"

If she let herself, she could still feel that sucker punch. "Oh, hell no."

"I suspect that puts you and me in the enviable position of being content with the here and now." He set his microgoggles aside.

"So, onto the work that, oddly, contents us. Both the victims and the method used suggest one killer. Another healthy young girl who'd barely begun to live. No sign of previous illegals use, no signs of alcohol abuse. Her last meal, enjoyed, I hope, about four hours before death, was pizza and a fizzy lemonade."

He walked back to the sink to rinse the blood from his hands, picked up his coffee.

"She'd recently ingested a twenty-four-hour pregnancy blocker."

"She had a boyfriend—a couple of condoms in her bag, and his parents were out of town for the weekend."

"Ah well." After walking back, he laid a sympathetic hand on Arlie's shoulder. "The best-laid plans." Then he smiled as Peabody came in.

"I'm still not late!" she insisted.

"No, you're not late. Same general area for the injection," Eve added.

"Yes. Slightly lower on the left biceps than the first victim."

"The second's taller. She thought she'd gotten stung by a wasp. She had a thing about wasps."

"A sharp, quick sting." Morris nodded. "Yes, I can see that. From the site, he takes little care with the penetration. In fact, the opposite."

"He wants them to feel it."

"And they certainly would have. My initial analysis, which the lab will confirm, is the same mix of illegals as was used on Jenna Harbough. The needle itself was certainly dirty, and again coated as before. Her system would have reacted in the same way, or very nearly the same. Only minutes between injection, the onset of symptoms, and death."

"And that's the only thing that connects them. I can't find anything else." Wouldn't find, she was nearly sure of it. "Arlie Dillon was Upper East, Jenna Harbough Lower West. Different schools, different interests, different lifestyles."

"Other than their age and gender, their basic health," Morris commented, "physically they're not similar."

"It's not how they look, but what they are. And where."

"In a crowd," Peabody put in. "And when? At night, in a crowd. A loud, crowded area."

"With a lot of teenage girls to choose from. The victim only has one parent in the mix. Her mother. No sibs."

"Ah." Morris let out a sigh. "More pain. I'll contact her when Arlie's ready. I don't expect Arlie to tell me any more to guide your way, Dallas. But if she does, you'll know when I do."

"I'm going to hit the lab, see if I can squeeze something out there."

"I'll wish you luck," he told her as she and Peabody started out. "With nothing linking them but method and murderer, we all worry we'll stand here like this again tomorrow. Or soon after."

She didn't worry, Eve thought, because if they didn't find more, she had no doubt they'd stand there again.

Peabody trotted to keep up. "McNab headed straight in to work on the club feed."

"Good. Unless the bastard got in the same way he got out, he'll be on the feed somewhere."

"Shit! You think he came in through the window?"

"Not impossible. But it's riskier than just sliding in with a group. And harder," she added. "The way the window tilts, harder to squirm in, and time it so nobody's in there when you squirm.

"He's on that damn feed."

She slid behind the wheel, tapped her fingers on it. "Lab first. It's early, but that gives us a jump on nagging Dickhead, and we can nudge Harvo."

"Did you get anything from the mother?"

"Enough to tell me the two victims didn't know each other. It's not impossible, but again unlikely, the killer knew them both. I sent everything to Mira, asked for a consult."

That would help clarify angles. It always did.

"I think he needs attention—that's part of it all. He killed the first during an Avenue A performance. They're a big deal, and that's going to generate media."

"Last night's event? Another big deal," Peabody confirmed. "Draws a big crowd, with whole lots of bunches of people live streaming it. A lot of publicity."

"I bet he recorded it. And I'd bet your month's pay and mine he's done the same with all the media on the murders."

"I really need my month's pay. We bought a new bed and it's— I'll get to that later. But I really need my pay, because new bed, and this cocotte I want so ultra bad. Plus, we have to outfit our new, amazing powder room. We have a powder room! And stuff. But since it sounds like a sure thing . . . Except sure things can be sucker bets."

Winding down, Peabody frowned.

"This is why I don't gamble. How do you know a sure thing from a sucker bet?"

Simple, Eve thought. "They're all sucker bets. Just ask Santiago's cowboy hat."

That got a laugh.

"Then I'm a sucker because I'm laying my month's pay on the line with yours, because yeah, he's watching the media on this. He's swimming in it."

Since she had Roarke's cash in her pocket, Eve turned into a lot near the lab.

"Why?"

"Why is he swimming in it? Well . . . He couldn't hang around and watch them die, right? This is the next best thing. And if he didn't know them, which probably not, he gets to know them. The reports lay all that out. And it'll all be how tragic, how horrible, and he'll swim in it because he made it happen."

"All bets are sucker bets, but your money's safe because that's absolutely right."

"I'm going to say I just doubled my money and buy that cocotte."

As they walked to the lab, Eve tried to resist, ordered herself not to even consider asking. Then gave up.

"What the hell is a cocotte?"

"It's a pot. A French cooking pot. I bet Summerset's got one. I want it for my fabulous kitchen, but it's like nine hundred dollars, so—

Eve stopped dead. "Nine hundred dollars? For a pan?"

"A pot. A French pot."

"Does the price include going to France to buy it?"

"If only," Peabody said dreamily. "But since I doubled my money, I can afford it. Now I just have to decide what color. I may go for the red, because big pop of color there. But the blue is so gorgeous."

Eve put her hands over her ears and walked into the lab.

Early, yes, she thought, but already a hive of activity. That gave her a boost.

She made her way to Chief Lab Tech Dick Berenski's workstation. Resorting to bribes became routine too often when dealing with Dickhead. But when the case involved kids, she could usually count on him moving without the added incentive.

His egg-shaped head bent over his work while his long, spidery fingers crawled over a keyboard.

When Eve approached, he looked up, scowled at her.

"How about giving me more than five fucking minutes on a fucking Monday morning?"

"Jenna Harbough, age sixteen, died Saturday night. Arlie Dillon, age seventeen, died last night. A lot longer than five minutes."

"Yeah, yeah, some of us had the weekend off, and spent it at the beach with a big, busty blonde in a tiny red bikini."

"You wear a tiny red bikini?"

"Har! The blonde wore one. On and off," he said with a leer.

"I guess it's just their bad luck these two teenage girls won't ever hang on the beach again."

"Yeah, yeah." But this time he muttered it. "The weekend crew DNA'd your puke, right? And I'm checking their tox on the first vic, running the second. I got Morris's report here says the first wasn't a user."

"She wasn't, and I've just come from Morris. Neither was the second."

"Both of them—what I'm seeing, both of them—got a bomb jammed inside them. The heroin, that was enough to do it alone. Not Junk, the pure. You don't see the pure like this. Not seeing a cutting agent. I want to run them both again, but I don't see it. Then there's ketamine. See that?"

He pointed to his screen with symbols and equations Eve couldn't have deciphered with a stunner to her throat. So she said, "Okay."

"Given the first vic's size and weight, enough of that to take her down if not out. Then you've got Rohypnol."

"You're sure of that?"

"I'm looking at it, aren't I? Threw in a roofie."

"Fatal dose?"

"Nah, but he tossed it in. Enough to take her down again. Just this, I'd say he wanted to get her somewhere and rape her. But with the heroin? She wouldn't live long enough. Then you've got traces of fucking potassium chloride. It's overkill, it's all overkill. Sick, twisted bastard son of a bitch. Used an infected needle on top of it.

"See that?" The anger came through as he pointed to the screen again. "That's *Treponema pallidum*."

"Berenski, I'm just a cop."

"Ever had syphilis?"

"No, I have not."

"This is what causes it. What he did here, what I'm seeing here, is he coated the needle with *Treponema pallidum* bacteria—with a chemical booster for fast action. It ain't fatal, and she'd be dead before she showed any symptoms. But that's the infection at the injection site."

"A roofie and an STD," Eve murmured.

"It's the same formula, the same dosage in the second vic. The exact same down to the frigging microliter. I'm running them both again. See that? That's an agent, a compound, and what it does is it inhibits the enzymes in the bloodstream, the CYP3A. Can't do its job, so the drug works faster, the bloodstream absorbs more of it, gives it a bigger punch."

Careful, Eve thought. Took no chances.

"It had to work fast," she said. "He couldn't have them lucking out with medical intervention."

"Easier to dump some cyanide in their fizzy. This took work, precision— and I mean precision—knowledge, and some goddamn skill. It's fucking science. It's bad science, fucking mean science, but it's science."

"Yeah, it is. Where would he get the ingredients?"

"A goddamn lab." Visibly pissed, Berenski threw up his arms. "It's not just getting them. We don't have heroin this pure around here. You guys hit a gold mine like that on a raid, maybe somebody skims some. Or maybe he makes it his damn self."

Bang, Eve thought. That was a fresh bang.

"From poppies?"

"From freaking poppies. Research lab, biochem lab, medical lab. A roofie's not hard to come by, and you can score some Kettle on the street. But the rest?"

He shook his head. "Even if you have access, you need damn fine skill to make this mix. And a sick fuck brain, Dallas, to think it up."

"All right, appreciate it. I need to talk to Harvo about the fabric from the window at the first scene."

"Like she's got nothing else on her plate." Then he shrugged his shoulders, beetled his eyebrows. "Go ahead. I'm running these again."

"Peabody," Eve said as they wound through the lab, "find out if we've hit a gold mine on an illegals raid in the last three years."

"I think we'd have heard if the NYPSD confiscated a hunk of pure heroin, but I'll tag Detective Strong in Illegals."

With a nod, Eve kept winding to Harvo's workspace.

The Queen of Hair and Fiber had a chin-length bob of blue hair today, about the same shade as Morris's tie. She wore a pink T-shirt where what looked like a rat in a lab coat held a smoking petri dish and wore a maniacal grin.

Below it read:

BEWARE THE LAB RATS!
THEY'RE SMARTER THAN YOU.

With it she wore blue baggies and pink air sneaks.

"Hey, Dallas. Running your Saturday night fiber now. Nothing came to me on the Sunday night thing."

"Nothing to send."

"You know, I was thinking of hitting the Battle of the Bands Sunday, but I zipped to the Hamptons. My cousin's boyfriend's sister had a place up there for a couple weeks, did an open house deal for the weekend. Pretty frosty."

Swiveling, she placed a speck of fiber on a slide under her scope.

"I can tell you by eyeballing this, it's a cheap, synthetic blend. I'm going to say from pants, and new ones. Nothing the killer had in his closet for a while, nothing he washed."

"You can tell that by eyeballing?"

She grinned, much like her cartoon lab rat.

"That's why I wear the crown. But we'll verify that."

She straightened. "Window frame, right?"

"Right."

"Gonna be pants. I know they're working on trying to get a partial on the scuff marks on the wall. So he boosted up. Maybe you catch your sleeve, part of your shirt, but pants, that's more likely if you're going out headfirst. You want to see where you're going, make sure nobody's out there, so headfirst."

"You bucking for my job, Harvo?"

Smiling, Harvo tapped the top of her head. "I like it here, in my queendom, with my crown."

She swiveled again when one of her machines beeped.

"Yeah, got your cheap synthetic blend, cheap black dye, sizing's pretty damn stiff, so new. It's pants. Could be a jacket, but it's too hot for that in a club, so pants. That much sizing in a shirt? Nope. Wash this fabric a few times, you're going to fade the dye, break down the sizing, and the fabric's going to fail after, oh, a dozen washes. Cheap shit, right off the rack."

"The one wit says black baggies."

"Sure, cheap, new baggies, so probably a little stiff—not the kind of drape you want in baggies. Doofus-wear."

"Or dooser?"

Considering, Harvo tilted her head. "Well, most doosers are fashion-forward and strutty with it. That's the dick part of it. But the one you're looking for isn't."

"If he's a teenager?"

Harvo puffed out her cheeks. "Used to be one myself. You're a teen on a really low budget, you might have to settle. But most would scrimp, save, beg, whatever, to get a decent pair if they're going to see Avenue A at Club Rock It.

"Kids judge, Dallas, and judge hard. Doofus? You don't know any better because doofus. If he's wearing this . . . Hang on."

One more swivel, and she used her desk 'link.

"Hey, pal, how's the partial coming? Uh-huh. Oh yeah. Dallas is right here, so I'll pass that. Dog and fizz? I'm in. Cha."

She turned to Eve. "My footwear counterpart thinks he's going to pull a partial. No way for a full, but a partial, and if it rolls, he should have a brand or range of brands for you by noon. When we're grabbing lunch."

"I appreciate it, Harvo. All around."

"We all live to serve, right? The protect part's strictly on you."

"Yeah. Well, cha."

She wound her way back as Peabody came her way.

"Plenty of Junk, no pure. Not in over five years. Harvo?"

"Cheap, synthetic baggies. Or most likely baggies. She called them doofus-wear."

"The cheap ones don't hang right. Plus, they don't last for shit. I bought a pair once for gardening or shopwork. Not even good for rags after a dozen washes."

"That fits what she says. Would you wear a pair to a club?"

"Oh, eternal mortification hell no. My budget was so tight when I came to New York it cut off my air, but I'd have died of embarrassment wearing those out anywhere."

"So either he can't afford better or doesn't know any better. They were new, so he bought them deliberately. He wanted to blend, so if he knew better, he wouldn't have bought the cheap. And he had to plan, so time to squeeze the budget enough for decent."

"So he's fashion-declined. Unlikely to have friends who'd tell him how to dress."

"Among other things." As they walked, Eve's 'link signaled a text. "Mira. She's reading the file now. She'll let me know when she has a window for the consult."

"We know a little more about him."

"Yeah. Start on the labs. He's got to be young or look it. Maybe he's a chem major—top grades. Maybe he's a lab rat or an intern. Pure heroin. Where's he getting it? Or how's he making it? Growing his own poppies?"

"You'd need a hell of a lot, wouldn't you?"

"I don't know enough about it, but I'm going to find out."

She paid the ridiculous parking fee.

"I need a cash machine."

"It looked like you had plenty."

"It's Roarke's."

"Isn't most of the cash in all the world Roarke's?"

"Sure seems like it," Eve muttered. "I'll hit one at Central."

"I know a little about harvesting medicinals. We didn't do opium!" she said after Eve's stony stare. "But I know a little, so I'm looking it up. You need opium poppies," Peabody began, reading off her PPC. "Okay, a lot of steps. It takes about three months to grow and flower, then the petals fall and you've got the pod. The pod's the ovary, where you get the opium. Then you have to cut the pod a certain way, with this curved knife, and extract the opium. It like drips out, secretes for a few days."

"Time-consuming. Exacting."

Down, Berenski said, to the microliter exacting.

"Yeah, and there's more. So when the sap oxidizes, it makes a resin. You have to collect that with another knife and make it into bricks and wrap that up. And then there's boiling and drying and more. Finally, you have to make a solution if you're going to inject it, so you have to liquify it, boil it to get it in a syringe.

"And okay, like ten tons of the raw opium comes down to, after all this, about one ton of heroin."

"If he's making his own, he's got land or a greenhouse and the facilities to go through the long, exacting process. But he doesn't need a ton, does he? A couple of pounds would more than do."

"Maybe he's just buying it."

"Cheap synthetic baggies. Pure heroin costs a lot more than a good pair of pants. Add the other drugs in."

Eve changed angles. "Or, if he could afford but just didn't know better, it's science—his science. He had to come up with the formula. He knows his science, and can either make the stuff or peel off enough to experiment with it."

She pulled into the garage at Central. "Start on the lab angle. I'm going to hit a cash machine, then try EDD, see where they stand."

She drew out the exact amount Roarke had given her and put it in the pocket opposite the one she'd already pulled cash from.

They'd deal later.

She took the glides and thinking time to EDD, and found McNab and Feeney in the lab.

"We may have him," Feeney said immediately.

"Where?"

Eve studied the screen and pointed before Feeney could answer. "This guy here. You can't see his face, or much else because he's keeping behind these two. Taller. And this one broad with it. He's what, five-six?"

"That's my take, and we can verify. We just hit. Time stamp's twenty-one-twenty-three."

"McNab, see if you can ID any of the group he's blending with."

McNab, bony hips twitching to his inner beat, nodded. "Working that now."

"Black baggies, I can see that. Can't see the footwear, the shirt. His fucking face. But . . . brown hair, right?"

"Reads brown. Can't get a gauge on the length, 'cept it looks long in the front. This here?"

He froze the screen. "The way the hair falls over his face. Maybe wearing shades from how it falls, but it's only a partial between the two guys in front of him.

"Can't get skin color. He's careful. But we don't have the baggies, height, hair color, and that front length coming out again, so we may have him."

McNab did a little dance in his not-cheap canary-yellow baggies. "Got two of them, Dallas. Sending names and contact info to your e's now. I interviewed these two. They came with a group of five, all guys, between, ah, fifteen and seventeen. Came for the music and the babes."

"Give me a sec."

He pulled out his portable, checked his notes.

"Yeah, yeah. One of these two, and two others in the group, danced with the vic and her friends. One time. Sort of together but not, but made some conversation."

"Good. This is good."

"I want to run all of it, then run it again," Feeney told her. "Make damn sure."

"Yeah, but this is good. It's a strong good. Send me the names, McNab. I'll contact for follow-up. We know more, so maybe we'll get more. They're working on the possible print off the scuff. Harvo said cheap synthetic blend on the fibers. And I've got the full formula for the cocktail injected. I'll copy you on my report."

"We'll get the bastard, kid."

She nodded at Feeney, then headed out.

She believed that. She'd always believed she'd track the bastard down. But would they get him before she stood with Morris over another teen-age girl?

She swung into Homicide, and even with her mind elsewhere had to wince at Jenkinson's tie.

Today's offering had what she thought might be magic wands scat-tered all over a bloodred background. Each one shot a different glittery stream of color.

"LT." He signaled her, forcing her to move closer to the eye burn. "My esteemed partner and I . . ."

He trailed off as Detective Reineke hiked up his pants leg to show off the white rabbit peeking out of a magic hat.

"Sweet color-blind Jesus."

"We're closing one we hit at oh-five hundred this morning." Jenkinson fluttered his tie. "Investigative magic."

"So you say."

"Damn straight. We're clear if you need any assist on the two girls."

"Peabody, share the load on the chem lab angle with the two magi-cians. I need ten minutes—fifteen," she corrected, "then we're in the field. Follow-up interviews. We may have him coming in with a group, hiding his sorry ass behind them."

"That's big!"

"It's something. We get more, it's big. Add in approximately five-six, brown hair. If they get any other details or sightings, we'll add those.

"Fifteen. Be ready to roll out."

In her office, she hit coffee, then updated her board and book. She copied Mira, her commander, Feeney, and McNab on everything.

When she contacted the first boy, she found them both together at their summer job. Working at a deli only a few blocks away.

One more good, she thought, and walked back into the bullpen.

"Let's go, Peabody. Detective Sergeant."

Jenkinson looked over, sent her a grin. "Lieutenant, sir!"

"Watch the kids while I'm gone."

"As always."

Peabody waited until they were out of earshot. "I actually like today's tie."

"Don't make me hurt you," Eve warned, and took the glides down.

Chapter Eleven

E ve weighed the four-block walk against the morning traffic and parking issue.

"We're walking. It's only four blocks."

"Okay, sure, but it's raining."

"Oh, rain! In that case, we're walking. We'll be talking to Hank Kajinski and Devin Spruce, both seventeen, both working at the Corner Deli."

"I know that place. They make incredible cheese blintzes, and their matzo ball soup's seriously mag."

"We're not going there for lunch, Peabody."

When they reached the main lobby, Eve headed for the doors, and the rain.

A slow, steady sky drip that turned the city into a sauna.

People huddled under umbrellas—some, Eve thought, bought hastily from a street vendor who sold them at a premium at the first drip. Others, shoulders hunched, trudged along scowling like the wet equaled a personal affront.

She watched a woman, legs scissoring despite the heels, dashing up the sidewalk with a shopping bag over her head.

And vehicular traffic, as she'd predicted, crept inch by inch with horns blasting.

"You'd think a little rain ranked as one of those biblical plagues, like, what is it, locusts."

"Or water turning to blood."

"That's ridiculous." Wasn't it? "That's a plague?"

"It's a popular one. One of Egypt's ten, and one of the seven predicted in Revelation."

"How do you know this stuff?"

"Oh, just things you pick up."

"I'd put them right down again," Eve decided. "We have to deal with enough blood without worrying about it spurting out of the shower."

"Okay, that's guaranteed to give me daymares the next time I take one." Peabody jerked her head right. "The guy across the street's selling fold-up umbrellas for fifty bucks."

"Yeah, I saw him. Anybody stupid enough to pay that deserves to get hosed. Plus, he'd make us before we crossed the street, and I'm damned if I'm chasing him. And we're here."

The Corner Deli actually stood on the corner. Most of the breakfast or bagel-and-schmear-to-go crowd had come and gone, but a few lingered on stools at the spotless white counter, or waited out the rain (good luck with that) over coffee and one of Peabody's blintzes at an equally spotless postage-stamp-sized table.

The place smelled of baked bread, of pickles and onions and boiled eggs. And somehow it all combined into a single, appealing aroma.

Hank Kajinski was working the display counter and currently boxing up a round of rye for a waiting customer.

Eve judged him as six-one, with youthful vid-star looks, the kind that would cast him as the high school quarterback. Thick blond hair under his clear cap, bright blue eyes, just the hint of a summer tan, square-jawed, and lankily built.

Eve waited until he'd rung up the customer and turned with a flashing smile.

"Good morning. How can I help you?"

She held up her badge.

"Oh, right! Should've recognized you guys. I saw the vid. I mean, who didn't?"

"Who didn't," Eve agreed.

"Dev's in the back. I'll get him, but I gotta get somebody to cover the counter while—"

He broke off as a woman strode out. Middle sixties, Eve gauged, sturdily built, with improbably red hair filling her cap with curls. Her skin was so white Eve wondered if she glowed in the dark.

"You the cops?"

"Yes, ma'am. We need to—"

She pointed a finger at Eve. "What'd they do? And I don't want to hear any namby-pamby megillah."

"They're not in any kind of trouble."

"We don't put up with criminals and deadbeats in here."

"As far as I know, ma'am, they're neither. They may have seen an individual we're looking for, and have fully cooperated in our investigation. This is a follow-up interview, as we've uncovered new information."

"About these two?"

"Indirectly only."

"Jeez, we didn't do anything. I told you—"

Now that finger pointed at Hank. It bore a sharp, murderously red nail Eve imagined capable of slitting a throat with a single swipe.

"Hush! Go get Devin." She pointed across the room. "Take that table. I'll bring you a nosh."

"We're fine, thank you, but—"

"You sit in my place, you have a nosh."

Better to move things along, Eve decided, and walked to the table.

"Whatever it is," Peabody told her, "it'll be really good nosh."

Hank came out of the back with his friend. If Hank represented the high school quarterback, Devin could have stood as his defensive lineman, with his broad shoulders, tough build. He had smooth golden brown skin, a long blade of nose, and big, dreamy brown eyes. His hair, a kind of brassy gold at the crown, fell into pure black twists.

Both boys yanked off their caps as they sat, as if they weighed half a ton each.

"Sorry about that, Officers."

"Lieutenant," Eve corrected Hank. "Detective."

"Yeah, still sorry about that. My bubbe's a hard-ass."

"That's your grandmother?"

"Yeah." Hank flashed the smile. "She says it's her job to keep me, and Dev, too, on the straight and narrow, so we don't end up putzes like her sister's first ex-husband."

"We didn't tell her about being at the club that night, you know." Devin hunched his broad shoulders. "She'd worry. We told the other guy . . . Sorry, the other detective guy we'd seen the dead girl—I mean before," he said quickly. "Before that happened."

"Understood. You danced with her."

"Sort of." He glanced at Hank.

"There were three of them. Excellent babe-age."

From behind him, his bubbe gave him the flat of her hand over the back of his head. "You don't talk about girls that way. You show respect."

"Bubbe, it just means they were pretty. Like you." That smile blasted out. "You have the most excellent babe-age."

She gave him the flat of her hand again, but this time lightly, with affection. Then she set the tray she'd balanced on one hip on the table.

"You'll have some babka, fresh this morning, and some sweet tea."

Devin looked at her with those big, dreamy eyes. "Thanks, Bubbe."

She stroked a hand over the brassy crown of his head. "Now, you tell the police whatever they need to know. With respect! Then you get back to work. We don't pay for you to sit and eat babka."

When she walked away, Hank forked up a bite. "It's extreme. You gotta eat it, or she'll give you all kinds of grief. Plus, extreme."

"You danced with the victim and her two friends."

"Sure, and a bunch of other babes. We weren't there to hook, you know? Just swim. The music was tight and total. They, the babes, a unit, right, Dev?"

"Check it. I think Chaz danced with one of them again, just the one, but a unit. We didn't hang with them, or anything like that."

"Let's go back to when you got to the club. You came as . . . a unit."

"Five of us," Hank confirmed. "Me, Dev, Chaz, Orlo, and Jonah."

"When you got there, to the door, did anyone else come in with you?"

Dev shrugged, looked at Hank. "Maybe. We were all talking, and ribbing Orlo because he was supposed to come separate with his girlfriend, but she dumped him the day before. Harsh, man."

"Maybe someone who was right behind the two of you. Your three friends were just ahead of you. We have Chaz opening the door, going in first."

"I guess. I didn't pay attention. We were pretty jacked about seeing Avenue A for free. No cover or anything. We all went last summer, so we knew it would slay."

"The little guy?" Frowning, Hank squinted his eyes as if trying to see something in the distance.

And Eve felt the buzz.

"A little guy. Shorter than you, than both of you."

"Yeah."

"Can you describe him?"

"I didn't really see him—I mean, pay attention. I only sort of noticed because when Chaz opened the door, he kind of blocked it for a couple seconds."

"Yeah, yeah," Devin confirmed. "He did this drama pause, said like, 'Now it begins.'"

"That's it, so when I had to stop short, the little guy bumped into me from behind. No big, but I thought, Jesus, man, we got all night."

"How do you know it was a guy, or he was short?"

"Oh, right? I sort of halfway saw him slide in behind me and Dev when we were all walking up the block."

"What did you halfway see? Any detail at all."

"Well. Sad, sad baggies. Crap kicks, too. That sounds harsh, 'cause maybe that's the best he could do, but that's what I thought when I halfway saw him slide behind us."

"Can you estimate his height?"

"I dunno . . . maybe . . . About as tall as my sister. Maybe about."

"How tall is she?"

This time he just lifted his shoulders, and Eve glanced at Peabody.

When Peabody pulled out her PPC, Eve turned back to Hank. "Skin color?"

"A white guy. For sure, on that. I guess I saw his arms. Yeah, yeah, I did. Really white, so he was wearing a T-shirt. Maybe a tank type deal. I didn't pay attention."

"Hair color, eye color?" Eve asked, and Hank began to look distressed.

"Is this the guy who killed that girl?"

"It's someone we want to identify."

"Jesus, Jesus, I don't want to guess on something like this. I don't want to be wrong on it. I didn't pay attention. I just gave him a glance back, that's all. You didn't notice?" he asked Devin.

"Sorry, man, I didn't. I didn't see him at all."

"Hank." Peabody pulled out her trust-me voice. "You've already helped us by what you did notice."

"But he was our age. Shit, I don't know that for sure, either. I just figured. I don't know if I saw his face. I don't think so. I've got nothing in the banks that says I did. I more noticed his bags, right? And thought something like, here comes a doof."

Time to back off, Eve thought.

"I'm going to confirm what Detective Peabody just said. You've helped us a lot, you've told us details we didn't have. We appreciate your time and cooperation."

"Okay. Sorry that's all I got. And, um, you could maybe eat some of the babka? Bubbe'll be pissed if you don't."

"Right." Eve broke off a piece with her fork and sampled. And found herself eating a small bite of heaven.

"Well, God."

Hank gave her a weak version of his smile. "Told ya. We gotta get back."

The boys rose together and, pulling on their caps, headed back to the counter.

"I ate my entire slice," Peabody confessed. "I couldn't stop myself."

"Easy to see why. Height?"

"Hank's sister's ID lists hers at five-five."

"We'll call it, for now, between five-five and five-seven. He's white. Hank confirmed the cheap-ass baggies. Apparently to go with the crap kicks. And he told us more than he realized."

"That the guy who slid in behind him wasn't worth noticing."

Eve took a second bite of cake. The streusel topping it hit a grand slam.

"My pride nearly exceeds the magnificence of this babka. The minute he noticed the sad baggies, the one wearing them sank beneath notice."

Eve pulled some cash out of her pocket, laid it on the table.

"You're not leaving that half a slice of babka."

"We need to get back."

Peabody solved the issue by wrapping it in one of the disposable napkins. "I'll give it to McNab," she said as she slid it into her pocket.

They started the rainy walk back.

"We can confirm approximate height and race. That's not nothing. Contact the other three friends. It's doubtful they noticed him at all. Hank barely did and only because he walked up behind him. I'll add these details and contact Arlie's group. We could get lucky."

Her 'link signaled.

"Mira. She's got a window now. I'm taking it. Try Jenna's group on it, too," Eve said, and quickened her pace.

She finger-scooped some of the wet from her hair as she stepped back into Central. Ignoring the elevators, she took the glides to Mira's level.

Where the dragon waited.

"Dr. Mira will see you now. Don't you own an umbrella, Lieutenant?"

"Probably." Eve walked by the admin's desk, knocked briefly, then walked into Mira's office.

The NYPSD's top profiler and shrink sat behind her desk, but stood when Eve walked in.

"You were quick," Mira began. "And you've been out in the rain. I'll get you a towel."

"No, I'm fine."

Maybe a little soggy compared to the soft and sleek that was Mira. She had her mink-colored hair twisted up and back today. It suited the straight lines of the white dress and short black jacket.

Despite Eve's words, Mira stepped into the adjoining bath on her white shoes with their black cap at the toes, the high, skinny black heels, and came out with a towel.

Eve scrubbed it over her damp hair as Mira moved to the office Auto-Chef for what Eve knew would be flowery tea in delicate cups.

"Sit," Mira told her. "I've read the file."

"We have a little more." To protect the fabric on the blue scoop chair, Eve laid the towel over it before she sat. "EDD nailed him on the security feed. Not his face, not much of him, but the group he merged with to help avoid just that."

Because it was expected, Eve accepted the tea.

"Peabody and I just talked to two of the group. Only one, so far, noticed the unsub. And only to give us an approximate height. Between five-five and five-seven. And his race. White. He was sure on the race, reasonably sure of approximate height. The only other things he noticed were the cheap baggies, and he says crappy kicks."

"So he noticed the height and skin color, the pants, the shoes. Nothing else?"

"That's right, and he wanted to."

"After the lack of fashion status in the shoes and pants, the rest was beneath notice."

"That's our take, yeah."

Nodding, Mira sipped her tea. "And still nothing to connect the two victims?"

"No."

"I don't think you'll find anything."

"Neither do I. It's not who they are. It's what. Attractive teenage females. They don't notice him, either."

"Or if they do, with derision. Or worse? Pity. And he, so clever, so bright, so skilled—"

"Can't get laid," Eve finished.

Crossing her excellent legs, Mira nodded again. "An involuntary celibate. The additions of a date-rape drug and the STD bacteria certainly indicate a sexual revenge element. They served no other purpose, but had deep meaning for him, personally. He knew they'd die in minutes, but he gained the satisfaction of knowing he'd dosed and infected them. The use of a needle when a pressure syringe would have been more efficient represents penetration."

"Why not dose them and rape them? Infect or kill them while they're under? Is he impotent?"

As she considered, Mira wrapped one of the strands of her triple chain of black-and-white beads around a finger.

"That's possible, of course, but though he wants them, he despises them as much or more. He needs their notice, their willingness, even their gratitude. They owe him attention, owe him sex, and as they give him neither, they're to blame. They're to be despised, and eliminated. Eliminated in a way that demonstrates his cleverness, his skills and intelligence. His superiority."

"Both girls noticed him after he injected them."

"Yes, and I'm sure he wanted that, that one shining moment—after the penetration. Look at me. See me. You're giving me attention now, aren't you?"

"And so is everyone else," Eve added.

It occurred to her the way Mira smiled at her, sat back, showed a similar satisfaction to what she felt when Peabody hit the mark straight on.

"Sure, he wanted the crowd, the dark," Eve continued, "but there are plenty of venues that cater to under-twenty-ones. These two events? Specifically chosen, I think, for the media attention that would follow the murders. We're all paying attention to him now."

Setting the tea aside, she pushed up to pace. "Not just the girls he killed. Yeah, I get that shining moment for him. Needed, necessary, but hey, they're dead. All he has to do is turn on a screen and he can see and hear all the attention paid. To him, about him. About his . . . accomplishments."

"I agree. Still, the media attention after Jenna Harbough wasn't enough. He found his second victim the very next night. No cooling-off period, no reveling in his success."

"He'd already picked the time and place, scoped it out, researched."

"Yes," Mira agreed. "But he's young, Eve, and though organized, meticulous in his science, he lacks impulse control. I would give you a range of fifteen to twenty-two, and my instincts say he falls in line with the ages of his victims."

"The wits would've noticed if he was older—into his twenties. He could look younger than he is, but . . . I don't think so. He targets girls in his own age range because those are what he wants. And despises."

Mira waited, stayed silent as Eve slid her hands into her pockets.

"An incel, sexually deprived, so sexually obsessed. He has to know chemistry. I toyed with the idea he had someone helping him create the formula, access the ingredients for him. But that doesn't play. That's attention and focus. A mentor, a partner takes something away from him."

She shook her head. "It doesn't play."

"I think he's very much alone," Mira said. "He certainly sees himself that way. Alone, unappreciated. Above average, likely far above average intelligence, at least in this area. He's familiar with formulas, drugs, chemistry, and has found a way to access or create the ingredients he's chosen."

"Pure heroin. It takes months and careful work to go from flower to drug. But he can't afford good clothes for his shining moment? That doesn't play, either. He had to make it himself, almost had to because it makes it his."

"And the heroin alone would have been enough to accomplish death. The ketamine and the rest, they add a little flourish, don't they? It makes it his formula. A signature."

"Yeah." Eve let that settle in. "Yeah, a signature. His own creation."

"The bacteria and the Rohypnol add the sexual revenge. The potassium chloride—"

"He's executing them."

Mira's quiet blue eyes met Eve's as she nodded. "Exactly, for crimes committed against him. The girls he chose, more or less in the moment, represent all of them. All the ones who ignored him or taunted him or refused him."

"Or just didn't see him," Eve murmured.

"He's a white male, most likely between sixteen and eighteen, of superior intellect with highly honed skills. He's organized; he plans. But then he acts on impulse, in that moment. A misogynist, narcissist, emotionally stunted, socially inept. He knows what it is to be bullied and scorned, but that's nothing compared to being ignored.

"The kills, followed by the media attention, and no doubt aided by masturbation sate his sexual cravings, but not for long."

Eve nodded again because it confirmed her own thoughts. "At that age, a passing breeze has a guy thinking about sex. But this one? For this one it's not the desire that fuels him. It's the denial.

"Eventually, the needle won't be enough of a stand-in for his dick. He'll need to rape one before he kills her."

"The cravings build again, Eve, so eventually is likely sooner than later. He spends a great deal of his time alone, at his work. Parental attention, if any, is minimal. His father or father figure is likely something he only aspires to be. Sexually attractive to women, successful, admired. His mother or mother figure . . ."

Mira twisted the strand again. "There, he feels scorn at best."

"He's short for his age. A big brain, but weak, physically on the puny side. Not athletic. Nobody invites him to parties or to just hang. He doesn't have a circle, nobody to stand up for him. Or tell him how baggies are supposed to drape."

Sitting back, Mira sipped some tea. "You have a picture."

"When I was that age, I didn't want a circle. Actually, I never wanted one, yet it just happened. But at that age, I made sure I didn't. I know what it's like to be singled out and get the shit kicked out of you emotionally and/or physically."

"What did you do?"

"Learned to kick back, harder. Get through it and move on. He can't move on. I wanted to be left alone. He wants the opposite. Even a punch in the face is attention, isn't it? When you can't even get that? You've got nothing."

"That's interesting." Head angled, Mira set her teacup aside. "There may have been a teacher, an administrator, someone in charge who saw to it he was left alone. Stop the bullying, the taunting, the teasing—an effort to protect him. And he may have felt even more isolated."

"He's a killer. You don't kill this way unless it's in you. 'You think it's funny?' That's what Arlie's boyfriend heard her say after she thought she got stung by a wasp. He stood close enough for her to see him. See him smiling or laughing at her pain. He strutted off the dance floor after jabbing Jenna.

"Proud of himself," Eve concluded. "He's a sick, twisted, vicious little son of a bitch."

"Well. Not the clinical conclusions I'll write in my profile, but yes. Yes, he is. Look for exceptional students, science and math particularly, in accelerated courses. He may have skipped a grade along the way, or taken early college courses.

"His school records would include incidents of bullying, unless that, too, was ignored. And, Eve, it's possible he could afford better clothes, but simply didn't know the importance, at that age, of the right brand or style. Alternately, he may come from a financially stable family, but is kept on a strict budget."

"Someone could buy his clothes," Eve considered. "Pick them, hand them over."

"Ah, so baggies aren't on the approved list. Also possible," Mira agreed.

"He's got plans for another."

"I'm afraid I agree. And very soon."

"Summer. Most kids are out of school. Some working part-time, and all of them looking for something to do. Where's the action, where's the fun? Some music, some noise, some excitement. He just has to pick his spot."

"And there are so many."

"Yeah, there are. I appreciate you making time for this."

"How much sleep have you had in the last, what, thirty-six hours?"

"It has to be enough." But it made her think. "You know, if he's got a summer job, or the big brain copped him an internship—lab work's where I lean. He's not getting a lot of sleep, either. Maybe taking boosters to get through the day. Or making his own."

"Considering the amount of sleep most teenagers need, you're very likely right."

"It's good. That's good. He'll screw up somewhere. Not soon enough, maybe not soon enough, but he'll screw something up."

She pulled out her signaling 'link. "An incoming from the lab. The scuff marks. Got a partial. Kick It brand, Zoomers, men's size between six and seven. That's small, isn't it?"

"Dennis wears a ten, if that helps."

"Small feet, short guy. And even I know this brand is crap. Cheap soles, dye bleeds, so enough for the partial. Bet he's got blisters. Gotta get on this."

"Keep me informed."

"I will. Thanks again." She kept her 'link in her hand as she tagged Peabody. "Find out what stores in New York carry Kick It brand Zoomers. We're looking for men's size six to seven."

"Small feet, crap shoes."

"I know that much. Find more."

She cut Peabody off, grabbed a glide.

Already a mistake, she thought. Scuff marks, trace on the window frame. Little, tiny mistakes.

He'd make more.

"Peabody," she said when she turned into Homicide.

"I'm looking now."

"Try venues that sell the baggies and the shoes, T-shirts, too."

"I'll add it."

"Jenkinson?"

"We're working it, boss. Hell of a lot of labs in high schools and colleges in this fine city. We've got you a partial list."

"Keep going."

She turned into her office, went for coffee. Took a minute to glug some down.

The bacteria. Medical lab, research lab. Internship.

Poppies. You'd have to have a greenhouse, or some sort of area to grow them. Then somewhere to do all the other steps.

Months of work. Privacy? Maybe you could grow the flowers without anyone thinking why other than flowers. But you'd need a place for the rest.

Privacy.

She took another moment to drink, to organize her thoughts.

She'd update her board, her book, take some thinking time. Just five minutes.

Look over Jenkinson's list, she decided.

Then she'd make her own. Cross-check, and maybe.

Ten minutes into the work, she heard footsteps—two sets, unfamiliar. Jamie and Quilla stepped into her doorway.

"Really?" was all she could think of.

"Sorry to interrupt, Lieutenant."

"Then don't," she suggested.

"Sir." Jamie stuck with the formal. "Captain Feeney sent me. I'm actually—was actually—with Roarke today, but my supervisor said if I finished my work in progress I could shift to EDD. So I did, but the captain said I should get your permission to assist on the investigation."

The kid had skills. She needed skills.

"Then you have it. That doesn't explain you." She pointed at Quilla. "You're not an e-geek."

"Actually, she's got—"

Eve cut Jamie off with a look. "Was I addressing you, civilian intern?"

"No, sir."

"Jeez, harsh. I'm pretty good, he was going to say. But I'm here on a project, just bopped down with Jamie."

Eve started to say bop out again, but curiosity got her. "What project?"

"I've got permission, from the school and Nadine and Feeney, to do a story on EDD. I can do interviews as long as I don't, um, impede any work. And Feeney has to review and sign off on the final before I turn it in."

The kid had skills, too, in her area of interest. Besides, Eve thought, Feeney's decision.

"And since I bopped with Jamie, I was going to ask, once this one's done, if I can do one on Homicide."

"No."

"For the upperclassmen." Quilla rolled right on. "Some of the students, especially the year-rounders like me, give cops the hard eye. We've got reasons for it. So it's good to show cops are mostly just people, doing a job. And if some of them are assholes, most are working really hard to help."

"We deal with things in this division that aren't appropriate for students."

"Why? You have two girls, dead girls, on your board. They're just like me. Like us. Or like I am now, I guess. Like most of us are trying to be. We've got some assholes, too, but mostly we're trying. Like Dorian's trying. Shit, Dallas, you know what they did to her in that place. You got all those girls out of there. They raped them and drugged them and sold them. They killed Dorian's friend, and nearly killed her. How's what you do here inappropriate?"

Jamie stayed silent, but Eve caught the look, the smile. The pride again. Christ, it was everywhere.

"And to think I put Nadine onto you. Now I've got two of you."

"Nadine says she's just helping refine what I had when she took me on."

She heard Peabody coming. "I'll think about it." Much, much later.

"Hey, Jamie, hey, Quilla. I have a strong probable, Dallas. L&W."

"What the hell is that?"

"Losers and Wheezes," Quilla said. "A store," she continued. "Crap junk your cheap aunt Jane buys for your birthday since she doesn't know better, or doesn't really give a shit. I wouldn't even lift a pair of socks from a L&W." She waited a beat, shrugged. "Back when I maybe considered the possibility of lifting."

"Uh-huh." But since she had an expert on the matter, Eve pursued. "Did you notice anyone at the band thing wearing Losers and Wheezes?"

Quilla tipped her head so her purple hair fell over one eye. "Didn't stick if I did."

"Off the record."

Quilla shrugged again. "Okay."

"Short white guy, around sixteen. Black tee and baggies, Kick It Zoomers, probably black."

"Kick Its?" Now Jamie spoke up, and the interns rolled their eyes at each other. "Subzero. Maybe you buy them if you have to spend a day walking in mud, because they're gonna fall apart in a couple weeks anyway."

"If I got caught dead in a pair, I'd die a second time of humiliation."

Quilla's statement cracked Jamie up. They fist-bumped.

"It doesn't stick," Quilla said again. "But I'll look at the vid again."

"EDD has it."

"I'll look, too."

"Fine. Scram. Go do what you're here to do."

"You'll think about it?"

"I said I would. Go away."

"Think about what?" Peabody asked as they went away.

"I'm not thinking about it now. How many L&Ws?"

"Seven."

Eve got up. "It could be worse. Let's go check out the losers and wheezes."

Chapter Twelve

"They're really cute together."

In the elevator, already squeezed in with other cops, Eve turned to Peabody.

"Put that in my head, I'll kill you in your sleep."

"I don't sleep at Central."

"I'll break into your apartment."

"McNab's right there with me."

"I'm a cop, for Christ's sake. I'll kill you, quick and quiet, then plant evidence that implicates McNab. You'll be dead; he'll be in a cage for life."

"It could work," the uniform crowbarred in behind them speculated.

"Oh," Eve said, "it'll work. And after I allow a single tear to slide poignantly down my cheek at her memorial, I'll go home and drink an entire bottle of celebrational wine and never, ever think about what a pair of teenagers are doing with and to each other."

"I just said 'cute,'" Peabody mumbled.

Eve swiped a finger across her throat. "Quick and quiet."

"Our floor." The uniform muscled by her. "Use a knife out of their kitchen."

"Of course. Who's cute now?" Eve demanded.

"Nobody." Peabody hugged her elbows. "Absolutely nobody will ever be cute again."

Satisfied, Eve tolerated the crowd until they reached the garage. "Plug in the stores geographically. Both murders were downtown, but that's likely because the events were. Still, we'll start there."

In the car, Peabody started the program. "Just FYI, if I die of a slit throat in bed, there's a whole elevator full of cops who'd point at you."

"Which is why I'd wait until you got up, then bash you over the head with your fancy French cocotte."

"It's cast iron. That would do it. I'm still buying it."

"Your funeral."

"The first one's on Broadway."

Even Eve recognized how the franchise earned its sarcastic name after the first round. Aunt Janes and harried parents with snarly preteens made up the bulk of the customer base. The teens joining them seemed mostly interested in the cheap accessories—jewelry, sunshades, hair ties.

Music banged and boomed over the sound system while clerks shuffled along to refold stock heaped on display tables.

Signs, a forest of them, screamed FIFTY PERCENT OFF! SUMMER SALE! BUY TWO GET ONE FREE!

She got her first close-up look at the Kick Its. Yeah, she thought, he had blisters.

By the fourth stop, a post-Urban building in Midtown on Sixth, her head banged and boomed like the music, the same loop in every store.

"This is billed as their flagship," Peabody told her. "It's the biggest. Shoes and some activewear downstairs. Kids—like toddler to tween— upstairs. Everything else on the main."

"We'll try the shoes first. I notice you've yet to let out with one of your girlie squeals or longing sighs over any of the available merchandise."

"It really is crap," Peabody said as they started down. "And too young crap for me anyway. They sell—this store especially has a good crowd. But it looks like a lot of people saving some bucks because kids grow out of things almost as fast as you put the things on them.

"And Quilla's Aunt Janes," she added. "Plenty of the vics' and suspect's age group, but cheap sunshades and like that are a draw."

"Most of that age group has a limited discretionary income. I'd've been stuck with crap like this at that age."

"I'm lucky. Everybody sewed."

On the lower level, Eve hunted up a clerk, badged him.

"We're looking for a white male, middle teens, about five-six, who bought a pair of Kick It Zoomers."

He looked at her with tired eyes. "You're kidding me, right?"

Eve tapped her badge. "This says I'm not."

"Lady, do you know how many kids swarm through here pawing through everything? How many moms or dads drag a kid in here to try on a mountain of shoes?"

"It's Lieutenant, and no, I don't. I'm only looking for one, almost certainly alone. Size six to seven on the shoes."

"I can't tell you. Seriously."

"Seriously, how about you check and see when you moved a pair that matches that description?"

"Well, it'll get me off the floor."

As he walked away, Eve watched a woman with one hand in a death grip on a kid's arm—a boy, about twelve—shove a shoe at the clerk with the other.

"These, in the red. Size seven and a half."

"I'll check."

"And she has to be measured." She pointed at a girl of about eight sulking on a bench.

"I'll be right with you."

The clerk escaped.

"I don't want those!" The boy whined it in a tone that should have shattered glass in a three-block area. "I want Air Cats!"

"I'm not paying for Air Cats when you'll grow out of them in five minutes. You can have the damn Air Cats when your feet stop growing."

"See," Peabody murmured.

"Shalla, do you want the pink or the green sneaks?"

"I want Air Cats, too."

"Yeah, well, I want a vacation in Fiji. We're all going to have to live with our disappointments. Sit by your sister, Garret."

When he did, with a solid foot between them, the mother dropped into a chair. "Have kids, they told me. They'll fill your life with joy and adventure. Your heart will swell with love."

Closing her eyes, she breathed, then sighed.

"Let's get through this, okay, kids? Then we'll go get ice cream."

The clerk came out of the back, handed her a shoebox and a sympathetic smile. "Give me one more minute, and I'll measure your girl."

He crossed back to Eve. "Haven't sold a size seven in over a month. Three weeks ago on the six in red, five weeks in black. Two weeks ago, the last six and a half, and the new shipment hasn't come in."

"Let's try the six and a half. Color?"

"Last one was black. We've been out of the red and white for a while. Shipment hasn't come in, like I said."

"Do you remember selling that last pair?"

"Lady—Lieutenant," he corrected, "I'm lucky to remember my name after shift. Could've been Carleen, anyway. She rotates."

He circled his finger. "She's working activewear."

"All right. Appreciate it."

"Whatever."

"Let's find Carleen," Eve said as he went back to work.

They found her folding table stock. Barely older than the customer base, she had pink-streaked blond hair to her shoulders, a glinting nose stud, and a look of unspeakable boredom.

"Shoes? The worst. It's mostly the boppers, right? The eight to twelve, maybe thirteen, dragged in by Mom. Or Granny. They curl up their toes when you try to measure them. And whine. Sometimes they kick ya."

"This one would've been alone, around sixteen."

"Yeah, we get those. They mostly don't go into shoes in groups 'cause they don't want buds to know they're buying Kick Its or Sprints or Joe's."

"Two weeks ago, the last Kick It Zoomers, six and a half, in black."

"I don't know. I guess I sort of remember selling the last pair. Sort of remembering marking it in inventory because now we're out total, you know, and we've been waiting for the shipment."

"A white kid, about sixteen. Brown hair."

She poked out her bottom lip as she thought. "Maybe. Sort of maybe. We don't get them in shoes much over fourteen, maybe fifteen. Do better with activewear, but shoes, you know, that's status, and they're really thinking about that once they hit high school."

"Give me the sort of maybe."

"Excuse me." One of the Aunt Janes tapped Carleen on the shoulder. "Can you help me? I have a list." She held up her 'link displaying said list.

"Of course. Give me a minute," she told Eve, and led the woman away.

"He'd have gotten the baggies and tee on the main. See if you can track that down, Peabody. I'll wait, see if we get anything."

"It's the first sort of maybe. I'll hold on to that."

While Peabody went back up, Eve watched the parade.

Yeah, mostly moms or grannies, herding bored, excited, or fussy kids. A woman pushing a toddler in a stroller had another three in tow.

Potentially four, six, eight, ten.

Four kids, Eve thought, unsure whether to feel astonishment or deep pity.

She had an enormous net bag filled with clothes in the back of the stroller, and another hanging from one of its arms.

"Just shoes, gang, then we'll go check out."

She walked by Eve with the look of someone who'd been through one war and was braced for another.

She took a tag from Roarke, and immediately decided looking at his face on-screen was a major improvement over watching irritable kids and exhausted parents.

"Do you own L&W?" she asked before he could speak.

He took a long moment just to stare at her.

"I'm going to firmly believe you don't know how insulting that is. And I'm going to assume from the vicious music you're in one now. Have you tracked him there?"

"Maybe."

"Well then, good luck with it. I'm letting you know I'll likely be a bit late getting home."

"Anything to do with letting Jamie ditch you for EDD?"

"No. Was that a problem?"

"Another no. We hit some of that luck earlier, so I know he's white, about five-six, and was wearing Kick It Zoomers, size six to seven, cheap-ass black baggies, at least on the night of the first murder."

"Then L&W's the place to be, isn't it? Substandard apparel is their business. We had their like when I was a boy in Dublin. I wouldn't've pocketed a pair of socks inside those doors."

She had to laugh. "You and Quilla have more in common than I realized. She was with Jamie. She's doing a report on EDD."

"So I'm told. And she intends to try to tap you for one on Homicide."

"She already did. I'm thinking about it. Later."

With mild amusement in those fabulous eyes, he smiled at her. "Are you now?"

"Not now, later. Here comes my source. I don't know if I'll be late or not. It depends on if this lead pans out."

"Then I'll see you at home when we get there."

Eve pocketed the 'link.

"Sorry about that. Long list." Carleen whooshed out a breath. "Anyway, I'm thinking. Short white kid, I think white kid, alone. Dopey clothes."

"Dopey?"

"Well, like his mom made him dress for school or church or to visit snooty Aunt Martha. Honest, I can't tell you what clothes, just not what you usually see in here. Like pants—not bags or jeans or sweats. I think a button shirt, all pressed and whatever. I know not a tee or sports jersey. But what I remember is he had really good shoes. Dress shoes, not sneaks or kicks or airs. Quality though. Leather dress shoes, like you'd wear to church or like that.

"I remember because I thought if he could afford—or his parents could afford—good leather shoes, what the hell was he buying Kick Its for?"

She lowered her voice. "They're totally crap."

"So I'm told. Can you describe him?"

"It was a couple weeks ago. I swear they blur. And we were having a sale, so we were crushed. I'm not even sure he was a white kid, just pretty sure."

"Hair color, build?" Eve pressed.

"Sorry, got nothing. I mostly remember the shoes. I mean the ones he wore in."

"What about the shoes? Describe them."

"Well, brown leather dress loafers, with the tassel. I mean who puts a teenage kid in those? Lame. But real quality. Alan Stubens."

"You're sure about that? The brand?"

"Yeah. Most of the rest is maybe, but I'm solid on the shoes because I thought how you could buy fifty . . . nah, more like a hundred Kick Its for one pair of Stuben loafers."

"All right. I'm going to give you my card. If you remember anything else, any detail, contact me. If he comes in again, don't alert him. Go into the back and contact me."

"Well hell, what did he do?"

"Just contact me."

Eve took the steps up two at a time and found Peabody.

"Bombed," Peabody said. "But if he bought those items here, he paid cash. They checked. And the cams are overwritten every twenty-four."

"He bought them here. Carleen remembered him."

"Holy score! We get a description?"

"Not of him. She fixed on his clothes—quality, neat, conservative. And more, on the shoes he came in wearing. Run a search on what venues carry Alan Stuben dress loafers. Brown leather. With the stupid tassel."

"Stubens?" Peabody hustled after Eve. "Those are premium. It's going to be high-end boutiques, high-end department stores, or one of his stand-alones. I know there's a stand-alone on Madison. I think around Fifty-Third."

"Check. We can start there."

"Crap, it's still raining. Madison and Fifty-Fourth. And crap again, there are over sixty places that carry Stubens in the city, and four more at the Sky Mall. Another three dozen in Brooklyn. Then there's—"

"Let's just start with Manhattan."

Two hours later, they'd covered the first stand-alone, two major department stores, and three boutiques.

"Bombed." Peabody dropped into the passenger seat. "Coffee. Can I get coffee?"

Eve held up two fingers.

"You're as wiped as I am. You didn't threaten me when I let out girlie squeals and longing sighs in that last store. And the venues are closing soon for the day."

Sometimes you couldn't fight the clock, Eve admitted. And she was wiped.

"We pick it up tomorrow."

"I have to say it. They could've bought the shoes while traveling."

"They won't be his only pair. Maybe of that brand, maybe. Quality clothes and shoes—somebody's got the scratch to outfit him that way."

"If he wasn't a murderer, I'd feel sorry for him for having to dress like a rich doofus. You know what else? Unless he likes the doofus-wear, and why would he, the L&W haul makes him feel like he's got it."

"That could be part of it. I'm just like you. Smarter, better, cannier, but just like you. It's after shift. House or apartment?"

"First, mega thanks for not making me deal with the subway. The apartment. I need to crash for an hour."

"Pick a downtown venue, send it to me. We'll start there."

"They won't open until ten."

"Take the gift."

"Oh boy, will I! We're going to hit, Dallas. We have to hit. Who'd have thought we'd nail him over his shoes?"

"Scuff marks. First mistake. If he made one at the second scene, we just haven't found it yet. He made another wearing his dopey clothes in a place like L&W. They got noticed because they're out of place. Smarter to have bought good kicks or sneaks and the rest. Walk into a higher-end shop, nobody's going to notice. But he didn't know any better. Didn't think that one through."

"You're right, and I didn't think of that, either. But if they keep him on a really short leash, maybe that's all he could afford, in cash."

Eve shook her head. "They don't pay that much attention. If they did, they'd see him. They'd wonder what the hell he's doing growing poppies, or spending all that time in a lab—maybe his own, because they could afford it, and it keeps him out of their hair. They'd have seen he doesn't have friends, isn't dating, isn't . . . just isn't right."

"Didn't think of that, either."

"They'd have seen something twisted in him. They dress him in what they approve of, but they don't see what's inside the button-down shirts and pressed pants."

She pulled up in front of the apartment building.

"He doesn't give them any grief," Eve continued. "He's quiet, studious, gets exceptional grades. He keeps out of their hair.

"There was a woman in L&W with four kids, ranging probably from four to ten. I bet she pays more attention to every one of them than whoever's in charge pays to him."

"You're going to make me feel sorry for him again."

"Don't. They don't abuse him. They don't even neglect him. They just don't see what he is.

"Go crash."

"Gonna. You know, it's only weeks now until we move into the house. You can count it in weeks, and I'm so excited. And still, I'm going to miss this place."

"You'll get over it."

"Oh, bet your skinny lieutenant's ass. Thanks for the lift."

She drove uptown the way she'd driven downtown that morning. In steady, dreary rain.

She'd deal with the headache, she thought, by crashing herself for twenty or thirty minutes.

Let the worst of the fatigue drain, sleep the fog out.

Then take another good, hard look at where they stood.

She had more, considerably more, than she had when she'd left the house that morning. The picture of the killer had begun to coalesce in her mind.

He hated being short in stature when his intellect was so tall. He hated his clothes, hated his life. He was destined for so much more.

He despised the others his age for their shallow brains, their shallow interests. Despised them for their lack of interest in him, their inability to see all he was and would be.

But more, so much more, he despised what he most craved. The girls who ignored him.

He'd experimented, she thought, refining his weapon against them. A lab rat, a stray cat.

A scientist had to experiment, had to test his methods, the results. Keep records.

Yet whoever kept him, mother, father, guardian, didn't see.

How did he get out for the events? Did he have a curfew? Didn't they see the cheap clothes?

Maybe he snuck out. Maybe they trusted him to be compliant and never considered he'd leave the house.

She stopped at a red, closed her eyes. Then shook herself when she nearly nodded off. Though tempted to take the rest of the trip on auto, she knew herself well enough.

She'd end up dead out in the car parked inside the gates.

Maybe she was being too hard on whoever they were. Maybe they encouraged him to go out. Have a good time! Enjoy the music. Be home by midnight.

No. No. It didn't fit the rest.

So quiet, so polite, so bright.

That's what they'd say about him. The "they," and anyone who thought they knew him.

The neighbors, other relatives, shopkeepers, at least most of his teachers or tutors.

And while he desperately wanted them to see him, he made sure they didn't.

Relief swamped her when she drove through the gates. Even in the rain, the house looked beyond a dream. Lights gleaming in windows through the gloom, blossoms forming streaks of color and shape.

And quiet, she thought as she pulled up. Already the quiet after so much noise, such relentless movement.

She dragged herself out of the car, through the rain, and into the house, where Summerset and Galahad waited.

"You've had a long, wet day, Lieutenant."

She had nothing, so kept walking.

"Was there another? After last night?"

She glanced back as both the man and the cat watched her. "No. But there will be."

"She may be wet," Summerset told the cat, "but she's wrung herself dry. Go on now, go see to her. Roarke will be a little while yet."

In the bedroom, she dragged off her damp jacket and considered it done. As she had the day before, she dropped facedown on the bed.

Thirty minutes, she told herself, and went out.

She didn't feel the cat leap onto the bed, or spread himself over her ass to guard her.

When Roarke came in a half hour later, Summerset waited.

"She's upstairs. Exhausted."

"Small wonder."

"You're a bit fagged yourself. How was Philadelphia?"

"Dry, so there's something. And all's in place."

"That's good. After last night, I anticipated considerable fatigue. I made fresh pasta and meatballs."

"That will be very welcome, on both our counts. She's closer."

Understanding, Roarke laid a hand on Summerset's arm. "I had a brief update, and she's closer."

"Go tend to your wife." Summerset gave the hand on his shoulder a brief pat. "There's cherry pie for later."

"You've been busy."

"It kept my mind occupied."

"She'll find him."

"She will, and you'll help her."

"As I can."

Roarke walked up, made his way to the bedroom.

Galahad blinked his eyes open but maintained his perch.

"We'll both see to her now, won't we?"

He sat on the side of the bed, skimmed a hand lightly over her hair.

He took off his suit jacket, his tie, his shoes. Then lay down beside her. After setting his mental clock for ten minutes, he dropped into sleep with her.

Chapter Thirteen

She woke with a groan followed by a muttered curse.

"There she is."

At his voice, she turned her head enough to see Roarke—jeans and a tee—sitting on the sofa with his feet up, his PPC in his hand.

"Is there a half ton of cat on my ass?"

"There is indeed. I can't decide if he's there to guard you from any and all intruders or just keep you down until you got some sleep."

Reaching back, she scratched Galahad's head before rolling him off.

"You've been home awhile," she began, then checked the time. "Shit! It was supposed to be twenty minutes, thirty at the outside. I was out for over an hour."

"And benefited from it. Hungry?"

She sat up, scrubbed her hands over her face. "I had a nosh earlier. I guess a lot earlier."

"A nosh?"

"Jewish deli, slice of babka. It was really good. I could eat, but—"

"Spaghetti and meatballs?"

"I'd say that was hitting below the belt, but it's dead-on."

"There's cherry pie."

She had a weakness for all things pie.

"Looking out for me, pal?"

"Whenever I can, but this one's Summerset. He made it all today. He heard about the second girl. Cooking keeps his mind occupied."

She nodded, slid out of bed. "Murder does that with mine."

"We'll set up in your office. Have a meal, a glass of Chianti, and you'll tell me."

She started to nod again, then remembered and dug a hand in her pocket. As he rose, she held out the cash she'd pulled.

He looked at it, at her, with eyes suddenly and dangerously cool.

"Why in bloody hell would you want to start a row?"

"I don't. I've got too much to do to fight. So just listen, okay? Listen," she insisted. "I know we've been here before, and mostly resolved things. I get you think it's insulting, especially since you buy all my damn clothes, and whatever goes into the spaghetti I'm about to eat. But that's just not it."

"What is it then?"

"It's on me. Completely on me, and I hate that I can't at least shove a part of it on you. We could schedule a fight then, when I had more time, and"—she had to admit it—"I'd like that a hell of a lot better."

"Should I check my book?" he asked, all too politely.

Her hackles—whatever the hell they were—went up hard when he used that tone on her.

But.

"No, because, fuck it, it's on me. I've gotten careless, and that makes me feel stupid and, well, careless. I didn't run short before you. Maybe skimmed close to it, but I paid more attention. I had to. Okay, I've got to sort this out so I can pay the rent, and get some crap coffee, like that. Now I don't pay attention. Not enough. I forget to pay attention."

"You don't need to."

"But I do. I do need to. Do you want me to feel stupid?"

He only lifted his eyebrow. "It would seem that's in your hands, not mine."

"Oh, fucking fuck." Turning away, she tried counting to ten. Made it to five. "This money thing makes me feel stupid, and makes you feel insulted. Which would be in your hands, ace."

He slid his hands into his pockets, felt the gray button he carried.

A cheap suit, loose threads, and she'd given him a talisman he carried everywhere.

"I suppose it is. Regardless, it should be somewhere in your Marriage Rules, that what we have, we share. The good and the bad of it."

"It's probably in there," she muttered. Maybe she'd put an asterisk on that line to remove money from it—and that, she admitted, was on her, too.

"I just need to pay you back. It doesn't mean anything to you, a few hundred. But it does to me, especially since I damn well know I'm going to get comfortable and careless again. Then I'll feel stupid, and annoyed with both of us, when you peel off a few hundred and hand it to me like I'm . . ."

"My wife?"

She tried one more careful breath. "Your stupid, careless wife."

"You're neither of those things. *Hardheaded, hard-assed* come to mind."

Her eyes narrowed. "I'd say we're pretty evenly matched on that one."

"Difficult to disagree."

"I need to pay you back so it's not such a big stupid deal every time, for both of us. It's just a loan, not a 'Here, dumbass who can't keep enough cash in her pocket to pay for a slice of babka, let me peel off a few from the wad in the pocket of my zillion-dollar suit.'

"And it makes me feel more of a dumbass when I put the damn cash in the pocket of pants I not only didn't have to buy, I didn't have to think about buying. So I need to pay you back. That's it."

"Let me say this first. I enjoy filling your closet the way you never will. You shouldn't begrudge me my small pleasures."

"Only you would call that acreage of clothes in there small. And I'm standing here wearing stuff you put in there. I'm grateful for it."

She stopped, shoved at her hair.

"Shit, I probably should've said that sometime along the way, probably a few dozen times. I am grateful you like what I hate, and I don't have to carve out time for something I hate, like shopping."

"I don't need thanks," he began, but she shook her head.

"Yes, you do. It's not you paying for them, because, Jesus Christ, I don't want to think about what you paid for these boots. It's embarrassing. Even a little horrifying. Or it would be if I thought about it, so I try not to. It's not the money. It's the time and thought. I'm grateful for it."

"Darling Eve." He sighed it out, and his eyes had gone warm again. "You intrigue me, constantly. I know who you are, what you are, how you think, how you feel, and still, you intrigue me. Constantly."

He took a step toward her, cupped her face in his hands before brushing his lips to her.

"Take the money back, okay? I pulled enough."

"We'll make a deal, shall we? When you run short because you've been busy hunting a killer, or standing over the dead, you'll tell me. No bloody shite about it. Then you'll graciously accept a loan."

"A loan I could accept. The graciously might be a tough reach."

"Graciously," he repeated. "Then, when you've had time to deal with it, I'll graciously accept repayment."

"No bloody shite about it?"

"None."

"Okay, that's a deal." She held out a hand to shake on it. "Give me a little spread on the exact level of graciously."

He took her hand, kissed it. "I'll grade on the curve."

"Did we just avoid a big, ugly fight?"

"I'd say we cut short a spat."

"*Spat*'s a stupid word for actual adult people. We had a pissing match. Done now. Let's eat."

"Intrigued," Roarke repeated as they walked out. "Constantly."

She needed to do her updates, and had, by her mental schedule, fallen behind.

But he'd been right. The hour down had done its job.

The abbreviated pissing match hadn't hurt, she realized. That cleared the air like the nap had cleared her head.

Now she'd let the spaghetti and meatballs, a little wine, do the rest before she tackled it all again.

Besides, she shared that food and wine with the most excellent sounding board she knew. Something else to be grateful for.

While they ate, she started off with the morgue, shifted to the lab, wound back to the follow-up with Jake that she hadn't relayed to him.

"I know a lot of talented people don't hit, but I think she would have. She had the talent, the focus, and a hell of a lot of determination. He took that from her, erased her, her potential."

"Do you think that's part of it?" Roarke asked. "Erasing her potential?"

"Not specifically. He didn't know her. It wasn't, for him, who she was, but what. Attractive teenage girl. Her parents gave me the green to give Jake a copy of the demo. I figured it's going to make him feel worse, because he'll hear that potential."

She shrugged. "Anyway."

"A very busy morning for you."

"Oh, and not over. Consult with Mira, slice of babka."

"That must have been brilliant babka."

"Gotta say yeah. EDD hit—can't really see him, but we ID'd the group he merged with, which took us to the deli and the babka. One of the wits got a glance at him. Caucasian male, teenage male. But that's it unless something else shakes loose from the memory of that quick glance."

"It's more than you had."

"A lot more." She wound some pasta, had a moment to wonder what exactly went into noodles to make them close to the perfect food.

"Back to Mira," she said, and ate. "I can sum up her profile and my own conclusions. We're looking for a horny teenage boy who can't get laid, so hates what he lusts for. Which is not only sex but attention, validation of his superiority. He has knowledge, skills, and certainly interest in chemistry and drugs, must have access to equipment. He's a loner, the kind of kid nobody notices—except academically."

She stabbed a meatball. "He's going to shine there. Whoever's in charge of him dresses him like a doofus."

"Is that a brand name?"

She laughed, enjoyed the bite of meatball. "Clerk at L&W didn't remember him enough to give us a description, but she remembered his clothes because you don't see kids come in there wearing dress shirts and dress pants and tasseled loafers. Alan Stubens—she noticed the shoes when he took them off to try the Kick Its."

"Small wonder." Roarke handed her a slice of bread from the basket. "That's as big a step down as I can imagine."

"From the scuff marks we got the approximate size and the brand he wore at the club. From the clerk we've got his size—six and a half—and the brand he wore into the store. So far, we haven't hit on where he got the pricey ones."

"He could've sold the Stubens and bought at least three decent kicks or sneaks, add in the baggies, and he'd still have cab fare."

"So he didn't want to risk whoever's in charge asking him 'Where's your loafers?' Mostly? I think he didn't know any better. He's not in the club, the normie club, much less the chill club. He doesn't know L&W is Losers and Wheezes."

"And what, Lieutenant, does that tell you?"

"He goes to a fancy-pants private school or he's homeschooled with fancy-pants private tutors. Maybe a combo. Whoever's in charge of him doesn't see who he is. They only see what he wants them to see. He knows how to present himself to them—that's easy. Smart, quiet, polite, well-dressed."

"Trustworthy," Roarke added.

"That's key, yeah. So they're not poking around in his stuff, demanding what he did when he went out. He can run his experiments, hell, maybe grow his own poppies.

"He's got plenty of time to himself," Eve murmured. "Plenty of time on his own. Nobody says, 'Hey, let's go grab a slice after school,' or 'Let's party at my house.'"

"I'd have been lost without my mates as a boy."

"You were getting your ass kicked daily. We both know how that feels. He's not abused, not technically neglected. He's just not seen. He's cerebral, not athletic. Not that athletes can't have good brains, but he's short for his age. Maybe puny. Not chunky—kids notice that, too, so I think the wit would've said porky white kid, or something like that."

"He had to use his feet to boost up to the window."

Eve gestured with her fork. "Exactly. No core. He had to use his feet, enough pressure with them, to leave the marks on the wall."

"There was cruelty in the entire thing, but an extra flourish of cruelty in the roofie and bacteria. Your sexual elements. If you're right, and you no doubt are, and he's particularly bright, knowledgeable, he added those for spite. He'd know the police lab would analyze the formula he used."

"Making his point. The cops are scratching their heads, the media's in an uproar." Eve gestured up with her hand. "Everybody's paying attention now."

"He doesn't think you'll find him."

After eating the last bite, Eve set down her fork. "No?"

"He's so much smarter than you, than anyone with a badge. Cops are just low-paid public servants, after all. When they catch criminals, it's only because the criminals are even less bright than they are.

"Add the arrogance of youth, Eve, to the rest. And all that testosterone. The only way he can satisfy his needs is using his own hand. These girls who don't see him, don't want him? They're idiots who'd rather spread their legs for the barely literate jock because he can throw a football, or the bad boy in cheap boots and fake leather sneaking smokes in the loo."

Fascinated, Eve leaned back. "Keep going."

"You were a teenage girl. Would you have seen his type?"

"I did my best not to see anybody too close. You look too close, they look back. I didn't even consider banging anybody until I was in the Academy."

He blinked at her. "I don't believe you've mentioned that before."

"Not worth mentioning. But I'm not a good judge of what a typical teenage girl thinks about sex. And this is about him, and you seem to have an interesting take."

"I knew his type back then. Not the murderous, but those who felt entitled to what wasn't coming their way. You're a bit obsessed with sex at that age—well, more than a bit."

After picking up his wine, he leaned back.

"But there's a lightness to it, an excitement, a wonder the first time you have a girl's breast in your hand that doesn't lessen with the next time. But for this type, the obsession darkens and hardens."

"And the girls are to blame."

"Of course. Who else? They're frigid or teases or ballbusters, and their very lack of any respect only solidifies the resentment. What they want is subjugation, as the female's inferior, a vessel for their use. So they hate and demean. But under all that, I think, is fear."

"Fear of what?"

"The female, and their mystery, their otherness, and most of all, their power. I think, don't you, that some of those who start out like this, when and if they find a woman, they become abusers. Because the fear's always there, under it all. And the need," he added, "to prove they're in charge."

"Yeah, some of them, but I've never wound it around just this way. I'm giving you some of your 'intrigued.' So you knew some of the type."

"I don't recall any being particularly bright, as this one."

"You wouldn't have had any trouble getting a girl's tit in your hand."

He smiled, sipped his wine. "And still a wonder."

"How old were you when you got lucky?"

"You'd ask such a question when I'm trying to help you catch a murderer?"

"Satisfy my curiosity."

He drank more wine, and she saw what rarely showed on his face. Discomfort.

"Well, I didn't know my age as an exact thing."

"Ballpark it."

"Round about fifteen, I suppose. Give or take."

"For the tit or the whole bang?"

He smiled again. "Well now, one thing leads to another, doesn't it now? And if that's of any use, the type we're talking of tended, in my experience, to hang together. Feed each other's resentments. There are all manner of places in life, online, that feed that same resentment and attitude."

"He wouldn't join a group. Online, possibly, but I see him as more of a lurker. He doesn't participate. As much as he wants attention, he's too smart to go online and brag about what he's done, is doing."

She got up to clear. "When we find him, we'll find his records, logs, a journal. They'll be meticulous and detailed."

With the plates in her hands, she paused at the board.

"He didn't feel wonder when he jammed that needle in these girls."

"What did he feel?"

"Satisfaction. The kind you feel when you puncture somebody's tires because they were mean to you. Your teacher trashed your test score because you fucked around. You don't wait for him to come out and see the tires, you take off. Same thing with this, for him. The motive just as juvenile. It's the method and execution that takes it over that."

"But he won't brag to his mates about paying the teacher back. He has no mates."

"And," Eve added, "he's too smart. He's so above, in his mind, the others who go on bitching and strutting. And he's achieved a satisfaction they can only dream of. Twice."

"It doesn't last, does it? That satisfaction."

"No. He's already planned how and when to feel it again. And he'll need to use that roofie on its own before much longer. He'll need that power over the girl. 'I'll take what I want from you, what I'm entitled to. Then kill you.'"

She glanced back at him. "You thought of that, too."

"I did, yes."

"He's already planned for that, too. The where, maybe the when. But the where, he's got that worked out."

Knowing her, he laid a hand on her shoulder as much in comfort as support. "I'll take the dishes."

"Rules are rules. You got the food."

"I could begin updating your board then."

"Did you ever think you'd pass the time after a meal updating a murder board?"

"Not in my wildest."

When she came out—she'd caved as Roarke usually did and given Galahad a handful of cat treats—he was well into the update.

He had her system down, she thought.

Yeah, he knew who she was, what she was, how she thought, what she felt. Sometimes, she figured he knew all that better than she did. Or at least more clearly.

And he loved her anyway.

She walked over, put her arms around him, hugged hard and tight.

"This is for stuff, and especially the spaghetti, because I'm not hugging Summerset."

"I'll happily be his proxy. And I'll remind you there's pie."

"I might just let you, as proxy, get your hand on my tit for cherry pie. But later, both counts."

With her chin on his shoulder, she studied the board.

"I want him up there. I want him in the box. I want him in a cage. I can see him now. Doofus dooser incel psychopath who still doesn't shave. Short guy syndrome. Rich white kid snot, on the puny side. Something not right, not quite right in his eyes, but they don't see it. Or if they do, they figure it's all that smart, not all that sick."

Drawing back, she circled the board. "The teachers, tutors, they think: If only all the students were as bright and well-mannered as this kid. Work's always turned in on time, goes the extra mile."

She circled back, stood, hands in pockets. "Parent, parents, guardian, whoever's in charge. Busy life, professional, successful. That boy never gives me any trouble. I'm so lucky. Never talks back, never misses curfew. He'll have his pick of universities in a couple years.

"I bet there's a housekeeper or nanny or— Is middle teens too old for a nanny?"

"I would think so."

"Something like that. Because busy, professional, successful." Pausing, she played with that one. "Maybe that's who buys the clothes, takes care of selecting his clothes. Maybe an older person, trustworthy. But he's almost college age now, doesn't need someone sitting on him. He can come and go. He's got those exceptional grades, never misses curfew—if he has one."

"Wouldn't they want to know where he is, who he hangs with, what he does with his free time?"

"Library, study group. He'd lie smooth enough if he needs to. And he could have a way to come and go so they don't notice he's gone.

"If they've heard about the girls, and that's probable," Eve concluded, "it would never cross their minds he's responsible. Most adults just see a well-dressed, polite kid. It's the other kids who see him for the outsider, the not one of us. He can be cerebral, not astute but smart, and still know what they think of him."

"Rage builds."

"It builds," Eve agreed. "And I worry, not just that he'll kill again. That's inevitable if we don't find him first. I worry he'll have to escalate. The quick jab and escape, even with the media attention that follows, won't be enough."

"As you said, he'll want the girl."

"He'll need the experience, what they've all denied him. Incapacitate the girl, rape the girl, kill the girl."

He'd thought of it. Dreamed of it. But he held back.

He'd weighed risk and reward, and wisely, he thought, concluded risk weighed more, a great deal more.

But how would he know, for certain, conclusively, without the sample?

Rather than alleviating the craving, the successful conclusions of his project only increased it.

But tonight, he'd hold back again.

He'd added the trench coat tonight. He'd seen other kids wear similar in this venue, as it tended to be cold inside, even when crowded as it would be tonight.

Big night at the vids with the opening of what would surely be the summer's biggest hit, yet another ridiculous, scientifically impossible installment of the Defenders franchise.

A bunch of misfit aliens from across the galaxy, all gifted with absurd powers, who defended Earth from evil.

And all that utter nonsense.

Personally, he rooted for the evil, which tended to be more interesting.

He had nothing against fiction, but *science* fiction simply infuriated him. But the venue, the setup, the possibilities here, tonight, outweighed his fury and disgust.

He'd paid his entry fee in advance—in cash—one of the remote ticket sellers as soon as available. A premium price for the absurd, but well worth the investment.

Now he stood, just another idiot kid queued up with other idiots who'd paid far too much money to sit in a cold, loud theater stuffing overpriced, slime-covered popcorn in his face and slurping a watered-down fizzy.

Of course, he wouldn't do any of that.

Oh, he wanted to feel it all again. Wanted to hurry. Of course, he understood perfectly well that need to rush came from the boost he'd taken.

Not enough REM sleep could equal sloppy work.

He was never sloppy.

So he controlled himself, and he shuffled on with the rest, careful to keep his head down, angle himself away from any cams—which he'd already scoped out on previous visits.

Everyone packed together, so easy enough. He'd already picked two likely targets for his personal experiment. And entertainment.

Either the redheaded slut or the blond whore. Unless he saw something more appealing inside the lobby.

Neither of them would look at him twice, or if they did, with that not-worth-noticing look.

He'd make them notice soon enough. He closed his hand over the syringe in his pocket, imagined himself just jamming it into one of them. Either of them.

He took slow, deep breaths to bring his heart rate down.

Inside, the noise level grew, just as he'd anticipated. He had his 'link scanned for admission. Just another brainless kid. The cops would notice if he didn't follow through with admission.

He slouched along toward concessions with giggling girls, boys talking too loud, music playing the Defenders theme.

It banged in his head, reminded him of the club, of the park. The music, the memories, the booster, all revved in his system.

He had to deliberately loosen his fingers around the syringe.

Now they packed in for that popcorn, those fizzies, candy, chips, all that disgusting junk food.

Somebody bumped him from behind so he almost bumped into the redhead. She glanced back at him, through him, then went back to giggling and talking too loud with the masses.

You then, bitch. It's you.

And his fingers tightened again.

He followed the plan, kept close but not too close as she and her group ordered. Then he fell in with them as if he belonged.

Into the theater where, again as planned, the previews had already begun. He slipped off his sunshades, tucked them away. In the dark, following closer—he could smell her—her hair, her skin.

He slid the syringe out of his pocket.

He couldn't wait, just couldn't wait a minute more!

He had to jab through her jacket, but he'd accounted for that.

But when he pushed the needle into her, she shrieked. The sound sliced his eardrums. Sent his already raging heartbeat into a wild gallop that leaped into his throat.

It stole his breath.

The popcorn tub in her hand flew up; the contents rained down in a blizzard as she started to spin around. Something thudded on the floor, and liquid splashed on his shoes.

He saw her raise her fist, and he stumbled back as cold sweat coated his skin.

He fled, as planned, through the emergency exit. But not with the strutting satisfaction he'd imagined. He had to run, to shove, to push his way through the crowd as he heard her screaming:

"That asshole stabbed me!"

He was barely out the door when the houselights came up.

With his heart pounding, his ears ringing, his stomach churning, he kept running.

Chapter Fourteen

Private school, Eve thought as she looked over the lists Jenkinson and Reineke had generated. The killer she saw came from money and privilege and attended private school.

She'd start there.

She glanced up as Roarke came in from his adjoining office.

"How can I help?"

"I thought you had some stuff."

"I did, now it's done, so I no longer have some stuff." Stepping behind her, he rubbed at the knots in her shoulders. "It's near to half-nine, and I expect you want to put another hour or two in."

"I tapped Jenkinson and Reineke to dig into schools with a solid chemistry department, but I didn't have a chance to start on it."

"You'll want private schools, I imagine, from how you described him at dinner."

"That's where I want to start. I had them pull in universities, too, but

I'm pushing that down. He wants and hates what he sees. He's not killing college girls."

"How many do you have?"

"Two hundred and thirty-three. I can cut that back to two hundred and six by eliminating ones focused exclusively on the arts, theater, music."

"That would be a hundred and three for each of us."

"These are just in the city." Thinking of that, she reached for her coffee. "But he's not killing in Brooklyn or Queens. Not targeting girls in Yonkers or the Bronx."

"You start with the most probable." He kissed the top of her head.

"Yeah. Yeah," she repeated. "We eliminate female students, any male student under fifteen. Fourteen," she corrected. "Better to dig through more than miss. We bump down any athletes—he doesn't have the build or the time for that. Focus on Caucasian males, the honor students, the chemistry angle—or premed."

"Some of the private schools include boarding as an option, as we do at An Didean."

"I don't think he's boarding. Too much supervision with that. We'll set that aside for the second pass. We pull up the rosters and the—what is it?—yearbook thing. That'll have photos. If he's not top of the class, he's close to it. No clubs outside of his interest in chemistry."

Following her line, Roarke added, "He won't hold an office—class president, student council."

"Definitely not. Whatever we can't get to tonight, I'll dump on Peabody or whoever's clear tomorrow. Twenty each for now."

"I'll use your auxiliary. And your coffee," he added, "as it'll go nicely with the pie."

She'd forgotten about the pie, and now wanted it.

She used her command center to program coffee while Roarke dealt with pie.

"He's not an average student," she said over the first bite. "He's exceptional there. But"—Eve sent Roarke his twenty—"he'll stand out because he doesn't stand out.

"Were you ever in a yearbook thing?"

"I was rarely in school in any case, and for that? I most deliberately was not." He glanced over. "You?"

She shrugged. "I managed to slide out of it until the last one. The senior one."

"That I absolutely need to see."

"We're working."

"I'll find time for it when we're not."

She brought up the first roster, eliminated all female and nonbinary students and those outside the age group. As race wasn't included, she began the task of matching name to yearbook photo, then the photo to the brief student bio.

She found three potentials, none of whom hit a chord in her. But the right age, ace students, chemistry whizzes.

She eliminated the first with a quick scan of social media showing he was spending the summer with his family on their yacht mostly in the French Riviera.

She kicked the second off the list due to his summer courses at Oxford—England.

Which left her one potential after one school.

It would be a slog, she thought.

Her comm signaled.

Now her belly tightened along with her shoulders.

"Dallas."

Dispatch, Dallas, Lieutenant Eve. Incident at Roth's
Midtown Theaters. Female victim, age sixteen,
transported to Clinton Health Center.

"She's alive?"

Affirmative. Kiki Rosenburg, treated on-site prior to transport. Officers on scene. Officers at health center. Suspect believed to have fled the scene via an emergency exit. BOLO issued for Caucasian male, approximately sixteen, wearing a light-colored trench-style coat.

"What's the victim's status?"

Unknown at this time.

She pushed up as Roarke came back into the office with the jacket she'd tossed aside in the bedroom. "Have the officers hold the scene until Peabody, Detective Delia, arrives to take over. I'll inform her. I'll take the victim first. Dallas out."

"She's alive?"

"For now," Eve answered. She pulled out her 'link as they started out together.

Peabody answered with an "I'm awake!"

"Roth's Midtown Theaters. He tried for another. She's still alive. I'm heading to Clinton to talk to her. Get to Roth's, take the lead there."

"She's alive after the injection?"

"I don't have answers yet. Get there, get them. Take McNab. Get the security feed."

Outside, she jumped into the passenger seat as Roarke took the wheel.

"The Defenders," Peabody said. "*Return of the Three*—summer blockbuster. Some of us plan to go this weekend. Tonight's the opening. Dallas, that place would've been packed."

"Pull in Baxter and Trueheart—they're up. You need more, pull more. Suspect fled—wearing a trench coat this time. Out an emergency exit. I want that exit door gone over, every inch of it. All the security feeds, the ticket scanners."

"I've got it, I've got it. I'll tag the sweepers. We're not tagging the morgue, Dallas."

"Let's hope that holds. Get moving."

She shoved her 'link back in her pocket.

"He missed. Somehow he missed. She wouldn't have survived if he'd gotten that shit into her."

"It might be he bolloxed up the formula."

"No. No, he's careful there. He's exacting there. It was the execution. Some sort of fumble. The emergency exit was probably his planned escape route, but not this way. Something went wrong. He'll be shaken, angry. But it'll be her fault, not his."

"You're worried he'll try for her again?"

"We won't take chances, but no. She's spoiled it for him. And shaken or not, he knows we'll have cops on her. Right now, or when he can think again, he'll hope she doesn't make it. Delayed satisfaction's better than none."

"Vid opening, and as Peabody said, a summer blockbuster."

"What does a vid have to do with a block getting busted? Never mind."

"I won't," Roarke assured her. "He'd have to have his ticket scanned, cross the lobby. Unless he managed to get in the way he got out."

"Unlikely—set off alarms. Unless it's you. More, he'd need the time to select her, watch her, get close enough. His exit means they were in the theater. Dark, probably noisy. It's a good plan, all in all. But something went wrong."

He pulled up at the center's ER entrance. "Go, I'll park and find you."

"Kiki Rosenburg," she reminded him, and rushed to the doors.

She hated the smell of hospitals, the sickness, fear, and despair. And the sounds, weeping, wails, the slap of crepe-soled shoes on tile.

She grabbed the first medical she found.

"NYPSD. Kiki Rosenburg, MTs brought her in. Drug reaction."

"You'll need to see the—"

"I'm seeing you. Find out her status and where she is, so I can find out who tried to kill her."

"Jesus, this is hour twelve of a double for me. I need—"

"Got you beat."

The ER nurse might have worn scrubs adorned with cheerful daisies, but her eyes read tired and cranky.

"Fine. Wait here."

"Why would I do that?" Eve fell into step beside her. As they approached the registration desk, she glanced down a long hall.

And saw a uniform on a door.

"Never mind. I've got her."

As Eve started down, the nurse called out, "Hey! You can't just—"

"Watch me. Officer. Kiki Rosenburg."

"Her parents just got here, Lieutenant. Less than two minutes ago."

"She's still alive?"

"She was two minutes ago. Doc's in there, too, and a nurse, and my partner."

"Stay on the door. Expert consultant, civilian, is coming in. He can hold here with you."

She pushed the door open.

The doctor, an oddly perky-looking blonde in her white coat, and the nurse, green scrubs, fuzzy gray hair, both turned.

"Miss, you can't come in here."

Eve held up her badge to Dr. Perky. "Lieutenant, and I'm in here."

Two women, both middle forties, flanked Kiki. The kid's face, likely pale to begin with given the half a mile of red hair, looked nearly translucent. Pinprick pupils told Eve at least some of the heroin had gotten into her.

"How are you feeling, Kiki?"

"I don't feel so good."

"I'm sorry about that, but really glad to see you. You're her family?"

"Her moms," the women said in unison.

"That's an impressive bruise you got there on your arm, Kiki. How'd that happen?"

"Slipped off my airboard this afternoon, banged my arm good. Really hurt. Hey . . ." She gave Eve the smile of the high or drunk. "Are you Marlo Durn?"

"No."

"Look just like her."

"I get that sometimes. Ah, Moms, I'm Lieutenant Dallas."

"Ooooh, you're the other one. She's the other one, Mom."

"Yes, I know." The one on the left spoke first. "Connie Rosenburg, and my wife, Andrea Harris. It's like what happened to those two girls, isn't it?"

"Kiki's going to be fine," the doctor said, then looked at Eve to repeat it. "She's going to be fine. Why don't we step out for just a minute?"

"Sure. I need to talk to Kiki."

"Yes." Andrea gripped her daughter's hand. "She was with her brother and some friends. We sent them all down to the family waiting room."

"I'd like to talk to them, too."

"Please." Connie gripped Kiki's other hand. "We want to know what happened. Or could have. Because you're going to be fine, Kiki doll."

"I did some mega puking," Kiki told Eve.

"Glad to hear that, too. Officer, with me."

She stepped out with the doctor, nodded at Roarke.

"You and your partner can take a break," she said to the officer, then turned to Dr. Perky. "Are you going to release her?"

"Not tonight," the doctor said. "I want her overnight, observation, and another round of treatment."

"Take a break," Eve repeated to the officers. "Then you're on the kid until you're relieved. Take thirty now."

"Yes, sir."

Eve turned back to Dr. Perky. "I need to talk to Kiki. And I need her tox screen."

"Understood. Dr. Myler." She extended her hand. "I'll arrange for a copy of the tox screen as soon as possible. I want you to talk to Kiki. I'm thrilled you'll be able to talk to Kiki. Her moms just need a few minutes with her."

"Fine. The bruise on her arm. I bet if you tried to stick a needle there without a numbing agent, it would hurt like the fires of hell."

"You'd be right. I can only assume that's why he didn't succeed in getting a fatal dose into her."

"How much did he get in?"

"Enough to make her sick. The MTs administered an antidote quickly, and as medicals have been alerted, gave her a dose of antibiotics to, we hope, counteract the bacteria. The kid doesn't need a bout of syphilis. We've regulated her arrhythmia."

"She's strong and healthy," Myler added. "Young, strong, healthy, and while she wouldn't have considered it lucky at the time, she was very lucky the sick fucking bastard son of a bitch tried to inject on that bruise, and through two layers—shirtsleeve and jacket."

"And that's twenty bucks. Worth it." Myler blew out a breath. "It's twenty bucks every time I swear in multiples on shift."

"I'd need a beggar's license in under a week."

Myler shot out a smile as perky as her shiny blond ponytail. "I really liked the vid. I like even better finding out you're like that in reality. I'm going to go reassure her brother and friends. Don't overtire her, okay? She's a little high, but her system took a beating."

"I'll be as quick as possible. Then I want to talk to the rest of them."

"I'll be back to check on her. You can tell Nurse Cabot to take a break." Now she beamed the smile at Roarke. "I have to say you're even yummier than vid Roarke."

While she mentally rolled her eyes, Eve signaled to him. "With me."

Eve stepped back in. "Nurse Cabot, Dr. Myler said you could take a break while I speak with Kiki and her moms."

"You need me, you just press that button. Remember?"

"Check it. She's so nice," Kiki said when Cabot left. "Oooh, it's the other one of him. You're even prettier."

"How are you, Kiki?"

"Feel really . . . whoosh! I threw up a lot, and I think maybe I passed out. We were going to see *Return of the Three*, and we didn't. That's so bogus. David came with Pres, and I've got kind of a thing—maybe—for David, and Lola came with me, and she's abso got a thing for Pres. It was kind of a double, but that jerk stabbed me. It hurt really, really bad."

When Eve gave him a look that said keep going, Roarke stepped closer. "Where your arm's bruised there?"

"I guess. It hurt mega more than when I fell off my airboard this afternoon and rapped it. Mega more. I think I screamed and everything, and Pres is all 'What the hell, Keek?' And I screamed some more and tried to take off my jacket, and even that hurt. I didn't see blood, but he stabbed me all right.

"Then the lights came on, and way, way bright, and everyone's yelling, and I started feeling like whoa. And everybody looked funny with their faces all . . ." She circled and twisted her hands in the air. "And I booted, right in front of David, who's got to think I'm a wheeze now."

"I bet he doesn't."

Hope slid into her glassy eyes. "Really?"

"Not a bit of it."

"Your voice is pretty, too. Aamon of Thrune sort of talks like you."

"He's one of the Defenders," Andrea told Roarke.

"I'm aware, yes, and very flattered. Kiki, did you see who stabbed you?"

"It was all dark. My eyes feel funny. Do my eyes look funny?"

"You have lovely green eyes."

Obvious, to Eve, from Kiki's sigh, the girl was developing another thing.

"Golly. Maybe sort of saw him." She closed her eyes now. "Maybe sort of saw him, for a second. He wasn't tall like David. Not really tall like you. I think wearing a trench. Mostly flakers wear the trench in the summer anyway. So I guess a flaker. But he was running away, so I saw the trench."

"Not his face then?"

"It was dark. He had WTF eyes."

"Did he now? Did you see what color?"

"It was too dark, but his eyes were pow!" She widened her own. "WTF eyes. I spilled all my popcorn, and I was going to punch him right in the face for stabbing me. But he ran away. Flaker."

Losing her, Eve decided. The kid was wrung out.

"Kiki," she said, "had you ever seen him before?"

"Don't think so."

"Is there anything else you noticed about him? Any little thing?"

"Nuh-uh. Flaker. We didn't get to see the vid. Wish I'd punched him."

"So do I."

"She's so tired. I'm sorry," Connie added as she stroked that long red hair. "She's just been through so much."

"Don't be sorry. She was a big help. I'm very glad she's going to be all right. I'll need to talk with her again when she's feeling better. If you have any questions, need to talk to me, contact me at any time."

She dug for a card. "Crap, I'm out of cards."

Roarke pulled out one of his own. "I'll just put the Lieutenant's contact on the back for you."

"Thank you." Andrea swiped away a tear. "When she's more herself, she'll be thrilled to have met both of you."

Eve stepped out just as Myler came down the hall.

"She looks delicate," Eve said. "Probably the red hair adds to that. But she's not. She's tough, she's a tough girl."

"Was she able to help you?"

"Yeah. I'm going to want to follow up with her tomorrow."

"She'll be much more herself. We'll monitor her overnight, and she'll continue the course of antibiotics. A couple of days, she'll be back on her airboard."

"The one that saved her life."

With a perky smile, Myler nodded. "The very one. The waiting room's down the hall, first right, then the glass-walled room on the left."

"She didn't tell her mothers about the spill from the airboard."

Eve nodded in agreement as she and Roarke walked down the hall. "They'd have treated it, and given her a safety lecture. She'd rather have the bruise, and thank Christ for it."

Behind the glass, the three kids sat in a huddled unit.

Eve doubted they'd be the only occupants for long, and hoped to get through the interviews while they were.

She recognized the brother. The red hair, a few shades darker than his sister's, fell in a tumble around his face. They shared the same bone structure.

When he saw her, he jolted to his feet. "Oh God. No. Kiki's dead!"

"She's fine," Eve said over the sudden wail of the girl between the two boys. "I just spoke with her."

"But you do dead people. We saw the vid, right?" He looked at his friends. "We all saw it."

"Didn't Dr. Myler just tell you she was going to be fine?"

"Yeah, but—"

"I'm telling you the same."

The other boy—must be David—pushed his hands through a mass of blue-streaked blond hair. "Somebody tried to kill her. That's really real?"

"Yes, and they failed. Kiki's pretty damn tired, but she was awake, and lucid, and pissed off she missed seeing the vid."

"Okay." Tears swirled in Pres's eyes for a moment. "Okay. Sorry. She can be a pain in my ass, but she's my sister. She's my little sister."

"It's okay, Pres." The girl took his hand. "It's going to be okay."

"I'm Lieutenant Dallas."

"Duh," said Pres, and managed a weak smile.

"I need to talk to you about what happened tonight. Would each of you state your full name and age for the record?"

"Wow, since she's really okay, this is chill. Presley Rosenburg. Eighteen."

"I'm Lola Nelson, seventeen."

"Lola, do your parents know where you are?"

"Oh yeah. I tagged them right away, said how something happened to Kiki and there were police and MTs and the police were bringing us to the hospital and they said I could stay because Kiki's moms were coming and how I should talk to the police if it helped Kiki. They love Kiki, and Pres, too."

Did all teenage girls talk in endless, run-on sentences? Eve wondered.

"You have parental permission to speak with me?"

"Yeah, sure. It's for Kiki."

"David Olmstead, eighteen."

"All right. Let's start with you, Presley. You, your sister, and your two friends were together?"

"Yeah, that's right. We scored four tickets a couple weeks ago for the opening—exclusive show, ten o'clock tonight. Last night was the big premiere, but that's for the cast and the bigwigs and the rich guys. Tonight was for real people. A hard score anyway, and some of the cast was supposed to come up for questions and stuff after the vid."

"We were really excited," Lola put in. "We're monster fans of the Defenders."

"You had to get on line even with the presells, so we got there like right after nine. We were still pretty far back, but it finally started moving."

"Did you notice anyone in a trench?"

"Sure. It's mostly flakers who wear them to the vids, but you're always going to have the flakers."

"A white guy, about Kiki's age. Short. Probably about five-six."

"Not really. Is he the one who stabbed her? I mean, she wasn't stabbed, but she thought she was. He used a needle syringe. I heard what the MTs said."

"Maybe he was behind us when we were getting the corn and drinks?" David posed it like a question, and Eve shifted her focus.

"You saw him?"

"Not so much. The trench, because if you're going to wear a trench, you've got to beat it up some, right? And I just noticed this one was like right out of the box or whatever. And the doofus shoes."

"What kind of doofus shoes?"

"Kick Its or Joe's or one of those. I just remember because he's the one who ran. He shoved right by us and ran when Kiki screamed."

"What color was his hair?"

"I don't know. I didn't bother to look at him when we were getting the corn. We were all talking and figuring out what we wanted, and I just noticed the trench and the shoes. In the theater, when it happened, it was dark, and it happened so fast."

"He pushed me."

"He pushed you, Lola?"

"I think. Kiki yelled and screamed. Man, her popcorn went flying, and her jumbo fizzy went splat all over, and I was turning around, and Pres, you said, like, 'What the hell, Keek,' and he, well, not really pushed, but more like . . ."

She jabbed out with both elbows.

"Like 'Out of my way, bitch.'" With a wince, she put her fingers to her lips. "Sorry about the 'bitch.' I didn't think of it because Kiki was screaming and trying to yank her jacket off, and there was fizzy all over my pants and shoes."

"Everyone was yelling to shut up," Pres continued. "And I was embarrassed and pissed off at her. I shouldn't've been."

"You didn't know."

"She was screaming and pulling off her jacket and yelling 'Is there blood, is there blood?'"

"He hit the emergency exit, because the alarm went off," David added, "and the lights all came on."

"They were going to kick us out, I think, but Kiki got sick all over the place." Lola shuddered. "And she kept saying he had a knife, he stabbed me, and how her arm was on fire. Then the MTs came, and the police. No, right before, Kiki went whack and tore the sleeve of her new shirt."

"I saw the bruise, and there was a red mark on it." Presley shut his eyes. "I thought she had been stabbed, but when the MTs came, and I heard them say about the drugs, and remembered about those girls, what happened. I thought she was dying. I thought Kiki was dying."

"She's not. And she, along with all of you, are going to help us find him."

She wanted to go over it all again, try to pry out more details. But the moms came in, and this time Pres didn't stop the tears.

"She's okay." Audrey went to him and, though he stood a head taller, gathered him in. "They're moving her to a room, just for the night. Just to monitor."

Connie spoke quietly to Eve. "Dr. Myler said she has the copy of the toxicology screen for you, also the names and contacts of the MTs who treated her if you need them."

"That's helpful, thank you. As I said, I'll have to contact you for follow-ups."

"Whatever we can do to help you stop this monster."

On the way out, Eve picked up the tox report and the contacts.

Then she stepped into the summer night and took a good clear breath.

"You'll want to walk a bit, and we're not far." Knowing her, Roarke slid an arm around her waist. "To the theater?"

"Yeah. She got lucky. That kid got lucky. He goes for the other arm, I'm notifying those two women tonight."

"He didn't, and she'll be fine. She strikes me as not only tough, as you said, but resilient."

"Maybe tomorrow she'll remember more. And David? People don't always realize what they've seen. I'm going to see if he'll work with Yancy on a sketch. Kiki, too. She saw his eyes, his what-the-fuck eyes, so maybe."

When they got to the car, she stood one more moment, just breathing the smell of hospital out of her lungs.

Coffee, she thought, she wanted a whole lot of coffee to combat the fatigue trying to creep back.

"Didn't know to beat up the trench. Didn't know trenches at vids are for flakers."

"Did you?"

"The beat-up part, sure. But teenage social levels are strange and changeable. Maybe he got it at L&W with the shoes and shit. I need to check if they carry them."

She got in the car. "Anyway, it's more, and I didn't have to stand over a dead girl for three nights running."

A bud that would never bloom. Kiki Rosenburg would have a chance to bloom.

"Big mistake on his part. I need to see where he tried to kill her, and the distance from there to the emergency exit.

"Didn't have as much time as he counted on," she calculated. "Jab her, sneer, walk away. Shove open the emergency doors and out. Don't care about the alarm. That's just more confusion—he thinks. People might see him sliding out, but they'll just see some kid in a trench. He'd have already scoped out the cams on the doors, in the lobby. We won't see his face, but we'll get more.

"Every time, just a little more. And this time the more comes without a girl on a slab."

"He didn't know to jam the alarm. Easy enough to do," Roarke told her. "Emergency exit doors are as basic as they come. Just put together a jammer, or buy one off the street. Your escape's silent then. Silent's always better."

"It is, isn't it? Nobody notices a thing then. You're right."

She programmed coffee because she might have missed that little detail.

"He either didn't know to, or know how to. Most teens have a pretty solid or at least basic knowledge of e's. He doesn't. Not enough for this."

She let that roll as he pulled up behind a cruiser at the theater. "That's more of the more."

Chapter Fifteen

Inside the brightly lit lobby that smelled of the substance pretending to be butter they squirted on popcorn (it wasn't all that bad), uniformed officers escorted small groups of civilians from theaters to the exit.

She recognized one, stopped him. "Where are my detectives, Officer Hurley?"

"You got Baxter and Trueheart in theater three. Flick in there ended 'round right before the attack in theater one, so it was already emptied out. Peabody's in one. The e-geek's up in the security hub."

She shot Roarke a look, and he peeled off to find McNab.

"Do you know who was first on scene?"

"That'd be Hernadez and Blicker. They're in with Peabody. Kid still breathing?"

"She is, and she's going to stay that way."

"Lucky break, all around."

She headed to the main theater.

The lights flooded there, too, and the noise level spiked with nervous laughter, quick shouts all underlined with buzzing conversation.

"Quiet down!" Eve ordered before she moved to Peabody and a group of three.

"Okay, you're free to go. We appreciate your patience and cooperation."

"Yeah, right." One of the three—all male, all about Jamie's age to Eve's eye—sneered as he pushed up. "Like we had a choice."

"The girl in the hospital sure didn't have one," Eve commented.

"She spoiled things for everybody. Screaming like she got chopped with an axe."

"Come on, Jerry." One of his friends nudged him. And didn't budge him.

"Then the cops lock us up in here like criminals. Shit, they hauled the screamer out, didn't they? But instead of watching the vid we paid for, the one we've been waiting a damn year for, we're stuck in here with nothing."

"That's a sad story. I can feel my heart bleeding."

"You know what we paid for these tickets, for the reserved seating?"

"Management will honor all tickets dated for tonight at another showing," Peabody reminded him. "Or afford a full refund."

"Yeah, like that makes up for it. Cops are assholes."

"Are you twenty-one, Jerry?"

"What's it to you?"

"Well, it appears to me you haven't reached that legal age as yet, and you've spent some of your time in here nipping off whatever's in the bottle in your coat pocket."

Deliberately, Eve took a sniff. "My guess is gin."

The flush that rose up his throat and into his face equaled the perfect tell.

"I don't know what you're talking about."

"I may be an asshole cop, but I know gin when I smell it on some whiny fuckhead's breath. No alcohol permitted in this theater. Add the underage element, and you and your pals—who've wisely stayed quiet—could end up spending some time in the tank.

"You've got two choices," she continued. "The tank's one of them, and given the hour, you probably won't be able to post bail until the morning. You might find spending the night in the tank educational. Second choice is to take a tip from your friends. Say nothing and walk away."

She stepped aside so he could. He took the second choice.

"You know," Eve observed, "it may not be tonight, but Jerry's eventually going to have that educational experience.

"Status."

"First, what's Rosenburg's status?"

"She was awake, reasonably lucid, and her doctor says she'll make a full recovery."

"Excellent news." Peabody eased back in her seat, rubbed at her tired eyes. "Next, I knew he'd been drinking, and he was a fuckwit, but I thought it more practical to just get through the interview and move him along in the interest of time."

"Agreed. I, however, enjoy making a little time for fuckwits. Next?"

"We've been through several who state they saw someone run out the emergency exit, the one on this side, and those accounts vary. A male, a female, a kid, an old guy, Black, white, big, small. You know how it goes."

"Yeah."

"But we may have something from a wit who was working the concession stand. Sharlie Weaver, age twenty-three. She noticed the vic because of the hair. Really long, thick, straight, and really red."

"That's accurate."

"She's been thinking about going red—Sharlie—so she got a good look. And remembers there was someone in a trench just behind her. She assumed with the same group, as he approached the concessions more or less with them, but walked away without ordering anything when they had their snacks."

"Did she see his face?"

"Again, she only noticed him because she was looking at the victim's hair, but she noticed the trench because—I quote—'the rest of the group weren't flakers.' She said he had his head down when they walked away, and he was wearing shades."

"Shades? At ten at night? Inside?"

"It's a look, Dallas. But she's pretty sure she caught a glimpse of his profile. She definitely ID'd him as white and about the same height as the redhead. She thinks his hair was brown, and—again quoting—'floppy,' flopping over his face so she didn't really see it."

"It's a wig."

"You think?"

"His clothes, Peabody. Button shirt, expensive dress shoes—freaking tassel—quality pants. Who's going to put him in those and let his hair flop around? A wig, longer than his hair, helping to hide his face. Shades do the same. We need her to work with Yancy."

"She's willing, and I sent him a text on it. He can make time tomorrow."

"I have another for him. One of the vic's group noticed the trench. He said it looked out-of-the-box new."

"Okay, that plays in. You never want a trench to look new. Makes you a wheeze."

"Right. Yancy may be able to tease more out of him. I'll arrange it. And the vic, when her doctor clears her for it. She got the best look at him."

"The sweepers processed the door, and there are a crapload of prints on it. Fingerprints, handprints, partials, shoe scuffs from kicking at the base. But if he sealed up—"

"Why? You can hit a door like that with your hip, your ass, your shoulder. Unless you're panicked and running, which he was. So maybe a mistake."

She nodded her chin toward the spill of popcorn and fizzy in the center aisle. "That's where he hit her. And that's a mistake, too. Why not wait until they moved farther down? They had reserved seats. So they'd have walked six, seven more rows down. He'd have been closer to his escape route. Too eager," she murmured. "Wired up on it, and maybe a booster with it. Couldn't wait. Needed to feel it again."

"He knocked into people when he ran. So far nobody he bumped or shoved could add anything solid. It was dark, it happened fast."

"We only need one. Look, I'll send Hurley in. He can help with the interviews. I want to check in with Baxter and Trueheart."

"Theater three, they took half of mine in there."

Eve moved on to three.

A smaller space, and a smaller group. With two detectives working, they'd processed more, released more.

She walked to Trueheart. "Excuse me. I need a minute, Detective."

"Yes, sir. Just hang one minute," he said to a group of five as he rose and stepped away with Eve.

"Sir, the victim?"

"Full recovery expected."

A smile moved over his earnest, all-American face. "That's good news. I may have more. This group here? The girl three in—Annabelle Joan Pierce, goes by A.J.—states she heard the screaming, started to turn around. She couldn't really see what was going on because the aisle was still crowded. Then somebody plowed right into her, knocked her into her friend—the girl on her left. And dominoes. A.J. states she tried to catch her balance and ended up in the lap of a guy in the aisle seat."

"Can she describe the one who plowed into her?"

"Darkish hair—she thinks brown, but can't say light, medium. On the long side, at least in front. Falling over his face."

"Shades?"

"No, sir."

WTF eyes, Kiki had said. He'd taken them off when they got into the theater. House lights off.

"Wearing a trench—gray or tan, not black. Lighter. No facial hair. She thinks a short guy, small build. Short, Caucasian. I'm trying to get more, but I think if she could work with Yancy."

"Yeah. He's going to be busy. Where was she when she got knocked?"

"She said they were nearly to their seats. They were in row ten."

Was it irony, Eve wondered, or some other thing when the best potential witness would have sat in the same row as the target?

"You've got a rapport going with this group?"

"Yes, sir, I think I do."

"Then stick with it. I'll line up Yancy."

She walked down to the front and Baxter.

"Give me a minute, gang, my boss is here." He added a grin that served as a wink. "We're almost done."

He rose and walked aside with Eve.

"The kid?"

"Got lucky. She's going to be fine. Got anything?"

"Plenty who heard the commotion and were pretty pissed about it. I talked to a couple of groups who were already seated and close enough to see the popcorn fly. One close enough the fizzy she dropped splatted over his new airboots. He was pissed at that, then he realized she was screaming somebody stabbed her, and thought the fizzy was her blood. Half passed out."

When he scanned the theater, Eve knew he did a head count just as she had on entering.

"Plenty who saw the trench coat fly by, but—"

"Descriptions vary."

"Oh, they do." Baxter let out a sigh. "They do."

"Trueheart has a good lead."

"My boy hit?"

"He's got another I'm going to push on Yancy. When you finish this group, move into theater one with Peabody. Trueheart can handle the rest of these. If McNab's freed up, I'll toss him in here or there, depending. Once you're clear, go home. You can write it up in the morning."

"Tonight, tomorrow." He shrugged. "I've got the time. I was on a date, about to seal the deal." He laid a hand on his heart. "The personal sacrifices we make in the pursuit of justice."

"Huh. I was told shortly ago that all cops are assholes."

"Sometimes you need an asshole to pursue justice."

"That's a good one," Eve decided, and went to hunt up her e-geeks.

She found McNab popping out of the elevator.

"We got some pieces of him, Dallas. Out on line, then in bolting from the emergency exit. Even bolting, he kept his head down. More of his hair though. Medium brown in a boarder's do."

"What is that?"

"Airboarder's do. It's not especially in now. Long in the front, sort of diagonal." McNab swiped the flat of his hand from his left temple, across his eyes to the bottom of his right ear. "Shorter on the sides. In the back, you can go for a stub tail, but his is loose, just past collar length."

"It's going to be a wig."

"Hey, you know, I wondered."

"Why?"

"Well, on the bolt, we did a freeze, and it looked a little—Roarke called it askew."

"He ran into some people. That could cause askew. Shades?"

"Can't tell you on the flight, but pretty sure affirmative on entry. Light gray trench, and—Roarke again—pristine. The black baggies and Kick Its. Kept his hands in his pockets on line, really worked on looking chill.

"He'd sidestep every few minutes. A lot do—is it moving yet, how many more in front of me? But he was scoping for his target. The vic and her group were about six feet ahead of him."

"Lobby cams?"

"Plenty of blank spots there, and he stayed inside the pack, the crowd. We can see him moving and maneuvering until he's directly behind the vic and her group. But there's no decent angle on him."

McNab did a long scan of the lobby and the cameras. "He's been in here before, knew the layout."

"Yeah, he does his homework. Give Trueheart a hand in three. Baxter's with Peabody. I've got two wits, maybe three with one from the first murder. Trueheart has one, Peabody has one who all saw pieces of him again. I'm setting them up with Yancy. It wouldn't hurt to find a few more."

"You got that."

"Is Roarke still upstairs?"

"Yeah, he's talking to the manager. As far as wits go, she's out. She was taking a personal call in her office when it went down."

"Wait, what about the ticket scanners? If we know approximately what time he moved to a scanner for entry, can we trace from that?"

"Scanner code doesn't carry personal data. It's like a verification, and you could track it to where it generated, but that's about it."

"Where it generated's more info."

"That's why, being an e-man, I'm having them upload the scans for the time frame. It may not help catch him, but it's more to pile on in the box, then in court."

"Copy me on that. Which you were going to do," Eve said. "Sorry. I know you've got a brain in there."

"And we're working on the third night of basically double shifts. Brains get sizzled. I'll go talk to some kids."

She opted for the stairs, then stopped halfway up as Roarke started down.

"McNab briefed me. Did you get anything else from the manager?"

"Not that applies to the investigation. She was in her office and didn't come down until after the assistant manager—who was in the back, behind concessions, unboxing more candy and such—notified her of the situation. She's hoping, of course, you'll clear the building so they can hold tomorrow's shows."

"If I get the clearance from the sweepers, we'll be done. Jesus, you don't own this place, do you?"

"I would have given you that information."

"Trying to buy it? Is that why you were talking to the manager?"

"No. I did persuade her to arrange a private viewing of *Return of the Three* for Kiki—when she's well enough—her friends, their families."

She said nothing for a moment.

He would think of that.

Of course he would think of that.

She shifted, stood hipshot. "What about the popcorn?"

"All they can eat."

"How much did it cost you?"

"Not to worry, darling. We can still afford spaghetti and meatballs."

She brushed a hand over his. "I'm on duty. But when I'm not . . . I'm going to give Peabody a hand with the last of the possible witnesses."

"Should I try to scare up some coffee?"

She considered, but she trusted vid theater coffee much less than its popcorn.

"Better off with the cold stuff."

"I'll take care of it."

Sometime after one in the morning, she stepped outside with Roarke and her detectives.

"Peabody, Yancy says he'll go to the wits. They're usually more comfortable in their own environment. Line them up for him, make sure you have parental permission for the minors."

"An ocean of wits." Tired, visibly fading, Peabody rubbed her eyes. "And a piss-trickle who saw enough to follow up."

"This time yesterday, we didn't have that. Or a survivor. Anybody needs a ride, we can pull in a couple cruisers."

"I've got a car waiting." Roarke held up a hand and a burly all-terrain slid up along the curb. "The driver can make the rounds for you."

"Sweet." Baxter gave Trueheart a pat on the back. "Let's get you home, young man."

"We're heading downtown. You'd be the first stop. Pops."

"Getting a sassy mouth on him. You hear that?" On a wide smile, Baxter squared his shoulders, puffed out his chest. "Makes me proud. Tomorrow, LT. Thanks for the lift, Roarke."

"Come on, She-Body. You're asleep on your feet."

"Pretty much. Thanks. Night."

"Appreciate that. Cruisers would've got them there, but this gives them a chance to unwind together."

"And after a long day for all. Off duty now, are you, Lieutenant?"

"As much as I ever am."

"And after, you said."

"Not in front of the crime scene."

She walked down the sidewalk with him toward the car.

"This'll do."

On the sidewalk, just after one in the morning, on a hot, sticky summer night, she wrapped her arms around him. She kissed him long, slow, deep. Pressing in more when she felt his hand fist on the back of her jacket.

"All that," he murmured, "for arranging a viewing?"

"No, all that for thinking of it, for knowing how much it'll mean, how much it'll push the ugly of what happened away. Then arranging it."

She drew him back, kissed him again.

"For that."

"She looked so fragile, yet under that, so strong." Bringing Eve's hands to his lips, he kissed them. "I've seen you look the same."

"Not tonight." She got in the car, stretched out her legs. "I'm tired. I'm damn tired, but I've got a buzz. Because she lived, he ran, and we're closer."

"Mistakes, as you said before. He made them."

"He won't sleep well tonight. He'll go over and over it. He'll watch the media reports hoping he got enough in her."

"Wouldn't he know he didn't?"

"Yeah, but he'd hope. Maybe she had a bad reaction to what he did get in her. Maybe the MTs didn't get there fast enough. Maybe. Hope. Sweat."

Settling back, she looked over at him. "He didn't make a mistake. Impossible. Too smart, too prepared. He got away clean, didn't he? Sure he did. Nobody got a good look at him. Wig, shades, trench.

"But he's sweating on it, going over and over his steps. He won't sleep well tonight, but I will."

In fact, she thought, she could drift right off now.

"Are we still on for that weekend on the island as soon as?"

"As soon as," he agreed, and drove through the gates.

"Gonna work the private school angle hard," she muttered. "I'm going to know him when I see him. I really think I'll know him. And maybe we'll get a picture tomorrow. Yancy's gold, so maybe."

"Will he try again? Not with Kiki, with another."

"He has to." She slid out of the car. "Tonight was a failure. Scientific mind, right?"

As they walked into the house, Roarke slid an arm around her waist.

"Of the mad variety, I'd say."

"I sucked at science, but even I know when an experiment or project hits a snag, you go over it step-by-step, maybe make some tweaks. Then you do it again."

"Maybe he'll take a few days to do that going over and tweaking."

As they walked into the bedroom, she shook her head. "He's still a teenage boy. They're impatient. They want gratification, and they want it now. Add in the rest, the craving, the misogyny, the arrogance, all that?"

She stripped off her jacket, her weapon harness. Sat and thought about drumming up the energy to take off her boots.

When Roarke did it for her, she smiled.

"I could go for some hot, sweaty sex with you, but I don't think I've got a round in me."

"Happily, I'm not a teenage boy, and can wait for that gratification."

"Appreciate it. And add to all I said, he's already got the next time and place picked. He's scoped it out, done his research, his calculations. He's not going to let some stupid little bitch who couldn't hold still for two seconds ruin all his work."

Knowing her preference when she only wanted sleep, he handed her a nightshirt.

"Thanks. I'll bang you like a marching band on the island."

"A marching band?"

"They got drums, right? Lots of drums. Bang, boom, bang. And Jesus, McNab was right. The brain can sizzle."

"In you go now."

When she rolled into bed, the cat rolled, then padded his way up to turn a couple lazy circles before settling again.

"He's awake now," she murmured when Roarke slipped in beside her. "Staring at the ceiling, going over those steps, considering those tweaks. And under the fear, because it's there, the fear, he aches. He aches like an addict jonesing for a hit. Because he missed, and instead of gratification, instead of release and pleasure, there's that craving. Eating away."

She curled herself against Roarke as the cat curled himself against her back.

"Sleep now."

"Oh yeah," she agreed, and dropped right out.

Someone else didn't sleep, but lay, just as she'd imagined, staring at the ceiling. Aching in the dark.

He'd done everything right, everything according to plan.

All he'd found from the media flashes told him she'd been transported to a hospital. Not even her name, not that he gave a good damn about her name. But it was the one he'd chosen, the redhead. The media said an incident at the theater, the opening of the idiotic vid.

She'd die at the hospital then. Even the partial dose should take her down. They wouldn't know why—just some trampy girl going down—so how could they treat her in time to counteract what he'd gotten into her?

Life support maybe, but brain-dead.

The jacket, that must've done it.

But no, he'd gotten the needle through. He'd felt it go into her. She'd screamed so loud! So fast!

As if he'd hacked her with a machete.

Neither of the others had reacted that way. A sting, yes, a quick prick. He wanted them to feel it or he'd have used a numbing agent. But she'd screamed, started to spin around the instant the needle went in.

He'd had to pull it out and run. No choice there.

It didn't matter, couldn't matter. For the next he'd make sure she had bare arms, like the first two sluts.

Maybe take a little more time picking her out. There'd be plenty of time. He'd already planned it so meticulously. The next step. How and where.

He knew just what he'd do to her, do with her, before he finished her.

So exciting, the anticipation, so fulfilling.

It would be his first time. Not hers, of course. They were all whores. But it would be her last.

Chapter Sixteen

The next time Eve opened her eyes, Roarke sat, the cat sprawled across the lap of his perfect slate-gray suit, scanning something on a tablet.

On-screen, the usual indecipherable stock reports scrolled by on mute.

Light streamed in the sky window overhead and showed her a happy blue sky.

"How did it get to be morning again?"

"There you have that pesky rotation of the Earth. You didn't sleep long, but you slept well."

"I slept like a . . . I was going to say rock because people say that, but it's stupid. Rocks don't sleep."

"But they're usually very still and quiet."

Mostly, she thought as she got up. Except for earthquakes, avalanches, mudslides, volcanos.

She hit the coffee first, then the shower.

When she came out, breakfast waited under warming domes, and Roarke had banished the cat.

Galahad stretched out in a sunny patch on the floor and eyed the warming domes with avarice.

"So what was it this morning? Buy, sell? Sell, buy?"

"Neither, as it happens, but a very satisfying progress report on a project in Kyoto, then some details on the beginnings of one in Sydney."

"And they're on opposite time because of the pesky rotation."

"See there, you're getting it."

He removed the domes on what turned out to be frittatas. Colorful ones, she noted, sure to contain lots of healthy things.

"What's the deal you've got with spinach? Do you own the world's supply of it?"

He poured her another cup of coffee. "You're a slender woman who all too often works herself into the ground and neglects eating during her workday. Iron matters. There's bacon in there as well."

She swore she saw Galahad's ears twitch at the word *bacon*.

Since she shared that affection, she sampled. "Got a little heat on it. Not bad."

Since she also had a dish of summer berries, she couldn't really complain.

"I'm wearing black today, so no comments. They're having Jenna Harbough's memorial, and unless I'm about to tackle this bastard, we need to monitor."

"Do you think he'll be there?"

"I don't. He's done with her. She served her purpose. But if I'm wrong about that, and he shows . . . I think I'll know him. I know that sounds—"

"As if you think you'll know him. And I believe you will," Roarke added.

"I will. If I see him at the memorial today, I think I'll know him. If I see him in the school stuff, I think I'll know him."

As she ate, she considered. "He's worn a wig—either because he thinks it helps him blend or for the disguise. Both. Plus, the style hides his face. Under it? His hair might be the same color, or close, but the style's not. His is conservatively cut, short, neat, parted on the side, ruler straight."

"That's very specific."

"It goes with the shoes, the clothes. He gets it cut at a high-end barber shop. Maybe a salon, but I lean toward the barber."

"Because salons give off at least a whiff of the feminine, and he wouldn't tolerate that."

"Exactly."

"Not as many of those as private schools, but."

"Yeah, but. Plenty of them. But it's an angle." One that needed following. "And besides the hair, it's going to be the eyes. His eyes, they're going to be wrong. And I'll know it."

Reaching over, she gave the black silk of his hair a tug. "Who does this?"

"In the last couple of years, Trina. She'll come to me."

"I bet." And thinking of the hard-ass stylist, Eve shoved her fingers through her own hair.

It was fine, just fine.

"And I bet she doesn't bitch at you when she does."

He smiled. "About what?"

"'Didn't I tell you to use that face gunk? You've only got one face! You're a dead cop, you oughta know skin's alive. You gotta feed it. Your hair needed a trim two weeks ago.' Then she slathers that sheep cum all over my hair."

He nearly choked on his frittata. "Sheep cum?"

"It looks like sheep cum."

"This begs the question," he decided. "Have you ever encountered the cum of sheep?"

"Not so far, but if I do, it'll look just like what Trina slathers all over my hair." After her last bite, she wagged her fork at him. "Your family has sheep. I bet they'd back me up on it."

"Well then, that will be quite the conversation starter over Thanksgiving dinner when they visit. I'll make a note."

"They'll back me up," she insisted. "Anyway, he doesn't go to Trina. Her place doesn't approach the bomb zone area of conservative."

She pushed up. "Black."

And went into her closet.

Roarke stacked the plates under the domes, then pointed at the cat. "Knock these off again, and there'll be no treats for you later. Mark my words."

"He's a cat, Roarke," Eve called out. "Do you figure cats understand the concept of *later*?"

"This one best learn to."

Black made it easy—or easier, considering her myriad choices. She slapped it all together, including boots, lightweight despite their good, thick soles.

In case she got the chance to chase the bastard down and tackle him.

When she came out to strap on her weapon harness, Roarke gave her a long look.

"No comments," she reminded him.

"Even if I say you look respectful, for the memorial, while still looking formidable and utterly in charge?"

She swung on her jacket. "Okay, those comments are admissible. I'm heading straight in," she said as she grabbed her pocket items. "I want to be there before Whitney contacts me, orders me up to his office."

"You're expecting that?"

"Two murders, one attempt in three days. He's going to bring up inviting the feds to assist. He has to."

"And your response?"

"Oh, hell no. But with more respect and diplomacy. I want to dig into the schools, hard and deep. Plus I want to look over the security feed from the theater, start the barber shop angle. Nag the crap out of the lab on the door prints. I still need to go through Arlie Dillon's room, and hopefully follow up with Kiki Rosenburg."

"So a full day of work before you start."

"If he doesn't hit again tonight, he will tomorrow. And if he hits again, kills again, and slides away, we'll have to call in the feds. We'll need them."

"You're all but breathing down his neck now, so my bet remains on you." He cupped her chin, tapped his thumb in its shallow dent before he kissed her.

"Tag me, will you, before you make that tackle. I'd like to be there if I can manage it. And see you take care of my cop."

"Affirmative to both. He's going for it," she added as she walked out.

When Roarke glanced back, the cat stopped his oh-so-casual walk toward the table. He turned, sat, shot up a leg, and began to wash diligently.

"Mind your step, mate, or we'll think about replacing you with a nice, obedient hound."

At the word *hound*, Galahad sent one searing look over his shoulder.

"Consider that," Roarke advised.

Maybe it was a gift from the universe, or maybe she'd fallen into the perfect window, but traffic streamed right along all the way downtown.

She pulled into the garage at Central a solid twenty minutes ahead of shift. Time, she thought as she strode to the elevator, to do her updates, write up a report from the attack on Kiki Rosenburg. Maybe start a city-wide search on the upscale barbers.

Her luck held as she rode up to Homicide with barely any stops and starts, shuffle-ons, shuffle-offs.

In her office, she hit the coffee before setting up the barber search on auto. She updated her board and book while it ran, and considered the next logical steps in the day.

The incoming from the commander's office told her what that first step would be.

She had the full complement of detectives in the bullpen when she walked out. And Jenkinson's tie.

She couldn't say for sure, but she thought they called the color fuchsia. If fuchsia was irradiated. White fuchsia-eyed rabbits hopped over it.

She imagined they had really sharp, pointed teeth under their sly smiles.

They made her wonder why she always felt compelled to look.

"Peabody, check on Rosenburg, contact her parents and Arlie Dillon's mother. Find out when it's convenient for us to take a look at their rooms."

"Detective Sergeant Rabbit."

Jenkinson grinned at her. "Yes, boss."

"Are you clear?"

"Just tying up some paperwork."

"Good." She took out her PPC. "I've got a list of upscale barbers. You and Reineke can start checking them out. Looking for a Caucasian male, about sixteen. You have the current description of the subject. Hair color unknown. It's a wig," she said when he frowned at her.

"Well, shit. Sure it is."

"Conservative cut. It's probably regular, say once a month. He may or may not be accompanied by a parent or guardian. Polite, well-mannered, well-dressed."

"We've got it, Loo."

"I'm with Whitney."

"We got it," Jenkinson said as she walked out. "Don't let him push the feds in yet."

And yet another reason she'd wanted him to take the promotion to DS.

This time she took the glides to give herself the time and room to think. She glanced at her 'link, read the brief text from Peabody.

Before you get to Whitney, Kiki's condition's good. Scheduled for tests this morning, and should be released before noon.

Roger that.

Outside Whitney's office, his admin gestured Eve straight in.

He sat at his desk, his gray suit shades lighter than Roarke's, the shoulders in it as broad as a fullback's. A mug of coffee steamed at his elbow.

His wide dark face had more lines than it had when she'd made rank, and his close-cropped black hair more threads of white.

But somehow they added dignity to power.

"Sir."

"Lieutenant. Coffee?"

"No, sir, thank you."

"Can't blame you. Do you have a status on the third victim?"

"They're hoping to release her before noon. We'll interview her again, as she saw him, and might remember more details. We have other witnesses from the theater, Commander, and Yancy will work with them."

"Yes, I skimmed your report. As of now, after two murders and one attempted, we don't have a full description, much less an identification."

"No, sir. However—"

"Three's the magic number, Dallas. You know that as well as I do."

"Yes, sir."

"Convince me why we shouldn't pick up the magic wand and bring in the FBI. I know you. It's not about power or pecking order, it's not about who gets the collar and credit. We can request Special Agent Teasdale. You've worked well with her in the past."

"Yes, sir, and it may come to that. I don't want to bring in federal investigators at this time, take time to read them in, agree on tactics and strategies, because we're close.

"He's made mistakes, starting with the first murder. They're our advantage, Commander, and more so since he doesn't realize or understand he's made them. As simple as the shoes," she began, and ran through it, point by point.

"If anyone can finesse more details from the wits," Eve finished, "it's Yancy."

"We agree there. Private schools, barbers, the shoes. Good angles, logical." On a pause, he sipped his coffee. "Time-consuming to pursue."

"Commander, we're close. We've systematically narrowed the gap and will narrow it more today. I know him. I've got everything but his face and his name, and we're close there. Teasdale's good, she's solid, but she doesn't know him. By the time she does, we'll have him."

His eyes, always direct, held hers. "All of that's based largely on your instincts."

"Yes, sir."

"I've never had a cop under my command with better ones."

He rose, walked to the windows where the city he protected and served carried on its daily business.

"I'll give the lab time with the prints, and you time to follow up on these angles. Forty-eight hours. If he kills another girl, that time ends immediately."

"Yes, sir."

"What does your gut tell you, Dallas? Will he try again tonight?"

"Yes, sir, I believe he'll need to."

Still watching the city, Whitney nodded. "My gut says the same, so you have that time. You have it because the feds can't do more than you and your team within that window. And you have the momentum."

He turned back. "Wrap him up, Lieutenant."

She headed back down, using her 'link to push on the prints, then tagged Feeney.

"Whatever you need, kid," he said before she could speak.

"I've got a long list of private schools, and criteria I'm looking for. If I could send you part of that list."

"Send it. McNab says the kid from last night's okay."

"She is. Whitney gave us forty-eight before bringing in the feds."

"Yeah." Feeney sighed, scratched his chin. "That had to be coming."

"I think he'll try again tonight, so cut that time down to more like twelve hours."

"I'll pull Callendar in on it. Look, send us the whole deal on the schools. You've got other angles, right? Work them; we'll work this."

"Thanks. The minute I'm back at my desk."

She clicked off, thought about the wig. Boarder style, brown. One more angle to work.

When she turned into Homicide, Peabody hailed her.

"Kiki's mom—Connie—tagged me back just a minute ago. She said if we can get to their place after twelve-thirty—just let them know—we can talk to her again. And Kiki wants to work with Yancy. She says Kiki's pissed, and eager."

"Mom One—Connie—cried just a little because she says that means Kiki's back. Her girl doesn't take any crap."

"Good to hear. Harbough's memorial's at noon, so we'll go after that."

"Arlie Dillon's mom said she'd be out all morning, from about nine to about noon. She's making arrangements. Asked if we could do this while she's out, and she'll leave the key with a neighbor. I said we could just master in if that was easier, and she was fine with it."

"We'll head there after I clear up some things."

"And Mira's in your office."

"Yeah, saves me a trip."

In a suit of the same happy blue as the sky, Mira stood at Eve's board drinking coffee.

"I helped myself."

"I'm going to do the same. I was going to ask for a quick consult."

"I assumed. I'm told the girl from last night is recovering."

"Recovered, from the sounds of it. No fall off an airboard's ever been so lucky. But I think it was more."

"Yes. And now I'm taking your only decent chair." Mira sat at the desk. "He rushed it. I read your report on my way in—you started early. He only needed to wait another minute, perhaps two, before his target made her way to her row. And that would've cut the distance to his escape route in half."

"He just couldn't wait."

"No. There's still a boy inside the killer, with a boy's impatience now that he's begun, now that he's succeeded twice. You added a note in there about Roarke's take on the door alarm. I find that valid as well."

"He's smart, maybe brilliant in his area of interest. But outside that? He's not. A jammer in one pocket, the syringe in the other. Kill the girl, hit the jammer, get out, no alarm. Sure, somebody would have seen him, but probably thought nothing of it. She's not going to react for several minutes, probably after she's in her seat."

"Most teenagers I know are very well versed in e's. It's just routine for them. But, as you wrote, he's not. Very likely no arcades, no vid games as part of his routine."

Mira paused, drank some coffee. "Then clearly he panicked. Instead of attempting to lose himself in the crowd, even for a moment or two, he bolted, knocking people aside, drawing attention on his way out, then through the door."

"The kid inside the killer again."

"Exactly," Mira affirmed. "And it's the child who won't take stock, not fully, of where he went wrong. Who won't stop at least for a few days, a week, to let it all settle down, to let himself fully calm.

"He'll be harder on the next girl, Eve. If he can find a way to incapacitate her, he will. If he can find a way to do that, lure her away, he'll rape her if he's able, physically abuse her, make her pay for his failure, before he kills her."

"He'd risk that now, this soon?"

"I believe he has to. He can't accept failure, not in his area of expertise. Not when he's planned so minutely, and succeeded. It's another rejection. The girl last night rejected him. She didn't submit; more, she put him in peril. He had to run."

Eve paced to her window, back again. "He had to pull out before he finished. If the needle stands in for his dick, he barely penetrated, had to pull out."

"And the frustration, the rage, is very physical. He'll need release."

"We've already run like crimes, that's SOP. Jenna was his first, I'm sure of it. Do you think he's raped or attempted rape before?"

"I don't. If so, he'd have had a plan for Jenna Harbough. Drug her drink, get her away from her friends. This is different. Something he's been imagining, working up to. Something he may never have attempted. But the girl last night rejected him, beat him, endangered him. Rape is about power—power, dominance, and punishment."

"Okay. I'll factor this in."

Mira rose. "If there's anything more I can do, any questions you have, I'll make time."

"I've got some leads. We're going to push them."

Because it felt like a race now, Eve thought as Mira left. She turned to the board again. A race until he had the dark on his side.

She couldn't let him win.

She sent Feeney the list and criteria, then went back to the bullpen.

"Move it, Peabody."

She took the glides at a jog.

Peabody raced to keep up. "Did Whitney—"

"He gave us forty-eight, but we don't have nearly that. The Dillon place first. You drive."

"Really?"

"I need to call in a favor with a fed. Mira says it's likely he'll change pattern with the next. Power and punishment. Rape, physical assault, then murder. I don't think he's tried rape before, but we're going to be sure."

She pulled out her 'link as they clanged down the steps to the garage. "Agent Teasdale, Lieutenant Dallas."

"Yes. Jenna Harbough, Arlie Dillon, Kiki Rosenburg."

"That's right." She got in the car as Peabody took the wheel. "I think we're close, but frankly, reading you in fully and coordinating will eat into the time I think I have before he hits again."

"Then what can I do for you, and them?"

"Dr. Mira believes after last night's miss, he'll escalate. He has access to Rohypnol. If he can use it, take her somewhere private enough, he'll rape her before he kills her. I don't believe he's raped or attempted rape previous. But if I'm wrong."

"Give me the best physical description of him you have, and I'll run it with those factors."

"I appreciate it."

"We work the same side, Lieutenant. Send me what you have, and I'll get back to you by this afternoon."

When she had, Eve put the 'link away. "Okay, we've got to cover every possibility. We'll make this search fast. I don't expect to find anything that links to him."

"Like with the prior rape, no chances taken."

"Right." When Peabody pulled up at the apartment building, Eve got out. "Wait." Though she said wait, she moved toward the building, pulled her 'link again as she mastered in.

"I need to talk to her," Eve began.

The dragon admin merely said, "One moment, Lieutenant."

And a moment later, Mira's face came on-screen.

"Eve?"

"Wouldn't he, at some point, need to know the victim? Someone he's seen, wanted? Someone who's rejected him, made fun of him, ignored him? Whatever. At some point, wouldn't he want that power over someone personal?"

"That's a very good point, and very possible. It's also possible that each of these girls, though they don't share coloring or build, represents someone who rejected him. And, I'm sorry, Eve, but his victims may simply represent all the ones who've ignored him."

"Okay, okay, so no easy answer there."

"I wish I could give you one. When you have him, we'll know that answer."

"All right. Thanks."

She mastered into the apartment.

"He's probably been rejected, or took it that way, plenty."

Eve nodded as she scanned the living area. It even looked sad now.

"Yeah, but . . . Why did I hold out for Big Bitch Brenda?"

"Who?"

Eve just waved that away. "She wasn't the only one who went at me at school, but . . . I waited, didn't I? I knew what I was doing under it all. She wasn't the only, but she was the worst. I wanted to kick the crap out of her, so I waited until I knew I could."

"You're going to have to tell me about Big Bitch Brenda sometime, but I see where you're going. He's got one picked who he's decided was the worst."

"Or one he wanted, sexually, more than the others."

"Or. He'll get to her when he knows he's ready."

"Or, again, when he can't hold out longer. It's not going to be this girl, but we'll do our job. Private school girl, someone he'd see every day. Who didn't bother to look back.

"Let's get this done, and move on."

Chapter Seventeen

Arlie's room wrapped the cheerful around chaos. A wildly floral spread covered the bed, and a half ton of pillows covered that. An enormous board crowded with sketches of designs commanded one wall. Curtains of shimmering blue spilled down the sides of the window.

A table stood in front of it, and on the table some sort of sewing machine Eve figured you'd need a degree in mechanical science to operate.

"Oh boy, that's one mag machine! Hanson Super Pro Portable," Peabody said, all but cooing over it. "And she's got a fully adjustable tailor's form. What I'd give for one of those! Looks like she was working on a few projects at once."

Eve saw piles of fabric, more sort of draped on the dummy, an open chest holding more.

"You can tell that?"

"Oh, sure. I mean, I don't work like this." Obviously unable to resist,

Peabody fingered some of the fabric. "Sure, I can bounce from a building project to a sewing one or knitting, crocheting, whatever, but I can't juggle two projects of the same type at once. Gotta follow through.

"My aunt Margo works like this, and basically so does Leonardo. These curtains, Dallas, the bedclothes, even some of these pillows? Handmade. Either she made them or her mother did. Probably some of each. It's excellent work."

"She's got a work/study area. Take that, see what you can find on her comp. I've got the closet."

No adjoining bath here, and a closet about half the size of Jenna Harbough's. But the cheerful chaos didn't continue in the closet. Clothes, carefully organized by type, coordinated by color, likely reflected the victim's deep respect for wardrobe.

They'd solved the small space by installing a closet system with rods at varying heights, strategically placed hooks, a long shelf over a rod for shoes and boots.

In the space, Eve found nothing but youthful style.

"She's got a lot of her design work on here," Peabody said. "It's pretty good, I think. Lots of flash. She's got files for school—last year's still on here. And she's bookmarked universities—ones with solid design departments. Looking for scholarships.

"Got a bunch of personal photos," Peabody added as she continued to search, "transferred from her 'link. Family stuff, friend stuff, a lot of her with the boyfriend. She has music downloaded. Probably played it while she worked or just hung around."

Peabody pushed back. "Most of her communications, her calendar, more photos and such, they'll be on her 'link. EDD already has that."

"No connection to the first victim, but I didn't expect to find it. Nothing that indicates she knew her killer. Her room's like Jenna's, but flipped."

That brought on a frown. "I don't get that."

"It's messy in here, chaotic, and her closet's like a tiny five-star boutique. Jenna's was the opposite. Neat room, messy closet. But they both had a particular passion, and aimed straight for it."

Shoving her hands in her pockets, Eve wandered the room.

"Is that it? Are we missing something, and this matters? Is that part of his motive, his method? Kill the girl with a dream? It couldn't be if it was of the moment, if it's random, and everything else says it is. But these two girls had common ground. No personal connection, but that singular dream, and the skill to go for it."

"Does Rosenburg have one?"

"None that shows, but we'll find out either way."

"Even if she does, I still don't see it, Dallas. The two victims live on opposite sides of the city, have no mutual friends or family. Yes, to the singular passion and skill—though Jenna's was, well, soaring skill, and Arlie's was solid, full of potential, but not as polished yet."

"They both had family support. That could play. Family paying attention."

"Okay. Still, their passions don't connect, either. It's a kind of narrow vision on each side. This is what I want." Peabody pressed her palms together, pointed them to one side of the room. "And the other, this is what I want." She pointed them to the opposite side.

"Public school for one, private for the other." And it mattered, Eve thought. Mattered because it provided no connection. "One rarely dates, the other has a boyfriend of several months, and he wasn't her first. No mutual clubs, no attending the same camps. But still, this is a communality, so we put it on the board."

Eve glanced around again. "Let's finish this up. We can check more shoe stores on the way back downtown."

On the journey they found two venues who'd sold the Stuben loafers, correct style, correct color within the last six months.

One to an eighty-year-old regular customer who bought them for himself, the other to a tourist from Ottawa.

"We cut the list more than by half now."

"Yeah," Eve agreed. "I think we pull some uniforms to handle the rest. The planet's revolving."

"Well, yeah, it has to or . . . Oh, like the clock's ticking."

"The clocks would still tick if the planet stopped revolving."

"I guess they would until . . . I'm not sure what happens if the Earth stops revolving, but it wouldn't be good. Maybe Teasdale will hit on something. Maybe the killings *were* the escalation, and he started with sexual assault. Then we have the shoes. We have Yancy. We may have his prints. Something's going to break, Dallas."

It had to.

"We've got enough time to swing by the lab before the memorial. Maybe an in-person shove will move things. Contact Uniform Carmichael. He can pick a couple of officers to start on the shoe hunt."

While Eve drove through traffic that had decided, probably gleefully, to thwart her at every turn, she tagged Feeney.

"I'm still in the field," she told him. "Any progress?"

"A lot of elimination, and that's progress. We've got a couple who may fit. Don't get a buzz from them, but they're a pretty close fit. You got a hell of a lot of schools, Dallas, and a hell of a lot of kids in them."

"Yeah. Send me the couple you've got. We pulled a couple out last night. I can start pushing on that later today."

"I'll send them, and any others who look possible."

"You got Jamie in there?"

"Roarke freed him up for the duration."

Another set of hands, another pair of eyes, another brain.

"How about you shift him over to universities, medical labs. Looking for the killer maybe taking a college course over the summer, or interning in a lab."

"I can do that."

"Appreciate it, Feeney. I'll get back to you."

Eve pushed through a yellow light as pedestrians did their best to flood the crosswalk in advance.

"Parent or guardian could be a doctor, a medical researcher, a lab rat. Not a police lab." Missing the next light, Eve hissed, braked. "You've got to be eighteen, and he's just not there. Plus, the screening, not that he couldn't get through it, but Dickhead's surely a dickhead, but he knows what we're looking for. He'd have flagged anyone who looked off."

"Dawber got past him," Peabody pointed out.

"Dawber got past everybody. But point taken."

She slogged her way to the lab.

Inside, the hive buzzed, as always.

She spotted Berenski at his station along with Garnet DeWinter—fashion dish and bone expert.

The fashion dish part wore a lavender lab coat over a plum-colored, body-conscious sheath. The skyscraper heels matched the coat. She'd tamed her hair, currently highlighted in copper, into a sleek twist that left her impressive face unframed.

She and Berenski appeared to be enjoying an animated conversation.

It paused when they spotted Eve.

DeWinter said, "Dallas."

Eve said, "DeWinter."

DeWinter smiled past her. "Hello, Peabody. I'm told the incident last night was attempted murder. I'm glad the victim survived. I hope you find who attacked her, who killed the other girls very soon."

"We're getting there," Eve said before Peabody could. "No bone work needed on this investigation."

"A good thing, as I'm hip-deep in one of my own. Remains found during demolition of a condemned building in Yonkers. Encased in one of the foundation columns after being bludgeoned, then shot in the back of the head twice. I've dated them at between a hundred and thirty and a hundred and thirty-five years old."

"Odds are whoever put them there's buried elsewhere by now."

"Very true, but no less fascinating. And we do need answers."

"Yeah, I need answers, too, and mine deal with the right now. Finger-prints, Berenski."

"I'll leave you three to discuss the right now. I appreciate the assist, Dick."

"Anytime, Garnet. You have a good one."

She sashayed off—at least that was the word that sprang to Eve's mind.

"Now, that's a woman who knows how to dress, how to act, and how to get shit done. You look pretty good, Peabody. You look like you're going to a funeral."

"Because I am. Jenna Harbough's."

His shoulders drooped. "Yeah. Well."

"Prints."

"I'm on them, for Christ's sake, and I've got my best man on them with me. You know how many prints were on that door?"

"I believe Peabody's term was a *crapload*."

"Yeah? Let me up that to a crap and a half load. We're pushing on it, damn it. I got a soft spot for little girls, so . . . Not that way. I ain't no perv or pedo."

"You're not a pedo," Eve said, and teased a smile out of him.

"Only get pervy with women over the legal age. It's taken some time to eliminate. Looks to me like they never wiped down the damn door, or hadn't in weeks. And it looks to me like a lot of the staff used it. See, they probably shut off the alarm, went out that way to catch a smoke or a snoot or try for a bang. You just prop it open while you're out there."

He slid down the counter on his stool, brought up an image on-screen. "Here's the section I'm working. A crapload, smeared prints, partials. I had a pal back in high school, right? He worked a vid place. Between shows, after the last one, they gotta clean the place because people are pigs. Trash they can't bother to toss in a bin, spilled drinks, and all that.

And they gotta police it before opening. So they sneak breaks out the back."

Eve had figured all that out due to the *crapload*, but didn't bother to point it out.

"I've eliminated seventy-three percent of this section, unless you want to tell me this fuckhead's employed there."

"No, I don't want to tell you that. He had to leave prints, Berenski. He was running, panicked. No reason for him to seal up like he did the first one."

She leaned closer to the screen. "He knew he'd have to grab the windowsill at the club, but here, all he'd need to do was rap the bar with his hip."

"We checked the bar first. What we can pull's staff. A couple partials, but wicked smeared. We're working to try to get something from them, but it's not likely."

"He's short." She put herself back in the theater, running for the door, shoving people aside. Full panic. "Maybe he doesn't hit the bar with his hands. Whole body slam, hands more up here. Or he's still got enough in him to remember the hip or side-body bump, but aren't you going to slap at the door? Instinct, flight instinct. People are screaming, yelling, the alarm goes off. And you're panicked, you're going to shove at the door.

"Can you bring up the whole thing?"

"Yeah, yeah. You're keeping me from doing the work you're bitching at me to do."

"Just bring it up, prints illuminated."

When he did, she felt the air deflate in her lungs. She'd have rated it two craploads of prints.

"Can you concentrate on this area? Say from the edge of the door to about a foot in, and factoring his height, below six feet. He could've slapped at it above his own head, but where are you going to shove at a door you want open fast?"

"Where it cracks open," Peabody finished. "Close to the opening."

"Prints on top of prints," Eve muttered. "Look, Berenski, I can see this is a bitch of a job, but I know he's going to be there. If he follows pattern, he'll go after another kid tonight, and she may not be as lucky as the last one."

"Prints on top of prints," he repeated. "Smeared, blurred, partials, fingers, palms, side of the hand. I'll shift to this section, but you gotta understand we need to separate, clean up, match, ID, eliminate. Unless we get lucky, it won't be fast."

You're there, she thought, studying the image on-screen.

"Let's all get lucky," she said, and left him to it.

"It could be faster than he thinks." Outside, Peabody climbed into the car. "They have all the staff prints now, that cuts some of the ID time."

"He was right. Nobody's wiped that damn door down for weeks. Maybe longer. But he was running, knocking people over. No way in hell he didn't put a hand on that door. We just have to hope he left an identifiable print.

"Plug in Haven Funeral Home, Peabody. Why do they call them homes? Nobody lives there."

"For comfort, I guess. Free-Agers bury their dead. I mean it's a choice, because choice rules, but mostly that's the way. Back to the earth. The Harboughs went with cremation. I guess that's natural, too."

"Death's natural. Murder's not."

"Which way do you want it? I mean a hundred years from now when you die peacefully in your sleep."

"What do I care? I'll be dead. All this stuff isn't for the dead anyway. It's for the living. A stone in the ground, ashes tossed in the air or kept in an urn. And that one's creepy. It's just creepy. It's all for the living. And they're entitled to it."

"I don't know how anyone gets over burying their child."

"They don't. They just get through it."

When they arrived, the room was filled with people sitting in long pews, and more standing behind them. The summer light streamed in windows, beamed on flower displays.

A woman in a black dress stood at a podium while the screen behind her showed photos of Jenna.

The baby, the toddler, the little girl. She recognized the music that played, as Peabody had played it in Jenna's room. So her own voice accompanied the moments of her short life.

When the music stopped, when the screen froze on a photo of Jenna, a pretty, smiling teenager, the woman invited others to step up and relate a memory.

Eve tuned it out, had to, and studied the room.

She saw Louise and Charles, seated together just behind the family. She saw Nadine and Jake near the back, and not surprisingly, she realized, his bandmates, along with the very pregnant wife of one, the longtime cohab of another.

Jenna's friends, their parents, ranged between.

A lot of people, and plenty of them in Jenna's age group. More friends, schoolmates, neighbors.

She spotted a couple of males with what she now thought of as boarder hair, but one was mixed race, and even though he remained seated, she judged him at around six feet.

The other sat in the family area. Blond hair and closer to twenty than sixteen.

A few short, more military-style cuts, but none of them fit. Just didn't fit.

When the service ended, the woman in black announced a reception in another area. The family would join those who chose to attend shortly.

Eve watched people file out, some weeping, some clutching hands, and hoped for the buzz she didn't expect to come.

"I thought you'd be here." With Jake, Nadine stepped up to her. "And you wouldn't be standing like this if he'd come."

"No."

"The girl from last night's okay?"

Eve nodded at Jake. "She is. We're going there next. She was released today."

"Okay, good. I wanted to say something to the family, but I don't know if this is the time for it. I don't want to go into the reception. Feels wrong."

"You brought the whole band."

"We all felt . . ."

"Exactly the right thing to do. Hang on a minute."

Eve walked down to where the family stood with Charles and Louise.

"Mr. Harbough, Dr. Harbough, my partner and I wanted to pay our respects."

"Thank you. The girl from last night," Julia began.

"She's home by now, doing very well. We're closer. I can only tell you I believe we're closer to finding him."

"She'd never say that if it wasn't true." Charles laid a hand on Julia's arm.

Julia laid her hand over it. "You and Louise have been a huge help the last few days. We've been leaning hard."

"No." Louise shook her head. "We've leaned on each other."

"We had Shane's brother take our parents to the privacy room. They needed a few minutes. Louise, would you and Charles mind taking Reed into the reception?"

"Of course not."

"But, Mom, it's Jake Kincade. It's Avenue A. They came." It wasn't excitement in his voice, but gratitude, Eve noted. "They came for Jenna."

"I see. But you go on with Charles and Louise, okay? We won't be long."

"Jake would like to speak with you, but he doesn't want to intrude."

"It's not an intrusion." Together they walked toward where he stood with Nadine.

"Thank you so much for coming. Thank all of you so much."

"Ma'am. I'm—we're—so sorry."

"Julia. Julia and Shane. I was the first person to hold her, then we held her together, didn't we, Shane?"

"We did. I was terrified, but we did."

"And you were the last to hold her. You held her when I couldn't, when she needed holding. We'll never forget you were there for her."

Julia put her arms around him, let out a long sigh.

Obviously struggling, Shane cleared his throat. "Jenna admired you, so much. All of you. Avenue A? That was the bar of excellence—she called it that. The bar of excellence she wanted to reach. I've asked myself what it could mean that you were with her when she left us. I have to believe it was a gift. I need to believe that."

"It was. Meeting you was such a dream of hers." Julia stepped back again. "Having you hear her music another dream."

"I did. I mean, the demo you let Dallas copy for me. I listened—we listened. It's . . . we'd like to produce it."

"I'm sorry?"

"We'd like to produce and release it."

"Avenue A wants to record Jenna's song?"

"No, ma'am—Doctor—Julia."

He fumbled a bit, Eve noted, and looked at his bandmates.

"Produce it. It's a good-quality demo. We can punch it up a little, but it's hers, and her voice is perfect for it. Pure. This isn't the time, I'm sorry—"

"I don't know if you could have chosen a better time. Is this offer . . . even if it is obligation—"

"It's not. If this hadn't happened, and she'd gotten the demo to me? We'd . . ."

He looked toward his bandmates again.

"We'd have brought her into the studio," Renn finished. "Done that punching up."

"She had the magic," Art added. "The shine."

"We've been around long enough to know when a hit falls into our lap," Mac added. "Shit, I didn't mean it that way exactly. I mean, it's not about the money. It's hers."

"Scholarship," Leon finished. "We talked about how we could, if it's okay with you, start a scholarship in her name with our part of it."

"She's got more. You don't write something like this and not have more. Maybe she doesn't have anything as polished." Jake gripped Nadine's hand when she slid hers into his. "We could work it. If she didn't add vocals, we'd record it. Unless you—"

He broke off when Julia held up a hand and turned away.

"I'm sorry. We're sorry. This is intrusive."

Swiping at her eyes, Julia turned back. "You're offering our daughter all of her dreams. All of them. I don't have words."

"*Thank you*'s not enough," Shane managed. "It's not even close. Yes. Our answer's yes to everything. We'll figure it all out, okay? Thank you." He worked his way down the band, gripping hands. "Thank you. We need to . . . We'll figure it out."

"When you're ready."

Julia kissed Jake's cheek. "Shane's right. A gift."

When they walked out, Mac pressed his hands to his eyes. "Man, I need a minute. Outside. We'll be outside."

Jake stayed where he was, looked directly at Eve. "You're going to get him."

"Yes. We're going to get him. You know how I'm so sure of that? I knew when I sent you the demo copy, this is what you'd do. You'd have done the first part even if it was crappy, which it isn't. I follow my instincts, so I know who you are. I'll know him, too. Now we have to get back to it."

"You did a good thing," Peabody added before she followed Eve out. "Made me cry."

"Me, too," Nadine murmured, then turned to face him. "I've got good instincts, too, but I didn't know you were going to do this."

"I didn't say anything because . . ."

"You needed to ask them first. You needed to talk to the group, get on the same page, make sure you all knew what you wanted to do for the right reasons. Then ask her parents. I know how you work, Jake."

"Guess you do."

"We've been together for a while now."

"A nice while."

"We're careful what we say to each other, sophisticated urbanites that we are."

It made him smile. "*Urbanites* hits it. I think *sophisticated* misses me."

"Nope. Here we are, a pair of sophisticated—and I'll add experienced—urbanites. So we've been careful in this nice while. I'm going to toss that away right now and tell you I love you. I love who you are. I'm completely and deeply in love with you. And don't care that that gives you an advantage."

He stared at her for what seemed like forever. "Okay. Well, it's a weird sort of time and place for this."

"And yet, here we are."

"Here we are. But I don't see my advantage, since I love you. I'm completely and deeply in love with you. I think it's a draw. There's just one thing."

"What would that be?"

"I don't want to kiss you the way I really need to in here. It feels disrespectful. So let's go outside."

"Outside, it is. But you'd better make it good."

Outside, as Peabody strapped into the passenger seat, she watched Jake pull Nadine into a kiss.

"Aw, look at that. Sweet. And there's Mac still leaking some, but they're all applauding. And . . . ooooh! Look, look! He's doing the 'lift you right off your feet, turn you around' lip-lock. I *love* those! Don't you love those? It makes me all gooey."

"Jesus, Peabody, give them some privacy."

"If they want privacy, they should get a room."

"Yeah, you've got a point."

As Eve merged with traffic, Peabody craned her head to watch.

"That's a damn good kiss."

Eve flicked a glance in the rearview.

She couldn't argue.

"Get your head back in the job, Peabody, before it snaps off your neck. Let the Rosenburgs know we're on our way."

Chapter Eighteen

The Rosenburgs' townhouse murmured dignity with its softly faded brick. It added cheerful with window boxes housing a rainbow of flowers spilling and spiking. They flanked a door painted I Dare You Red.

Solid security, Eve noted.

Presley answered the door. From the shadows under his eyes, he hadn't slept much or well, but the fear that had lived in them the night before had faded.

He said, "Um, hi. We're all in the back. I guess you didn't catch him yet."

"We're working on it."

They passed what Eve decided they used as a formal living space. Soft, warm colors, more flowers, furniture carefully arranged to encourage conversation. Across the hall a home office held a desk, a small, sleek data and communication unit, and floating shelves crammed with memorabilia and framed photos.

Eve heard the mix of voices, a quick giggle, and smelled what could only be pizza.

"We came straight from the hospital, then Kiki took one of her forever showers. Now everybody's starving."

Formality and business ended when the hall opened up to where, Eve deduced, the family really lived.

A similar layout to what Mavis would have, on a smaller scale, the space spread out with a serious kitchen. It lacked Mavis's wildly happy colors and settled on white, gleaming stainless steel, and a lot of black hardware. Kiki and her two friends sprawled in the lounge area on a big L-shaped sofa in the same red as the front door. The enormous wall screen currently presented a family photo with the moms and teens mugging for the camera on a beach.

Shoes littered the floor. No one seemed to notice or mind that a dog disguised as a mop held one clamped between his paws.

Connie, a white bib apron over the clothes she'd worn the night before, slid a pizza out of what looked like an actual pizza oven. Andrea filled tall glasses with lemonade.

"Kiki's hungry," she said with tears sparkling in her eyes.

"Starving!" Kiki corrected. "Hospital food is totally ugh. Plus, Mom's the best cook on- or off-planet."

"It's what I do."

It was, as Connie Rosenburg made her living as head chef at a restaurant far too upscale and snooty for pizza. Andrea made hers as a hardscape designer. For, Eve had learned on her run of both of them, one of Roarke's many business tentacles.

"I hope you're hungry." Andrea beamed at Eve and Peabody as she sliced the pie.

"I appreciate that, but we need to . . ." She trailed off, mildly astonished when Connie began to toss dough in the air.

The trio on the couch came out of their slump to applaud, then rose as a unit to descend on the table at the left of the kitchen.

"Please sit." Connie gave the dough another stylish toss. "We know you have to ask more questions, but the kids need to eat."

"Rough night," Presley added.

"And this is my I Almost Got Murdered reward."

"Kiki."

"Well, I did." Kiki shrugged at Andrea's head shake. "They were all really nice at the hospital," she added for Eve. "But I don't ever want to go back."

"I know the feeling."

"Have you ever almost got murdered?"

"It comes with the job."

"Then I don't ever want to be a cop, either. How come you are?"

"It's what I do."

"Eat," Andrea ordered as she set the pizza on the table.

Nobody had to tell the teenagers twice. Resilience, Eve thought as they snagged slices.

"Please," Andrea added, using a server to more delicately slide slices onto the plates already in front of Eve and Peabody.

It smelled like glory wrapped in heaven.

"Thanks." As she turned to Kiki, the girl pointed at her with one hand, shoved pizza in her mouth with the other.

"You're like married to the richest guy on- or off-planet, right? We saw the vid and all. I was kind of out of it before."

"The almost-getting-murdered thing."

"That." She grinned. "Now I'm eating pizza. Anyway, we all saw the vid."

"It was totally mag, but I thought mostly made-up." David gulped down lemonade. "Now I guess maybe not."

"Maybe not. Kiki—"

"Do you know what he did? The totally richest guy? We get a private showing." She grinned again, but like Andrea, tears sparkled in her eyes. "He made it so we can all go to see *Return*. The doctor said tomorrow because I have to rest and all today. Plus, it has to be in the morning, like ten o'clock before the theater even opens, because they're mostly sold out and all that this week."

"It's really solid of him," Presley said. "He doesn't even know us."

"It's what he does." Eve gave up, picked up the pizza. After one bite she decided Kiki hadn't exaggerated her mother's talents by much.

"This is amazing." Taking Eve's cue, Peabody ate.

"Told ya. Anyway, he didn't have to do something so nice. I sort of remember him from last night. Because he's got that voice and that face. I mean, yum-yum."

"Kiki!" But Andrea laughed as she said it.

"True is true." Lola lifted her shoulders. "Add yum three."

"It means a lot, to all of us." Connie ladled sauce onto a third round of dough.

"I'll let him know. Kiki—"

"So how come you—"

"Kiki." Connie cut her off. "Lieutenant Dallas and Detective Peabody have a job to do. A very serious job. And it isn't answering your questions."

With the warning, she set the second pizza on the table, then stroked a hand over her daughter's hair.

"Sorry."

"No problem. We're glad you've recovered, and because you have, because you're all here, we'd like to go over what happened. What you remember. Take us through it again."

Kiki grabbed another slice.

"Okay, well, after we got in—and that took a while even though we

had tickets—and we got our vid food, we went in. They had previews going, and we started down to our seats. Then it felt like somebody stabbed
me." She rubbed a hand on her arm. "I'd kind of banged up my arm trying a change-up on a loop. Fail!"

But she laughed as she ate.

"I didn't think it was that bad, and they fixed that up at the hospital. Con-
TU-sion." She rolled her eyes. "But when he stuck me with the needle, it
practically exploded. It really hurt, and I honest to God thought somebody
stabbed me. I was so pissed. I know I swung around. I was going to punch
that asshole."

"Ignoring the language rules only lasts so long," Connie warned.

"It should be at least twenty-four hours. I think I screamed."

"You did." Lola nodded. "Like split the ears open. And you kept
screaming."

"I thought somebody stuck a knife in my arm, so screaming's required.
And he sort of stumbled back, all surprised and whatever."

"You saw his eyes."

"Giant WTF eyes." She mimed them.

"Was his mouth open like that, too?"

"I—I guess, yeah. Yeah, now that you say it. Mom said a police artist's
coming in a while, but I don't know if I can make a real picture."

"That's Detective Yancy's job."

"I guess. He started shoving and running. I was going to run after
him and punch him, but it was too crowded. And I had on my favorite
jacket, and I was trying to take it off, looking down at the sleeve because
I thought there'd be blood all over it. But there wasn't. And everyone was
yelling, and I'd spilled my popcorn and fizzy."

"The light came on," Presley added. "And everybody was yelling, and
they were going to kick us out for, you know, creating a disturbance."

"Then I didn't feel right, and I got sick. The yelling was so loud my
head started banging, and my arm was on fire, then my legs felt wrong.

I don't remember much after. It gets blurry, then I was in the ambulance."

"Let's go back. You saw his face when you turned. He was behind you."

"I started to turn," Kiki corrected. "He was kind of beside me and behind. Beside my bad arm."

"Did he say anything?"

"No. Maybe. It was loud, then I was screaming. Nothing's ever hurt like that did. I remember that. I *really* remember that."

"David, you saw him when you were getting popcorn."

"Sort of. Pieces of him. The shoes, the trench. I think sunshades. I tried to go back in my head."

"A white kid."

"Yeah, short dude. I was just sort of glancing around like you do when you're waiting. But mostly the four of us were talking and getting the vid snacks. I didn't pay attention. He was just some dude with crappy shoes who didn't know enough to beat up his trench. Trying to look chill."

"Fail," Kiki said, and made him smile.

"Major fail."

With the third pizza on the table, the moms took a seat.

"David's parents are fine with him working with the police artist, too." Connie slid a slice onto her plate.

"We appreciate that. Kiki, can you think of anyone who reminds you of him? Someone at school, at the boarder park, around the neighborhood?"

"No, not . . . Barry Finklestein!"

The name had Lola letting out a wild giggle.

"From school?" Eve pressed.

"Yeah. It wasn't him, for abso-poso, but you said remind me. And not so much me, but what David said."

"Tell me about Barry."

"Oh man, I don't want to get him in trouble. It really wasn't him."

"We've got that, so you won't. Why does he remind you?"

"Well, he's short, and not just white, but pasty-like. And he's short, pudgy, too."

"That's unkind, Kiki."

"Mom, I'm just trying to answer."

"He is, Ms. R." Lola backed her up.

"So, short and white and carrying some extra weight. That's why he reminds you."

"Some of it. I don't think the murdering guy was pudgy."

"No." David shook his head. "He wasn't. I think I'd have noticed that. I remember Barry. He wouldn't have known to beat up his trench."

"He wouldn't! That's what I mean. I don't think he has one, but he dresses like his aunt Matilda picks out his clothes. I mean, he's just clue-less. He's got a real brain. I mean he's super smart, but clueless on real stuff."

"Aces everything. I mean everything. He can be a real . . . Twenty-four hours on the language rules?"

Andrea just waved a hand at her son.

"A real shit about it. Brags a lot if he can get anyone to listen. Even the nerds mostly ignore him. He wouldn't get bullied so much if he'd just shut up about how smart he is."

"We don't bully him," Kiki said quickly. "I swear. We don't roll that way, and if we did? He's not worth the time. Anyway, I'd have recognized him for sure."

"But he's a type?"

Kiki shot up a finger. "Yeah, that's it. Going off David, and what I sort of saw. He's a type. Without the pimples. Barry's always got at least one exploding on his face. Dude! There's treatment for that."

"And the one who attacked you had clear skin?"

"I . . . Yeah. I think, yeah."

Saw more of him than you think. And Yancy would dig it out.

She went another round, nudging here, nudging there, but accepted she'd gotten all she'd get.

"We appreciate your time and cooperation," Eve began, "and the pizza."

"I wish I'd punched him," Kiki murmured. "Not just for me, but for those two other girls. We talked about going to Club Rock It the other night, but it was Meem's—our great-grandmother's—birthday. I wouldn't have had the bruise if he'd picked me then. I read about her, the one he killed, this morning.

"You were out talking to the doctor," Kiki told her mothers. "And I looked it up. They had her memorial today. Jenna Harbough, she was my age. And I looked up the second one, Arlie Dillon. Hers is day after tomorrow."

"That's right."

"Do you think I could go to that, maybe tell her mom I'm sorry about what happened to her? And maybe, sometime, talk to the first girl's mom and dad and tell them?"

"Oh, Kiki." Andrea's eyes streamed. "That's so kind. I'm just not sure if it's appropriate, but it's so kind."

"I'm sure. We've spoken to Jenna's parents, to Arlie's mother. It is kind," Eve said, "and appropriate. And I think they'd very much appreciate you making that gesture."

"Can I go?"

The two women joined hands. "We'll all go," Connie said. "Would you mind, Lieutenant, checking with them first? We don't want to overstep."

Eve glanced at Peabody, who nodded. "I'll do that, and get back to you."

Kiki looked Eve dead in the eye. "You're going to get him, aren't you?"

"I'll repeat. It's what we do."

"That nearly teared me up," Peabody said when they stepped outside. "You think a girl that age doesn't think beyond the moment, and a lot of times it's true. But she's thought of what her own family would go through if he'd succeeded. And that led her to think what others are going through."

"She's tough. And you know, if she'd managed to clock him? We'd have his ass. He'd have been down."

She got behind the wheel. "And she saw more than she thinks."

"Yeah, I got that. Yancy will slide it out of her. And there's the wit from concessions, there's David, there's A.J., there's Hank. We may just have a face to work with."

"He's a type." She stayed parked while she rolled it around. "We knew that, but it helps our survivor sees it that way. A type. I wonder if our teenage killer has an aunt Matilda who picks out his clothes."

"You're not looking at this Barry Finklestein."

"No. She'd have recognized him. On line for a while? Yeah, you do glance around some. If she'd seen somebody she knew—and clearly disdains—she'd have said something to Lola, at least. But the type. Smart but clueless.

"Check with the two victims' families about Kiki reaching out. We'll push on the goddamn shoes."

"That pizza," Peabody said as Eve pulled away from the curb. "I ate two slices. Couldn't help it. I should've thought of doing a pizza oven in my mag-o new kitchen. Too late for that, but you know, I could build one."

"Build an oven? What the hell, Peabody?"

"I could. Outside, with the grill. Do a kind of outdoor kitchen. Brick-oven pizza! Maybe wood burning. Man, that would be a really fun project."

"Your definition of *fun* doesn't approach the same universe as my definition of *fun*."

"You'd have fun eating pizza made in my new wood-burning brick pizza oven."

. "There is that. Make the tags."

They spent over an hour pushing on the shoes. The single lead they gleaned from that took them to a twelve-year-old boy—inches shorter than five-six—whose mother bought them for him to wear to his All-State Orchestra competition the previous spring.

He played the piccolo. They placed second.

Since she verified he, his parents, and his two younger siblings had spent the weekend at an amusement park upstate, she had no trouble crossing him off the suspect list.

Pulling into Central's garage, about to deem the damn shoes a dead end, she got a tag.

"Three hits, Lieutenant," Officer Carmichael told her.

"Gimme."

"Arnold Post, age fifty-two, bought a pair, size eleven for himself, and a size seven for his son, Junior, age sixteen. Matched set, in April. Second hit, three pair, size six and a half, charged to Kevin J. Fromer, black brogues, navy ankle boots, and the loafers. All last March. Last hit, five pair, sir. Black lace-up, brown brogues with buckle, ankle boots, black, navy house skids, and the loafers. Charged to Allisandra Charro in March."

"Send me the addresses. We'll take them."

"Yes, sir. We're only a few blocks from the Post residence if you want to us to take that one."

"Take it. Send the other two."

She backed out of her parking space. "Who buys five pair of shoes at one time?"

"Me, if I could."

"Plug in the addresses, then do a run on all three."

"Fromer's closest." Peabody programmed the address. "Charro's uptown. Okay, okay, Arnold Post. One marriage, one divorce, one offspring—that would be Arnold Junior. CFO Livingston Wine and Spirits. No criminal, a handful of civil suits. Junior attends Breckinridge Academy. He's five-eight, Dallas. Decent grades, but not the big brain sort. Caucasian, blond and blue. Good-looking kid, on the smirky side."

Needed to check it out, Eve thought, but he didn't buzz.

"Fromer."

"Two marriages, one divorce. Second marriage going into year twenty, so it looks like it stuck. Two offspring from that: son, Lance, age seventeen; daughter, Marnie, age thirteen. Fromer's an estate attorney. Spouse, Arlene, maintained professional mother status until two years ago when she went back to work as an event planner. Runs her own shop.

"The son, Lance, comes in at five-eleven. That's above our range, and he's mixed race."

"We check it out anyway."

"The last, Allisandra Charro, age forty-one, single. Hell, Dallas, she's a professional shopper."

"So are half the people in this city at this very moment in time."

"I mean that's her job. She shops for people who don't want to. Like Roarke does for you. But for a living, not for fun. I don't get it."

"Shopping? Neither do I."

"No, I mean, don't you—not you specifically, obviously—want to browse, see what's out there? I mean, you tell somebody you want a black, bucket-style handbag, and they bring you one. How do you know it's the one you really, really want without seeing the vast universe of black, bucket-style handbags first?"

Eve took a moment to wonder why anyone wanted a purse that looked like a bucket, then let it go.

"She bought the shoes for somebody. She'd have records. She has to. It fits, too, doesn't it? Parents or guardians don't want to take the time to shop for the kid. Hire somebody to take care of it. Fromer first. We're nearly there. But the personal shopper fits."

Fromer wasn't home, but his event-planning wife was.

A tall, almost majestic blonde in a sharp white suit, she frowned at the badges. "Is there some sort of trouble? You just caught me. I have a meeting."

"You may be able to help us in an investigation. Is your son at home, Ms. Fromer?"

"Lance? No. He's spending the week at the beach with some friends. Is he all right? Is there—"

"I'm sure he's fine. Your husband charged a pair of these shoes." Eve held up her 'link.

"Those?" She laughed, and Eve heard the relief. "Not for himself or for Lance. Way too conservative for my guys."

"They were charged to Mr. Fromer's account, purchased at Dellan's."

"When?"

"In March."

"March, March." Frowning again, she took out her 'link, flipped through its calendar. "Oh, Mickey's birthday. Our nephew. I swear the kid will probably grow up to be president. I think Kevin picked up three pair. The kid's a shoe hound, and those are what he wanted. Thirteenth birthday," she added. "So we splurged on him some. What's this about?"

"Is it possible for us to talk to Mickey?"

"Sure. But he lives with his mom in Toledo. Kate's a widow, and the last few years have been tough. So we splurged on Mickey. I really don't understand why it matters to the police."

"As it turns out, it doesn't. Thank you for your time."

They walked back to the car.

"Mickey may be an odd kid wishing for conservative designer shoes," Peabody said, "but I don't think he flew from Toledo to New York to kill girls."

"Personal shopper."

En route, Officer Shelby, partnered with Carmichael, tagged her. "No dice with Post, Lieutenant. The kid was home, still sweating from a pickup game in the park. He said his dad bought him the ugly old man shoes to wear to a wedding, so he had to. Otherwise, no way. Kid had no problem showing us his closet in the dump heap he calls a room. He's got three pair of well-worn kicks—good ones—plus the newer ones he had on his feet. And the loafers, stuffed in the back. Barely worn.

"In addition, sir, on the night of the first murder, he was at the Yankees game—verified that—with his dad and some friends. Second murder, he was at his grandparents' for Sunday dinner, then, according to him, the adults played cards for hours, and he and his cousin chilled with some screen time.

"He doesn't ring, Lieutenant."

"Got that. Fromer was a bust, but we're heading to Charro's."

"Personal shopper—we checked. That's got a ring."

"It does."

"Do you want us to keep at it? We've still got some on the list."

"Yeah, finish it out, cross it off, then head back to Central. Dallas out. Check with Yancy, Peabody, see where he is in this. Text," she added. "He'll answer when he's not in the middle with a wit."

"I think we're going to get a face," Peabody said as she texted. "We've got a handful of witnesses who at least caught a glimpse."

Pieces, Eve thought. But they had to put those pieces together.

"He answered quick. He just got to Kiki. He worked with Hank from the first murder, with the concession worker and A.J. from the attempt. He made a little progress, but not enough to give us yet. He'll tag us back after he's worked with Kiki and David."

"That'll have to do."

But the day was sliding away.

He'd have plans, Eve thought.

The professional shopper did well enough to have an apartment on Riverside Drive in a sleek gold tower with a burly doorman who scowled at Eve's DLE.

Badging him improved her mood, marginally.

"It sits where I put it."

"Yeah, yeah, I got the word."

Which meant the golden tower belonged to Roarke.

"Nobody dead inside, is there?"

"Not that I know of."

She beat him to the door and entered a lobby as sleek as the exterior. Muted gold here, veining through the black marble floors. Flowers cascaded in snowy white from an urn on a central table.

A black desk trimmed in gold was tucked into the back wall with a backdrop of water sliding down a reflective surface in glittering streams.

A woman with white-blond hair in a short, severely angled cut smiled.

"Welcome to the Gilded Tower. How may I help you?"

A single, ink-black eyebrow shot up at Eve's badge.

"I'm sorry, Lieutenant, I didn't recognize you initially. What can I do for you and Detective Peabody?"

"Allisandra Charro."

"Ms. Charro is a resident. I believe the thirty-eighth floor. Let me check for you, but I don't believe she's in at the moment. Yes, 3802. I believe she left this morning just after ten, and as far as I know hasn't returned. Should I call up?"

"Appreciate it."

"Happy to help. No, she doesn't answer. Ms. Charro is rarely in this time of day. Her business keeps her quite busy."

"Do you have any idea where she went, or when she'll be back?"

"I'm sorry, I don't. Occasionally she returns before the end of my shift, at five. But more often I only see her in the morning when she leaves. I do have a 'link number, in the event we need to contact her."

Save us time accessing it, Eve thought. "We could use that."

The clerk took a card from her slot, selected a pen, and neatly wrote the name and number on the back.

"In the event you're unable to reach her and she returns, should I give her a message?"

"Card, Peabody. It's very important she contact me as soon as possible."

"I'll certainly relay that, or see that my colleague does so if she doesn't return before I leave. I'm sorry I couldn't be of more help."

"You did fine. Thanks."

Outside under the silent scowl of the doorman, Eve pulled out her 'link. She made the tag from the sidewalk as pedestrians swam by.

"This is Allisandra." She all but sang it.

"Ms. Charro, Lieutenant Dallas, NYPSD."

"So I see on the display. What can I do for you, Lieutenant Dallas?"

"Alan Stuben tasseled loafers, size six and a half, brown leather."

Charro's narrow face, wide brown eyes, perfect red lips all showed only bafflement. "You'd like me to purchase a pair of Stubens for you?"

"No, I want to know who you bought them for in March."

"Well, a shiny personal dream dulls. When I saw the display I thought, at last, Dallas wants me to dress her."

"I like handling that myself. The Stubens."

"Lieutenant, I can't possibly tell you that off the top of my head. Last March? Months ago. And I do have a long list of clients. I'm good at what I do."

"How many teenage boys do you shop for?"

"More accurately, I'm shopping for their parent for them, but quite a number. Teenage boys, particularly, rarely enjoy shopping. Parents who can afford me would rather pay out than drag said teenage boy through the shops. The dragging through rarely ends well."

"I wouldn't know, but I need a name."

"I'll look it up when I get back to my office and my records. I'm in New Jersey, with a client. I should be leaving within the hour."

"He's short, around five-six. Caucasian."

"I'd tell you if I could. Why wouldn't I? Very often I don't see the teenager or child, just have measurements, sizes, and so on. It varies. If alterations are needed, they have their own tailor, or I arrange one."

"You bought him five pair of Stubens on that single trip in March."

Charro gave her a long look. "Again, I can't tell you."

"You buy his clothes, too. Conservative, button-down clothes."

"Given the Stubens, I'd expect so. Private schools, which many of my clients patronize, often have strict dress codes, if they don't require specific uniforms. I dress a great many young men between thirteen and nineteen."

"He's about sixteen."

"Lieutenant, I understand this is important, honestly. But the longer you keep me on this 'link trying to jog something I can't possibly jog, the longer it'll be until I can finish here and come back to check my records."

Damn it, Eve thought. She was right.

"Contact me as soon as you have the information."

Eve clicked off.

"Damn it! She's the conduit. I know it."

"We may be close, but I don't see we've got probable cause for a warrant to get into her place and go through the records ourselves."

"No. Let's get back to Central. We're going to get that face, and we're going to get a name. We'll start pushing on where else Charro does her personal shopping. High-end venues that carry clothes in his size."

An hour, she'd said, and Yancy would need at least that.

So they'd keep at the job until.

Chapter Nineteen

She'd barely pulled away from the curb when she spotted the street thief and his oblivious target. The woman with a tower of gold-streaked red hair and a rat-sized dog on a leash carried three shopping bags. She wore mile-high pink heels with tiny grass-green polka dots and a tiny dress that reversed the color scheme. She'd gone with a white purse smothered in polka dots of both colors.

She wore it cross-body, but it bumped carelessly behind her left hip while she chatted away on her sparkly purple 'link.

She might as well have added a sign saying: PICK ME!

Eve watched the thief, casual walk, long, many-pocketed vest over black baggies and a black tee, slide by her.

He continued his casual walk. She continued to mince (it seemed to fit) in the opposite direction. Her purse no longer bumped at the back of her hip.

She figured people who could afford all those polka dots could afford to buy a clue. But.

Impulse had her swinging back toward the curb.

"Take the wheel."

Stunned, Peabody looked up from her PPC. "What—"

She didn't have time for more before Eve leaped out of the car.

The thief, not nearly as oblivious as Ms. Polka Dot, snapped his head around. Recognizing he was now a target, he changed the casual walk to a full-out run.

Eve pointed at the cranky doorman, then at the purse-less woman about to turn toward the building, then at the Running Man.

He might have been cranky, but he'd obviously bought a few clues in his time, and nodded.

"Get 'em, sister!"

Long legs stretched; good boots slapped the pavement. She felt her muscles sing a happy tune as she ran in the blazing summer sun.

He had some moves, she noted, and he had speed.

But then, so did she, and she wasn't weighed down—right side interior vest pocket—by a polka-dot purse and whatever treasures it held.

For form because, hell, he already knew, she shouted, "Police!"

That turned a few heads, but her quarry kicked it into the next gear.

So did she.

She caught him in front of an Italian bistro where people sat under big umbrellas drinking wine, nibbling on pasta, or drinking coffee out of thimble-sized cups.

She grabbed his arm, blocked his instinctive and wild swing.

He panted like a horse after a hard gallop, and his face shined, red as a pickled beet, with sweat.

"Okay, you got me." He rasped it out as he sank down to sit on the sidewalk. "Frog-jumping Jesus, I haven't had to run like that in years."

On closer inspection, Eve judged him as solidly in his sixties. "You've still got some fast feet."

He shook his head. "Not like I used to. Back when, I was lightning."

"Maybe time to find another line of work."

Now he shrugged. "It's what I got. Hey, any way I can get some water?"

"You run again, you know I'll catch you."

"I'm done."

She signaled a waitress, who looked right, left, then pointed to herself.

"Yeah, you. Get this guy some water and call for the beat cops. Lieutenant Dallas." She pointed at herself, then the wheezing man on the sidewalk. "Purse snatcher."

"You're Dallas? Heard of you." The thief slapped his hands to the side of his head and shook it. "Shit, shit, shouldn't have gotten out of bed this morning."

He continued to pant and wheeze, but his color faded down to pink so she figured she wouldn't have to send for MTs.

The waitress brought the water in a fancy glass with ice. Thinking what a world, Eve took it, then crouched down.

"You did me a favor. I needed some stress relief and the run did it. I'm going to forget the swing."

He gulped water. "Appreciate that." He sighed. "I mean, did you see the mark? A walking ad for Pinch My Purse Please."

While she couldn't disagree, Eve thought better than to vocalize it.

"Let's have it."

He drained the water, handed the empty glass to Eve, who handed it back to the hovering waitress.

He took the polka-dot bag and a gold bracelet studded with pink and green stones out of the right interior pocket of the vest.

She'd missed the bracelet.

Yeah, he still had some moves.

"Is that it?"

He spread his vest open. "I already passed on today's take. You know,

I was just stretching my legs before I headed home, thinking maybe I'd stop for an Italian ice. Frigging hot one. Then I spotted Polka Dot Queen. I mean, she was like a frigging billboard. Bad luck. But at least I got bagged by a serious cop. Lloyd Mesner."

He offered a hand. Amused, Eve took it, then hauled him to his feet as a pair of beat cops hustled their way.

She dealt with it, had them log the bag and the bracelet as returned to owner. Then walked the block and a half back to the apartment building.

Peabody stood at the door with the doorman.

"She's waiting in the lobby," Peabody told her.

No longer cranky, the doorman grinned at Eve. "You got some legs on you, sister."

"That's Lieutenant Sister," she said, and went inside.

The redhead sat with the rat dog in her lap and shopping bags at her feet. She sipped pale, straw-colored wine out of a fancy glass.

"Ma'am," Eve began.

"Oh my God, my purse! The strap! The strap's broken."

Snipped, Eve thought. Quick and slick.

"I just bought that purse last week! Do you know how much that purse cost?"

"No, ma'am, but I need you to identify same, and the contents and this bracelet, as—"

"My bracelet!" The screech hit a register that made Eve's ears ring. "Is it damaged?"

"I don't believe so. If you'd note down the property, as yours, returned to you, and sign." Eve held out her PPC.

"I can't be bothered with that. I'm far too upset. I have to have my purse repaired now, and it's brand-new!"

She rose with the wine, the dog, clutching the purse under her arm. "Have my bags sent up," she snapped at the desk clerk. "I'm very upset."

Eve watched her mince her way to the elevator. "You're welcome," she called out.

She pulled out her communicator as she walked back to the doors. "Let him go. That's right, the mark won't take the time to file a report. I'm not wasting mine. Put him on a minute. Yeah, I said put him on. Lloyd? Learn a lesson. You're too old for this. Dallas out."

She went out where Peabody and the doorman—Kyle—held a conversation about carpentry.

Apparently, Kyle's father made his living with that particular skill, but Kyle never got a handle on it.

"If you see that guy again—Lloyd Mesner—tell him Dallas is watching."

"Can do."

"One thing? The Polka Dot Woman: Is she always a fuckhead, or was it just today's trauma?"

Kyle's lips twitched. "I shouldn't say, seeing as building policy is never gossip about guests. But taking that as an official inquiry? Always."

"Figured." Eve walked back to the car. When Peabody got in, Eve sighed contentedly. "Well, that was fun."

"You jump out in the street, tell me to take the wheel when you zoom off like a rocket." She paused. "Actually, it was fun."

Eve glanced at her wrist unit as she drove. "Didn't take long. Charro's still in New Jersey, Yancy's working with Kiki and David. We head back, try the shop angle. If Charro's got as many clients as she says, we should get some hits.

"How does it work? The personal shopping gig?"

"I've never had the wonder and privilege of trying it on either side. I'll see what Charro does."

Peabody took out her PPC, reading as they traveled downtown.

"For a new client, she does a consultation—no charge—in their home or place of business. She'll also do remote consults. She verifies sizes, measurements, blah blah. I can click on a form here—a sample it looks like—dealing with colors, styles, lifestyle, price points, fabrics, hobbies, career, travel. Lots of stuff."

"By the time you do all that, you could just go out and buy what the hell you wanted."

"The idea is she gets to know you. You know, the *personal* in *personal shopper*. She brings a selection to you. Just want a suit? Fine. Want an entire seasonal wardrobe? Also fine. She sets it all up, helps you put pieces together, brings accessories, and if desired, jewelry selections with bonded security. Items are charged to her business account, or borrowed. Once the selections are made, she charges the client for the purchases, adds her fee. Travel expenses additional if outside Manhattan."

"What's the fee?"

"Ten percent of purchase—with a grand as minimum."

"I'm betting she gets that from the venues, too. You bet your ass she does from venues she uses regularly."

"I bet you're right. At least a ten percent discount on what she buys for clients, or herself. Think about it. She buys those five pair of Stubens. That's over seven K right there, one stop. She gets seven hundred and change from the venue, and another seven from the client. That's a solid fifteen hundred, more depending, for one stop. Then she writes off her travel, car service, cab fare, whatever she uses."

Peabody sat back. "If I ever turn in my papers, I want this gig. Oh wow! She'll travel with clients—at their expense, natch. Paris, Milan, London, Tokyo, and more, and she'll arrange private showings from designers on request."

Eve pulled into the garage. "Let's find out where she shops for teenage boys who dress like old, clueless accountants who never get laid."

That made Peabody snicker on the way to the elevator.

"It's no wonder he doesn't know how to shop for himself, how to buy things that make him look like a regular teenager. He's probably never shopped for himself, or on his own."

As they got in the elevator, Peabody tapped her PPC. "Charro provides her services for babies, toddlers, and on up the scale."

"How long has she been doing this?"

"Oh, right. Let's see." Working, Peabody shuffled back as the elevator stopped for more cops. "Okay, eleven years, with another six working in the industry in other capacities."

After the third stop, Eve pushed out for the glides.

"Start with specialty venues. Men's shops that carry boys' wear. Shops geared to teens, but upscale. Then department stores, high-end. Large purchases. Would he still be growing?"

"Maybe. Pretty sure he would've been last year, the year before."

"We look at that. Five pair of shoes at one go, figure that wardrobe deal, or a chunk of it. Button-down shirt. If you're buying a button-down shirt, you might as well buy half a dozen, different colors."

Peabody pointed an accusatory finger. "You know more about shopping than you admit."

"No, that's buying, and efficient. Efficient means she makes more profit. The client wants conservative, button-down shirts. You provide. Trousers, same deal. No baggies, no skin pants, maybe, possibly some sweats, but again, high-end. Black, gray, brown, tan, nothing outside the lines."

"I got it."

When she walked into the bullpen, she spotted Quilla sitting on the edge of Jenkinson's desk. And she smelled brownies.

Quilla pushed up, offered an easy and innocent smile.

Eve jerked her thumb toward her office for Quilla, then, eyes narrowed, pointed at Jenkinson.

He shrugged and brushed brownie crumbs off his irradiated rabbits.

"I did not give you the go on interviews with my squad."

"I wasn't. We were just talking. I heard he got a promotion."

"So you brought him brownies."

"I brought enough for everybody. Well, except you and Peabody, because, man, they wolfed."

Molded by Nadine, Eve thought.

"Quilla, I don't have time for this, or you."

"You weren't even here, and I just came down after I finished my interviews in EDD." Quilla pushed at her purple hair. "Well, I still have to put it all together, edit, work on the narration, polish, but—"

"Quilla, go away."

"But wait. I heard how you found where he got the shoes."

"That's not for public consumption."

"I *know* that." That earned a double eye roll. "Jeez. Like I'd blab about it so he gets to kill more girls. So I was talking to Mouser—you know, Dorian's friend, the new kid."

"You talked to him about official police business?"

"It wasn't blabbing. I wanted his, like, expert opinion. He was on the street longer than me. Longer than anybody I know. He knows stuff. And I talked to Jamie about it."

"Jesus." At wit's end, Eve scrubbed her hands over her face.

"Jamie already knows official stuff, and we're hanging out. Sort of maybe dating a little. He's really smart, and he's decent. I mean, it can't really go anywhere because he wants to be a cop, and I'm going to be an investigative reporter, so, you know, won't work. But I like hanging with somebody smart and decent. I never really did before, and without the school, without Nadine, I probably never would have.

"And I need to go to college."

To Eve's intense dismay, Quilla's eyes filled. "Nadine says I need a good education. She's going to pay for me to go to college. I'm going to work for scholarships so it doesn't sting so much, but I'm going to college. I mean I have to finish at An Didean first, but then.

"Can I have a Coke?"

Trying to ignore the headache creeping back, Eve waved at her Auto-Chef.

"Sorry, it sort of closes me up right here." Quilla pressed a hand under her throat. "I never should've been here, like this, and I wouldn't be if not for you, and Roarke, and Nadine. I could've ended up like the girls behind the wall, or the girls on your board. So I need to help."

She cracked the tube, downed some Coke Eve hadn't known was stocked.

"So I talked to Mouser because he knows stuff. Like where the snooty rich kids shop, especially the doofs, and he said . . ."

Pausing, she eyed Eve. "This has to be confidential. I mean like he's a source, right? You won't bust him down or anything, right? I should've said that first."

"I won't bust him down."

"Okay, good. He said he knew places like that where you could keep it low and wait, then maybe snag a wallet, and snag a shopping bag full of snoot clothes. He said how he'd rather wear rags, but you could sell them, or sometimes you needed them like a costume so you could . . ."

Pausing, Quilla pressed her lips together. "But never mind that part."

"Okay. You got a list?"

Digging into a pocket, Quilla pulled out a disc. "Names, addresses. Most are downtown, because that was Mouser's turf. Before," she said. "But they have Midtown and uptown branches. Some of them."

"Okay, I'll check them out."

"Do you think it'll help?"

"It does help. Now go away so I can work. And next time," she called out, "if you bring brownies to soften up my squad, you'd better have one for me."

"Check it," Quilla said, and hurried away.

Eve turned to the AutoChef, thinking coffee, then changed it to a Pepsi, since the temp control in her office wasn't quite beating the heat.

She sat and plugged in Quilla's list.

"Might as well try it."

She hit on the first one. Yes, Allisandra Charro often shopped there for clients. But the adrenaline rush proved temporary. None of the sizes worked, not even close.

It took time, but when she hit another, the sizes seemed reasonably compatible.

"Would you have the name of the client, or an address, other than Ms. Charro's, for delivery?"

"I'd have to check on that, and I'm not certain I can disclose that information."

"I can get a warrant, then I can come into your fancy store, flashing my badge around and scaring off your fancy customers. Or you can check and give me what I need."

The response came stiffly. "One moment please."

Eve waited a moment, then two, then three.

"Deliveries for one of Ms. Charro's clients are occasionally sent directly to a Ms. Tasha Grimley. Other client selections are delivered to Ms. Charro."

She read off a Park Avenue address for Grimley.

"Thanks."

Eve ran Tasha Grimley—forty-six, married, sixteen years to Paul Grimley, two offspring.

Eve latched onto the son, age fifteen. And deflated when his ID shot came on-screen.

Dark skin, definitely not a white kid. Laughing bright green eyes, mile-wide smile.

A quick dive, just in case, informed her his interests lay in electronics and lacrosse. Team captain.

So athletic and popular.

She moved on.

And switched back to coffee.

As she felt the time leaking away, she tagged Charro again.

"Where the hell are you?"

"Stuck in traffic, after a very long day. The cursed tunnel's backed up, so unless you can do something about that, I'll be at least another half hour."

"Since you're sitting there, think. Caucasian male, fifteen to seventeen, around five-six, small feet. Hard-line conservative clothes."

"Lieutenant, as I explained, I often work through the parents, grandparents, guardians, and a great many of my clients simply send me a list I spring off of. If I ever get out of this tunnel and home—and I could probably walk faster at this rate."

"Do that."

Charro just laughed. "Not in these shoes. It'll take me five minutes to look at my records on those Stubens and give you a name. Believe me, I want to do that to get you off my back so I can have a very large adult beverage."

Eve considered. "You have a driver?"

"Of course I have a driver."

"I need the make and model of the vehicle, the color, the plates."

"What for?"

"To arrange for a police escort once you're through the tunnel. Get me the data on the car. Now."

"Good God, who is this kid?" But the screen shifted as Charro scooted forward and talked to her driver.

With the information, Eve pulled strings, hard and fast.

It would save some time. Not a lot, she admitted, but every minute counted.

She needed that face. She needed that name.

"Charro, you still there?"

"Eyes wide, mouth agape."

"I'm going to send you a list of shops. Flag any you don't use. I think that'll be fewer than the ones you do."

"I can do that."

"Flag them, send it back. Make it quick."

Eve clicked up, pushed up and paced.

Close, so close, she *knew* it. But maybe not close enough if he tried to take another life tonight.

Another girl on her board? Like Jenna, Arlie, Kiki.

Like Quilla.

And all she could do? Wait. Wait for that name, that face. She'd pushed all the angles she could, and now had to wait for someone else to bring her an answer.

Charro worked fast, and as Eve expected, only two shops rated flags.

She sat down to try the next when her 'link signaled.

Special Agent Teasdale.

"Dallas."

"Lieutenant, I'm sorry it's taken me so long to get back to you."

"If you'd hit, you'd have gotten back sooner."

"I'm sorry to say that's true. I've got no like crimes for you. On the single one that skirted the outside, the perpetrator—age eighteen now—is in prison.

"I hope you've made better progress."

"We've made progress, and I appreciate the assist." She looked at her board, thought of the next girl. "If we don't have it solid in a couple of hours, I'd like to read you in."

"Of course. Good hunting."

Eve clicked off, and started down the list.

When her 'link signaled again, she snagged it.

Yancy.

"Dallas."

"I'm sending you the best I've got, but you need to know I had to put pieces together from all the wits, so . . ."

He let it trail off as his vid-star face and head full of dark curls filled her screen.

"You were right, Kiki saw more than she thought, but she saw it in a darkened theater and with a jolt of pain. I hope it's enough to run face rec."

It had to be, she thought, as she heard the incoming on her comp.

She brought it up, stared.

And that vital next piece fell into place.

"That's him. Jesus Christ, Yancy, that's him. I know it."

Hadn't she been sure, dead sure, she'd know the face?

"It's rougher than I'd like. I'm heading in to see if I can refine it, at least a little. But I knew you'd want the sketch as soon as I finished."

"I did. I do. You've got him here. You've got enough of him here for me to know it's him. Good work. Thanks."

She cut him off, started to program for face rec, then realized she had a potential shortcut.

If she could figure out how to navigate it.

She had the yearbooks. She just needed to figure out how to run the sketch against the damn yearbooks. If he wasn't in there—but he was, she knew it—she could run it standard.

"Computer." Dragging a hand through her hair, she kept it fisted there as she tried to figure out how to voice a command that would tell it to do what she wanted it to do.

Waiting . . . The computer said, not at all helpfully.

"Ah, copy and bring up files from my home unit and its auxiliary containing—hold, wait."

She'd need the documents, the names, the codes, the something.

Fuck!

"Having trouble there?"

She never heard him coming—nothing new about that—but she all but leaped up and dragged Roarke into her office.

"Sit there, talk later. I need the yearbooks to run against this sketch."

"So there he is. He looks . . . so ordinary, except for the eyes."

"Ordinary, forgettable, but the eyes are off. Kiki, at least, saw that. Make it work."

"I can do that. Seems I timed this well," he added as he worked the keyboard and swipe rather than the voice command.

She'd have never figured that out, Eve admitted, and leaned over his shoulder as the split screen ran faces by.

"It may take a bit of time."

Taking him at his word, she hurried out to the bullpen.

"Peabody, we've got a face. We're running it. Contact Reo, get her ready to get us warrants. Arrest, search and seizure once we have a name and address."

She went back to her office, where Roarke drank her coffee and watched the faces fly.

"Weak jaw," she said. "Still got some baby fat in the cheeks. Nose just a little too big for symmetry, thin mouth, then the eyes. No pretty boy, this one. And the eyes—"

"Aren't a boy's at all, are they? They're years older than the face."

"That's right. That's right." She grabbed her signaling 'link.

"Dallas."

"Allisandra, home after a wild and exhilarating ride. I believe my driver was nearly as thrilled as I was."

"Give me a damn name."

"Happy to. I purchased those shoes, as well as many pieces over the last several years, for the son of Dr. Nolan Bryce. I have the son as—"

"Francis Bryce," Eve said when the yearbook photo hit and matched.

"That's correct. I haven't been to the residence often, and not in some time, as the client most usually requests straight delivery, or has me package and messenger. But I recall it's a lovely home."

She read off an address on the Upper East Side.

"Thanks."

"Listen—"

But Eve cut her off.

"Let's move. Peabody," she called out as she half jogged into the bullpen. "Francis Bryce, father Dr. Nolan Bryce." She added the address.

"Move it, and get those warrants."

"Go get him, Loo!" Jenkinson called out.

"Fucking A," Eve responded as she ran to the glides.

Chapter Twenty

"Peabody, run the father."

"Already am."

"You drive," Eve said to Roarke. "What are you doing here?"

"Some business downtown, and you're nearing end of shift. Seems I timed it well. Yancy came through then?"

"Yancy, Kiki, David, bits and pieces." She jogged and weaved her way down the glide. "And Charro."

"Charro?"

"Personal shopper—the shoes. Actually, Quilla had a good angle I was working. What have you got, Peabody?"

"Some mild nausea from reading while running down this glide. Dr. Nolan Bryce, Caucasian, age fifty-three, head of Grant and Frisker Pharmaceutical's research lab, New York branch. One marriage, one divorce. Mariella Reeder, now deceased."

Peabody looked up when Eve banged through the garage door and down the metal stairs. "She OD'd, Junk cocktail—needle syringe. Five years ago. She had a sheet."

"Highlights," Eve said as they got into the car.

"Possession, assault, resisting, unlicensed solicitation. First bust . . . twelve years ago. Mandatory rehab."

"Didn't take."

"Not even a little," Peabody confirmed. "She did the ninety—swank center. Busted just under a year later. Another rehab stint. Barely made it six months. Did thirty inside, another ninety in rehab, another thirty in a halfway house."

"He'd have been about four, wouldn't he, when this began." Roarke glanced at Eve as he pushed through traffic. "Younger, certainly, when she started using, but about that when his mother spent long lengths of time away."

Before she could speak, he shook his head and skimmed around a corner. "It gives him no right to kill, nor does it make him an object of pity—at least not mine. But it's a foundational issue, isn't it now? His mother wanted the drug more than him."

"So he kills girls with the drug—a purer version—who wouldn't look at him twice. Or once," she corrected. "He can spend the rest of his life in a cage working out his foundational issue."

"Third bust," Peabody continued, "less than three months after she left the halfway house. Got three to five, served four, ninety in halfway. Bryce divorced her while she was inside, and was given full custody of the minor son."

"Quick, rounding math?" Roarke breezed through a yellow. "She OD'd shortly after her release, and he'd have been roughly eleven."

"That's accurate math," Peabody told him. "No criminal on the doctor, Dallas. He's squeaky clean. Plenty of money here. Not Roarke plenty, but plenty. Family money in addition to his income. He's got the house here, a boat, country club membership, a place in the Hamptons.

"Not to be pissy, but he didn't pass on his looks to his son. The doctor's dreamy."

"Not pissy, relevant." Eve had Nolan Bryce on her own screen. "The father's got looks. So did the mother. The addiction took care of that, but she started out with them. And the son lost the DNA lottery. He's short, soft, ordinary, mouse-brown hair, dead brown eyes.

"Flip back through Francis Bryce's ID shots," she suggested. "His eyes have always been off. Foundational issues, sure. But some are born psychopaths."

At the incoming signal, Eve gave a satisfied nod. "Reo came through." She printed out the warrants.

"And again, excellent timing." Roarke pulled into a No Parking zone, engaged the On Duty light.

A good, solid brick house, Eve noted. Three stories, square on the corner, with a short flight of brick steps leading to the double entrance doors.

Flat roof, and what looked like a roof garden on it. Maybe Francis grew his poppies up there, she thought.

She got out, took a long look.

"Smart enough to have one of your security systems."

"So it is. Do you want to me get through it?"

"We'll start with a knock. On record."

Knowing the security cam would pick them up anyway, Eve approached the door. Rather than the knock, she pressed the buzzer, and recognized the voice that answered seconds later as a droid. Female.

"Good evening. How may I assist you?"

"You can assist us by opening the door." She held up her badge. "NYPSD."

"Dr. Bryce is not in residence at this time."

"Scan the badge. Scan this warrant authorizing us to search the premises, and open the door."

"One moment please."

Eve waited for the scan, calculated thirty seconds before she gave Roarke the go to cut through security and locks.

The droid barely made it.

"I have verified your identification and the warrant. One moment."

Locks disengaged, and the door opened.

The droid, built to replicate an attractive blond female in her forties, stepped back. It wore a simple, straight-lined black suit and low-heeled pumps.

"You are authorized to enter. How may I assist you?"

Scanning the foyer, Eve slid a hand under her jacket to the butt of her weapon. "Is Francis Bryce in residence?"

"He is not at this time."

"Is anyone else here?"

"I am alone on the premises at this time."

"Where is Francis?"

"I don't have that information."

"When did he leave the house?"

The droid's bright blue eyes fixed as it processed the answer. "Seventeen minutes, twenty-eight seconds ago."

"Son of a bitch. Did he contact a car service, call for a cab?"

"I don't have that information."

"Peabody, tag somebody in the bullpen to check on that, three-block radius from this location. Where is Dr. Nolan Bryce?"

"Dr. Bryce is attending a medical conference in Las Vegas."

"When did he leave?"

"Eight days ago."

"When's he due back?"

"In six days. He extended his time away for a short vacation. Shall I contact him?"

"No. Where does Francis grow his poppies?"

"I'm sorry. I cannot process that question."

"Does Francis use the roof garden?"

"I cannot verify. My services are not required in that area."

"Peabody, go grab the field kits, then clear as you go, and check it out. Where else on the premises aren't your services required?"

"In Master Francis's laboratory, study, and recreational space."

Master Francis. Christ.

"Where is that?"

"His laboratory, study, and recreational space is on the lower level."

"The basement. Show me."

"I'm sorry. I'm not programmed to enter that area."

"Show me how to get to it. With me," she told Roarke. "There's going to be science and IT stuff you'll recognize that I won't."

"That area can be accessed by steps in the utility area or by the elevator. However, both are secured and only Master Francis has access."

"Show me," Eve repeated. "I've got my own master with me."

It led them to the staircase—classic, straight lines. Under it the wood-paneled door of an elevator nestled.

The droid spoke again when Eve pressed the elevator button.

"It will go up to the second and third floor, but not down without Master Francis's authorization. I can attempt to notify him."

"No." Stepping aside, Eve let Roarke go to work on the block. "Why attempt?"

"Master Francis values his privacy. He often uses the privacy setting on his 'link."

"Clear to go," Roarke told her.

Peabody brought Eve her field kit. "I'm on the roof."

"Great." Eve sealed up. "Roarke." She tossed him the Seal-It. "Take the droid back to wherever the door going down is. Come down that way after you shut it down. I don't want it rebooting and notifying Master fucking Francis or the father."

"You don't want to contact the father?"

"Whatever he thinks or feels about the son, he's still the father. Basic instinct when he finds out cops are looking for his son would most likely push him to contact the son."

"True enough. I'll meet you down there."

As the doors closed, her communicator signaled. "What did you find?"

"A really excellent greenhouse. Compact but really mag. And it's locked up tight. I really, seriously, totally don't want to break the glass. I can't see clearly through it. It's vented, but the vents are too high for me to reach."

"Come back in, find his bedroom, and start there. I'll send Roarke up to deal with the greenhouse locks."

"On my way. No luck on a cab or car service, Dallas."

"He's careful. Get on the bedroom."

The elevator opened to pitch-dark.

"Lights on," Eve ordered, but the dark remained. "Shit!"

Blocking the elevator door with her body, she used the light inside. Contacted Roarke.

"He's got the lights blocked down here. Paranoid fucker. I've got a flashlight, but it won't be enough."

"Give me a minute."

It didn't take much longer for the lights—a lot of light—to snap on.

It looked like a fancy studio apartment with its creamy white walls and dark wood floors. An entertainment screen dominated the wall across from a gel couch in navy, a couple of oversized chairs in navy-and-white stripes.

A mini-kitchen area held a full-sized AutoChef and friggie, a sink. The droid might not work down here, Eve thought, but good old Francis kept it spotless.

Though she didn't hear Roarke come down, she sensed him, and turned.

"Hangout area, rich boy's hangout. Looks innocent. I doubt he makes much use of it. He's too busy to flop down and play games or watch a vid."

"The door to the steps? Very serious locks. Hardly needed for innocence."

She walked to a door, opened it. "John. Let's try that one."

Through an alcove, another door, another lock.

"I should mention," Roarke began as he dealt with the lock, "he or his father installed alarms on the elevator block and the door to the steps. I deactivated them."

"I vote for Master Francis."

"As do I. They'd signal his 'link. Won't now, of course." He opened the door for her.

"I didn't see any cams in the hang space. Or in here," she said. "Study area. More like an office. Good desk, state-of-the-art comp system, leather chairs, beverage station."

She gave one of the desk drawers a tug. "Locked. He takes no chances. I bet the comp's triggered, too."

"I can deal with that."

"It really was good timing. But hold off." She pointed to another locked door. "Hang space, study space. This? It's just a pass-through. In there's going to be the real work area."

"I wonder how an adult could allow a boy— Sixteen, isn't he?"

"Seventeen in September."

"How he could allow all of this. The locks and blocks. I don't know much about parenting, but I know bloody red flags when I see them."

"With you there."

He eased the door open. "Hold," he told her. "Cams in here, and I'll wager a sensor that will, again, send an alert to his 'link. This may take more than a minute."

With no choice, she shut down impatience. "Do what you gotta."

She stepped back to give him room, did another pass through the study area.

All drawers locked. No photos, no memorabilia, no fiddle toys. He used the comp, she thought. But she'd bet Roarke's excellent ass he used that exclusively for schoolwork.

The money shot was the lab.

She heard Peabody coming.

"Wow, hell of a space for a teenager. He's got his own apartment down here, basically. Which explains the bedroom."

"What about it?"

"Bed, a pair of nightstands, matching lamps, reading chair, dresser, big closet, en suite. He's got a shit-ton of clothes, all along the lines of the Stubens. Make that a rich old clueless accountant. And there's nothing, Dallas.

"No mess, no personal things, no sign of a teenager. No tablet, no doo-dles, no posters on the walls. Neatly hung or folded clothes, neatly lined-up shoes. And none of them were baggies, cheap or otherwise, or Kick Its. No trench, no wig."

"He's wearing them. He's hunting."

"We're in," Roarke told her. "And yes, this is his real work."

And that real work held a space larger than the hangout area. It had two command centers on either side, each with an electronic board very like what Central had in their conference rooms.

The lab itself made her think Dickhead would rub his hands together in envious delight.

The two long counters formed an aisle. She could visualize Francis slid-ing along in his wheeled work chair, making murderous use of the vials, the beakers, the petri dishes, the scopes and screens.

A glass-walled cabinet, locked, of course, held more, a glass-door cold box yet more.

"He has to be pilfering some of this from the pharmaceutical com-pany. His father's lab. It's all labeled," Eve pointed out. "And I may not be up on all the scientific terms for this crap, but I got enough to know he has controlled substances in here."

"He's making more. Over here, Dallas. It's like a personal refinery."

Eve walked to another workstation, frowned at the machines, the burners.

"See, he's got pods here, he's milking them. And then he's got these wrapped balls."

"Opium cakes," Roarke confirmed. "I've seen these. And no," he said at the unspoken question. "Absolutely never."

"I read up more on it," Peabody said. "You make the morphine from the cakes, boil them with lime, and you get the morphine on the surface, then you heat it up again—I think with ammonia, and he's got that right under the counter. And the molds. See the molds? That brown pasty stuff in them's morphine, and you make heroin from that."

"A great many steps, I think. But he appears to have all the necessary. And skill," Roarke added. "Foundational issues or not, he's wasted his brain, that skill, his obvious privilege to make the very thing that killed his mother. To use that to kill the innocent.

"No pity. None."

"We know what he does, and we know he's out preparing to do it again. Get me into the comps. He's meticulous. He'll have a timetable, an agenda. Put out a BOLO, Peabody. Maybe we'll get lucky and a sharp-eyed cop will spot him."

She checked her wrist unit.

"It'll be dark in a couple hours. He needs the dark. Peabody, get Mc-Nab or Feeney or Callendar up here. A lot of comps to sift through, asap."

"On it."

"Roarke, once you get me in, could you go up to the roof, deal with the locked greenhouse? We've got enough here, but let's do the full sweep. Damn it, Peabody, see who's in the bullpen, or off and not on a hot. We need more bodies to go through this house. Not enough time with just us to fully search it."

While Roarke and her partner worked, she pulled out her 'link.

"Commander Whitney, I need to update you. We've identified the subject, Francis Bryce, age sixteen, and are currently in his home lab. Among other things, we've found what appear to be opium cakes and the equipment needed to make heroin. The suspect isn't on the premises, and I believe he's on his way to another location and another target."

"What do you need?"

"I'm calling in assistance from EDD for his comp systems, and detectives to assist with the search of the residence. We've issued a BOLO."

"If you need more hands and eyes, you've got them."

"I'll let you know, sir." When Roarke signaled, gestured to the first comp, she nodded. "That's all the relevant information at this time."

"When you have more, give me more."

"Yes, sir. Dallas out. Peabody?"

"We've got McNab and Feeney, and a full complement of detectives. Jenkinson's rounding them up."

"Good. Damn it, he's even locked the drawers and cabinets in here. Roarke, before you check the greenhouse?" She sat at a command center. "Peabody, once they're open, check the drawers."

She searched documents. It didn't take her long to skip over some of them, as they contained formulas and equations she couldn't possibly decipher.

The lab could and would.

Moving on, she answered her 'link.

"Poppies," Roarke said. "Poppies will put them to sleep."

"What?"

"It's from *The Wizard of Oz*," Peabody said helpfully. "The Wicked Witch."

"He's no witch, but right now he has the edge on wicked. Come down, will you? I think this comp is straight science. I need to find the personal."

"He's got mini cans of Seal-It. Pressure syringes, scope slides. And mother lode. Needle syringes." With her own sealed hands, Peabody held one up. "A couple dozen, individually packaged. Manufactured by Grant-Frisker Pharm."

"Find the recycler, see if you can open it. Bag the contents. He may have used it to dispose of the weapons. Fucking science."

Sitting back, she rubbed her temples. "He's got some notes in here, and it's enough to get him for manufacturing controlled substances. And if I'm reading it right, the formula for the cocktail he used on the two victims. But there's nothing on where he plans to hit next, or notes on where he killed before."

"The gang's pulling up." Peabody slipped her comm back in her pocket. "I'll go let them in."

"No, I will. Keep going, and ask Roarke to get us into another comp station."

To save time, she took the elevator up. *Gang* had been the appropriate word, she thought when she opened the door.

"Got a bunch of cops for you, Loo." Jenkinson grinned with it.

"I can use them. Feeney and McNab, take the elevator—under the steps—down a level. He's got a bunch of comps, a couple tablets so far. He's wearing his kill clothes, so he's hunting, and he has a plan. We need to find it.

"The rest of you, spread out. Peabody's been through his room, but it's a big house. There's a greenhouse on the roof. Poppies. Seal up, get samples. If you can't get into any of the house e's, they can wait. He wouldn't put anything on them anyway.

"Droid in the back, deactivated. Leave it that way. We'll have the e-team see if it's got anything in its banks to pile on later."

"You heard her. Trueheart, go up for those samples," Jenkinson ordered. "Baxter, start on three, and Trueheart'll join you. Santiago, Carmichael, take the second floor, Reineke and me, we've got this one."

"I'm below," Eve told them. "He'll wait until dark. His last hit was before eleven, but we can't count on that. Let's find the fucker."

She went down, found McNab at the comp in the study area.

"Kid's got it made, and he kills girls? I'd've been doing something much else with girls at that age if I had free run down here."

"Bet you were always pretty."

He grinned, tried for a modest shrug as he worked. "Well, pretty enough to get Peabody."

"It wasn't the pretty. That may start the ball rolling, it doesn't keep it in play. Find something."

"What I'm finding is school stuff. Assignments, tests, papers, essays, and all that. And it looks like he's kept everything, going back to freaking kindergarten."

"Yeah, he would."

See how smart I am, how smart I've always been.

"Just make sure there's nothing buried under that. I'm thinking no. Just make sure, then switch over to the lab."

Feeney stood at one of the counters, digging into one comp. Roarke had the second command center.

"We're going to need bigger evidence boxes," Peabody told her. "He's got morphine, fentanyl, Rohypnol, ketamine, and lots more. And it looks like he's been making his own street drugs. Zeus, Whore, Erotica. He's labeled them all. Has a good supply of house-made Stay Up. I guess he's too embarrassed to buy that over the counter. Must use it when he . . ." She jerked her hand.

"Whacks off."

"Yeah, that. I bagged up the recycler. And he's got a medical waste container."

"Leave that one for the sweepers."

"Gladly. Dallas, I don't know anything about it, really, but he's got these hermetically sealed containers, and I think they might hold viruses or bacteria."

"We don't touch those. We call in a hazmat team, scientific lead on it."

"Even more gladly."

She checked her wrist unit again. Outside, she thought, dusk would be settling in.

"Just school stuff, Dallas. Where do you want me?"

Feeney answered McNab. "We found another tablet, take that. This unit here, it's science stuff. I got some of it, and he'd have a lot of explaining to do with just this."

Science, she thought. Berenski would be off duty, but . . .

She contacted Whitney.

"Sir, we've found numerous chemicals and controlled substances at this location. Illegal substances. We're calling in a specialty team to handle what may be samples of viruses and/or bacteria. We've also found various formulas on his electronics we're not equipped to decipher. I realize Chief Berenski is off duty at this time, but we'll need the lab to prepare for what we'll send them."

"I'll take care of it."

"Thank you, sir."

"Passcoded," McNab said of the tablet. "Fail-safe. Take a couple minutes."

"Roarke?"

"Working on it," he told Eve. Since he'd taken off his jacket, rolled up his sleeves, and tied back his hair, she knew he was deep in work mode. "He knew enough to cover his tracks, but not very bloody well. I'm getting there."

She had to force herself not to tell him to get there faster.

Maybe he had a hidey-hole after all. It didn't make sense considering the security he'd put on his work area, but maybe.

She started hunting for it. A panel, a secret door, anything.

"Lieutenant."

She spun around toward Roarke.

"On-screen," he said, and Jenna Harbough's ID shot filled it.

"He uploaded this the day after he killed her. Along with media reports. And her social media accounts, as much about her as he could find. Including her obituary.

"There are notes, again logged the day after her death."

He brought them up.

> The first project successfully completed. The formula worked perfectly, allowing me time to leave by the preplanned exit. The subject, now identified as Jenna Harbough, reacted swiftly upon injection. She looked at me, and yes! She saw me. I had expected her to collapse inside the club, but, in what I consider a bonus, she managed to stumble out to the alley and die, the media reports, in Jake Kincade's arms.
>
> Girls, born whores, love to spread their legs for his type. Tall, a lot of hair, guitar-playing, brainless hulk. But she saw me first.
>
> After another successful project or two, at least two, I have a way to make certain the one I pick sees me last.

"Evil son of a fuck," Feeney muttered.

"There's another document, on Arlie Dillon. It's much the same," Roarke said, and brought it up.

"Kiki Rosenburg?"

"Yes, but there's a change there. No photo, no name. Just Third Project/Fail. And his notes."

> Every project, no matter how meticulously planned, how carefully each step is built, will have a failure. Circumstances, timing, an unanticipated event. Science learns from failures as much as from successes.

Perhaps more.

I believe the location chosen contributed to the failure. A crowded interior space. Although the first project achieved the desired results in such a space, this, due to the theater aisle, proved too constricted. And the cool temperature contributed, rather than the overwarm club, as the subject wore a jacket. This may have hindered the injection.

Yet this doesn't explain the subject's extreme reaction. Her screams nearly split my skull! She swung around so quickly, screaming that scream. I think she intended to strike me, and I was forced to run to my planned exit.

Accuracy, and one must be accurate, forces me to admit I was very shocked and frightened, and had to force myself not to run or look as panicked as I was when I gained the outside.

She, too, looked at me. She saw me. In this case, this is worrisome. Or was. The facts:

The theater was dark—more accurately dim, but enough. The cut of my wig obscures much of my face, and is much darker than my own hair. The trench coat obscures my build. And the subject was far too hysterical—as females tend to be—to have gotten a clear look.

I am, of course, disappointed, but only more determined. I find this setback only pushes me forward. Not only forward, but upward. The next project will succeed. The next subject will see my face clearly (and last), will know my voice. She will give me what her type refuses to give me.

The first injection will ensure that.

The second will end her.

I wonder who she'll be. Not that her name will matter, until after, for my logs.

"That's it? Nothing about when or where?"

"Not that I've found, no. I'll keep at it."

"Well, fuck me finally! I'm in."

On a huff of air, McNab opened the tablet. "He had to have paid an e-geek to secure this, because it was prime work. Just standard on the school comp, and . . . Shit, it's a journal. First date's three years ago."

"Go to the last entry." Eve strode across the room, hovered at his shoulder.

"I've got it. Logged today."

"'Leaving now,'" Eve read. "'It will take time to get there, and to ensure success, I need to be sure I've selected the most optimum location for tonight's project.'

"Go back, go back. We need that location."

"Wait, wait. Okay, bullshit, snotty-ass bullshit bragging." McNab skimmed through as quickly as possible.

"Stop!" Eve ordered. "'The first time I went to Coney Island, I was not quite five. My mother took me. I was so happy she would take me on what she called an adventure. I didn't understand then that she met her dealer there, got high. When I got sick on the rides, she laughed and laughed. I cried.

"'I never went back until June third of this year when I realized it would serve as the perfect place for my triumph. Since then I've visited that amusement park, the site of my childish humiliation, twelve times. I've wandered it during the day when it looks tawdry, and at night when the lights play false color and joy.'"

"What kid talks like that?" McNab wondered.

"He does. 'I had planned to wait another week or even two before turning humiliation into triumph, but last night's error convinces me it's time. One must weigh the risks against the rewards.

"'Even if she screams, as the subject did last night, who will notice? She will give me what I deserve. And then I will return the favor.'

"Coney Island. Round them up, Peabody. You've got the van, Feeney?"

"A van's too slow." Roarke pushed to his feet. "I can have a jet-copter here in minutes."

"Where the hell would you land it?"

"There's room on the roof."

She thought of how much she hated flying. And thought of the traffic creeping into Brooklyn.

"Do it. Peabody, get some uniforms to sit on this place, and call the sweepers to process every-damn-thing and start transporting to the lab. Move it and do it."

"Moving and doing."

"Feeney."

"I'll get some boys down here to haul in the e's. We're with you."

Good, she thought as she ran up the stairs. Coney Island wasn't a crowded theater. It was acres. Boardwalk, beaches, rides, arcades.

But now, she was the hunter.

Chapter Twenty-one

Francis Bryce knew he looked, in the vernacular, frosty. The hair, the shades, the clothes. He'd even worn the trench because he thought it added a little cachet.

Maybe the shoes had rubbed blisters on his heels, his toes, but that was the price he had to pay to blend in with the masses.

And he'd treated them, applied NuSkin.

He'd planned tonight so well, every step. He'd done his research, his due diligence, calculated the timing.

When he thought of the humiliation and ridicule he'd suffered here as a child, it seemed all the more vital he experience his triumph as a man in this place.

He had Seal-It for his hands. He'd taken a couple of his father's condoms. It wouldn't do to leave any of his DNA in or on the lucky slut he chose tonight.

As an added precaution he'd walked a full ten blocks from home be-

fore hailing a cab. He'd had the cab take him as far as SoHo before getting out, walking again, then hailing another to take him into Brooklyn.

Another walk, a third cab to Coney Island.

Not that the police had the slimmest clue, but 28.35 grams of preven-
tion equaled 0.4536 liters of cure.

He'd do the same on his return. No public transportation, with their
intrusive cameras.

Even with walking and switching cabs, he arrived at the amusement
park before dark.

Understanding the value of blending in, he bought a Coney Island dog,
a fizzy. Disgusting, of course, though he had to admit the first bite was
delicious. Still, by the time he'd walked, wandered, and finished the dog,
he felt vaguely nauseated.

His mother had bought him a dog on that long-ago visit. And blue
cotton candy.

*Sit on that bench, Francis. Sit right there like a good boy and eat your
candy. Mommy just needs to talk to this man for a minute. Then we'll ride
all the rides!*

Her dealer, he thought, though he hadn't known that at the time. He'd
sat, obedient, and fascinated by the texture of the blue fluff on the paper
cone.

He found that taste so sweet, sting-his-teeth sweet, but ate it anyway.

Then she'd been so bright and happy. High as Ben Franklin's kite.
He'd ridden kiddie rides. Some she could ride with him, and did with her
hair blowing while she went *Wooo!*

Then the bumpy cars, the revolving carousel, the spinning teacups,
the swaying mini-Ferris wheel, the rocking rocket ships had combined to
purge his stomach.

Other kids had giggled or made noises of disgust. And his mother had
laughed and laughed.

Oh, Francis, isn't that just like you! Puking up a fun afternoon.

He'd never gone on an amusement ride again.

Until.

Now dusk settled at last, and those of his age group began filtering in. For the most part, his on-site research proved, afternoons were for kids with their nannies or grannies or a parent or two. Families—a lot of tourists there who took selfies in front of the classic Wonder Wheel.

In daylight hours, he'd often observe old people—especially men—sitting on benches, looking out over the beach. Probably dreaming of the life they could have had if they'd had brains or luck or a whore wife who didn't bitch and complain constantly.

They were at the end of the road anyway, so too late for them.

He was at the beginning of his road. In one year, one month, one week and three days, he'd turn eighteen. University waited, and he already had his pick there.

He'd wait until he was into his sophomore year before arranging a tragic accident for his father. Then all the money would be his, the house would be his. He'd sell the boat due to his mal de mer along with the house in the Hamptons, as he had no interest there.

He could do whatever he wanted, whenever he wanted. He could buy as many whores as he wanted.

And make them do whatever he wanted.

He really wanted to experience—using the inaccurate vernacular—a blow job.

But tonight, he'd experience intercourse. He'd earned it. He deserved it.

Tonight, he'd finally know what it was like to have female breasts in his hands, to slide his tongue inside a girl's mouth, to shove his erection inside her.

To penetrate her, dominate her. To hurt her with his body while hers gave his pleasure.

As thinking of it gave him that erection, he was grateful for the trench.

The lights gleamed and flashed now and brought that—for him—false sense of excitement and a kind of tawdry glamour.

Screams streamed down from the Cyclone as its cars and passengers dived down a run, looped around a loop.

Insanity, as far as he was concerned.

Air guns popped as idiots fired at various animals or cartoon villains, all to win some cheap prize. The Wonder Wheel circled. More screams from the G-Force with its passengers strapped to a spinning wheel that twisted, inverted.

It made him feel queasy just to look at it.

He considered several possibilities. Long-legged girls in their tiny shorts and skimpy tops, so obviously asking for what he was so anxious to give them.

But most traveled in packs, and many had boys with them. Tall jocks with empty brains, slouching hoodlums with smirking mouths.

He had several options for cutting one from the herd, but preferred finding a satisfactory selection who walked alone. He kept his eye on the restrooms, though for some reason females often traveled in packs even there.

He only needed one, but he had standards. She must be pleasing to his eye, in face and figure. She must not be taller than he was.

But he grew impatient, and jittery with it, nearly settled for one who carried more weight in her hips than he liked, another whose mouth looked pinched and ears too big.

He found it frustrating that the ones who pleased his eye, met his standards so rarely walked alone. For this most important project, he couldn't approach one who had companions.

Then he saw her, and could barely believe his luck. That is, if he believed in luck at all.

He *knew* her!

Delaney—she went by Del—Brooke. She attended his school, actually had a reasonably intelligent brain. Black hair that fell in waves, golden brown eyes, perfect features. Long legs, but she met his height requirement, as he had at least an inch on her.

She wore blue shorts to show off those legs, legs with excellent muscle tone, as she captained the school's swim team. A tiny white top with skinny straps to show off those swimmer's shoulders.

He'd been her lab partner once, and they'd worked well enough together. But when he'd suggested they meet for coffee, she'd looked at him with pity that barely disguised derision, and told him she was seeing someone.

Lies, just another lie. And he *knew* she'd tittered about it with her friends after.

Here, an opportunity to have all he wanted presented itself.

And though she talked on her 'link, for the moment, she walked alone.

He slid a hand into the right pocket of his trench. The first syringe, the one filled with his own formula, one he'd termed Compliance.

He imagined trademarking it one day.

It would make her, obviously, compliant, open to suggestion, malleable, a bit sleepy.

This time, he'd coated the needle with a numbing agent. She'd feel a prick, of course, but little more than that.

Then his formula would do the rest.

He nudged off the safety on the needle, and approached her.

Eve spent the flight working on the logistics of the operation.

"You've got copies of his face and the sketch where he's wearing the wig. He'll be wearing it. Black baggies, black Kick Its, probably a black tee. The trench, as we didn't find it at the residence.

"Ditch the ties. Not you, Jenkinson. Yours makes you look right at home at a carnival. Peabody, lose the jacket. Your shirt's long enough to cover your sidearm. You're with McNab. He always looks at home at a carnival."

Though she didn't like knowing she stood over sky, she stood, pointed to the screen and its image of the park.

"Santiago, Carmichael, take the north side. Jenkinson, Reineke, take the east, and try to look less like cops. Peabody, McNab, the south. Feeney, do the crisscross, and Roarke and I will go straight down the middle heading west. Skip the kiddie area. He isn't interested in that."

"Two minutes," Roarke called out.

"You've got earbuds, use them. Keep in contact. The locals should be in place, along the beachfront, entrances, exits. Remember, he's armed. The syringe is lethal."

She sat, strapped in. "McNab, any more on the journal?"

"There's a hell of a lot of crazy and ugly, LT, and whoever prosecutes this is going to do cartwheels, but he doesn't say where, the exact location in the park. Just how he's going to start off his senior year with—he writes—metaphorically, a bang. And how he'll enjoy the screams as he ejaculates into a female. He actually writes like that. It's whack."

She felt the copter's descent in her gut.

"Pattern here is to write the details afterward, like a report. I'm back to last March when he goes off bragging about successfully creating a formula. He calls it Compliance. Here's a quote.

"'The popular term is date-rape drug, but rape is a lie perpetuated by women in their endless quest to emasculate men, to deny us our rights.' It's how he thinks," McNab concluded.

"He can spend the rest of his life thinking like that, in a cage where his 'rights' will be severely limited."

She glanced toward the front and saw the lights, the iconic wheel turning, flashing, with the buildings spearing up ahead, the sand and water spreading behind.

Then the water came very, very close, so she turned her head and just let herself breathe through the beach landing.

Glad that part was over, she unstrapped, stood.

"We're go. Let's find the fucker, save the girl."

While they worked their way to the entrance with its big, grinning-face logo, she coordinated with the local cops. For now, she wanted them as backup only. She already had ten cops and a consultant going in.

Enough, she thought, to cover the park, and maybe not get made as cops too quickly. The locals covered the beach areas, the ins and outs.

"Have to cover the beaches, the city areas in case he plans to lure her out. But he's inside."

The two cops on the entrance nodded her in.

"He wouldn't do this on one of the exterior rides." Roarke took her hand as he spoke, then just smiled as she started to tug it free. "Try to look less like a cop," he reminded her.

"Right."

"But we have dark rides as well."

That reminded her he had a financial interest in the park. In both parks.

"Dark rides?"

"Interior thrill rides. Murderer's Row, the Tunnel of Terror, Well of Woe, and Final Battle. All age twelve and up without an adult."

"A lot of screaming in those?"

"That's what they're designed for, after all."

"We'll start there."

"Let's see then. I believe it's this way to Murderer's Row."

She scanned crowds as they went, focusing on the younger set. Plenty of screams out here, too, she thought, and wondered why in the name of humanity people paid to scream.

No cams on the entrance of the ride where one-seater cars trundled into the mouth of a structure made to resemble a prison. Over the mouth, a man wearing the old-timey black-and-white-striped con suit bared his teeth in a maniacal grin and swung an axe.

"It's a prison break, you see," Roarke told her. "Escaped prisoners looking for blood and/or hostages."

"Single-rider cars. Not this. He needs to be with her, right with her. Not this one."

But she checked with the attendant anyway.

She tapped her earbud when Carmichael spoke. "Attendant at the Shoot 'Em Up Arcade thinks he saw him. Teenage attendant, says he noticed because of the trench, and it's too hot for one. Plus, he walked by a few times, alone, so the kid thought he was probably a pickpocket and kept an eye out."

"When did he spot him last?"

"He's not sure, but less than a half hour."

"Keep looking. That's good, it's good," she said to Roarke. "He's here, and less than thirty ago, he was alone. What's next?"

This time Roarke had a park map on his 'link. "Well of Woe."

The Well looked like a big, walled hole in the ground, and cars—room for three—descended at, to her eye, an insanely steep angle.

"What's the deal?"

"A bit like a series of escape rooms with various obstacles, dangers including giant insects, a fire-breathing dragon, booby traps, evil sorcerer. And not this," he realized. "If you get through one room successfully, you go into the next. If whoever's in there hasn't gotten through, you'd team up."

"Not this," she agreed, but checked before she stepped back from the echoes of screams and wild laughter.

"All right then, we're on to the Tunnel of Terror."

"Which is?" she asked as he led the way.

"Haunted, overrun with vampires, zombies, name your monster. If

I remember right, and it's been some time, the tracks circle and snake, climb up, then drop down abruptly into the dark. Various horror vid sound effects, perhaps the brush of skeletal fingers over your face, the red-eyes of a giant spider hurtling toward you in a sudden flash of light."

"Who thinks of stuff like that?"

"Well now, I had a bit to do with the design here, so I remember some of it. If you're paying for terror, the tunnel ought to provide it. Just over there."

Shortly after the Shoot 'Em Up attendant spotted Francis, Francis spotted the girl.

He had a plan.

Put away the 'link, bitch. Put it away.

She stopped a moment, a hand on one hip, and laughed. Then as he wished, she slid the 'link into her tiny purse.

When she started to walk again, he came up beside her, slid the needle in—delicately this time. Then swatted the air.

"Sorry! You had a bee land on you."

"I think it stung me. Shit!" Frowning, she rubbed at her arm.

"Are you allergic?" he asked, all concern, then looked at her face. "Oh, hey! Hi. It's Francis, from school?"

"Oh yeah, hi." Still frowning, she gave her arm another rub.

"Are you here by yourself?"

"No. I'm meeting some friends. They're getting on line at the Cyclone, so—"

"I was heading for that myself. It's such an iconic ride, isn't it? Have you had a good summer so far?"

"Uh, yeah. Actually pretty mag." She'd quickened her pace, obviously hoping to shake him off. Now, as the drug began its work, she slowed. "Um, you?"

"Absolutely! I've had a simply glorious summer, and it's only going to get better. Let's go this way."

"What?"

"This way."

She shrank back at first when he put his arm around her, then turned as he did.

"We're going to take a ride. You like rides, don't you, Delaney?"

"I like rides. I'm going to ride with my friends."

"I'm your friend now."

"I feel funny."

He slid his hand up from her waist, toward her breast. "You feel marvelous. You're excited to be with me."

At the tunnel, he got on line with her. Only about a dozen ahead of them, and that was fine. It gave him more time to prep her.

"We're going to get on this ride. It's what you want." He slid his hand over the curve of her ass. His heart pounded; his mouth went dry. "Like you want me to touch you. Say it, Delaney. Say, 'Francis, touch me.'"

"Francis, touch me."

"That's right." He put his mouth to her ear, and the scent of her nearly turned his knees to liquid. "When we get inside, in the dark, I'll touch you. You'll come with me, into the dark, and let me touch you wherever I want. We'll have intercourse. You want that. You want to have sex with me. Whisper that, in my ear."

She put her mouth to his ear. Compliant. "I want to have sex with you."

Then she looked around, her eyes glazed, confused. "I—I'm meeting my friends."

"No. I'm what you want, bitch, and don't forget it."

He kept her tight against him, and his head down as they held out their wrists for the scanner.

He nudged her into the car first, then sat close.

He'd chosen this ride for several reasons. The dark, the screams, the length—eight full minutes—and the small platform behind a wall of fake bones and severed heads.

In exactly two minutes after the ride began, he needed to get her out, behind the wall, on the platform, with its emergency exit just waiting for his escape when he'd finished with her.

The ride began with a shuddering descent. And the dark.

"Put your hand on my penis. Rub it. Rub it, whore."

He shoved up her top, yanked at her bra so he could, at last, at last, feel the female breast.

"You like that, don't you?"

"It hurts. You're hurting me."

"That's what you want. Say it. Say, 'Hurt me, Francis.'"

He didn't see the tears leaking out of her eyes. "Hurt me, Francis."

The screams began, and the crazed laughter, the groans and howls and moans.

Eve took one look at the Tunnel of Terror, and thought: Yes.

The dark, the size of the cars, the screams that echoed up.

She pushed her way to the attendant.

"This boy. Has he gotten on, with a girl?"

"Lady, I'm doing a job here."

She shoved her badge in his face. "So am I. Look at him. Have you seen him, with a girl?"

"The doof in the trench with the iced little chick? All over her." He shook his head. "Can't see why she's with a doof. They're on now."

"How long ago?"

"I dunno. Few minutes. A couple."

"Hit the lights. Stop the ride." While the attendant gaped, she tapped her earbud. "Tunnel of Terror. He's on it. He's got the girl. Move! I said hit the damn lights, now."

"But—"

Before Roarke could speak, she grabbed the attendant by the shirt.

"Lights, now, or I charge you with accessory to rape and attempted murder."

"Holy shit, I'm just doing a job."

He hit the lights and the brakes for the ride. Shouts of protest rose up.

Eve saw the steep, narrow platform beside the tracks, and started down.

"Cover the exits to this ride. Emergency exits. Call for MTs. He gave her something to get her on. Francis Bryce," she shouted, and swatted at whatever dangled from the ceiling. "This is the police. You're surrounded. Move away from the girl."

If they were too late to stop the rape, please God, let her be alive.

"There's a platform coming up on the left," Roarke told her. "Behind the wall of doom. First emergency exit."

He'd had to practically lift her out of the car, but excitement gave him strength. She didn't struggle, but went limp. And there were tears in her voice.

"It's dark. I can't see."

"Don't worry about it."

He took the penlight out of his pocket. It wouldn't do to step wrong.

"Move your whore ass!"

Filled with power, he shoved her onto the platform. Pulsing with power, he fell on her, then tore at her top.

"I want you to put my penis in your mouth, but we only have six minutes, so we'll just have intercourse."

He pushed her down. "No, that's not what they say, the ones you lie down for. We're going to fuck. I'm going to fuck you. Say it. Say: 'Fuck me, Francis. Fuck me hard.'"

"I—I don't want to."

He slapped her, first with the palm of his hand, then with the back. And that felt marvelous.

"But you will. Scream. I want you to scream while I take what you wouldn't give me. You won't fight me, you can't, but you can scream."

When she did, he went so hard he wondered he didn't implode.

Pushing up, he started unbuttoning the baggies. "Now say what I told you."

She choked out a sob.

And lights filled the tunnel.

Stunned, he dropped to his knees, slapped a hand over her mouth. "Shut up. Don't make a sound. If you do, I'll kill you."

Her eyes, so big and tawny, stared at him. His penis was so hard it hurt.

Just a glitch, he thought. A stupid glitch. It would go dark any second, and then.

"Francis Bryce, this is the police!"

Disbelief flooded him. His ears rang, and his breath began to hitch.

He fumbled in the trench for the second syringe, but he could hear them coming, closer. Closer.

As he had at the theater, he panicked. Throwing his body at the emergency exit, he ran.

Eve heard the weeping, soft and desolate under the shouted objections and catcalls of riders. And the shrill of the alarm on the emergency door.

She stepped over, skirted the wall.

Alive. One injection mark, so she should stay that way.

"You're okay. We're the police. Roarke, take the girl."

"He's got that second syringe. You bloody well mind my cop."

Then she was gone, out the door.

Roarke knelt down to the girl, who trembled and wept. "There now, darling, you're safe."

"Kill me if I make a sound," she whispered.

"He won't hurt you again. There's a promise."

Since he'd left his jacket behind and her shirt was in tatters, he took off his own. "Let's put this on now, all right? What's your name?"

"Del."

"There you are, Del. Can you walk?"

"I don't know."

"Well, never mind that," he said, and lifted her into his arms.

As he carried her out, she pressed her face to his shoulder and wept.

Her team hadn't converged on the exits before Eve shoved out.

But she saw Francis—the trench, the hair—heading toward the giant Ferris wheel in a limping run.

Hoping the girl had managed to kick him in the balls, she sprinted after.

"In pursuit. Suspect's running northeast from the tunnel ride to the Ferris wheel. Never mind. I've got him."

She supposed it rated as anti-climactic how easily she caught him after such a frustrating hunt. But she tackled him on the fairway, and actually heard him say, "Oof!" as he went down.

He kicked, humped his body, squirmed while people crowded around.

"Get back. Police. Move back!"

She started to reach for restraints, then pulled her stunner instead.

With one hand, she pressed it to the side of his neck. The other, she clamped on his wrist. He struggled to turn the syringe in his hand, the needle shining sharp in the festive lights.

"Drop it, you little bastard, or you'll get a jolt you won't forget."

"I wasn't finished!" But his fingers uncurled.

"Trust me, you're done."

"Sorry we weren't closer, LT."

She glanced up as she pulled Francis's hands behind his back.

"Don't touch that." She nodded toward the syringe. "I need to check if he's got a safety in his pocket somewhere."

"We had a bet going," Santiago told her. "If someone else spotted him, called for backup, who'd get there first."

She just stared at them as she clipped on the restraints.

"Had to call it a tie."

"Yeah." Carmichael confirmed it. "It was . . . Well, oh, my, my."

While Francis started to blubber, Eve looked back to where a bare-chested Roarke carried the girl wrapped in his shirt.

"Don't piss me off, Detective."

"Just admiring and envying your taste. Sir. Here come the medicals."

"Good. And here's the safety." She handed it to Santiago. "Be careful. The needle's probably coated, and you don't want what it's got. Francis Bryce, you're under arrest for the murder of Jenna Harbough, a human being, for the murder of Arlie Dillon, a human being. For the attempted murder of Kiki Rosenburg."

When she hauled him to his feet, he spat at her. "Bitch, you're all bitches!"

"Wow." She used the sleeve of her jacket to swipe the spittle from her cheek, and wasn't the least sorry to see he'd bashed his nose on the fall. It dribbled blood.

And his wig sat crooked now.

"That's called assaulting an officer, so we'll add that in. Also the attempted rape, also the use of a date-rape drug, and a whole crapload of other charges we'll make official when you're booked."

The eyes, she thought, even with tears streaming out of them, the eyes were wrong.

Yes, some were just born twisted.

"Meanwhile, you have the right to remain silent."

"Fuck you, whore!"

"Keep it up." She tapped her lapel. "Record's on. You have the right to legal counsel," she continued, unfazed, and read off the rest of the Revised Miranda.

"I need somebody to transport him to Central while we clean things up here."

"We got him," Jenkinson said.

Reineke nodded. "Be a pleasure. Come on, young sir. We'll escort you to your first cage in what will be a long line of them."

"I want to go home! You'd better get your hands off me! Do you know who my father is?"

Perp-walking him away, Jenkinson turned and grinned. "Who's your daddy?"

She would have laughed, but she spotted Roarke walking toward her. He wore a black tee, which would've been fine. Except for the park logo of the silly face with its wide, toothy grin.

"Are you kidding me?"

"She didn't want to let go of the shirt. McNab ran off and got it for me."

"It would be McNab."

"Peabody's with the girl in the ambulance. Delaney Brooke. Del. Whatever he used on her is wearing off."

"I need to talk to her." She turned. "Let's get that ride blocked off. We can use local sweepers to process, and . . ."

She trailed off at the look from Feeney. "Sorry, you know what to do. I'll be with the girl."

As she walked off, Feeney clapped his hands. "All right, boys and girls. Let's get things done."

Chapter Twenty-two

Eve walked over to the ambulance. Peabody sat inside with the victim, talking softly. The locals set up a perimeter to keep the crowd away, but three girls stood beside the ambulance in a kind of teary group hug.

Eve signaled to one of the MTs.

"Status?"

"We need to take her in, get a full workup, but she's stable, and she's lucid. BP's still a little high, but she's coming out of it. We can do a surface scan with the mobile."

His dark, rawboned face tightened. "He dosed her. Injection site, left biceps. Rohypnol, but other additives we need the lab to identify. She's got some bruises, but he didn't rape her. Didn't get the chance."

"Give me a few minutes with her."

"Go ahead. You got him, right? I got a kid her age."

"We got him."

When Eve climbed in, Peabody turned back to Del.

"Del, this is Lieutenant Dallas."

"You were there. The lights came on all of a sudden, then you were there. You went after Francis."

"That's right. He's in custody now." Pretty brunette, Eve noted, about sixteen, with brown eyes still on the glassy side. "He told you his name?"

"No. Maybe, but I mean he didn't have to. I know him from school. His hair's different, but I know him from school."

"You know him? Did you meet him here?"

"Not on purpose. He's creepy. Even before this, he's just creepy."

Her gaze shifted to the open doors of the ambulance. "Oh!" And reached out a hand.

Roarke climbed in, sat, took it.

"You saved me. He saved me." Her eyes filled as she leaned into Roarke. "I couldn't stop him. Francis. He was going to rape me, and I couldn't stop him. He tore my shirt and squeezed my boobs so hard. He made me put my hand on him, down there. You know. And say things. I couldn't stop him. It was like watching myself and screaming inside, but doing whatever he said even though I didn't want to."

She dropped her head. "He said like come with me, and I did."

"Del, none of this is your fault. None of it. He dosed you, used a date-rape drug on you. This is not your fault."

She stared at Peabody. "You're sure?"

"Abso-poso," Peabody said, and got a smile.

"Can you tell me what happened?" Eve brought Del's attention back to her. "As much as you remember."

"I can remember it all because it's like I said. Like I was standing and watching him and me. I was walking toward the Cyclone. That's where my friends were waiting, and I felt this pinch or sting in my arm. Then Francis was right there, beside me, waving a hand. He said I'd had a bee on me."

She went through it, with more detail than Eve could have hoped for.

As she did, Del gripped Roarke's hand with her left, clutched his shirt around her with her right.

"You caught him. I heard them say you caught him."

"We caught him. We'll need to talk with you again," Eve told her.

"They said I needed to go to the hospital even though I feel mostly all right now. My parents are coming. But my friends . . ."

"The three girls outside? If you want, we can arrange transportation for them, to the hospital."

"Really? That would be mag. He . . . he won't come back to school, will he?"

"No."

"You've got my card, Del, if you just need to talk. If your parents have any questions, they can contact me or Lieutenant Dallas. I'm going to go take care of getting that transpo."

"Thanks, Detective Peabody. Thank you for catching him," she said to Eve. "I knew he could be mean. I could see it in the way he looked at me, or other girls, sometimes. But I didn't know he could do this."

She leaned into Roarke. "Thank you for saving me."

"It was my very great pleasure." When Roarke kissed her hand, Del's eyes went from a little glassy to very dreamy.

By the time she got back to Central, Eve didn't expect to see Jenkinson and Reineke.

But there they were, playing cards at Jenkinson's desk.

"You're off duty," she told them.

"Got that. It's why I'm crushing Reineke at gin."

"Had a lucky streak. Mine's coming due."

"Prisoner secured?"

"Oh yeah." Jenkinson tipped back in his chair. "Took his one call on the way in. To his father. Cried like a man-baby."

"All trembly with it," Reineke added.

"Terrible mistake, police roughed him up, under arrest. He had the call on mute so we couldn't hear what the father had to say, but he's on his way. Kid got all smirky after the call. His father's coming, and he'll fix our asses good."

"Golly. Now I'm all trembly."

Jenkinson snorted out a laugh at Eve. "Getting the best lawyer money can buy. We're all going to pay, but the bitch who bloodied his nose—that would be you, boss."

"Yes, I am that bitch."

"She's going to pay more. He lost some of that . . . would you call it bravado, partner?"

"I would. Bravado."

"He lost that during booking, and when we closed the cage door. Juvie section, considering, but that won't be where he ends up."

"No, it won't. Good work. Now somebody get Roarke a shirt without a face on it. Then go home. I'll write this up and wait for the father."

"You ain't obliged to wait, Dallas. Past midnight now," Jenkinson pointed out. "His old man can wait until morning."

"Yeah, but I want a sense of things there before we take on the kid tomorrow."

Plus, she had her second—or maybe it was third—wind, she thought as she walked into her office. And straight to coffee.

She sat and started her report, one that would fill in the details and expand on her brief update to her commander.

Suspect in custody. Victim alive and stable.

She'd made headway when Roarke walked in wearing a gray T-shirt with NYPSD across the chest.

"And this is better?"

"Miles. You don't have to wait through this."

"I'm sticking, and apparently Peabody and McNab are as well. They've gone down to the Eatery to get something that passes for a meal. You're going to eat as well, and so, by God, am I. I suppose, considering the time and place, it's pizza."

She decided not to mention she'd had a slice—a homemade slice—that afternoon.

She double decided when the scent of it hit her very empty stomach.

"We've got at least an hour," Roarke told her.

"How do you know?"

"I deduced given the circumstances, Dr. Nolan Bryce would book a private shuttle in Vegas, and do so quickly. And indeed, found one booked in his name. It should land in New York in about fifty minutes. He's booked a car service to bring him to Central."

Eve got up, sat on the floor. "This is where we eat when I have company."

He didn't bother to sigh, just sat and set the pizza between them. "You're never going to accept a bigger office, are you?"

"Nope."

"Ah well, this one suits you, doesn't it?"

Riding on her second or third wind, she smiled at him. "Look at you, master of the universe, sitting on the floor of a cop shop, eating pizza, and wearing a borrowed shirt."

"And all for love."

She reached out for his hand. "When this is wrapped, it's you and me. Sun, sand, sea, and sex."

"I want the sex in or on all of the first three, and elsewhere."

"I'm in." Munching on pizza, she looked up at her board. "He wanted sex, but not the intimacy, the unity, the sharing of bodies, minds, certainly not hearts. He'd have killed her after, because that—destroying, eliminating, punishing—that's the main thing. He hates them, the girls. Women, females. He feels superior to the boys—men, males—but he hates the girls."

"He'd have hurt this one. Del. Before he used that second syringe, he'd have hurt her. That's what he is. She? An attractive vessel for his hate and rage."

"Mira will sort through the whys—I've sent her a request to observe when I have him in the box." She shrugged. "But the whys are pretty clear. What he made Del say and do, allow him to do? He's entitled. He's better and smarter, comes from money and privilege, and he's psychotic. They should all do what he wants, when he wants. If they don't? They deserve to be forced, and they deserve to die."

"Not yet seventeen," Roarke murmured. "And planning to kill his father."

"It puts the money in his hands. The power of it. He doesn't love. He's incapable of genuine feeling. So I want a sense of the father. Didn't he see? If not, why not?

"Nobody's using Interview, so I'm going to put the father in there. I want to set it up. I want to show him what we found in that lab, on those comps, in that journal."

"Are you thinking of charging him? Neglect, accessory?"

"I want to get a sense," she repeated.

He helped her set up as she wanted in Interview A, then stepped back as Peabody and McNab returned. She laid out her strategy.

Her comm signaled.

"Send him up," Eve responded. "He's here. Alone. I wondered if he'd talk a lawyer into coming in with him. Peabody, you can handle the e's?"

Peabody shot two thumbs up.

"Any trouble there," McNab put in, "just signal. We're in Observation."

When the men walked off, Eve laid down her files, unsealed evidence boxes. Then she went out to wait for the elevator.

When it opened, Bryce rushed out. He wore khakis, a pale blue golf shirt, and looked both harried and stressed.

"Dr. Bryce. Lieutenant Dallas."

"I want to see my son. I want to see Francis."

"He's locked down for the night. I can arrange for you to see him at eight tomorrow morning."

"He's not staying in a cell overnight! I'll pay his bail until this horrible mistake is corrected."

"Dr. Bryce, he won't have a bail hearing until tomorrow, and my experience tells me bail will be denied. Do you understand the charges against your son?"

"I don't understand anything!" Against a golden summer tan, his light green eyes glittered with anger and fear.

"If you'll step in here, we'll explain it to you."

Bryce drew himself up, a tall man who hadn't passed his height to his son. "Francis is only sixteen. You can't lock him in a cell."

"He's charged with two counts of first-degree murder, one count of attempted murder, one count of sexual assault and attempted rape."

"That's just ridiculous. Francis is—"

"Also charged with multiple counts of creating, possessing, and using illegal substances, lethal substances, on others without their consent. Please come with me."

She led him to Interview. "This is my partner, Detective Peabody. Have a seat, Dr. Bryce. Francis has an exceptional knowledge of chemistry, correct?"

"He's brilliant, but that hardly—"

"Please sit." Eve did so herself. "When's the last time you were in his home lab?"

Bryce dragged a hand through his thick mane of sun-streaked brown hair, and sat. "It's his space. Privacy is very important to Francis. I don't want to get into this, except to say his mother developed an addiction."

"To heroin."

"Yes." When he folded his hands on the table, his knuckles went white. "She wasn't able to conquer that addiction, and eventually it killed her.

When we were separated and early in our divorce, she would bribe or bully her way past the nanny, and take things, valuables, from the house, from Francis's room, to sell. Eventually, I replaced the nannies with a droid, as they can't be bribed or bullied. Privacy is important to Francis, and it's little to ask after what he dealt with."

"I see. Peabody, let's give Dr. Bryce a look at his son's home lab."

She brought up the recording, and as planned zoomed in on the glass-walled cabinet. Under the summer tan, Bryce went very pale.

"You'd recognize the names of these substances. Some are labeled by your company."

"I—he shouldn't have these. He—I—he must have taken them from the lab. He occasionally interns there. I'd never permit him to take these, to experiment with these. I'll see they're removed, immediately."

"Already done, and in evidence. You see the equipment on the work-station? And do you recognize the wrapped cakes, the molds?"

Now the pallor took on a gray tinge. "Oh my God. Oh God. Is he using? I've never, I swear to you, seen a single sign. I know the signs. I lived with them."

"There's no evidence he'd used illegals on himself. There is quite a bit of evidence that he's created a lethal substance which he's used on others.

"Show him the formulas, Peabody. Side by side. On the left is the for-mula from your son's lab computer. On the right, the tox reports on Jenna Harbough, age sixteen, and Arlie Dillon, age seventeen. Your son injected Jenna, without her knowledge or consent, on Saturday night, and Arlie, without hers, on Sunday night. They died, painfully, within minutes."

"He wouldn't. There has to be some mistake." But Bryce's breath had quickened. "He couldn't."

"You haven't heard about the murders, Dr. Bryce?"

"I was at a medical conference until yesterday. I was taking a few days off after . . . He didn't want to go. He rarely does."

"So he stayed home alone."

"He's almost seventeen, and he's never . . . Another year, he'll be in college. He's never given me a moment's trouble. He excels in school, has already been accepted by ten universities. He's quiet, prefers his own company, but . . ."

Eve took the baggies, trench, wig, shades, shoes from an evidence box. "Do you recognize any of these?"

"No. Those aren't his." Relief flooded his voice, his face. "You've mistaken him for someone else. Francis wouldn't wear anything like that. I actually bought him pants like that a couple of times, pants like a lot of them wear. He returned them. He's a bit fussy about his clothes. I ended up hiring a personal shopper, as he didn't like what I'd choose, and disliked shopping.

"He's fussy," Bryce repeated. "And yes, somewhat socially awkward. But you're talking about murder."

She'd gotten a sense, Eve decided, of a father who didn't know his son. Of a father who trusted and indulged his son because he didn't see him for what he was.

But he would, she thought, and continued.

"He attempted to inject Kiki Rosenburg on Monday night, but was unsuccessful. She only got a very small dose. We have witnesses who saw him wearing these, at the scene of Jenna Harbough's murder, at the scene of the attack on Kiki Rosenburg."

She paused, just a beat, to let that sink in.

"And these are what he was wearing tonight when he dosed another girl, this time with a date-rape drug of his own making. He had that empty syringe and a second loaded with the lethal dose in his possession when he was captured."

"This isn't my son. Francis is well-mannered, well-educated. He's quiet, studious."

"Notes, Peabody, on Jenna and Arlie. You'll see he chose these two girls at random, though he'd worked out a very careful plan. He didn't know them. The photos, copies of media reports, his personal notes, were added the day after each was killed."

The relief had died. Even the fear had faded against a kind of desperate disbelief.

"You're making him into a monster."

"I'm not making him into anything. I'm giving you facts and evidence."

"You're telling me my boy's a monster. He's—he's never been violent. Wouldn't even play sports. He's shy, but always polite. How can he be a monster? How could he do these things you're telling me he did?"

"I can only tell you he did them, and planned to do more. Journal entry, Peabody. This is from the tablet taken from his lab."

Bryce seemed to shrink into himself as he read. "But—he wanted to kill me? That can't be. For money? It can't—we've never had a hard word between us. What can I do?"

Bryce covered his face with his hands. "What have I done? What can I do?"

Eve didn't have the answers.

"You didn't show him all of it," Peabody pointed out.

"I didn't need to. He'd had enough. This wasn't neglect, but indulgence. He saw what he wanted to see, what Francis wanted him to see, and trusted his son. Go home, get some sleep. We'll give him his eight A.M. visitation, give the lawyer his time, get Mira and Reo in here. Say ten for Interview. Just be here in time to prep for it."

"Can do. Home, sleep, morning prep. We saved the girl, Dallas, and the others who could've come after."

"We'll drop you," Roarke said as he came out of Observation with McNab.

"Actually, I'd like the walk. A little fresh air, some unwind time. You up for that?" she asked McNab.

"As long as it's with you. We'll take the boxes back to Evidence, Dallas."

"Thanks."

When they'd hauled the boxes out, she secured the Interview room, flagged it as in use.

With the first, second, and third wind depleted, she fell asleep in the car, and only woke when Roarke lifted her out.

"Thanks. Don't let me oversleep, okay? I have to set all this up for tomorrow, write up the interview with Bryce."

"Not to worry. I'm rearranging things and going in with you. I need to see the end of it. And, as foolish as it may sound, I want to stand witness for Del."

It didn't sound foolish at all.

"She got to you, didn't she?"

"She did, yes."

When he set her on the bed where the cat sprawled, she reached for her boots. "How about you rearrange and I arrange, and after I cook this little psycho in the box, and I will, we take off for the island and those four *s*'s?"

"Done."

She stripped down, got into bed. And was asleep again before Roarke put his arm around her and the cat curled up at her back.

In the morning after he programmed omelets—loaded with ham and cheese and, maybe like a kiss on the cheek, no spinach—he gestured to her closet.

"I have a suggestion. You'll enrage and intimidate him just by being you, but why not pile on a bit?"

"I'm listening."

"T-shirt. You have excellent, leanly muscled arms. A vest. Let's show off the weapon as well as the arms. Go with straight-leg pants, ankle boots with laces."

"Combat ready."

"In a sense."

She looked at him in his black T-shirt and jeans. "And you with no suit."

"I'm counting on you to do that cooking. No need for a suit on the island."

"And the meeting you took before dawn?"

"I'm the boss." He shrugged. "I wear what I like."

True enough, she thought, and went in to peruse her closet. Black and white, she decided. The absence of color made a statement, too. Black pants, thick-soled laced boots, white tee, black leather vest.

"A woman of power and authority. He'll detest you," Roarke said when she came out.

"Counting on it."

She strapped on her weapon, grabbed the rest. "Let's do this."

In the car, she contacted APA Cher Reo.

"He's got the money for a solid lawyer."

Reo, who'd somehow worked her fluffy blond hair into a short, stylish braid, nodded. "And he's got one. Marshall Derwood. He's very good, and he's also not even a little bit stupid. I've spent the last hour going through the evidence, the statements, and I'm not finished. Holy mama, Dallas. Derwood will know we've got this locked."

"He could try for insanity."

"He may try, but he won't get it. I just got off with Mira, and she agrees. She'll factor in what she observes in Interview, but with what we have, he doesn't reach the bar of legal insanity. He certainly will try to deal down given Bryce's age, but—"

"No."

"And agreed. Two girls the same age are dead, two others were attacked. He spent a couple years on this so-called project. The boss is in full agreement. He's tried as an adult. He's a stone-cold killer, and I don't give a skinny rat's ass for his feels about how the girls won't bang him.

"You play him," Reo added, "and we'll lock his teen-killer ass away."

"There's a deal. See you at Central."

When they got there and she walked into the bullpen, she paused. She didn't even let Jenkinson's frosted pink-and-blue-cupcake tie bother her.

"Santiago, Carmichael?"

"Caught one, about four hundred hours. Pity the saps."

She actually did. "Pass it to them if I'm not around when they come in. Good work on the Bryce investigation."

"Are you taking him this morning?" Baxter asked.

"Ten, Interview A."

"Fry him up, boss." Jenkinson grinned. "Fry him up good." Then he pointed at Roarke. "No suit?"

"After I fry him up," Eve said, "I'm taking a couple of days."

"You got it coming."

"Detective Sergeant, after we fry him up, take Detective Peabody off the roll for the rest of the week. On call, off the roll."

"Yes, sir. She's got it coming, too."

Eve went into her office, organized her thoughts, put more files together, then sent a just-arrived Peabody down for evidence boxes.

Reo, with the braid and in a slim red dress, breezed in.

"Coffee." Without waiting for an answer, she crossed to the AutoChef. "I just had a brief conversation with Marshall Derwood. It appears Dr. Bryce had an even briefer one with his son. I don't know what was said, but the doctor was visibly shaken. I saw that for myself before Derwood asked him to leave us alone."

"He saw the monster."

"That may be. Derwood broached diminished capacity. Sixteen, frontal lobe's not fully formed, mother was an addict, OD'd, busy father, bullied in school."

"Gosh, this is breaking my heart. Of course he had to kill those girls."

"Right." Reo eased down on the corner of the desk, a better bet than the ass-biting visitor's chair. "He had to try, that's his job. And I called bullshit, which is mine. He tried his first deal. Juvie, mandatory counseling, five years' probation upon release."

"Oh please."

Reo batted her pretty eyes.

"I believe I said about the same in about the same dismissive tone. His next move will be to try for twenty, on-planet, pointing out that the boy—and he'll make sure to call him that—will have spent more time in prison than he's currently spent alive."

"Two girls aren't alive, two more were attacked and traumatized."

"Which is why there'll be no such deal. He knows this. He has to try. He knows I'll be observing, so he may pause the interview to take that swing. He will miss.

"I can't say what the father's told him, what the son's told him. But you'll do what you do, then I'll do what I do."

"He may pause to take that swing, but I know Francis Bryce, and before I'm finished, he's going to admit to all of it. On record."

She pushed up as she heard footsteps. She knew Nadine's stride.

And when the reporter stepped in, along with Jake and, damn it, Quilla, she simply said, "No."

"I've already reported on the arrest. It's all over the media—along with vids taken by several civilians who witnessed your takedown."

Nadine held up a hand for peace. "I anticipate you're going to take him into Interview this morning. I'm not going to ask you for a one-on-one—though I wouldn't turn it down. We just need to be here."

"You can't observe." Eve pointed to each in turn. "Civilian, reporter, minor."

"We're not asking that, either. We just need to be here. I know you can kick us out. I'm asking you not to."

Eve rubbed the back of her neck. "Go down to the Eatery or somewhere. You'll get word when we're done. You were helpful," she said to Quilla.

342   J. D. ROBB

"I was?"

"Yes. You get your interview in Homicide."

Quilla pumped both fists in the air. "Score!"

"When Detective Sergeant Jenkinson tells you it's convenient. I stand for Jenna now, Jake. And for all of them. You stand down now."

He nodded. "He's really a kid?"

"Age doesn't matter with monsters."

"Come on, gang." Reo began herding them out. "Dallas has to do her thing so I can do mine. Quilla, I love that shade of purple in your hair."

"You'd look mag in it."

"Maybe next vacation I'll try it. Gotta look serious in court."

And in Interview, Eve thought, frying up a monster.

Chapter Twenty-three

F rancis didn't wear orange well, and the shadows under his eyes made it seem all the more wrong.

Beside him, his lawyer looked sharp and savvy, golden brown skin, a wave of curly black hair, a serious dark gray suit.

On the other side of Francis, his father looked pale, exhausted, and miserable.

"Record on," Eve began, and watched that hateful rage fill Francis's eyes as she read the necessary into the record.

"Dr. Bryce, as I'm sure your son's attorney has informed you, you are allowed in this interview due to your son's age. However, you will be required to leave if you interfere with this interview."

"As you state, Lieutenant, my client is a minor, a child, and should be treated as such."

"You want to be babied, Francis?" Her voice was a verbal sneer. "You came to the wrong place. Your client had the skill, the capacity, the intellect, and the murderous purpose to cook heroin, from the poppies on."

She tossed crime scene photos on the table.

"To then devise a lethal formula. Peabody."

Peabody brought up the formula, on-screen.

"This is an entry from Francis Bryce's computer, from his lab," Peabody said. "Along with the tox reports on Jenna Harbough, Arlie Dillon, Kiki Rosenburg, and the contents of the second syringe on his person after the attack on Delaney Brooke."

"As you see, they match," Eve continued.

"This is a tragedy for all involved. My client's mother was an addict. The boy spent his first formative years living with her addiction, then her death from an overdose. Clearly, this trauma affected him emotionally, mentally."

"Want to hide behind Mommy now, Francis?"

"Please direct your questions to me, Lieutenant. My client isn't required to speak."

"I bet he's got a lot to say though. He likes to think he's so much smarter than anyone else. So much better."

"I know," Francis whispered. "I know I am."

"Quiet now." Derwood patted Francis on the arm, and was shrugged away.

"Not as smart as he thinks." Eve spoke directly to the lawyer. "Hell, we made his stupid shoes inside hours. Not strong enough to boost himself out of a bathroom window."

At that Peabody brought up the wall with scuff marks.

"Worse, they're doofus shoes. No self-respecting kid, with the money, would wear them. Add the cheap baggies. What did the first witness call him, Peabody? The one who saw him walking off the dance floor at Club Rock It after he jabbed that lethal dose into Jenna Harbough?"

"Dooser. It's a combination of *dick* and *loser*."

Eve kept her attention on the lawyer, but she heard Francis's breath suck in, then quicken.

"Kids noticed the doofus, dooser clothes. His big brain wasn't smart enough to dress like a normal teenager, and he was too physically weak to get out of the club clean.

"But he did this first."

Eve put Jenna's crime scene photo on the table, angled it so Francis could see.

"His early childhood—"

"Jenna had an early childhood, too. She'll never be an adult. Neither will Arlie Dillon. He made sure they saw him. After he stuck that needle in them, he made sure they saw him. Because girls don't look at him. I mean, why would they? But he made sure these two did before their short life ended by his hand.

"You want me to feel sorry for him because his mother was a junkie. Bullshit." She slapped Arlie's photo on the table. "Tell that to her mother. He plotted, he planned, and it didn't matter who they were as long as they were pretty teenage girls. The kind of girls who wouldn't look twice at him, avoided him, wouldn't give him what he wanted."

"Lieutenant, we intend to engage a top child psychiatrist to examine the boy."

"Fine with me. We've got our top shrink observing this interview."

Jerking, Francis looked up at the camera. "I told you no! I told you no psychiatrists, no therapists. I said no!"

"Francis." Bryce reached out to him, jolted back when his son slapped his hand away.

"I said no!" Rhythmically, Francis beat his fists on the table. "I will not have it! I have rights!"

You see the monster now, Eve thought. And he terrifies you.

"We're trying to help you."

"Help me? Oh, that's rich! If this is your idea of help, I can help myself, thank you *very* much for nothing! This is the best you can do?" He jerked a thumb toward Derwood. "This mealymouthed excuse for an attorney? 'The boy' this, 'the boy' that. I'm a man!"

He turned on Derwood. "You're letting this bitch run all over you when you should be filing charges against her for police brutality. She bloodied my nose, bruised my wrist." Now he turned on his father.

"I spent the night in a cell like an animal, and what do you do? You leave me there, then you come in and start on how I have issues, how I'm sick, how you love me and you'll do everything you can to get me help. And you hire this idiot? Get out, *Derwood.* I'm smarter than you on my worst day. I can handle this idiot female myself."

"Francis." Derwood spoke with enviable patience. "You're understandably overwrought. We'll suspend this interview while we—"

The fists banged again.

"I said get out. Get out, *Derwood.* Do you have a problem comprehending a simple, declarative sentence? Let's try another. You're fired."

"I do not have a problem with comprehension, but your father hired me."

"He can get out, too. Love me? Oh yes, yes, that's rich. You love having the sluts fall all over you. Sluts just like my mother."

"Francis!" Bryce's look spoke of genuine shock. "I never brought a woman home. You didn't like it. I never—"

"But you got hot and sweaty with plenty of them, didn't you? I'm not stupid! They'd spread out for you because of how you look, and because you have money. I should've killed you first."

"Don't speak again," Derwood snapped. "Lieutenant—"

"You're useless," Francis said, his tone deliberately bored. "I said get out. I can file for emancipation, and I will. I'll have your money one day, *Dad.* And all that comes with it. Then all the years I said, 'yes, sir,' 'no, sir,' and pretended to be fascinated by your work—which doesn't hold a candle to mine—will be worth it. But now, I'm going to say what I've wanted to as long as I can remember. Go to hell."

Bryce got to his feet. His body shook. "You're my son, and I love you. And now I'm terribly, terribly afraid you have to pay for your choices, your actions."

He looked down at the photos. "You have to pay. I'll help you, all I can. All you allow, but you have to pay for what you've done."

Francis feigned a yawn. "Sorry, did you say something? I wasn't listening."

"Lieutenant, you have parental permission to continue the interview. Mr. Derwood no longer represents my son. Mr. Derwood, please come with me."

"Dr. Bryce, there are things I can do to—"

"No. No, I don't think there are." Grief lived in every word. "And if there are, I don't believe you should. Please, come with me."

Derwood got up. "Francis, you're making a mistake."

He aimed those dead eyes at the lawyer. "I don't make mistakes."

"Dr. Bryce and legal counsel, former, exiting Interview."

Eve shifted, smiled at Francis. "So."

"Fuck you. I don't know why I never used that word before last night. It's a fine, flexible Anglo-Saxon word."

"I'm fond of it myself. Let's start with Jenna Harbough."

"I don't know who that is." He widened his eyes, did his best to fill them with innocence. "I've never seen her before. I've never been in that club you talked about. I found those shoes yesterday, and I thought maybe I'd look chill in them."

"For somebody who everybody says is so smart, that's a dumbass play, Francis. The clerk who sold them to you remembers you."

"You must be lying. Police can and do lie. Store clerks don't remember some kid buying shoes."

"I thought you were a man," Peabody commented.

"Oh, I am."

"Well, the clerk remembers you," Eve told him, "kid or man, and your fancy Stuben loafers, with tassels. The button-down shirt, the dress pants." Eve shook her head. "Really, Francis, wearing old man designer shoes to buy cheap kicks? Makes you stand out."

"I'm hardly the only individual in the city who has Stuben loafers."

"With tassels," Peabody added. "And you're probably the only teenager who wears them to shop at L&W."

"Well, it's called Losers and Wheezes for a reason." Eve smiled at the quick, hot flush that burned over Francis's face.

"Didn't know that, did you? Where'd you get the wig? MHF? Major Hair Fail?"

"I found it, all of it. I went for a walk and I found this bag with all of it in there. I wondered how it would look."

"Handy it was all your sizes."

He sneered at Peabody. "It was. That's why I wanted to see how it all looked."

"And you put all that gear on last night before you went to Coney Island to kill Delaney."

"I know her. We go to school together. Why would I hurt Delaney? We were lab partners once. I don't know what happened." He widened his eyes again, but in them lived the vicious. "I think I had a kind of breakdown. I put the outfit on and the wig. And I was like someone else. The next thing I remember is there were all these lights, and people. And then you knocked me down."

"And the syringes just happened to be in your pockets?"

He shrugged. "I don't remember."

"You really are stupid."

"I said fuck you. My IQ is easily the sum of both of yours combined."

"Monumentally stupid, plus short, dopey-looking, bad hair. You got it all. No wonder you can't get laid."

"Shut your mouth, bitch."

"Guess what, you pissant, you're not in charge here. I am. I'm in charge. I have the authority."

She got to her feet, leaned in close. "I'm in charge. You're free to shut up if you want while I tell you what you are. Loser. I don't add the *dick* because I don't have to look at it to know it's very, very tiny. Here's a tip. Jerking off constantly won't make it bigger."

"Get out. You're a whore. Just another whore trying to emasculate men, pretending she can do a man's job. I don't want a whore cop talking to me."

"I'm in charge. You're nothing here. Nothing out there, either. Nothing anywhere. Girls don't go for the nothings like you. Those bitches, those stupid bitches."

She rounded the table, then shoved the photos closer under his face. "They'd barely look at you, hardly speak to you. And when they did, they'd look at you with disgust, speak to you with pity. Pity, from them? When you're their superior."

"I am. I am superior."

"You deserved their attention!" Eve whipped out the words. "Their respect. Hell, their adoration. But those whores, bitches, sluts ignored you, rejected you. Again and again. You wanted inside them, and they wouldn't even look at you."

"I have a right. I'm entitled."

"You have a right to their attention. You're entitled to do what you want with their bodies."

"It hurt and angered you," Peabody put in, "they wouldn't give you what you're entitled to. But with your intellect and skill, your dedication to the project, you found a way to take what you deserved."

"Women are weak," he said simply. "But conniving creatures nonetheless. Men are stronger, physically, mentally, certainly emotionally, to the female. Though they manipulate and maneuver to attempt to make us less, we're superior. I'm vastly superior to those moronic jocks, the leather-clad idiots those weak-minded tramps lie down with."

"You hate them, those weak-minded tramps," Eve said. "But you want them. Want them, but despise them. Jenna, out there shaking her ass on the dance floor, showing herself off. Asking for it, wasn't she? You made her pay for making you want what you hate. You had to make her pay."

"Get the hell away from me."

"How did it feel? You couldn't jab your cock in her, but with the needle you could penetrate her. Did that get you off, Francis? And knowing you'd be one of the last people she saw. No more shaking her ass, showing herself off. Did knowing that get you hard?

"How did it feel?"

"Amazing! Vindicating! Orgasmic! Everything I'd hoped and more. They connive to make us desire them, then they refuse, they walk away. But she saw me. She felt me. Then I was the one who walked away."

Eve flicked a glance at the camera before she walked back around the table.

"Did you intend to kill her?"

"Are you an idiot? Of course. She saw me."

"And Arlie Dillon."

"She let that brainless moron put his hands all over her. Oooh, a wasp, a wasp!" He threw back his head and laughed. "I almost stayed to watch her die, but that would have been a mistake. I don't make mistakes."

"The theater was a mistake."

"It was not. It was an unforeseen complication, and it only pushed me further along my timetable."

"To Coney Island."

"Do you know how much time, skill, exacting work it took to create the proper formula? Of course you don't. How could you? I deserved a reward for all my time, my work, my focus, my dedication."

"You deserved to rape Delaney Brooke."

He let out a sigh that spoke of mild annoyance.

"In the first place, rape is a lie perpetuated by women to deny men their right to intercourse. Secondly, it wouldn't have been rape, even by your skewed definition. She was compliant. And I didn't know Delaney would be there."

"It didn't matter who you raped. Raped, Francis. It's rape when you inject someone with a drug that takes away their free will."

"You can call it rape. That's just a word women use to control men's natural instincts. She let me touch her—she told me to. She touched me. She told me to fuck her. You can call it whatever you want."

"And I do. So does the law. You had the second syringe. Did you intend to kill her with it?"

"She saw me! How did you get to be a lieutenant when you're so slow and stupid? On your back, like the rest of your kind. Legs spread, whoring to take a man's job."

He beat his fists again. "I was nearly there. You spoiled it all! I had her on her back, and I was so hard! She was ready, all soft and weepy.

"You took that from me. I'll kill you for it one day."

"If I had a dollar for every time some schmuck says that to me, I'd have a bunch of million dollars. You, Peabody?"

"Maybe about half a million. You've been on the job longer, and it adds up."

"Long enough to know Francis here has confessed, on record, to murder, attempted murder, attempted rape, and so on."

"So what?" He shrugged, and with it could almost have passed for a normal teenager.

Except for the eyes.

"Wait . . . let me rephrase. So the fuck what? I'm sixteen. I'll be out in less than two years. I have the first hit of my trust fund coming to me at eighteen, too. I can go where I want, do what I want.

"I believe I'll take a gap year. I'd have earned it."

Keep right on thinking that, Eve decided.

"In that case, let's take it back, go over some details. Science is all about the details."

"As if you know anything about science."

"You'll educate me. Want a drink for this round, Francis? A soda?"

"I don't drink that swill. Spring water, flat, room temperature."

"Peabody, would you mind? I'll take some swill. Peabody, exiting Interview."

"I will kill you." He spoke matter-of-factly. "Not right away after I get out. I'll want that downtime first. I'll have money so I'll have all the whores I want. You won't know when I'm coming, or how I'll come. Maybe I'll keep you alive awhile, maybe fuck you first. If I'm in the mood."

"Do you think that scares me? My cat's got a bigger dick than you."

He went very white, then very red. "I'll kill you very, very slowly. I'll make an experiment out of it. Out of you."

"Keep talking. It's really going to help at your sentencing hearing."

"Peabody, reentering Interview," Peabody announced. "Water, flat." She set the tube in front of Francis, then a tube of Pepsi in front of Eve before sitting with her Diet Pepsi.

And reading the room, the waves of hate, the waves of disgust, said, "Did I miss something?"

"Nothing important. Okay, Francis, why don't we start with the poppies?"

It took a very long time. He had a great deal to say, and finally someone to hear it. However many times he threatened her or Peabody during the extensive interview, he showed pride with it. Pride in what he called his accomplishments.

When they came out, Eve saw Bryce sitting on a bench, his head in his hands.

"I'll talk to him. Let's get Francis back in a cage."

"We've got that." Baxter and Trueheart stepped out. "The boy and I'll take him down. Both of you have spent enough time with him. We were in Observation for a while."

"Appreciate it." She walked down to the bench. "Dr. Bryce."

He looked up at her with eyes red-rimmed and desolate. "Is it over?"

"This part is. You should go home. There's nothing you can do here. Is there someone I can contact for you?"

"No. No one right now. I've sat here while he was in that room, and I've thought of a thousand ways I could have done things differently. A thousand things from the time he was born until I walked out of that room today."

She sat beside him. "Dr. Bryce. In my experience with someone like Francis? Nothing you'd have done differently would have changed him."

"I shouldn't have let him lock so many doors."

"Maybe not. But he'd have found another way."

"When his mother died . . . When I had to tell him his mother died, he never shed a tear. At the time, I was relieved. I thought, she's been out of his life for so long now, he doesn't feel the loss. But I see now, that was a warning of what he lacks inside."

He shuddered out a breath.

"Now I think . . . Those girls. Their families. What he's done to them. Lieutenant. Oh God."

He feels the loss, Eve thought when he looked at her. And always would.

"I know he has to pay for what he did, but I have to try to help him. He's my son, my only child, and I don't know how to begin to help him."

"Dr. Mira. She has a sterling reputation as a psychiatrist. You don't have to take my word on that. You can look her up. She'll be holding an interview with him in the next day or two. She'll talk to you."

"All right. I never saw it in him until today. I never saw it."

"He didn't let you see it. Can I arrange transportation for you?"

"No. No, thank you. I'm going to walk awhile, then call for a car."

Shoulders tight, mind exhausted, she sat where she was a moment before sending Nadine a text.

Done. Full confession. Tell Jake Jenna got justice. I
need to write it up, then I need to get away from this for
a while. Jenkinson might give you a one-on-one. Don't
ask me now.

I won't. We're all wrung out. Dallas, thanks. From
all of us, thanks.

She got up, walked to Reo and Mira.

"That was difficult," Mira began. "It's difficult to see such an active psychopath inside a young body. A challenge to find the key to unlock the psychopath for all to see.

"You and Peabody did an exceptional job in there."

"Difficult to see, yeah. But the job was easier than I expected. He's educated, he's got intellect, but his arrogance, his narcissism blocks any actual smarts. It was never about getting laid. He could have paid for a fake ID, hit on a street LC. It was about hurting them, and showing them he could take what he wanted. And using his famed intellect to do it."

"Yes."

"You and Peabody made my job easy," Reo told her. "We're going to push for consecutive life terms, off-planet. Three consecutive life terms. And we're going to get it. That's a very dangerous individual."

She gave Eve's arm a squeeze. "I'm going to go start pushing. And you should find a horizontal space and get some sleep."

"As soon as possible. Thanks."

She walked to her office. Roarke stood from her desk, took the two steps toward her, and folded her into his arms.

"Oh. Well. I shouldn't do this now. I still have to write it up and update Whitney."

"He was in Observation long enough to know you did the job. And you need this now."

"I guess I do." And she could have stayed as they were for hours. "But I still have to write it up. We have to pack."

"That's done. Bags, such as they are, on the shuttle."

"Okay, check that off. I need to make some stops on the way."

"To the families, and the girls."

"They deserve to hear it in person, not on a media report. Del will be thrilled to see you. I need to check if she's still in the hospital."

"She's home. She texted me."

"Good, then— Texted you? You gave her your contact?"

"I did."

"Softie."

"In this case, apparently so."

Those eyes, he thought, so like Eve's after a nightmare.

"Write your report, then we'll make those stops." He kissed her. "I'll wait in the bullpen."

After the report, after the stops, Roarke piloted the shuttle himself. Their just-you-and-me time began then and there. While he flew, she slept. Still in her in-charge outfit, including, he noted, her thick-soled boots, with her weapon still strapped on.

No dreams, he thought. Not now. And not, he hoped, for the few days they'd have alone together.

She stirred when he landed. Then sat up, shook herself awake.

"Are we there?"

"We are. I'll grab the bags."

"I've got mine. It sure doesn't weigh much."

"You won't need much, will you now, for those four *s*'s."

"Guess not."

Shouldering her bag, she climbed off the shuttle.

And oh, oh, oh, the warm tropical air. The white sand, the impossibly blue sky and sea with palms so green, so gently waving.

And the lovely house, the only house on the island, with its huge windows and tile roof, its long decks. The stately veranda where they could sit, look over the colorful plants and grasses, then over the sand to the sea.

A sparkling pool stretched behind the house, with chairs and loungers under a vine-smothered pergola. At night it would all sparkle with pretty lights, and under a sky filled with stars, a tropical white moon.

Just now, she thought heaven couldn't look more beautiful.

He'd have had supplies brought in, and the staff, a quick shuttle flight away, would have prepared everything.

She watched a bird, colorful as the plants, wing by, heard the sea gently rolling toward the white sand beach, then away again into its own rich blue heart.

Every drop of tension and stress drained out of her, from the top of her head to the soles of her feet.

"We'll have a glass of wine, won't we?"

"I vote for a bottle." She lifted a hand to his cheek. "You look a little tired. You hardly ever do."

"I'd say we put a month into less than a week."

"Feels like it."

When he opened the door, she dropped her bag on the white tile floor. Fresh flowers filled vases and turned the air into a garden. Sparkling glass brought the views into the wide-open space, empty of anyone but them.

She tugged his bag free, dropped it, then boosted herself up, wrapped her legs around his waist.

"'Links on emergency contact only."

"Already done."

"I haven't, but I will." Completely content, she ran a hand through his hair. "I say the fourth *s* starts now if you're not too tired."

"I think I can manage that."

When he kissed her, she knew he could, and would. So she fell into the kiss, into him, as they held on to each other in the wide-open space, with the breeze blowing through the door of the house on an island where there was no one but the two of them.

NORA ROBERTS

For the latest news, exclusive extracts and unmissable competitions, visit

 /NoraRobertsJDRobb
www.fallintothestory.com